LIFE AMONG GIANTS

LIFE AMONG GIANTS

A NOVEL BY

Bill Roorbach

ALGONQUIN BOOKS OF CHAPEL HILL   2012

Published by
Algonquin Books of Chapel Hill
Post Office Box 2225
Chapel Hill, North Carolina 27515-2225

a division of
Workman Publishing
225 Varick Street
New York, New York 10014

This is a work of fiction. While, as in all fiction, the literary perceptions
and insights are based on experience, all names, characters, places, and incidents
either are products of the author's imagination or are used fictitiously.

LIBRARY OF CONGRESS CATALOGING-IN-PUBLICATION DATA
Roorbach, Bill.
   Life among giants : a novel / by Bill Roorbach. — 1st ed.
      p. cm.
   ISBN 978-1-61620-076-3
   1. Murder victims' families — Connecticut —Fiction.   2. Murder —
Investigation —Fiction.   3. Quarterbacks (Football) —Fiction.
   4. Ballerinas —Fiction. I. Title.
   PS3568.O6345L54 2012
   813'.54 —dc23   2012016965

10 9 8 7 6 5 4 3 2 1
First Edition

For my dancers

LIFE AMONG GIANTS

PART ONE

My Dancer

1

I have a thing about last meals. Not as in prisoners about to be executed—they know it's going to be their last. But as in just about everyone else, most all of us. Whatever's coming, there's going to be that last thing we eat. My folks, for example. They did pretty well in the last-meal department, beautiful restaurant, family all around them, perfect sandwiches made by someone who truly cared about food. Lunch, as it happened. Their last meal, I mean. For my sister it was breakfast, but that was years later, and I'll get to all that. The point is, I like to eat every meal as if it were the last, as if I knew it were the last: savor every bite, be there with the food, make sure it's good, really worthy. And though it's an impossible proposition, I try to take life that way, too: every bite my last.

MY FATHER TOLD me I could do what I set my mind to, though it hadn't been true for him. Mom told me not to expect everything to go my way, probably because of her own bad luck with Dad. She wasn't a mom to coddle you; she thought once you were ten you could make lunch for yourself. And we did, Katy and I, wild inventions, often edible. Dad ate what we offered, never a complaint.

He wasn't one of those fathers who did it all for a kid; he liked to stand back and watch, ready to give a standing ovation, but ready to withhold it, too. My mother was tough on Katy, pushed her toward tennis stardom. The same mom took no particular interest in my football career, hoped I'd pick up a more useful hobby, like gardening. And Mom and I spent hours in the borders around our modest house most Sunday mornings—the azaleas were our church. Who knew what Kate and Dad were up to? Always in cahoots, as my mother liked to say.

But Mom was Dad's one true love: Barbara Barton Hochmeyer, a real prize, her wedding photos like glamour shots, his only great success knocking her up to produce Katy, he wasn't shy to tell us, the very boy Mom's father dreaded: no-college Nicky H. She was a formidable woman, all right, tall and broad in the shoulders, a tennis star in her day, club champion to the end, always organized and scheduled and ready to go. Nick was slicker, looked for leeway, wasn't one for a plan. Words were their sharpest weapons, and they didn't need more than a few. She called him inept; he called her unloving. *Kaboom!* Their fights were like boxing matches—all the moves well practiced, weeks of workouts in preparation, strategies stored up, sucker punches in desperation.

Figurative punches, I mean.

He apologized elaborately after bouts of anger, after errors, after outlandish deceptions, foolish decisions, all of which were frequent. Mom wasn't one to apologize—Mom was always right—but quietly she'd wear a tight dress he loved, or bake him one of the oddball pies he liked: gooseberry, mincemeat, quince. And the two of them were constantly up to their bedroom, where they made way too much noise, lovers till the end.

KATY AND I had a private world. The cellar was the crater made by the crash of our spaceship, the old stone stairs a rock-climb to the dangerous new planet above. The object was to make it to the attic, collect the magic cloak (a sable cape that had belonged to our grandma) and get back downstairs unnoticed by the natives, great fun during our parents' frequent parties: Mr. Coussens sniffing his way through Mom's underwear drawer, Mrs. Paumgartner slipping a porcelain bunny into her purse, the pockets of all those coats piled on the bed unsafe from our alien feelers: diaphragms, strange syringes, once even a revolver, pretty pearl handle, polished steel barrel, chambers fully loaded. My big sister and I passed it back and forth—surprisingly heavy.

On family trips back to Mom's lakeside Michigan from our corporate Connecticut, Kate and I were the backseat duo—barely a year apart— always some elaborate card trick or dance routine (no seat belts, not in those days). The motel rooms we shared inspired proto-sex games: Monster in the Dark, Cannibal, the Blob. But at Sleeping Bear Dunes National

Seashore, summer of 1964, Katy stopped playing. Later in the week, as we sat bobbing bored on a raft, she said, "I've got hair." And pulled the crotch of her suit aside briefly to show me, frank kid.

She was even then a girl who harbored secrets, parceling them out on a need-to-know basis. She was a shoplifter in junior high, a Freon sniffer freshman year, a medicine-cabinet bandit after that, a dealer of hashish at times, small amounts in glassine envelopes she showed me the way she'd shown me her pubes: frankly, briefly, with the understanding it wasn't for me. Before long I was making pipes for her from every odd material in the house, gifts in adoration, though I never liked to smoke. Also—and this seems more important in hindsight—she had what she called "magnificent thoughts": sometimes she saw the world as if from high above. Looking off bridges she could feel her wings flex. Looking at the sea she grew fins. These big moods were balanced by weeks of darkness, bleak pronouncements, irritability, furtive movements.

Her most ironclad secret was boys. Tim Hayes was the only one I actually encountered, a kid I knew as the leather-jacket guy. Home early from freshman football one inclement afternoon I walked in on them, he naked, she fully clothed (still wearing her rain slicker, in fact), her face flushed dark. Arousal filled her pink bedroom as if with smoke, stung my eyes and caught in my throat as I made my escape: I'd been seen. Later, Katy pledged me to secrecy. "I made him *strip*." To what end, she didn't say.

My sister was what I knew about sex before I dated. In fact, she was what I knew about girls, period. Lady Kate sank into a kind of simmering monthly funk that I knew to be womanly in some way: she gave off actual heat, owned special items, left spots of blood on the bathroom tiles.

I came into the high school as into a foreign country, looked to Katy for guidance, but very little guidance was forthcoming. Where I wanted only to fit in, she was falling out. To all appearances we were a team, the clean-cut Hochmeyer kids, sharply dressed, serious students, successful athletes, sunny smiles, good deeds. And I *believed* in those things, felt them readily as our identity. But my sister clearly did not believe or feel the same.

Half the guys on the freshman football team had crushes on her, asked me how to proceed, asked me to put in a good word, asked me to set them

up. Of course I didn't: what would Katy want with my jerky pals? She
didn't really have boyfriends at all, not as far as I knew. Yet as soon as
the pill became available, she was on it, a circular month's supply hidden
among the dust balls under my dresser: Mom never searched *my* room
for anything, ever.

And Kate's friends might have been a source of dates for me, but they
were the tennis girls, a tight-knit crowd with muscular legs, deep tans, and
lanky, bespectacled boyfriends from the local country clubs. Otherwise,
oddballs: she ate lunch with Giant Janine the goiter girl, who spat food
and often burst into tears; she stood at the bus line with Mark O'Meara,
the thalidomide boy, unafraid to grasp the tiny hands that grew from his
shoulders; she idolized June Harrison, who played piano well despite the
wheelchair, spent nights at her house. She courted drama, was enamored
of difference.

She in her own heart was a freak, is my guess now.

Otherwise, why all the secrets?

IN OUR NICE stone house—three bedrooms, huge yard sloping to willow-
wept water, one-car garage—we thought of ourselves as of modest means.
Because across the pond, on what was called the High Side, there loomed
an immutable example of what it was to be truly rich: a mansion the size
of an embassy. In winter, you could see the far-flung wings of it across
the ice and occasionally the movements of its tenant, the world-famous
ballerina Sylphide (say it in the French manner: sill-*feeeed*, as many *e*'s as
you wish), whose even more famous husband, the English rocker Dabney
Stryker-Stewart, had died on the Merritt Parkway (as everyone in the
world knows), piling his Shelby GT Mustang at eighty-some miles per
hour into the abutment of one of those handsome Depression-era WPA
bridges. But the body wasn't with the car, didn't show up for two full
days, found flopped by a muddy stream nearly half a mile from the accident scene. Had Dabney wandered dazed from the crash? Or was there
foul play?

Despite months and then years and even decades of conjecture and
investigation and conspiracy theory, answers were not forthcoming. The
sorrow and disbelief (some say madness) on Sylphide's veil-shadowed

face in the famous photo of her standing at his graveside in Newcastle, England—well, it still haunts me, haunts everyone, the closing visual bracket on an era that begins with John-John Kennedy saluting at the graveside of his dad.

There'd been another person at the High Side, too, Dabney's child from a previous marriage, just as famous as his father and step-mom: Linsey the *Life* magazine boy, visited for a photo shoot every year on his birthday, both physically and mentally deformed, as we would have said it then, anyway, profoundly challenged (fetal-alcohol syndrome is my diagnosis in hindsight—the abandoning birth mother was a lush and a leech, famously). He was sweet as a puppy, small and soft and helpless, those huge eyes, but with a weird sense of humor and sly smile, a secret nasty streak the rest of us delighted in. He'd been a vexed and cross-eyed fixture in my classes from kindergarten straight through, the richest kid in the public schools, mainstreamed before mainstreaming was even a concept, all because the private day schools in the area wouldn't have him, and his stepmother—the greatest ballerina in the history of the world—wouldn't allow him to be institutionalized. The superintendent of Westport schools was happy to oblige, as were Linsey's teachers: the boy wasn't charming, but you got to hobnob with the famous parents.

By the early sixties, Sylphide and Dabney had become the world's own royal couple, their courtship and subsequent wedding a glimmering fairy tale. He bought her various castles and mansions and retreats around the world, but the High Side became their home base. The permanent move to the U.S. from London came with her elevation in 1964 to principal of the New York City Ballet (George Balanchine her longtime mentor and devoted fan—"Her *sweetness* of thought," he famously wrote, "her *sweetness* of motion and lineament emerges from the very core of her soul, moves ever outward"—of course I'm working from Google for my quotations), and was followed by Dabney's megaplatinum album *Dancer* (the only album at the time other than *Meet the Beatles* to contain more than one number-one single, four in fact; I'm still always catching his melodies in waiting rooms and elevators). The beloved in all the songs was Sylphide, or so we thought, and that's her on the wildly controversial original album cover (the cover that got pulled after two weeks in favor of the safer and more familiar airplane image), that sleek, modest, achingly shy nymph fleeing naked into the forest with an almost taunting glance over her shoulder, blond hair streaming sweetly, misty golden light, her high, pretty fanny more plain lovable than erotic.

But then, I was just eleven.

My big sister was to become well acquainted with the dancer. By the time I finished junior year Kate had, in fact, babysat and tutored and contained Linsey for nearly four years. She'd been pledged to utmost discretion, became insufferable about her constant contact with fame. She was stingy with the free *Swan Lake* and Dabney Stewart-Stryker tickets and hoarded amusing or shocking inside stories (dinner parties attended by Mick Jagger or Julie Christie or Muhammad Ali, even the likes of Twiggy; Marlon Brando naked with three girls in the High Side pool, no one swimming). Katy's closets were filled with old Nehru jackets and worn-out guitar straps, her summers with exotic jaunts, three weeks here, four weeks there, various points in Europe or Africa, trips to famous Japanese and Brazilian and Australian cities during every school vacation and often *during* school, the lucky duck. The Prince and Princess needed her, and of course the puppy-eyed Princeling most of all.

ONE WEDNESDAY EVENING in my senior year, Kate off at college, one especially wonderful Wednesday in the especially warm October of 1970, just as Mom and Dad and I were sitting down to an especially wonderful dinner (fishsticks and frozen French fries, plenty of ketchup, mounds of canned peas), several black cars pulled into our cul-de-sac and parked neatly along the curb. Two men from each car headed for our different doorways. We could see them coming every step of the way. If we'd been armed and dangerous, they'd have been toast. Dad was calm, simply let the main guys in the front door. "FBI," one of them announced. Another offered him sheaves of papers, which he didn't take. They let him gather a few things—toothbrush, fresh underwear—and then they took him away, multiple felonies connected to his work at Dolus Financial. (Yes, *that* Dolus Financial, the one that all these years later has collapsed under its own weight despite some 15 billion in federal cash.)

"Dad's had some trouble at work," Mom said when he was gone, no particular emotion. "Bail has been set very high."

Later I heard her cursing him out in her room. "Fucking asshole" was the exact phrase, repeated endlessly, Bar-Bar someone who never swore, except on the tennis court.

A FEW DAYS later (October 30, 1970, to be exact), Dad's court-appointed lawyer—a portly sycophant named McBee—met us at the courtroom steps, gazed up at me.

"Ozymandias," he said darkly.

I knew what he was saying, more or less, knew my Shelley from Honors English. "It just means I hit my head a lot," I said.

"Seven feet?"

"Only six eight," I told him.

McBee wheezed, sighed, gave us our marching orders: "Okay, just as I discussed with your mom. You kids, you must look solemn. Pretend it's his funeral. Look one part pissed, two parts forgiving, like people who are going to put your old man on the straight and narrow. Got it?"

My sister put on a face—pissed forgiveness is hard to do—and of course kept putting it on, and soon I couldn't stop giggling. Kate wasn't laughing much in those days, kept the straightest face possible, which just made things the worse for me. Mom was plainly irritated with her, but said nothing, just as she'd said nothing about Katy's tennis clothes, which were hardly appropriate for the occasion. They hadn't seen each other since Katy had left home for her first year at "New Haven" (you weren't supposed to say the name of the school), and maybe Mom just couldn't admit that her daughter looked great.

Katy's new boyfriend was there, Jack Cross, who (shockingly enough) was her professor. He was a stoic guy with wild hair and posh court-day clothing, meeting Mom for the first time. Solicitous, he took the old lady's arm, shot Kate a look that froze her. And silenced me, too. Because, well, I'd met him before.

Plenty of secrets in our family.

Under the dome of the stately courthouse lobby (still not so grand as the High Side foyer), Mom brushed her hair and pinned it into a bun, made her face up in a tiny mirror, reclaimed her gorgeous poise. The courtroom itself was just plain, nothing but cinderblocks and workaday furniture, the judge at a table in shirtsleeves, not what I'd pictured.

Mom and Kate and I took seats in the front row. Jack sat in the row behind us. He was Dad's age, Mom's age, craggy as a sea cliff. My mother had asked if I thought he and Kate were sleeping together. Unlikely, I told her. Kate, who'd never even had a boyfriend? Sleeping with a professor? Easy lies. Because I knew more, a lot more. Kate basically lived at Jack's beautiful house, for example. And I'd visited them there. I'd liked him for not mentioning my height, a feat few could manage. He'd even loaned me a car to take home to our family. That was the kind of man he was, someone with extra cars. Dad had lost ours. The kind of man who lost them. For Mom's sake I'd said the loan was from Katy's roommate, true enough, as far as it went.

The judge shuffled papers. He looked like an insect. People came and went, whispered to him, whispered to one another. Kate wasn't the only one with a new love. My mind wandered over Emily Bright's brown skin, her soft and secret hair, a whole night of her kisses and long hands, Emily in the shower, Emily in my little bed all night while Mom was away managing Dad's crisis, wreaking her vicious serve on defense and prosecution alike. Two cops brought him out in his rumpled business clothes, handcuffs in front. He definitely looked like a guy who'd been in jail, dusty and pallid, badly mussed. He scanned the room back over his shoulder, couldn't find us.

McBee approached the bench with the sandy-haired prosecutor, said a few quiet sentences. The prosecutor said several more—nothing we could make out—and the judge nodded. He looked to Dad. Dad said a long, long paragraph, almost silent, his back to us, his posture weary, carefully remorseful. When he was done the judge made a sign and two Afro-American men the size of NFL tackles stepped to Dad's side. The judge instructed them, didn't look at my father. They nodded seriously. A bailiff came in, removed Dad's handcuffs. Exhausted smiles all around. The gavel.

Dad had gone state's witness. He turned to us, looking unhappy as ever. He shuffled over to the docket gate. "Lunch," he said.

Katy leapt to him and hugged him with all her strength, which was considerable. Dad teared up, choked and sobbed. Mom joined them, offered hugs, too, less voluble. She wasn't buying the tears. Professor Cross waited for the exact moment, found it, shook my father's hand. I could see from the brisk quality of the shake and greeting that they already knew one another, too, more secrets.

The prosecutor sidled over before I could join the greeting, gave Dad ten fond slaps on the shoulder. "We'll be getting to know each other very well," he said. He gave Katy a long look, the way certain kinds of men did, up and down, down and up, wry twinkle when he got to her eyes.

Katy didn't turn away but took him on.

"State Champions," he said to me, tearing his eyes from hers, a guy who must have played football himself, years back.

"Yessir," I said.

"You're even bigger than they say. Gonna repeat this year?" Dishonest eyes, a guy on the take, something you could see from a vantage point high as mine.

I didn't feel any need to explain I'd quit the team. "Sure," I said.

Mom accepted a folder of papers from McBee, who looked proud of himself. And finally it was time to go. With the big African-American guys—Dad's security detail—we formed a phalanx around the old man, made our way out to the parking lot. He said, "They're paying for the best restaurant around. It's all approved."

My mother made a show of not being impressed.

Dad rode with his guards. We dutifully followed. The restaurant was called Les Jardins, and it was very fancy, all right, acres of garden, empty fountains. Empty parking lots, too, and an empty dining room—it wasn't even eleven o'clock yet. At our lace-and-lantern table, under the staid textures of what Dad said were real medieval tapestries, we ordered Bloody Marys, though Kate and I were underage. When his drink arrived, Dad looked happy for the only time so far that day. He chugged it down and ordered another before the waiter, working around the table, had even managed to put mine in front of me.

"Love this place," Dad said. The bodyguards stood in two corners of the room, deadly serious, no lunch for them. The Bloody Marys were like salads, spears of celery, slices of green and red pepper, home-pickled pole beans. Emily the night before with Mom away was our first time, my first time, and I couldn't stop thinking of her skin, the skin on her inside, too, endless minute visions, her brown skin, and pink, her kisses, the nipples of her breasts like knots to untie with your tongue.

No prices on the menu.

Mom choked down sudden rage, I could see it.

Jack said, "These are going to be difficult weeks."

We sat in silence, empty dining room soon to fill, clatter from the kitchen, biting our celery stalks.

"How's your tennis, Katy?" Dad said suddenly in his investments voice, loud and jovial, always disastrous.

"Good," Katy said, not buying.

Same voice: "No, I mean, give us the works. Who the heck have you played? What are the rankings? How awful is your coach? Bring us through the season."

Mom writhed, rankled.

Which inspired Katy. She took Dad's cue and held forth. Her coach was brilliant, she'd been seeded high. Dad signaled for a third drink, or maybe it was his fourth, or even fifth, impossible to keep up with him. We all slaughtered a basket of bread, speared our tiny salads. Just the previous weekend, Dad not yet in jail, Kate had played the longest match in the history of the Hanover Classic, but lost finally to the top seed—a girl from Penn.

"I cried," my sister said.

"She howled," Jack said.

"Oh, honey," Mom said, not very warmly.

"I'm sorry," Dad said. And then he laughed, booming mirth, vodka hitting the old brain, bones all sore from jail, laughed his hollow laugh, deeply all alone inside his misery.

The meals arrived, really gorgeous, simple BLTs, thick, flavorful bacon like I'd never had, slices of tomato thick as steaks, crisp, fresh-picked lettuce from the gardens beyond. We ate in the silence, Mom's silence, except a single moment in which Jack cleared his throat. But he thought better of whatever it was he was planning to say, and we all looked back to our food.

The waiter cleared the table efficiently, dropped dessert menus in front of us. No other diners had arrived. The place was like church.

"So, state's evidence," I said. I just wanted to jumpstart a conversation, the one we really should be having.

"I'm not allowed to say much," Dad said. He nodded toward the bigger of the guards.

"But he'll be free when it's all done," said Mom, no apparent joy in the thought.

"Get my good name back," Dad said.

"They're treating you very well," said Jack. He was a philosopher with a famous book and plush towels in his house, that's all I knew.

"Daddy's got valuable information," Kate said wryly. Her neck, her arms, even her wrists were thicker than when she'd left home, more muscular, much healthier: college sports.

"Always something to sell," said Mom, mocking.

"Didn't we agree . . ." Dad said, but he trailed off.

Mom pounced: "We agreed on *lots* of things. We have always agreed on *everything*. And look, just *look* where we *are*."

Kate slammed her water glass down on the polished table. "Just get off his back," she said.

And Mom said, "Don't *you* start."

Jack said, "Of course we're all tense. Couple of deep breaths here."

Mom puffed and fumed, but Jack had a way about him.

Dad said, "I'm thinking cognac."

"If you want to know," Kate began.

Cutting her off, gentleman Jack said, "I'd really better get Kate back to campus. The tennis van leaves for Ithaca at two. She's supposed to travel with the team if at all possible. Your girl gets another crack at Miss Penn again this weekend, if all goes well."

"We leave at three," Kate said, sudden wince.

He'd kicked her leg under the table. "I believe it's two," he said.

"No dessert?" Dad said. He wasn't oblivious, though, and let them get up and go without protest, just an overly long hug for Kate, and a kiss on her hair. She kissed him back, on his cheek, his ear. They whispered to one another, patted at each other, always in league. He held her out for a look, straightened her collar, gave a tidying tug at the pockets of her tiny skirt. Once again, tears started to his eyes, but this time continued to flow. More hugs.

"These have been tough days," he said over her shoulder.

"Not only for you," Mom said.

"Always selfless," Kate said to her bitterly.

"Don't force your backhand," Mom said brightly, as if it were just tennis advice.

"Good afternoon," Jack said, enormous warmth. You could certainly see why Katy liked him, forty-year-old genie with a famous book about love. "Wonderful to meet you, Mrs. Hochmeyer."

Mom patted at her hair. "Yes, Professor, lovely."

I felt glad when Jack and Kate were gone. Much of the tension dissipated the second the restaurant's perfect front door shut perfectly behind them. And nice to have my parents to myself.

We dug into dessert, which was a huge piece of chocolate cake to share.

Presently, the check came, and Dad proffered the credit card he'd been given by the state. The three of us talked logistics, nothing more interesting than that. I would drive Mom and myself home to Westport in the loaned Volvo. Dad's new bodyguards would take him to his secret location. Apparently the judge thought the old man's life was in danger. Mom would join Dad in a few more days, get him settled in his rooty-toot lodgings (as he called them—this was before anyone had ever heard the phrase "witness protection program"), then she would come home to me. This or that undisclosed town around Danbury would be his home and his life for the next several months; he had to remain under guard. There were people who wanted him to stay quiet. What people, what crimes, these were not discussed, not for the children to know, though of course I'd read the papers: half of middle management at Dolus Investments had been indicted for hundreds of counts of dozens of crimes, from fraud and extortion to murder and back again, also gross embezzlement. Dad's bosses had been portrayed as victims, Dad as a ringleader. Not true, I knew, impossible: Dad was a follower, never in front.

Mom would be allowed to visit him, but only under escort, a night or two maybe a couple of times a week, occasionally longer. And while she was away I'd attend school as always. Take the school bus. Go to the store—our neighbor Mrs. Paumgartner would be glad to drive me. Get the mail. Keep the house neat. They trusted me *implicitly*, was the exact word. Lugubrious talk like that, talk I could barely stay with, my one thought being that I'd have any number of nights with Emily, making love with Emily all over our house, this lithe, lanky girl who knew too much: mouth and tongue, hips and thighs, breasts and hands, smoothest brown skin.

Outside, one of the guards hustled off to get the government car, which he'd parked down the hill in a gravel lot hidden among rhododendrons. Mom admired the selection of mums in the breezeway—those mums, I'll never forget them, all dried out in lines of flower pots, rare colors, apparently, splashes of blood and brains and bruises. The second guard crossed his arms, closed his eyes in the nice sun. His name was Theo, suddenly comes to me, *Theo.* Dad and Mom stood apart, fury spent, some semblance of peace arising, some old redolence of love.

Oh, man. I'd rather not go on.

But:

A new-looking silver sedan pulled into the drive, swung around very slowly under the portico, stopped. A man in a crisp blue suit got out, blue tie dotted with hundreds of golden fleur-de-lis, cocky grin.

"Kaiser?" my Dad said clearly.

Smoothly, the man pulled a large black handgun out from under his jacket, the barrel a black hole sucking in everything. He aimed it casually, pulled the trigger, shot Dad in the face, shot him again in the chest. The bangs didn't seem loud enough to be real. I thought it was all a joke, had to be a joke, Daddy's stupid jokes, the man still grinning. Time went into suspension. The place was lit in sparkles, dust motes, forever lit. The bodyguard fumbled in his own jacket, couldn't get his weapon out. My mother made an impossibly slow hop, caught Dad as he was falling, fell with him in a blooming mound of their nice clothes.

"Nicholas," she said, almost conversationally. Then incredulous: *"Nicholas."*

And then, and then, and then, as I was making my own hop toward them, the man shot *her,* three bullets, three pops, efficient trajectory, making sure my dad was dead, that's all; Mom was just in the way.

The guard still couldn't get his gun out, stepped forward anyway with a shout, and the man shot him, too, dropped him. In the moment's vast illogic, Dad and not the shooter seemed the dangerous one to me, someone who pulled bullets to himself and his loved ones with his big negative magnetism. So it was no heroic act when I finally got my body to lunge at the shooter, a big leap on longest legs even as he aimed his weapon at my face, *click-click-click,* empty magazine, or whatever it's called, at any rate no bullets. I would have had him, too, but tripped over my parents' tangled legs, landed on my mother bodily, lay on her heavily, and she on Dad, a bleeding, stinking pile.

I looked up into the coldest eyes I'd ever seen, clambered up in that tangle of legs, like breaking a tackle. Kaiser didn't like leaving me alive, that I could see, but he'd already used too much time, must have known he wasn't going to prevail in hand-to-hand combat with the likes of me. He slid easily back into his car, shut his door almost gently. The transmission clacked into gear like any transmission. I dove at the car, luckily missing: I would have hung on till my skin was peeled off, every scrap. The shooter drove away neither slow nor fast, crunch of groomed gravel.

I grabbed a pot of mums—heavy, cold, plenty awkward—held it like a football as time resumed full speed, spun, cocked my arm, calm quarterback, spun and fired that thing in a perfect spiral after the retreating car, watched it smash that wide rear window.

But the shooter just kept going.

2

The perfect drinks, the perfect salads (down to perfect individual slices of radish, clearest memory, a bit of the red skin pulled into the white of the glistening core by the edge of a prep cook's knife). And the perfect sandwiches, so neatly made on white toast, perfect, perfect, and served with perfect china-lavender ramekins of house-made mayonnaise, tiny spreading knives plated in gold. It was really, *really* good food, unforgettable down to the last details, details I'd linger over for the rest of my life. So simple: *pommes frites,* those BLTs, tiny cups of lobster bisque. "Sherry," my mother said, tasting the soup, that palate of hers. And then dessert. I've never since had chocolate cake like that, a celebration in itself where no celebration was possible.

I linger over the people, too, except for my father, whom I just can't ever quite stand to conjure. Jack, though. That confident presence, the élan with which he handled the tension—tension was just something to be expected, he seemed to say, as if conflict were a gift. And my mother, of course. I linger over her. But reluctantly, memory going cloudier, Mom in her best little smart suit, short tweed skirt, great gams, Mom in her perfect makeup, her hair in a perfect coil glistening with lacquer, secret pins. And Katy. How strong she looked in her tennis clothes! How buff she'd become, new bracelet on her wrist, her easy access to perfect rage, no transitions for her, lightning bolts igniting the barn when all around the sky is clear, those long fingers, the quick blue eyes, the skin of her face, the faint freckles, her straight teeth, the scar on her lip (a bicycle fall), the very slight but permanent impression therefore of a sneer.

It's Kate I have to start with, Kate where the story really begins, though she would disagree.

WHEN DABNEY STRYKER-STEWART died (on April 7, 1970, according to Wikipedia, so six months or so before my parents' own catastrophe that October), my sister cried as if he'd been *her* husband and not the great ballerina's. Our robust girl became a wraith walking the hallways of Staples High, and it was a good thing she'd already been accepted at Yale. She locked herself in her room every afternoon, wouldn't come out on weekends, refused to go back to the High Side, not even to collect her belongings, her accusations getting wilder and wilder as the weeks went on, hysterics giving way to paranoid fantasies: the dancer was out to get her, would have her killed!

What?

Yes, Sylphide! The dancer had forced Linsey away to England, where he was in custody of his awful grandmother, who was a witch! As for poor Mom, Katy decided she was in on whatever the conspiracy was supposed to be, wouldn't eat food if Mom had touched it, wouldn't ride in the car with her. My father said it was the shock, that it would pass. My mother didn't let on what *she* thought, for fear of saying something unkind, as she put it, which was her way of being unkind.

Kate, meanwhile, was failing to pack for college. Mom entreated her. Dad still said she'd come around. Four in the morning, five, she'd ghost into my room, wake me just by the queer force of the things she couldn't tell me, these long silences as she sat on my desk tugging at her hair or inspecting the moons of her fingernails. Here and there she'd murmur answers to my queries: the dancer had stolen valuable belongings from her (never anything specific, though I pressed); the dancer had called her a slut (no particular context cited, and the idiom more like Kate's than any international ballerina's); the dancer had put weights in the handles of Kate's tennis rackets (oh, sister, no); the dancer had bugged Kate's room with microphones (I couldn't find any, of course, but searched thoroughly through two separate dawns at Kate's forceful behest).

Therapy, medication—those things were uncommon back then, and were certainly not things we talked about in my family. Psychiatrists were for crazy people, not for any of us. There were normal people and then there were people with character issues. We Hochmeyers, of course, were the normal people. So Kate pined and mourned and slammed doors and made accusations in cycles of delusional intensity, thoroughly retreated as summer wore on.

I could understand her being upset. Dabney and his band had planned a very fancy world tour for the new album, including two whole months in South Korea, Hong Kong, and Japan; there had in fact been discussion of Kate's deferring matriculation at Yale for a year so she could continue to care for Linsey as he traveled with the rockers past the summer: India, Indonesia, Australia. A glamorous vision of her future had died, and not only Dabney.

I WAS INVOLVED in my own little drama. In early July, Coach Powers had sent out a mimeographed memo about the summer practice schedule for football, stern handwritten note at the end: HAIRCUTS MANDATORY!

That was aimed at Jimpie Johnson, who had managed to grow a huge bush of curly hair since the end of our last season, and at me. I was no hippie, and no Samson, either, and certainly not a rebel. I didn't care about my hair, and in fact my then-longtime girlfriend, Jinnie Bellwether, liked to rub her hands on a new buzz cut like nobody's business. But I didn't go to the barbershop, and I didn't go, my hair sneaking down into my eyes, over my ears, into my collar. I could take my shirt off and lean my head back and feel the ends of it on my shoulders, nice.

Dad, still alive (still alive!), sat up with me in the nights before my announcement, marched me through the consequences step by step, but I was firm: no haircut. I meant to stand by Jimpie and surely the whole team would stand by us. Dad's angle was reassuring, too, delivered with a hot grin as he sat on the edge of my bed: "What's Powerless going to do? Cut his championship quarterback? His all-state fullback?"

COACH CUT BOTH of us, is what he did. He'd made a public stand, so he was stuck. After a week, best friend or no, Jimpie gave in and went back to practice with his head shaved. I hung on, could hardly say why. I hung on even when Coach Powers tapped Wes Fielding, a promising freshman, to be quarterback two weeks into summer practice. I hung on even when Jinnie Bellwether dumped me, end of August, and even when she took up with Jimp the first week of school. She was a football girl to the core, and I was off the team.

If all these years later the decision seems momentous, the breaching of some kind of fateful dam, an unleashing of the floods of destiny, it certainly didn't seem that way then. It just seemed right. I was a kid who stuck to his guns, my father liked to say, but it seems more to the point that I was a kid with a father who did not stick to his. My reasons seemed diamond sharp back then, but they were quixotic at best, deeply vague. I was a kid who loved football. Why would I quit? Maybe I just meant to please Kate, not that she gave any sign of caring, or maybe I was compelled to echo her withdrawal from all things. Anyway, without football practice to worry about, I had time to do good deeds, the stuff my mother was always on me to do but never gave me credit for, stuff that made me feel happy: dog walking at the animal shelter, clean-up after a flood at the YMCA, youth night at the old folks' home.

I could also sit with Kate, pat her back, tell her things were going to be okay, even though I didn't believe it. Just about the time I thought she was going to break down completely (she barely slept, barely ate, didn't talk, never laughed), she straightened herself up, appeared for dinner showered and dressed and shining bright, two suitcases tightly packed, her tennis bag stuffed and ready.

"What'd I tell you," my father said. And the next morning he drove her the fifty miles to New Haven, where she took up residence in her college (as they called the dorms up there), took up residence, in fact, on Saturday, August 26, 1970.

WHICH DATE I remember perfectly, because that same afternoon I took it upon myself to rescue the bereaved widow next door. This was less saintly than I was prepared to admit: like my mom, I'd been jealous of Kate's connection with Sylphide. Here was a chance to forge my own.

Dabney (so we had learned in the "People" section of *Time* magazine) had made some kind of mess of his last will and testament—apparently he'd written two versions. The newer one turned the mansion and everything in it over to Sylphide, but every penny else, including the rights to his songs—a vast fortune—went to Linsey, with specific instruction that the boy be remanded to the custody of his grandmother (so much for Kate's theories about the matter), Dabney's blighted mother back in Newcastle-upon-Tyne, where Dabney himself had famously worked as a coal miner into his early twenties, writing his heartsick songs at night.

It all happened instantaneously after Dabney was dead: Linsey was flown to England under escort and in a firestorm of publicity. There were photos in the *Daily News,* photos in *Newsweek,* photos in *The Saturday Evening Post,* editorials (all of them arguing for the return of the beloved boy to his stepmom); there were the dancer's ever-so-gentle public queries about the motives of her in-laws and ungentle countercharges (which sounded, in fact, a lot like Kate's ideas, all wrong: the dancer was a piranha, a gold-digger, a careless parent, a fake). The legal system, immune to the great ballerina's delicacy, her magical kindness and obvious honesty, oblivious of her inability in grief to dance and so make a living (my own take on the matter), froze all assets indefinitely, so that she couldn't even sell belongings to pay for daily life.

And after a season without funds, the High Side was visibly in trouble. Sylphide, we knew from *The New York Times,* had had to let go the High Side's groundskeepers, cooks, maids, drivers, and finally the famous little butler. From my bedroom window I could see that the glorious gardens were overgrown. The vintage Bentley sagged in the driveway under a layer of old rain-patterned pollen and acorn caps. The daily deliveries of food and liquor and flowers and the streams of guests had stopped.

After a long look at Dabney's old album cover—a really long look, that nymph both fleeing and beckoning, that exquisite form, that open, angelic face, that dancer's *derriere*—I ferried our lawn mower across the pond in Dad's aluminum rowboat (the closest he'd gotten to his dream of a yacht). On the far bank I unloaded quickly, set to work mowing, stopping often to clear the discharge gate on the machine, my fingers turning green. I pulled my shirt off, paced the great, dewy expanse of lawn, a whole sweaty morning in hot sun. If nothing else, I was getting a workout. I pushed the mower, I daydreamed, I made my way toward the mansion, stripe by stripe of lawn, more and more intricate as I got closer. In a tremendous sugar maple growing inside their walled garden, I spotted the remains of a tree fort Kate had often mentioned, a leafy palace for the kids of the Chlorine Baron, the industrialist who'd built the High Side during the Roaring Twenties on his profits from industrial chemicals and home cleaning products, also the poison gases used by the enemy in World War I.

The front yard was ornately planted. I made my way around the rhododendrons and azaleas, ducked under wild branches (but no matter, at my height I was always ducking), doubled and tripled back, going for every blade, taking the opportunity to examine the famous building, almost a mausoleum: leaded windows, iron shutters, massive lintel stones, an elegant but forbidding entryway, heavy oaken door looming at the top of a flight of ancient steps, the whole setup imported from Europe block by block, remnants of a feudal castle. Last pass, I killed the mower and studied the door, black iron straps and vast hinges, massive knocker held in a life-sized lion's mouth, really enormous.

There was a bang and creak up there, and suddenly the door swung open with a momentum of its own. Framed by the blackness behind her, the ballerina appeared, hugging herself sleepily, dense bathrobe faint green. She was smaller and much more delicate than she'd seemed onstage those few times Kate had coughed up tickets, more airy and light and ephemeral than even on the famous album cover. And certainly less beautiful, not particularly beautiful at all. I cowered, all but bowing, soaked in sweat, filthy, embarrassed.

"I'm sorry," she said.

"I'm just mowing," I said.

She gave a small but grateful nod.

"I'm Katy's brother," I said. "David."

"I thought it is Lizard, no?"

"That's what they call me at school."

"Ah," she said seriously, even somberly. "In Norway, *firfisle*."

"Fur-feez-ul," I repeated, best I could do, as serious as she.

"You are taller than anyone is saying," she said, all matter-of-fact, famous Scandinavian lilt. Her gaze lingered briefly on my belly, which in those days was hard as any marble god's. I was used to comments about my size, used to being stared at, and used to people being a foot and more shorter than I. But even as tiny as she was, at the top of the stairs the dancer towered over me, her greatness like sunshine up there, her sorrow like clouds.

I said, "I just wanted to help."

Apologetically she said, "I can't pay."

"It's okay," I said. "Neighbors help neighbors. You know."

She seemed to consider that, brightened. "I am wondering if you can help me with one thing more."

I tried to take the wide stone steps gracefully, even if three at a time, followed her into the enormous foyer, past the grand stone staircase and through a hidden door, down a hallway into the spacious, restaurant-grade kitchen. We floated right to the stove, where a teapot waited cold.

She handed me a box of matches, gazed up at me. She said, "I can't make the fire to light."

Those startling celadon eyes, always mentioned by the press! (I'd paid attention to every word ever written.) Eyes the color of oxidized copper, or what my mom called sea-foam green, full of light and a penetrating intelligence. Pale, spare eyebrows, open and generous face, her nose tall and thin, cut like glass. Her lips thin, too, and parted in supplication, and I saw as I broke her stare that a front tooth was chipped. She was short, I kept realizing, really quite short. She had breasts under that robe and all the rest of a female body. And she had *bad skin,* acne-scarred and shining. Which was what I'd tell Mom when I got home. The dancer's unassailable beauty in photographs, her imposing beauty onstage, that towering presence, they were illusory! She was really only a girl, not very much older than Katy and her friends, or me. She smelled of bed sheets more than anything, like someone who'd been ailing, smelled of what must be jasmine—always her scent, according to Kate, who found it nauseating.

Not I.

I lit a match, turned the knob, waited. Nothing. "The gas is off," I said.

"Off?" said the world's greatest dancer.

I looked into green light of her eyes a second too long, like rocketing past the earth's atmosphere and into the realm of stars. Helpfully I said, "You have to have gas to make the burners work. It comes in through a pipe. Did you pay your bill?"

She studied me, trying to understand. My heart fled to her helplessness.

The dancer had no equipment for living in this world. When tears came to her eyes, tears came to my own.

"Oh, for me," she said cryptically, and then something urgent in Norwegian, a song of a sentence, a woman troubled about much more than her gas bill. Abruptly she reached up to hug me, or rather, reached up to *be* hugged the way a child might. I leaned and put my arms about her as best I could, more than surprised, intensely aware of my naked, sweaty, grass-stained chest against her cheek as she pressed back. "Oh, Firfisle," she said, rising up on her tiptoes, balance enough for both of us. "Firfisle-mine."

We breathed there in front of the ten-burner stainless-steel stovetop five minutes or so, a monumentally long embrace, the multiple fragrances of her rising to my nostrils—a little sweat, a little liniment, that smell of bed—just about the most awkward five minutes of my life. I wondered when it would be okay to let go.

"I am hating it, to be alone," she said finally.

"Me too," I said. And then I flushed with the truth of it: my former teammates, and Jinnie, and most of all, my sister, Kate, all lost.

THE NEXT WEEK, entirely out of the ether, a message arrived from the head football coach at Princeton, "Rumbling Rick" Keshevsky himself, a crisp piece of bond paper folded into a shorter note from no less a personage than the president of the university. The letters took some deciphering, but after several readings it became clear that based on my junior-year game stats and my perfect grades they were offering me early acceptance and a full academic scholarship, plus room and board.

It wasn't that I'd forgotten meeting the Princeton scouts, wasn't that I'd forgotten my Princeton dream; it was that I'd assumed I'd blown it, quitting the Staples High Wreckers. Had wanted to blow it, no doubt. But the letter made it clear they knew all about Coach Powers and my hair, my getting axed: didn't matter—they'd had their eye on me for years. I was pleased but not jumping up and down, nothing like that, mostly I was just surprised. I really had very little sense of the honor of the thing, had always taken my physical prowess for granted, just something I'd been born with, nothing to be particularly proud of, not something to peddle in exchange for status. Long hair or no, I was one of the best high-school quarterbacks in the country, something to this day it's hard to keep in mind. Jock or not, I was an academic star, as well, on course to be valedictorian, a kid who read philosophy on his own, a kid who translated Latin poetry (looking for the sexy bits, but still). Of *course* Princeton wanted me.

My high-school-dropout father, always the salesman, put on his best pair of penny loafers and his most collegiate sweater and drove me down to South Jersey—he wouldn't let me go on my own, wouldn't let me not go. He steered the big highways with one hand on my knee, a squeeze every twenty miles or so, not a word between us. The two of us were shown around campus by a simpering series of assistant football coaches. I was being courted, stroked, seduced, nothing subtle about it. I wasn't impressed—not with myself, not with the school, not with any of their blandishments.

But my dad glowed, handed his business card to each new professor and coach and admissions dean, shook hands vigorously, talked too loudly, led with his bulky, oft-broken nose, cranked up his sparkling but damaged charm, left me in the background, where, as it happened, I was content to be.

Rumbling Rick, though, was too imposing for that treatment. His office was a cave in the bowels of the football stadium, steel door like a prison gate; he answered Dad's knocking only at length, filled the archway—chiseled face, chin like a truck grille. He ignored my father, took my hand in his two Princeton tiger paws, pulled me in, squeezed my biceps, unembarassedly pulled a leather-covered stepstool between us and stood on it so he could look directly into my eyes.

"Son," he said, "a little haircut shouldn't come between great men. You can play in braids and ribbons as far as I'm concerned. First-string quarterback by sophomore year! Can you give me a yes today?"

From out in the alcove my Dad said, "Yes. Yes, he can."

Keshevsky ignored him, could see the ambivalence in my face. Gently, he said, "Yes, no, Hochmeyer, take your time, make your own decision. But come out and practice with us today. Those boys want to see you in action."

The 1970 season at Princeton would start in two weeks. I was intensely aware that I was still only going to be a high-school kid. Quitting the Wreckers had made me different; nothing that had been important before had remained important after. And meeting Sylphide had turned me one notch again in the direction of this undefined thing I seemed to be straining toward, nothing to do with hair, more to do with the ambiguities I'd begun to notice in the world, a new feeling that nothing was black or white, nothing either/or, that no one could truly lose or win. I thought of the dancer's not exactly delicate hands on me there in front of her kitchen stove. I was no gridiron brute, took no pleasure in my own powers, didn't need to stomp anyone, didn't want to play out my father's dreams, or Coach Keshevsky's, these stale old guys with their failing testosterone.

But there was no way around it. I dressed for practice and worked out with the college fellows, shadowing the quarterback, Matt Morrissey, my once hero, a senior everyone knew was going to play for the Green Bay Packers. In a scrimmage Coach Keshevsky let me take the helm of the freshman team. The varsity drubbed us, of course, and the real first-year quarterback, left on the sidelines, was visibly pissed. I ran plays perfunctorily, completed a dozen solid passes, slowly got inspired, ran for the only freshman touchdown—an arrogant quarterback sneak against the coach's call, purposefully knocking over my own man, the enormous freshman center (guy from Hawaii, later to do well in the bigs), using his bulk as a ramp to launch myself over the opposing line, then dancing through the secondary, breaking one tackle, two, head fakes, spins, straight-arm right, straight-arm left, lots of simple ducking, and then, all alone out there, a colossus racing seventy-nine yards with the whole varsity defense chasing me, the best tackling team in the Ivy League.

So what?

Rumbling Rick was stern with me after, of course—I'd gone against orders—but I just gazed at him, nothing to say, this little tyrant without his stool. I was through apologizing to coaches. As a parting gift—a little more incentive towards my decision—Keshevsky gave me an envelope with six box-seat tickets to the upcoming game at Yale—the opponent's homecoming. "Closer to Westport for you," he said in a way that was warm and cold all at once.

"Hey," said my dad.

I was indifferent until I had the obvious thought: I could invite Katy to her own homecoming game. Of course the coach would have known where she went to school, would have known everything there was to know about me, including my plans to major in Philosophy and Culture, a new field being pioneered at Princeton, as it happened. But none of that would have occurred to me then, the extent of a coach's manipulation.

He said, "Okay, mister. No more bullcrap. Time to grunt or get off the pot. Can I tell the boys yes? Can I give Professor Lunkins the good news?"

Lunkins was the chairman of the philosophy department. From him I'd had three stirring letters in a week. "I need some time to think," I said.

"Nothing to think about," said my father.

"He'll *think*," said Rumbling Rick approvingly.

Dad drew himself up, handed over a business card, barked in imitation of the coach: "Mr. Keshevsky—Rumbling Rick, if I may—telephone me at your leisure. Have *I* got investments for *you*!"

CRUISING UP THE Jersey Turnpike on the way home Dad and I laughed about the coach's face at that moment—his dismay, disgust, disdain for my father all barely hidden—but I must have let on that I'd been embarrassed.

Pop said, "I know, I know. You think it's extortion. You think I'm using you. But, buddy, you've got to be fighting all the time. All the time, fighting. Because why, David?"

I mocked him mildly: "Because 'Opportunity Could Be Right in Front of You.'" Sign in his boss's office apparently, oft quoted.

"Exactly right. And I've got to be sharp these days, believe you me. Mr. Perdhomme is up my ass every second with a hot glowing poker, David. You should see the scars. I've got to be on my toes! No, not good enough. I have to be on my goddamned *toenails*!"

"Especially in these times," I said unhappily, since that was going to be the next line.

And those were bad times indeed. Kate's tuition at Yale was an issue, I'd come to understand. We hadn't had beef for dinner in weeks. Only a couple of months before, Dad had lost a briefcase with negotiable bonds inside, also his entire collection of illegal gold coins, also his raw diamonds, his vaunted Yangtze River pearls, all his paranoid investments, stuff he could physically touch, keep in sight, keep protected from man and market: gone.

That briefcase!

He'd been bringing it to the office vault for safekeeping, he said, one of his occasional paroxysms of insecurity, and managed to *leave it on the train,* just another in a long series of self-imposed disasters. All the humor drained from his face as he remembered it now: "My fucking pearls! How could I be so stupid?"

I didn't want him crying. I said what I'd said a dozen times before: "It could have happened to anyone."

But he did cry, first just a little, his lip quivering, and then he was sobbing. He pulled over on a patch of grass, all there was for a shoulder on the Merritt Parkway, folded himself into the steering wheel, really broken.

"Dad?" I said.

"Never be a loser like me, David. Please, please, please. Don't say no to Princeton, David."

"Oh, Pop." I patted his back. "You're no loser." And because I knew I had to be plain, I added, "And as for Princeton, we'll see."

I was too big for the car (too big for a lot of things, come to think of it), sat there cramped and uncomfortable patting at his back, no further gesture I could make, just waiting him out. It had never been close to this bad, and, painful truth, for the first time he did seem like a loser to me. Finally he spoke, blubbering: "Mr. Perdhomme's got my ass in the fire, son. He's a bad oyster. If I come up a suicide, don't believe it!"

"Oh, come on, Dad. Mr. Perdhomme? Suicide?" Like my mom, I wasn't one for his histrionics.

He knew it, too, tried to be funny: "Unless it's by martini. Then you'll know it was real. That's my weapon of choice, David. If I'm dead of olives, you know I was depressed." Then coldly serious, another big sob: "Anything else, go after that little prick Perdhomme. You hear me? Make that little prick pay!"

"I'll make him pay," I said gently. Humor thy father. Pat, pat, pat his back.

THE NEXT DAY I called Coach Keshevsky, told him yes.

My future as a winner secure, at least in Dad's view, I awaited the start of the Staples High school year, doing good deeds (mucking kennels at the ASPCA, litter at the cemetery, repairs at the Historical Society), my hair long enough for a baby ponytail, of which I was secretly vain. My father had no friends left, but every waiter and gas attendant, every neighbor too slow to avoid him, everyone he met, anyone who would listen, heard the news about Princeton. My mother had a different style. She seeded the story with a certain few friends, and the whole thing—my early acceptance, the unbelievable scholarship money, probable position on the varsity team as early as sophomore year, no need for a haircut—traveled in the way of such things till it reached Coach Powers' cauliflower ear.

Among my old teammates I still had vestigial friends (Jimpie not among them), and it was Carl Little, a huge tackle, smart in science, devastating on defense, that telephoned. "Congratulations," he said straight off. I'd taken the call on the illegal extension Dad had wired in the basement, where in my capacity as post-football saint I'd been building new window boxes for a nursing home up in Weston. "Coach says congratulations, too. And I'm supposed to kind of sweet-talk you and spit on my hands and pull on your dick and so forth, Lizard, but here it is straight: the old general needs your ass and he's ready to make a deal. He's got to save face. You're making him look like a shithead. Which he is, of course. Don't get me wrong."

"Tell him forget it."

"Lizard, you fucking won the war!"

"Tell Coach I'm taking ballet."

A FEW DAYS later a fellow in a tidy suit pulled Sylphide's freshly buffed silver Bentley into our cul-de-sac. Emerging well-buttoned and dignified, he clicked smartly up our flagstone walk, presented himself at our door, knocking formally though it was wide open. I stood there in a towel staring down at him, my hair wet and stringing around my shoulders.

He regarded me without judgment, taking in my size, and said, "Mr. Hochmeyer?"

"He's at work."

"Mr. Lizard Hochmeyer?"

"Oh, okay, that's me."

He went on to explain with further formality (and a partly conquered working-class Boston accent) that he was employed by Sylphide. Which, of course, I knew. Kate had told me all about this guy, Sylphide's butler, Desmond: soul of discretion, heart of a lion, mind like an IBM computing machine taking up whole air-conditioned rooms, as organized as a military parade. A person who could have run a bank, yet who'd taken this subservient position. This sacrifice he'd undertaken willingly for the good of the world, said his posture. In his eye, though, was something a little misplaced, slightly furtive.

I said what my mother would have said, and in her knowing tone, too: "I thought all the staff had been let go over there."

He smiled briefly. "Let us simply say, sir, that funding has been restored. I am the houseman. The others will be back on the job shortly, as well."

"Ah," I said, "Did Sylphide win her lawsuit?" I wanted gossip for Mom, whose attention could be won by such things.

The little butler—shorter even than Sylphide—smiled despite himself, his eyes darting. "I didn't say that. I said only that funding has been restored. Madame has sent you a gift, along with a check for your services during the brief absence of the groundsmen." He handed me a fragrant, gilt-edged envelope.

I'd thought I'd heard a lawn-mowing rig over there! Genuinely nonplussed, I said, "Oh, I don't want pay." I'd had plans to mow more, dreams of further impromptu visits with the dancer. I could not forget the feel of her cheek on my chest.

But the little man didn't hear. As I towered there in my towel, he clicked back to the car and opened its trunk, wrestled with a large, flat parcel wrapped in kraft paper. This he handed up to me with a bow I took to be ironical. He looked me over one more time, said a complimentary, "You, sir, are *gargantuan.*"

"Two meters," I said. "We measured me in math class last year."

He approved of the metric system, sized me up, sized me down. Soon he'd be building me a coffin. "Your torso, it's a *keystone,*" he sighed, those eyes darting. Suddenly professional again, he spun on heel, clicked to the car, and drove off stately, not more than fifteen miles per hour.

Only when he was gone did I tear open the fragrant envelope. Inside was nothing I wanted, just a large check and an invoice in my own name, neatly typed, an accurate computation of the hours I'd put in mowing and a contractor's hourly rate, princely. I opened the parcel next and found a large photograph in a walnut frame: President Kennedy and Dabney himself, the two of them grinning as after a joke, touching one another's shoulders. The president had signed it over to the rocker in black ink with "Great Vigor," the famous Kennedy catchphrase that comedians had made into a joke.

I trotted up to my room with the treasure, hid it in my closet, knowing my mom would never let me keep such a gift: she'd see it as the addled gesture of a woman in mourning. I preferred to see it as a promise of friendship.

I looked at President Kennedy and Dabney a lot over the next few weeks—two dead men—trying to discern in the image or frame or scrawl of presidential handwriting a message beyond thanks from Sylphide, but nothing was forthcoming. No invitation seemed implied, and without one I couldn't get myself to go back over to the High Side.

Meanwhile, the parties across the pond resumed, the deliveries of dresses in huge boxes and liquor and sculptures in ice, the constant in-rushing of guests, the perpetual music—from the most delicate chamber quartet on the lawn to live, roaring rock 'n' roll barely muffled inside the great walls, Dabney's world of friends and hangers-on, all of them paying tribute to the great man at Sylphide's expense, or at least that's how *Look* magazine and I saw it, gentle Sylphide a victim of her husband's wild life.

ALTOGETHER, I FELT like a new kid in school. I suffered no great regret when I saw the football team at practice or heard the roar of the sixth-period pep rallies on Fridays. The only thing that made me really feel the pain was sight of Jimpie, or worse, Jimp with Jinnie, the supercilious way they ignored me, her hand in the back pocket of his jeans.

In light of my stand against haircuts, I'd become a hero of the dress code. The artsy, intellectual crowd had taken an interest in me at lunch-time, and among them was Emily Bright, whom I'd known since grade school. Emily was also a tall person, very shy, known to be difficult, a hurt look behind granny glasses, long dresses, long legs hidden. She was angular, awkward, not everyone's idea of a beauty, certainly not mine (no one but Jinnie would do for me). But she'd been voted Anti–Homecoming Queen in our junior year. The hippie types loved her, had invented a comical "anti" tradition around her.

Emily was in my math class—Honors Calculus—and sat just in front of me, an accident of Mr. Ramsey's seating chart. Her hair was unbelievably rich and black, fragrant, thick and long like a thoroughbred's tail, always in a braid. She seemed short in a chair, her height all in her legs. One warm day she wore a kind of jumper that left her upper arms bare, her dark, smooth skin laid over boyish muscles. When she raised her hand to answer Mr. Ramsey's questions, her wing muscles rose, too, the skin of her shoulder folding. I spied the tuft of tidy, private hair under her arm and caught her scent, something in the category of vanilla, with an agreeable tinge of root, like a forest plant I'd tasted once in Boy Scouts.

I tapped her shoulder sometimes to ask a manufactured question about the math, just to see her face. Her eyes were black and burned always. She'd turn unhappily, look me over, smoldering. Did I want to get her in trouble? But Mr. Ramsey was oblivious, always writing on the chalkboard with the back of his ancient pinstriped suit to the class, *tap-tap-tap.* She didn't smile, didn't like my little jokes, not even the famous Mr. Ramsey face drawn on my fist, moving mouth and all, little black eyeglasses.

Walking through my life after noticing her, I could hardly breathe. Suddenly, I could think of nothing and no one but Emily. Sylphide's hug slipped from my mind, the vision of Sylphide on her steps faded, the Kennedy photo and the album cover ceased beating in my closet. Emily Bright, of all girls. Her mother was a South Korean national who barely spoke English when I'd met her at field days in grade school. Her father was Afro-American (everyone knew) and well educated (everyone said). He and Emily's mother had met when he was a serviceman in the Korean War (everyone explained). The whole family traveled to Korea each October for two weeks at a time, some kind of holiday there. Our sixth-grade teacher, Mr. Bobbins, told us that Emily was the product of something called miscegenation, which he said was the mixing of races (he pronounced this *rices*), and wrong, against God's law. Emily was right there in the front row, brightest kid in class. No one would accept her, said Mr.

Bobbins, with exaggerated tones of compassion, not the Negroes, not the Orientals, certainly not the Caucasians, and therein lay the tragedy of her existence. "Cruel but true," he said, then addressed her directly, pityingly: "Your parents should have thought of that."

Even then I knew enough to be shocked, we all did.

Emily, thoroughly self-contained, all of eleven years old, took her time standing, simply gathered her books, her pencils, her wooden, foreign box of lunch, and walked out. Whoa! Later, we learned she marched all the way home.

Several of us told our moms the whole thing, and these good women told a lot of other people, including Mr. LaRue, the principal. Mr. Bobbins was censured in some obscure way. At any rate, he didn't talk about the need to contain the Jews anymore, or about the communists inciting the Negroes. He stopped his ranting about Martin Luther King, too, and never said again that it was just as well that JFK was dead. (However, he still occasionally wondered aloud if Linsey Stryker-Stewart—not in our room that year, but next door—should have been euthanized at birth.)

The more obvious upshot of the whole incident was that Emily's parents took her out of public school and placed her in dance conservatory, a famous program that accepted without prejudice everyone of talent. She lived in Boston all the way through junior high and into high school, only to return to us in the middle of sophomore year, having been reported for curfew violations (out all night, was the rumor) by a jealous rival in her dorm.

Even gangly as she was, she became the reigning star of "Count" Vasily Derchenko's Westport School of Ballet, and was known to be taking class nearly daily at Lincoln Center in New York City, even occasionally dancing very small parts in very big productions. Suddenly I was the most ardent ballet fan in New England, or anti-fan, if that would get me closer. I made a point of dropping Sylphide's name in otherwise quotidian conversations with the drama crowd, hoped my connection to the famous dancer would get back to Emily.

One of the engines of my crush, of course, was that Emily wanted nothing to do with me. Sophomore year, she'd written a series of anti-establishment opinion pieces for the school paper, in one of which she attacked me as the leader of the football team, called me "reptilian." I'd been kind of hurt, found myself almost agreeing with her. The other guys immediately started calling me Lizard.

But I felt no anger toward her. In fact, it may have been her argument that had set me on the road to quitting the team. She'd written that the true test of physical strength came in restraint, equipoise, tenderness, compassion. Those were dancers' words, of course, concepts my battling father didn't know, a form of manhood coaches Powers and Keshevsky wouldn't recognize.

In study hall a kid I barely knew, Dwight Leonard, slipped me a copy of *Rolling Stone* magazine. On the cover was Sylphide, looking lost and bewildered in an office somewhere, a heartbreakingly lovely fairy tricked in from the woods for a photo shoot, her exquisite, muscular legs in ever-so-slightly wrinkled tights as she sat on a desk, faded leotard the only other cloth, perfect posture, grainy contrast, which hid the bad skin of her face. Inside was the story of her first performance since her husband's accident—not a ballet, just a single number in a recital to benefit a famous famine-relief foundation, something she'd agreed to long before. She'd leaped out onto the stage, made a few magnificent turns, and then just come to a stop, staring out at the crowd. After a few more phrases the orchestra had stopped too, and the room (Bradley Center in San Francisco, eighteen or nineteen hundred well-heeled people) just sat there in silence, long minutes. "We love you," someone in the balcony said finally—no need to shout. According to the article. The dancer had looked up there, looked up there a long time, then simply walked offstage.

"I have to have this," I said.

Dwight accepted the Kennedy half-dollar I carried for good luck.

I sat near Emily at lunch, opened my hard-won copy of *Rolling Stone*. And Emily noticed; you couldn't miss that cover shot of Sylphide. And you certainly couldn't miss me, pointing my toes as I read. Oh, Emily noticed and stood and picked up her dance bag and walked right past me and out the great doors to the bus loop where her mother waited to take her to the train station and the 12:41 to New York.

Emily had no need of me, no need of any of us.

□ □ □

IN THOSE DAYS, my mother was always off at tennis, the kitchen bulletin board papered deeply with schedules and tourney dates and lesson times, not the slightest letup since Kate had left.

One fine Saturday, Dad and I raked leaves, the first weekend he'd been home for six weeks. Apparently, things were going better at work. This, I simply intuited—it's not like we talked about our troubles. The poor guy had been putting in seven-day weeks, twelve- and fourteen-hour days, home on the late train to sleep, out on the early train, working his lips, chewing his nails. And something odd had happened. I'd driven him to the station Friday so as to have the car—dashed fantasies of driving off to Compo Beach for a walk with Emily—and he'd left his crappy replacement briefcase in the car, a cardboard thing already coming to pieces. When I returned with it, I spotted him climbing into the wrong train, opposite direction from New York.

I leaned on my rake, smelled the brisk air, felt the fall sunshine, couldn't help it: I thought about football. The team would be on the bus to Greenwich for a game they'd probably win—Greenwich was weak in those years. But then again, who did Staples have for a quarterback? No one but that scrawny Fielding kid, who'd gotten his chance from my abdication. If he won, he'd be a hero. Me, I was raking leaves. Dad made a show of pulling on his beloved work boots, his one connection with an identity he'd never had: paint-splashed, steel-toed, oil-proof soles, the leather worn and supple, lovingly waxed, the rawhide laces double-knotted, absurdly high heels.

"So where'd you go yesterday?" I said lightly.

"Yesterday what?"

"Yesterday morning. Without your briefcase. I came back to give it to you and you were getting on the New Haven train."

He laughed. And then he laughed more: busted. "I'll let you in on a secret," he said. "But don't you tell your mom. I was going to see a lady."

"Dad!"

"Not like you think, bud. I just had to do a little job for Mr. Perdhomme up in Bridgeport. Wooing a client, you know. Perdhomme knows where his bread is buttered. I practically gave the woman a massage. One of the Fricks, you bet she came around."

And before I could formulate the next question—Dad obviously lying—
he gave me a shove, retrieved his rake, shouted, "Last man to the Butt
cooks dinner!" The old stakes with rakes. He ran comically and took the
little west side of our modest lawn, leaving me with the big east side, re-
versing the advantage of my childhood, and we set to, herding leaves like
a couple of overcranked toys, real competition. He pressed his advantage,
wasn't a dad who was going to let you win. He was stout on top, slim on the
bottom, legs like a heron's, forty-four years old, stamina of a goat. The Butt
was a massive round boulder down at the edge of the pond, cracked down
the middle from all the fires we'd had there, from leaves to marshmal-
lows to Kate's troop of Girl Scouts, the ones who'd named it. The physical
exercise broke the gloomy mood. My father laughed and shouted taunts.

As we came around the house—scratch, scratch, scratch with the
rakes—I saw three large men in black clothes striding purposefully down
the High Side lawn toward the dam end of the pond. When they saw I'd
noticed them they visibly hurried, splashed heedlessly through the little
brook and high cattails. They were coming to see *us*.

I said, "Dad?"

The biggest guy broke from the others and jogged to put himself between us and the house. He stuffed his hand in the pocket of his sweat-
shirt, showed the grip of a black gun. My hands began to shake. Why
were armed men coming from *Sylphide's*? Why were armed men coming
at all? A gray-haired guy, clearly in charge, stepped up calmly. My father
pulled himself up to his full five ten—or maybe in his work boots it was
six feet—thrust himself into the guy's face. "State your business, Freddy."

Freddy put a hand on Dad's chest. "Nick, relax. Take a breath."

I was incredulous. "Dad! You *know* these guys?"

"They're goons," my father said, playing tough. You could see how it
was he'd gotten his nose broken so many times, little cockerel among the
roosters.

The third man was the High Side chauffeur, I suddenly realized, the
Chinese guy who had always dropped Linsey at school, a nervous hench-
man, if that's what he was, breakable as a twig.

Freddy turned to me, authoritative, not particularly scary: "You were
at the High Side the other day?"

"Ixnay," Dad said.

But I saw no need to be secretive, took a reasonable tone: "I tried to light Sylphide's stove for her. The gas was out. Oh, and I mowed the lawn. She asked me in. She was very sad, I thought."

"She ought to be sad," Freddy said. "She's missing some very important paintings."

Suddenly, Dad flung his rake to the ground, wheeled hard and threw a sucker punch into the chauffeur's delicate nose, turned and bolted, his comical trot, former track star with bad knees, working hard to lift those huge boots. The surprise gave him a couple of seconds head start—no thought of me, as I would later realize—and he trundled up the lawn toward the house with the biggest guy chugging along close behind.

Freddy seemed unconcerned about either Dad's escape or the bloodied chauffeur sprawled on the ground, so I flung my rake, too, raced up the hill after Dad and his pursuer. I tackled the big guy in the middle of Mom's thorny *Schneekoppe* roses. He was soft, pillowy, way out of shape, huffed and puffed beneath me, no fight in him.

Rescued, Dad leapt across the patio and into the house, slid the big doors shut, dropped the heavy locking bar in place. I could see him as he raced to the front of the house, where no doubt he was locking that door, too. For the first time, I understood all those deadbolts: Dad's paranoid dream was coming true. And I was on the wrong side of the doors. I got to my feet—the big goon wasn't going anyplace.

Freddy strolled up the lawn, the picture of nonchalance. "The paintings," he said. "I just want to get in your house, here, have a look around."

Suddenly, I thought I knew what was going on. "It was a *gift*," I said. "The *butler* brought it over. I'm happy to let you see it. I'm happy to return it, even, no big deal. I never even wanted it."

Confused, Freddy ran a hand back through his already smooth hair, said, "The butler? You mean our houseman? Desmond? A gift? A painting?"

"A picture."

"I'd better have a look."

It took a good deal of pounding and yelling at the back door, but my father eventually appeared. "No guns," he said, muffled.

Freddy yanked a big .45 out of his shirt and just dropped it on the glass patio table with a clank.

Dad raised the locking bar, slid the big glass door open.

"You leave your kid outside to fend for himself?" Freddy said.

"My kid's no kid," Dad said.

In my closet, I kicked Dabney's album cover out of view, and pants by shirt by sweater I unburied the huge photo of Dabney Stryker-Stewart mugging with JFK.

"What the hell, Son," my father said. I dug a little more and pulled out Sylphide's thank-you note, showed Freddy, showed Pop.

"So there it is," Dad said almost gleefully.

"There nothing is," Freddy said. And then he searched the house, Dad and I tagging after him, a half hour or more of his poking under our beds and behind our dressers, looking in every drawer, opening every suitcase and trunk in the attic, inspecting every closet and cabinet. He moved old furniture out of the way in the basement, opened every box down there. He made a slow circuit of the detached garage, even checked inside the car. And then he looked again—living room, bathrooms, dining room, back in the kitchen—no sign of whatever it was he wanted.

"That lady's a fruitcake," my father said.

"She's no fruitcake, Nick," Freddy said. "She's a distinguished person, and she is understandably upset." Then, sharp and sudden and precise, one quick hand, he grabbed my father's collar and pinched it tight. Warning me off with the other hand, he pulled Dad's face toward his till they were nose to nose. "Nick," he said, "If you can help me here, you best. You're hearing me? Paintings. Three. Stolen from the Stryker-Stewart collection. Not your son's beautiful photograph up there, and you fucking well know it. The lady is beside herself."

"What about us?" Dad said, half-heartedly pulling against Freddy's grip. "We're not beside ourself?"

"Why doesn't she just call the police?" I said helpfully. I reached and took Freddy's hand off Dad's collar, separated the two of them.

Freddy didn't protest. His point had been made.

We all stepped outside. The big goon was standing down by the Butt picking thorns from his face while the bloodied Chinese guy impassively looked on. Freddy turned his icy gaze upon me: "Lizard, young man, here's a little advice you'll want to hold on to as you and your dad here proceed through life: The police aren't always up to the job."

I returned the cold stare, an advantage in height of half a foot or more, felt no particular threat, looked down on him till he turned away. And that minuscule triumph is the thing I still hold on to: I had become my father's protector.

Freddy picked up his gun, aimed it vaguely at Dad. "Your shoes," he said.

"Oh, come on," my father said.

But there was the gun—no one was kidding—and so my father sat in one of the patio chairs, his whole frame shaking. He wouldn't cooperate beyond that, and so with my own hands I unlaced his heavy work boots, pulled them off his sweaty feet. One at a time, Freddy accepted them, held them as he might a pair of dead animals, turned and ambled down the lawn.

3

I couldn't stop thinking about how my father had locked me out of the house. The only way to make it seem okay was if you considered that he already knew Freddy and knew I'd be all right with him. But that left a lot of unsettled questions, and here I was already pretty well unsettled. I wanted to talk with Kate—she'd have some answers—but when I called her college I got nothing but a ringing phone, or worse, her suitemate Ling-Ling Po, who apparently found calls from family deeply irritating and insignificant. "You again!" And it wasn't like I could trot over to the High Side and ask the dancer what was going on. Earth-deep pounding had come from there all night, the bass lines of an endless rock 'n' roll evening: so much for needy hugs in her kitchen.

That Monday morning at school moved slow as snot down Linsey's lip unto lunchtime. And it didn't get better then, Jinnie and Jimp making out severely at the tables under the cafeteria's grand windows—the unofficial football section—lots of big, obvious laughs and smooches offered for my benefit, the rest of the team ignoring my entrance pointedly. I spotted Emily, but she ignored me, too, engrossed in conversation with an art boy named Mark Nussbaum, serious stuff. I got myself to math early to watch her arrive: not so much as a glance in my direction, whispering sleek skirt, homemade sweater, that fragrance of hers not from any perfumer.

Leaving school later, seated among a lot of younger kids on the Route Fifteen bus (no more football, no more daily practice, no more rides in the Jimpy-mobile—how the mighty had fallen!), I spied her by her car with someone. Him again, Nussbaum. I had them in my sights long enough to see him kiss her, all very sober, like communion at church. She put her hand on his face, said something ardent, drank from his lips.

When I got home, dejected, I found Mom blocking the stairs, same expression as when she found my Trojans back when Jinnie was mine. The condoms were still in my drawer because I never got to use them, truth be told.

"What does this mean!" Mom said, brandishing a silver-piped envelope, which she'd already ripped open.

I grabbed it away from her, tore it further, found a fragrant note on thick parchment, beautiful handwriting in rich fountain-pen bronze: Sylphide, telling me there was much to apologize for. Her frantic accusations were an embarrassment to everyone at the High Side. Very soon, she said, she'd make it up to me with an invitation. The paper smelled of her jasmine liniment, also sweat. The language of the note, however, smelled of Desmond, the hyperarticulate butler, or houseman, or whatever you were supposed to call him. I recognized his handwriting: blocky and formal, the kind you see on blueprints.

Mother breathed and pulled herself up. She was a formidable woman, all right. People often suggested that we were similar, but I never had her edge, the steely stare, the sharpness of features, the look of a falcon plummeting to a kill: "What *accusations?*"

My heart pounded in my throat. Dad and I had managed not to tell Mom the goon story. That was the way it worked in my family—cabals.

I attempted an end run, called up all my indignation: "What are you doing opening my mail?"

"I'm your mother, David Hochmeyer, and I'll open your mail when I see fit. Do not change the subject. Whose accusations?"

When you can't tell a little, tell it all, tell it at length, tell it so thoroughly you never get to the end: "You remember I mowed her lawn the other day?"

"I remember you didn't mow *ours.*"

AFTER HER LONG silence, almost a month since she'd left for college, a week after the incursion of the goons, Kate called collect during dinner. Dad refused charges and called her back, saving fifty precious cents. Their conversation was very brief, Dad mostly listening. Mom got on next, and after some initial bickering, she and Kate seemed to have a nice talk, Dad monitoring the call, three flips of the egg timer, nine whole minutes, note of discord at the end: Mom had asked Kate if she was seeing any boys. Kate didn't like questions like that. So, suddenly Mom was handing me the phone. I pulled it into the living room as far as I could on its wire, not far enough.

"It's good," Kate said, no preamble. "It's like you become who you were supposed to be all along without all the static and interference. If you don't want to listen you don't have to listen. There's no one to tell you to go to bed or wake up or eat lunch or iron your pleats, you know? I adore my English class, David. We write a paper every day. Every single day. And Greek philosophy—divine information, right? The stars are pinpricks in the outer shell of the universe. 'Is what is holy holy because the gods approve it, or do they approve it because it is holy?' The professor has us over to his house for dinner, he takes us to see movies. He's like my best friend here, I'm not kidding. And I've got tennis every morning. My coach sees things in the *minutest* detail. He's got me eating like crazy. I'm supposed to gain twenty-five pounds. It's ecstasy! Mexican food, right? It's all beans and rice and limes and hot peppers. Mom would shit! My coach, she's a health nut. 'I eat to live.' And I'm lifting weights. I feel so fucking *solid*. You hit a thousand balls at a time, same shot over and over. You should see my serve! It's a whole different game, David, college sports."

Our time was half used up. I didn't want to talk about football at Princeton, which is where she was leading, how football at Princeton was going to be harder than football at Staples. I said, "That guy Freddy was here from the High Side."

Silence. Then: "Yes, Daddy mentioned that."

"Oh?" Dad had mentioned no such thing, not that I'd heard.

"What the fuck were you doing at the High Side, David?"

"Sylphide couldn't light the stove."

"She couldn't light a Mobil station."

"I don't know. I like her."

"I've got news for you, brother, the whole world likes her."

"They took Dad's work boots."

"Oh, Daddy and his work boots. Like he's Paul Bunyan. Listen, you fucker. Don't go over there any more."

"Katy," I whispered. "Tell me what's going on."

"That's three minutes," Dad said.

"You ask Daddy what's going on," Kate said.

Dad started to pull on the phone cord, slowly increasing the pressure. Quickly, I said, "I've got tickets for the Yale–Princeton game. Want to come?"

"Don't you have any friends to invite?"

"I want *you*," I said.

"Three minutes," Dad said again.

"Fine," said Kate. "Just don't bring Mom. And nothing's going on."

MY MOTHER WATCHED from the car as I trudged up the grand stone steps to the High Side doors carrying President Kennedy and Dabney wrapped in string and brown paper. Mortified, I pulled a braided golden cord, heard a church's worth of bells and gongs. At length, the little tottering butler answered the door.

"Ah, Caliban," he said, craning to take me in, sniffing the air around me.

"Ariel," I said, looking down upon him.

He nodded approval: I knew my Shakespeare. He'd basically called me a monster and I him a fairy, both true enough, no great judgment implied. Behind him, deep in the High Side bowels, I could hear lush piano music, and someone counting over it.

I said, "My mom says I have to return this picture."

He gazed into my eyes dreamily. "Your mom," he said.

"Says I have to return this picture?"

He accepted the package, bid me wait, padded with it off across the great foyer, disappeared down a hallway.

The piano music abruptly stopped.

Then he was back. "Madame says she has not missed that photo, and will not, but would like in any case to replace it with something more to your liking." And he presented me with a teak case all fitted in brass, Dabney's initials inlaid delicately on the lid, opened it ceremoniously to reveal a pair of gorgeous old binoculars, polished, shining, clearly beloved.

"Swarovski," said the butler, "Crystal lenses, clear as night. Mr. Stryker-Stewart was a birdwatcher there for a week or two, one of his finer *enthusiasms*. We purchased these in Austria, as I recall. Thousands of dollars, you'll be happy to know. They've not been used." He shut the fine case and handed it over, peering into the open neck of my shirt, a blush coming to his cheeks. Soulfully, the piano music resumed, then the counting.

"Whoa," I said, weighing the wooden case in my hands.

Desmond nodded, let his gaze aspire to mine. Why couldn't Emily look at me like that? "Madame invites you to tea next Wednesday, guest of your choosing. You'll attend?"

"Oh, I couldn't," I said.

"Then the answer is yes," he replied, finding my collarbone again. His voice went timid: "Sir, if you don't mind. Could you. Strictly as a matter of scientific interest. Would you. Make a muscle for me?"

Jinnie had forever been asking me to make muscles for her. And I'd made a few for the mirror, truth be told. I was a kid who'd worked out for years, did my pushups a hundred at a time several times a day at any odd moment the spirit moved me, one arm, fingertips, handstand, you name it: pushups. I didn't want to encourage Desmond, but seeing an advantage, said, "Tell me first why Freddy took my father's work boots."

His eyes drifted to my hair, traced its new length. Absently, he said, "Work boots? I know nothing about Freddy's activities. And nothing about Nicholas."

"How do you know his name, then?"

"Through Katy of course. Now, a muscle?"

I rolled my T-shirt sleeve up over my shoulder, made a show of flexing, pumped the heavy binocular box like it was a dumbbell, turned my arm this way and that.

"May I?" he said.

"My dad," I said.

"He is not welcome here," Desmond said quickly, "neither in person nor in conversation," and reached up sighing to take his prize.

But I withheld it, evaded his pinching fingers, pushed my way out through the heavy doors, vaulted down the steps to my mother, realizing too late that I should've hidden the binoculars.

"Something a boy likes," I said, opening the case at her command.

She just shrugged. Binoculars were not President Kennedy; binoculars were fine.

I WAITED FOR an opening to ask Emily to tea at the High Side, blurted it at lunch, stupidly in front of Mark Nussbaum. He said no for her, proprietary, the three of us sitting all awkward at their lunch table. Emily didn't protest, let him speak for her as if she weren't one of the most forceful, independent girls in school. From her brightening I could tell she wanted to go—dearly wanted to meet Sylphide. But she and Mark must have had some kind of plan: neither of them was in school on the big day, no explanation.

So much for my fantasy date.

My actual date was lurking in the driveway when I moped my way off the school bus and down our little absurd cul-de-sac. Mom had gotten her hair done—horrors—it stood up on her head spiraled and shining like some kind of blond vase. Upstairs, the model warplanes of younger days turned on their threads over my bed. I put on a church shirt, plain white (bought by the half dozen from the Big Man shop in Bridgeport: collar twenty-two inches, sleeves thirty-eight), tied my church tie around my neck (extra long), patted the dust off my custom blue jeans (waist 38, inseam 46). I reached under a blanket box, pulled out Dabney's *Dancer* album, propped the thing between doorknob and molding, gazed lovingly. If you did the math—and I had—Sylphide had been nineteen or twenty when that photo was taken. That sprite dashing off into the woods! Barely older than Emily! I opened my pants, pulled at my suddenly leaping penis, special attention to Sylphide's streaming hair, the small of her back, her rump fantastical in veils of mist. I grew tremulous in seconds. My mother said my name in the hallway—otherwise she would have caught me—said my name and burst into the room as I turned my back on her and the great ballerina and tucked myself in even while ejaculating.

"Dog*gone* it!" Mom said, highest ire.

"All ready," I said, semen dripping copiously into my underwear.

She clacked her tongue. "Oh, David, *those* pants?"

Studied calm: "Yep, these."

❏ ❏ ❏

DESMOND, POINTEDLY NEUTRAL, showed us through the grand High Side foyer and into a large parlor—Madame would be with us shortly—and there my mother and I perched on real Queen Anne chairs (as she'd later declare, naming *every stick of furniture,* as my father put it). Quick glances at one another, long looks around the room. The ceiling was twenty miles above our heads, ornate plaster moldings gilded and polished, a forest-scene fresco up there, gorgeous, lots of fauns and cherubs and satyrs with pan pipes, fairy castle at the center. The walls were a startling deep blue, the woodwork all in perfect white, not a single spot or spider web, sparkling windows facing the front lawn I'd mowed heroically, all that rhododendron. At the far other end of the room a very long piano loomed, shiny black. Hanging high on the wall over it was a huge ridiculous oblong canvas, plain pink (Ellsworth Kelly, I'd learn later, not ridiculous at all), and several other paintings as well (Warhol, Kandinsky, Max Ernst, ditto), which were mere samples of Dabney's famous collection of modern and contemporary art. Just behind us, a patch of unfaded wall paint in the perfect shape of a large painting. The rectangular void set my heart to pounding.

I said, "Katy will kill us."

My mother sat up straighter yet. Judicious whisper: "Listen, Bub, all these years? Did Katy ever once invite me to meet these people?"

I whispered back. "Mom, come on, they had you in for dinner!"

"Dinner with Linsey and Kate is what I had! In the kitchen at a card table!"

"Didn't Dabney say hi?"

"Dabney stuck his head in, yes."

Famous snub story. I was baiting her. Mom had gone over there in furs and best jewelry.

She imitated the rocker: "'Yer ol' lady's a looker, she is!'"

"So now you're getting back at Kate."

"Ye gods and little fishes!" Mom said brightly so as to prove my observation had had no effect on her, and no basis in truth.

There was an actual wet spot on my trousers, now, and it was growing. I'd have to cover it to stand or avoid standing—it'd never dry with us sitting there drinking tea. The wave of mortification built into a wave of guilt. I had to bring Katy and Mom together, had to do it soon if Katy

were not to be lost to us both down Dad's warren of rat-holes. Suddenly a
solution presented itself. Hardly thinking, I said, "Mom, come up to the
football game with me in New Haven. Kate'll be there. I mean, I invited
Katy. Maybe a couple of her friends. And Dad could come, too, wouldn't
that be nice? A family day? We've got six tickets."

"'A looker!'" she said, British tones, wagging her head to imitate the
rocker.

Suddenly a rumpled tuxedo staggered into the room, landed on the
piano bench without acknowledging us, took a couple of big sniffs of air,
began softly to play. The guy had a large blue earring, something in my
sheltered existence I'd never seen on a man: queer? His nose was a like
a potato left in a drawer too long. He sniffed audibly at every pause in
the music.

"Chopin," my mother said, too pleased with herself.

Next a maid trotted in, dark eyes, dark hair, heavyset, black uniform,
white apron, a very friendly face, not a peep from her mouth, large silver
tray tinkling with china in her nervous arms. This she set carefully on
the low table in front of us. Desmond followed immediately, carrying a
sort of miniature samovar, and the two of them performed an elaborate
ritual that resulted in four perfect steaming teacups sitting prettily on
four matching plates, four teaspoons, four lace napkins. The parlor maid
hurried out, hurried back with an assortment of tiny cookies. The Chopin swelled.

Desmond put a hand on my shoulder, squeeze-squeeze, slipped something into my shirt pocket, all one smooth motion. He didn't break
character for a second, didn't catch my eye again, just snapped his heels
together for my mother's benefit, bowed and left us. She stared after him,
thoroughly impressed.

I took all my cookies in a handful, stuffed my mouth. The piano player
worked expressively—this was the real thing, very beautiful, Chopin at
concert pitch.

Surreptitiously I pulled the little card from my shirt pocket, just a
blank rectangle with the butler's famous block letters:

DO NOT FOLLOW IN YOUR
FATHER'S *FOOTPRINTS*.

Seconds later Sylphide popped in, damp hair combed out plain, sweat-shirt over a leotard, black tights, bare feet, not a trace of make-up on her face, acne scars for all the world to see, gentle smile for my mom (who rose and curtsied), something a little more ironic for me (who stayed put, hand over the front of his pants, feeling he'd been caught out). The great ballerina walked unnaturally, each step the result of thought, the effect more awkward than graceful, a quality of being a forest creature caught indoors. I cast down my mortal eyes. Her feet looked as if they'd been smashed and glued back together poorly, toes knobbed and bent. Clearly she'd been dancing before we came, and for hours.

"Guess who's home?" she said warmly, tiniest increment of a smile.

And Linsey tumbled into the room! He laughed to see me, his favorite classmate by dint of being Kate's brother, his former quarterback, too (he was the team equipment man, the only one of the fellows to quit on my behalf), bowled into my chair. No way around it, I had to stand, accept his sticky hug.

"Woo," he said, holding on tight, face ducked into my belly, deformed hands gripping my belt. He smelled of bologna and mustard. He wriggled to get closer to me.

"Sylphide," my mother said.

"Call me Tenke," the dancer said kindly.

"Wizard," Linsey said.

"Tenk-a," Mom repeated, like it was the most difficult foreign word. She stood up tall, seemed to measure herself against the tiny dancer. She was more than a decade and a half older, at the near end of her forties, but anyone would have guessed that they weren't far apart, Sylphide's world-weariness, perhaps, Mom's immaturity, like a couple of sisters who'd been dealt wildly divergent hands, and the unfairness was surely what dark-ened Mom's face, the same hurt look she got when losing at tennis, which was very, very seldom.

I pounded Linsey's back, like pounding a pillow, extricated myself from his grip, indicated he should hug my mom.

He blushed, took my hands instead. "Smell her," he said clearly.

No way to hide, I said, "Thank you for the binoculars, Tenke."

My mother shot me a look. Those *binoculars*. And who was I to call the dancer by her familiar name?

Sylphide was unperturbed: "Ah, *ja, ja*—I was thinking you'd like them. Dabney thought them treasure. Sometimes I was thinking he'd pay more attention to me if I were rainbow or robin redbreast or eclipse of the moon!"

"Oh, well, I doubt *that*," my mother said.

We took our seats. The piano mounted and mounted, the performer's heaving shoulders and flung fingers giving us a place to look—mounted yet more to the end of the movement, dropped away suddenly to a ringing silence. Mom and I picked up our teacups as if on cue in the quiet, found the tea on cue to be too hot, placed the cups back in their saucers.

"Eclipse of the moon," said Sylphide absently.

"Smelling smelly smells," Linsey said, such that I at least could understand it, apparently not taking to my mother's perfume.

Abruptly Mom said, "We're so sorry for your loss. Mr. Stryker-Stewart, I mean."

"Ah," said Sylphide. "I am sorry for it, too."

Exquisite timing, the parlor maid tripped in with a tinkling silver tray of little sandwiches on plates, dropped them in front of us. She poured more tea into each rattling cup. The second she was gone, Linsey and I lunged at the food. My mother ignored hers—such was her training—but Sylphide was only a beat behind Linsey and me. And when she saw my mother wasn't going to eat, she took that sandwich too, gobbled it unapologetically.

Linsey burped, a signature report.

Sylphide took no notice but pulled herself up, clapped her hands gaily. She said, "Georges, give us some acid rock for these long-haired boys, *ja?*"

I thought the piano player would be insulted, but in fact he leapt to his feet, comically kicking the piano bench away, threw his hands at the keyboard, the loud opening chords of "Manic Depression," the great Jimi Hendrix power song, complete with a cruel, raging bass line in the left hand, remarkable. Suddenly I recognized him: Georges Whiteside! From the Dabney Stryker-Stewart Band! Those ethereal organ chords on "Love Me Later," that famous crying solo that half the world can whistle? That was Georges! I still thought of him as a *teenager*, the lucky rocker he'd been on Ed Sullivan years before, all swagger and moxie. The guy in front of us had seemed more irritation than anything, a notch or two in

High Side service status below Desmond, little pot belly forming, cummerbund awry, leather pants straining at their buttons, hair unwashed in long strings around his shoulders. But suddenly his hands were wild animals again, this way and that up and down the keyboard.

"Kate would *love* this," my mother stated dryly, unable to love it on her own, struggling up and onto her very high heels, clapping off the beat, clearly feeling she'd lost her moment with the dancer. Linsey vaulted from his chair, spun monkey-style to Georges's side, patted the famous shoulder happily, then spun through the wide doorway and gone. The dancer rose like heat from her chair, glided to me, extended long hands, pulled me to my feet with surprising strength. My mother's eyes closed to slits and she turned profile, feigned an interest in Linsey's exit.

I had my own problems: the skin at the tip of my penis had glued itself to my underpants, tore itself from the cloth incrementally with exquisite, shrinking pain. Sylphide pulled me to her, placed her right hand on my back, started us around the room—she wasn't going to follow. Linsey came tumbling back in, hooting, chortling, dancing. Plainly, he'd wet his pants. In that, I supposed, we were brothers. I found myself dancing my partner backwards in an ungainly foxtrot, the great ballerina just as awkward as I, her bare feet barely escaping my brutish steps. She turned me this way, led me that, leaned at me confidingly in all the noise, perfectly pleasant smile, those green eyes, that pocked skin. The air of the room grew close with the smell of Linsey's pee, and jasmine, jasmine. I leaned down to hear whatever she would say, but she said nothing.

"Linsey must miss Katy," I said conversationally, but with the same impulse as my mother: bring the source of our guilt into the room.

The greatest ballerina of her time slid her hand up my back, gripped my neck, pulled me down so she could speak in my ear: "Let us not be talking of Kate."

We made a turn in front of Linsey, who lunged at us ungainly; we swept past my mother, who gave a needy wave. I leaned to the dancer's ear, flood of loyalty in my breast: "She says it's you who's trouble."

"*Ja,* well. I am forgiving her for that, too."

We lurched past the blank spot on the wall. Sylphide's pelvis was at my thigh, her face no higher than my chest. She pulled me close as the song reached its pinnacle, a crisis of black keys and white, Georges's hands sure and powerful, effortless crescendo. Then bang, it was done, steep silence. The dancer didn't let go of my fingers, didn't take her hand off my back—we stood there frozen like one of my mother's porcelain scenes, all these quaint and comical couples with no troubles of any kind. Except perhaps proportion: a giant and a nymph.

I was trying to form my words—poor Kate, battling such a personage—when one of Linsey's attendants appeared, a sleek Asian woman in a nurse's uniform. She pointed him out of the room, ignoring his protests, tough as slate, impassive. He butted her chest; she tugged him harder. He kicked off his piss-soaked loafers; she pulled his shirt over his head to subdue him. His belly was soft and white as bread dough, and his pants were soaked through. She gathered his shirttails in one little fist, expertly retrieved his shoes, led him away like a blindfolded prisoner.

"Katy was the only one who could control him," said Sylphide, but not to me. She let me go, almost thrust me away from her.

Mom worked to layer a look of pride over her frustration: I'd hogged our host just as Kate had done.

"We were *very* fond of her," said the dancer, no trace of irony, and taking my mother's arm as the Chopin began once again.

"Fond as soda pop," said my mother, ambiguous as always. The two of them sat close in the Queen Anne chairs, finally the intimate chat my mother had dreamed of.

"'Let's not be talking of Kate,'" I said unheard, almost happy to know that my sister and Sylphide had had some kind of falling out, that there really had been rancor between them and not only Kate's delusions. I slipped over near the piano and watched Georges closely, that famous craggy face, that rheumy gaze, the expressive hands, the presence of genius. Noticing me he bent harder to the keys, played with selfless attention, pure emotion: his heart had been broken, too.

MARK NUSSBAUM'S LITTLE friend Dwight rushed up to me as I ducked off the ignominious school bus. I mean, Dwight Leonard *charged* up to me like a hobbit, pimples first.

"Mark fucked up!" he hissed.

Emily!

I hustled to the student parking lot, found her slumped over the steering wheel of her nice little car, a boxy BMW her father's employer had loaned her as a reward for good grades. I waited till she'd finished crying, tapped on her window.

She turned angrily to see who, wiped at her eyes. I pointed at my wrist: time for homeroom. She shook her head, looked bitten. I twirled my fist to say *open the window*. But no.

Later I looked for her in the lunchroom, scanned the crowd. I could have any girl in that school, my mother was fond of saying. There was Patty DeMarco, her miniskirt rolled high at the waist to make it crotch-shot short for lunchtime. She'd given me half a hand job on a blind date back when she first came to town from the Bronx, ninth grade. I say half because I'd stopped her—some kind of embarrassment that I mistook for chivalry. I should have been nicer to her, after, but didn't know any better. Kelly Fenimore read a thick book at the dark end of the room. She was editor of the school paper, lab-beaker glasses, cutting wit, prim cardigan, ruffled blouse, breasts straining at the thin material like repressed thoughts. And Teensy Bowman, whom I'd kissed just once, back behind the YMCA after a dance in seventh grade, her shocking thick tongue. And Ally Mott, chubby Ally, whose pants I'd managed to unbutton in a make-out session freshman year, an après-school pool party, further moves thwarted by her cheerful, expert hands: she'd had a million boyfriends. And over there Petra Johanssen, the exchange student from Denmark, known to be dating some old-guy businessman from Greenwich, but always flirtatious with me, terrifying beauty, no known hobbies. All of them tomatoes, as my father would say. Why did I bother with Emily Bright, who wanted nothing to do with me?

I skipped out of the lunch line, trotted the long way around the school buildings to the student lot, found the girl back in her car—if she'd ever left—knuckles in her mouth. Again the faked smile. She rolled down her window, said, "I should have gone with you to tea."

Long pause as I groped for something to say: "Well. You had a date."

"Some date."

I let that sink in. "I don't see Mark around today."

"Mark is a little fucking prick."

The mouth on her! She opened her door hard into my knees, climbed out, a complicated unfolding of legs, perfect posture, none of the self-love of the football girls. Her dress that day was a gray-brown fuzzy thing like a pelt, unflattering, telling: it was the same garment she'd worn the day before. She noticed me looking, tugged at the hem.

"Want to take a lap?" I said. That was Staples High lingo for a stroll around the perimeter of the campus, not strictly off limits, yet suggestive— pot smokers took laps; class skippers took laps; lovers took laps.

"No," Emily said. But she began to walk.

Come spring, the lunchtime lawns and playing fields would be covered with kids again, but that day the air was crisp and almost cold, and Emily and I were alone out there except for Jerry Dice (a likable kid with rough edges, always getting picked up by the cops for small infractions like loiter- ing and shoplifting) and Jerry DeMarco (one of Patty's twelve brothers, a striving second-stringer on the football team), the two of them throwing a Frisbee. Emily hurried along, led me to a big ornamental boulder under cherry trees. We climbed it backwards together, an awkward process of shifting our butts up onto the high surface of the massive, cold thing, the shape of the rock putting us hip to hip in the end. I felt the bones of her.

"I hate fall," she said.

"I like the leaves," I said.

"Disgusting," she said, "everything dead and blowing around!" And then without transition, and apropos nothing obvious, she said, "My grandmother was a holy roller, like, a Jehovah's Witness. Door to door and everything, and Daddy did that, too, but he rejected the whole thing when he went into the army, duty and honor. Now his religion is, like, grounds- keeping and landscaping and ass-kissing. My mother is Buddhist— that you can't reject, you know, it's a mindset. She accepts my father's suffering. That's a joke, Lizard, don't be so serious. But she's Korean, too—no way she'll accept her own suffering. You're allowed to smile. I've got guilt from all sides, Buddhist guilt, Jehovah's Witness guilt, Korean guilt, Afro-American guilt. They're all a little different, so you never get a break, shame from all sides. I assume you're some kind of smug Protestant?"

"Guilty," I said.

Emily gave me a brief, pained smile, looked out across the lawns to the playing fields, disgusting leaves cartwheeling nowhere in the chill breeze. I felt the increasing warmth of her thigh. Sylphide's pale green eyes came to mind unbidden, vivid, as if she were spying on us. The two Jerrys ran through the cherry trees in front of us with loud shouts of greeting and long looks: What were we up to?

I waved, not Emily.

Same tone, she said, "My parents were away to see Chuck. He had some kind of ceremony at the academy." Chuck was her older brother, as I well knew, a West Point cadet. She pulled her braid around in front of her, turned it in her hands atop her thick dress. Her neck was marked by seven or eight hickies just shades darker than her skin. She meant me to see them, obviously, a kind of confession. She blurted the rest: "So I stayed over at Mark's. That was our plan. I don't know what I was think-ing. He was awful. He promised dinner. Vodka and orange juice. That was it. A few kisses and he's out to here, Lizard." Graphic hand gesture. "He ripped my dress." Briefly, she showed me a torn seam at her shoulder, then pointed out the safety pins she'd installed all the way down to her waist, glimpse of exposed skin in the breach, another hickey at her hip. She said, "I suppose it was all a lot of fun."

The first bell rang. I felt a surge of violence. I would have liked to have been there to pull him off her. But I felt tender, too: Emily had picked me as her confidant.

She said, "I should have gone to tea with you, is what I'm saying. Do you think there will be more chances?"

IN OUR OLD stone house, in my bright room, in my large closet, there was *The Dancer* cover to study. Out to here! I was. I saw masturbation as a weakness in those days of generalized adolescent guilt; it had to be all but accidental (awake from a dream in the night, or maybe rushing to dress before a tea party) for me to accede. And anyway, I wanted to be true to Emily. I put the album cover away, thumped downstairs, lifted the lids on all the pots, sniffed.

"What's got into you?" Mom said. "How'm I supposed to cook with you racketing around? Make yourself useful. You could finish those leaves, for one thing."

In the backyard I found no surcease but pulled my scattered leaf pile and Dad's together with the biggest rake we had, urged them furiously to the Butt, set a match to the huge pyre they made, watched the flames, the ascendant sparks. The familiar smoky fragrance was comforting, but only barely.

At dinner, Dad had a long, not exactly funny story about something complex that had gone wrong at work, a package of documents mailed instead of messengered, a missed deadline, an unusually lucrative contract canceled, several mid-level execs called on the carpet by the nasty Mr. Perdhomme—Dad himself among them—all followed by a week of gloom around the office, rumors that his whole team might be demoted or even let go. Then had come that day's news: the generous little firm that had canceled the contract—Tetron Mechanical—had been suddenly indicted as a Mafia money-laundering front, a long list of horrendous crimes, which Dad listed: "Threw one guy off the Brooklyn Bridge, just an accountant at a bakery, this guy. And chained four guys from a ticket agency together and hung them off the scaffolding at a job site. Yeah, yeah, Tetron Mechanical! And apparently these guys are tied to the Dick Fortin thing!" Dick Fortin was a Westport lawyer, everyone knew: gentle, peaceable man, he'd been taken from his office in broad daylight by two men in fake police uniforms, never to be seen again. Any firms doing business with Tetron had been named in the court papers, and indictments were set to roll. "So me and my half-assed colleagues have accidentally saved Concept Credit Corporation!" Dad stilled called it Concept though the name had been changed to Dolus Investments some five years before, sore point with Mom, who made a face. "Mr. Perdhomme owes me big time!" At the thought of all the missed carnage he laughed, and listed a few more grisly crimes. Which somehow seemed very funny. At least Mom and I laughed as he told us.

"And yet until now you've said nothing to us," Mom said, her laugh drying crisp.

And Dad said, "I wanted to spare you, is all." His beard was coming in scruffy, well beyond the usual shadow. Had he failed to shave that morning?

"Dad," I said. "Just tell us. What's going on?"

He said, "This is between your mom and me."

"And between you and Kate?" I said bravely.

"Kate nothing," he said.

"Honey," my mother said to me, her hardest look: I was way off base.

And quickly the discussion excluded me, drifted far from any secrets Kate and Dad might have: Mom wasn't going to put up with his lies anymore! Dad was doing his dead-level best to make a living for all of us! Mom was sick unto death of his self-righteous rubbish! Why couldn't he be a man and stand up to Perdhomme! Dad didn't understand how Mom could be so ungrateful, all the slaving he did for our sakes! Mom was sick of his floundering, and *what kind of man put all his earthly wealth in a briefcase and left it on a train!* That last sally marked a large escalation and the battle went thermonuclear, real shouting. Soon the dinner plates would be flying, if we had any left, these people who loved each other. I sauntered out into the living room, put on the TV—nothing but news—left it on loud and went to the front door to check the mail. No one had touched the pile. My heart pounded with the dark emotion of my parents' argument, the ugly picture of Mr. Perdhomme, all of that bile layered over dark visions of Emily and Mark. I thought a little desperately that maybe there'd be a *Life* magazine to look at before homework (a ton of math, a little Spanish). I seldom got actual mail. No *Life,* but under a grocery-store flyer there was a silver-piped envelope, fragrant, elegantly addressed to my mother. Sylphide!

I opened it carelessly—Mom had opened mine, after all—and read the note, breathing the fragrance as my mother shouted something to my father about *ineptitude,* and now, uh-oh, his haplessness, *haplessness!*

The butler's efficient, blocky handwriting, Sylphide's swooning scent:

> Dear Mrs. Hochmeyer: Thank you for your kind note. The answer is yes. Linsey and I will attend. And with your kind permission, the High Side will provide transportation and victuals for the Tailgating Picnic you describe so beautifully. We cannot wait for the game, and the chance to visit with Katy. And please let your Lizard know there is an eclipse of the full moon this very night at ten-fifteen, an excellent opportunity to try his new binoculars!

As if acting upon my own sudden flood of fury—Sylphide invited to *my* game at *Katy's* college behind both Katy's and my backs?— Dad stormed out of the house and shortly roared off in the Blue 'Bu. He wouldn't be home that night, I knew, might be gone for days. He'd take a late train into the city, which would force Mom to call a taxi to get to Westport Station in the morning if she wanted to use the car.

I took his place in the kitchen. "Mom!" I said.

"Don't shout," she spat. She looked very beautiful, flushed, young even, her eyes blazing, shades of Katy.

"What's this!" I said brandishing the letter.

Briefest pause as she took in the evidence. "Count yourself lucky," she said unrepentant.

"Those are *my* tickets!"

She took the note card away from me, took a deep breath: "Has Sylphide said yes? She's said yes! Wonderful!"

"Katy *hates* Sylphide."

"We don't know that," Mom said haughty.

But of course we did know that; we just didn't know why, and we wanted to, badly. Perhaps now we'd find out. A chance to visit, indeed! I groaned.

Mom took no notice, said, "We can't make *our* friends based on *Katy's* quirks."

I begged: "Quirks aren't the issue. Katy's going to tear our *throats* out!"

"Then that is Katy's prerogative," Mom said, followed by a little chirp of delight as she reread the dancer's note. She patted my shoulder queenly; one did not let the men in one's life slow one down. "Honey, I'm going to the club."

"Yes? And how're you going to get there? Dad took the car."

"Mrs. Miles and Mrs. Howley will pick me up presently. It's already planned. I'm not simply running off like certain other members of this family. If the ladies and I can find a fourth we'll play a late set of doubles."

"Double martinis, you mean."

That made her beam: the truth is funny.

Me, I wasn't going to smile for anyone. "Those are *my* tickets," I spewed. "Sylphide? *Linsey*? Kate, *Kate*? And *Dad*?"

"Don't forget *you*," she said, impossibly pleased with herself. "You're the guest of honor. And me of course, your ever-lovin' mom. The gang of six!"

"More like a circus act! You write back to Sylphide right now and tell her you made a mistake!"

But Mom was already bustling up the stairs: game, set, match.

ALONE IN THE house later, I tried again on my calculus homework, found the long problems I'd been happily solving for weeks unfathomable. Once again, I pulled out the little card from Desmond: "DO NOT FOLLOW IN YOUR FATHER'S *FOOTPRINTS*." Suddenly I noticed the emphasis, and understanding dawned: there'd been footprints on the High Side parlor floor, evidence in the case of the stolen paintings, the case that Freddy wouldn't take to the police. Freddy must think Dad took the paintings, which would have seemed absurd before I learned that Freddy knew Dad. And that Dad knew him. And if Dad knew Freddy and Freddy knew Dad and there were paintings missing, then Dad very likely *did* have something to do with their disappearance. And if Dad had spent enough time at the High Side with Dabney to get to know Freddy, then Kate had something to do with the missing paintings, too, as the only way Dad would have been allowed over there was with Kate. Kate would have the nerve for any caper, and had the power over Dad, too, could get him to do anything at all. But anything at all certainly would not include high crimes, even if such crimes might serve some purpose of hers.

All of us together at a football game!

Suddenly, thinking of New Haven, I realized where Dad had been going the morning he'd crossed over the platform without his briefcase. He'd been going to see Katy at Yale.

I paced the whole evening away, not another lick of homework, finally threw myself on my bed, warplanes overhead hanging on their threads: Messerschmitt, Zero, P-38, Spitfire, Flying Fortress, Mustang. You broke all the hundreds of little plastic pieces off of plastic trees, glued them together painstakingly, painted them, put the little decals on the wings, flew them with your hands all through the house. I counted tickets in my head, as no doubt Mom had done. She'd used them all, all right: Kate and me, Linsey and Sylphide, Mom and Dad—a mess from all angles—and right behind the Princeton bench. I lurched out of bed, assaulted the kitchen phone, dialed Kate's suite, Dad and the stupid phone bill be damned. Ling-Ling Po was perfunctory: she hadn't seen my sister in days, and no, she wasn't taking any messages.

Outside, the full moon rose. I retrieved Dabney's brilliant binoculars, stood swaying on the patio focusing them—never had I seen the moon so clearly. The edge of the disk against black outer space was jagged with craters, the center too bright to look at for long. Ten-fifteen came and went but there was certainly no eclipse in progress. And wouldn't Mr. Kerklin have told us about such a thing in physics class that afternoon?

It didn't take much to row across the pond to the High Side. I traversed the vast lawn, crouching and running to the wall of a lost garden, vaulted onto it easily, crept my way up the grown-in old ladder to the platform of the forsaken tree fort I'd spotted while mowing, protecting the binocs all the way. Up there, I had a clear view into a dimly lit bedroom—the only lights in the house, floor-to-ceiling glass doors that in summer would open out onto the large deck overlooking the pool. But nothing was happening, so much for my hunch. I focused on the full moon, picked out the same minor craters, grew bored. Definitely no eclipse. I thought of Linsey, asleep in some other wing of the house. Almost reluctantly then, I focused back on the large bed. Not much else to see: pair of ornate armoires, a blue-striped Queen Anne chair by the window, all lit by a studio spot, the effect through the glasses like looking at a stage set.

Just then, a man in a long red robe came in and out of view faster than I could focus. The spotlight went off, and there was nothing more to see, just the mansion bathed in moonlight. Eleven o'clock. So. The weird game was yet another illusion, and I was the one inventing it. I let the binoculars hang from my neck, started for the ladder, but turned at the advent of a powerful feeling. The studio spot blinked on, and this time Sylphide was there in its warmth, highlighted as if onstage, her pale skin tinted amber, her robe just a shade lighter. I put the glasses to my eyes. The man slipped in behind her and I saw it was Georges Whiteside. He'd dropped his robe. I could see his hairy shoulders. Sylphide accepted some kisses on the back of her neck, then seemed to shoo him. He walked out of view, barrel-chested, skinny-legged, high little butt embarrassing to me.

Sylphide straightened and stretched, let her hair out of its bun, shook it free. She appeared to be looking directly at me, but of course what she'd be seeing was her own reflection. I was a mirror, too, I realized suddenly, as purposefully placed as the bright spotlight. She'd known somehow she could count on me, and I'd known somehow how to proceed. My view was as clear as if I were on her deck, nose pressed to the glass, nearly as clear as if I were in the room, those excellent Austrian optics. She opened her robe, let it drop around her feet. Her pubic patch showed pale and trimmed leotard neat, her nipples pale, too, her belly taut and muscular. My involuntary hydraulics went into flow, all the levers pulled straight back. No chance of looking away now. Sylphide's hands went delicately behind her and she bent forward, shifting her hips to an obvious beat—a view for Georges—dancing as to music. Perhaps he was singing. I knew (as did the whole world) that his voice was low and lovely. Slowly she gyrated clear around, caressed herself, gave me the outlook Georges had had, the two halves of her butt, eerily familiar. Emily came to mind in her ripped dress, Mark's paw prints all over her.

Georges eased up behind the dancer. His expression was very serious as he massaged the wings of her back. He gave her coarse kisses on her shoulders. Tormented, I tugged at my pants to untangle myself, that's all. Sylphide lifted a knee gracefully, put a battered foot up on the Queen Anne chair. Her eyes never closed; she never turned back to look at him, skillfully cheated downstage, as actors say, gazed out at her audience. She adjusted her feet for better balance, that's all, one on the chair, one on the floor. Georges crouched, clearly starving, ate peaches right from the tree.

I found I could hold the heavy binoculars with one hand.

After a while Sylphide bucked and then bucked again and then suddenly folded in on herself, fell at the chair with no grace, caught her own weight, pushed Georges's head away, looked at her reflection and *gave a little wave* as Georges rose and lumbered around behind her, bent her to the chair. I died well before he did, an eruption with aftershocks, like nothing I'd ever experienced, the binoculars falling from my eyes, scales, too.

My mother had indeed gone for the double martinis, too much of a hangover to see me off to school. The car was not back in the driveway. What a Tuesday night we Hochmeyers had had, all secret from one another, Mom, me, Dad, Katy: school night, ha. Before bus time I'd tried my sister's college and just got Ling-Ling again, nasty as ever.

I waited in the high school parking lot.

Just at the bell Emily pulled up, climbed out of her car in a rush.

And suddenly there was Mark Nussbaum beside us. He spat in the dirt at my feet. To Emily, he said, "New boyfriend?"

Emily took a disgusted gulp of air, unleashed her foul mouth: "I told you, *dickhead,* I'm not having any boyfriends. I've had it with boyfriends. And I'm telling Lizard here the same: I'm not dating *anyone.*"

"You hear that?" Mark said pushing past her. He wasn't the little acerbic Mark I had vaguely known since junior high. Abruptly he took a step backward, wound up like a baseball pitcher, and *punched* me, a short shot too low to hurt much. I held my chin, stepped back in surprise.

Emily threw her hands over her mouth to cover a gasp.

"What the heck?" I said trying not to laugh.

Mark looked surprised himself, looked about to apologize—tricky—wound up again and took *another* shot, grazing my cheek. Maybe it looked bad—I did snap my head back to avoid the blow, but it was nothing at all, not to me at that age, twice his size and accustomed to being pulled down by overweight linemen and crushed to the ground, cleats to my face. Emily leapt between us, put both hands on Mark's chest, forcefully pushed him away. The homeroom bell rang, a long clattering. I turned and simply hurried away.

Linsey Stryker-Stewart was a savant of the emotions, always feeling things with you, or for you, even despite you. He was in Miss Butterman's history class with me, two periods into the school day, officially seated beside me. This was duty I'd volunteered for—the difficult but beloved kid had a partner in every class, a system that mostly worked. Your job was to help him find the right pages, help him get his special homework out, help him keep quiet or raise his hand to speak, help him get to his next class. Mostly, I found the assignment easy, oddly satisfying.

He only acted up when others did, or when some kind of storm was brewing, whether meteorological or human. He was the kid who got all A's just making crayon marks on a page and occasionally farting dramatically in class (you can imagine the laughter, his artist's pride), raising his hand to repeat key words of the lesson in uncanny tones, history as comedy: "Hammurabi-abi." Among the boys he was popular. The girls had got tired of him, mostly, all his kissing and slobber, innocent though it was, and despite the oddly handsome face, which was a freaky misprint of his father's, melted at the edges, slack. Anyway, they were rough on him, not that he noticed much.

That day he moaned for me, kept patting my shoulder. I couldn't shut him up, even with the formidable Miss Butterman staring us down. For two periods I'd been beside myself with jealousy, and Linsey felt it: Emily had given her attention to Mark Nussbaum, put her hands on him, anger all for him. I had to calm down so Linsey would, had to put Emily out of my mind.

Which worked. And class proceeded.

After, Emily was at the door as Linsey and I shuffled out at the back of the pack, her eyes blazing for me, for me alone, her long braid pulled over her shoulder, raveled in her hands. She dropped it to give me a short hug, said, "I want to say. You were so great. You just walked away. All that power and you chose not to use it!"

Linsey heard the same thing in her voice that I heard: he honked and spun around on his heels. "Schist!" he said, which we all knew meant *kiss.*

"Oh, Linsey, shut the fuck up," said Emily.

"Schist," he said again, delighted, demonstrating a proper pucker.

Without thinking it through, without thinking at all (and using a straight-arm to hold Linsey back from the girl), I said, "You know how you told me you wanted to meet Linsey's mom?"

And I invited Emily to the Yale game, a lot of stammering and extra phrases in explanation: ". . . Coach Keshevsky gave me tickets and . . ."

"Yes," she said cutting me off. "Yes, yes, yes." For access to the dancer, Emily would brave even the most medieval fare, and Linsey's slobber, too. She bumped against me quickly in lieu of a hug, brushed past the famous boy, and bounded off to French class, or whatever came next.

DAD WENT MISSING four nights, his record, and Mom had had it. Downstairs I heard her on the phone with Missy Stratton, her great divorced friend, what sounded from our end like advice on lawyers. But Dad returned the night before the Yale–Princeton game, all abashed and chastened and bearing the oddest possible gift, a Wollensak reel-to-reel tape recorder, no case, several boxes of blank 3M tape. "You can record anything," he said cheerfully. Maybe he hadn't noticed the little Dolus Investments logo stamped into the metal of the frame.

"Must have been heavy to carry all this way," my mother said, skeptical.

"It has a handle," said Dad. Their making up was as subtle as their fights were severe.

But Mom didn't miss much. "Nick, where's the car?"

"Stolen," said Dad simply. And then a lot else, a mudslide of words, the upshot being that the Blue 'Bu had been taken from Westport Station, where in his angry discombobulation those several nights before he'd managed to leave the keys in the ignition, all his own fault. "Not to worry," he said, "The good men of the Westport Police Department are on the case."

I imitated Freddy, his gravelly tones: *"The police aren't always up to the job."*

Dad tried a smile.

My mother didn't like my having private jokes with Dad, shut me down with a look. "And now, Nick, the truth: where have you been?"

He looked offended. "Holed up in my office, lonely as an astronaut. But I caught up on a lot of things and *singlehandedly* untied some of the knots the company was in with that Tetron thing and, tell you what? I'm back on Mr. Perdhomme's good side."

"Raise in the offing," Mom said tartly, but with a delicate glimmer of forgiveness that allowed me to breathe.

Dad, too. He said he understood why we'd given his ticket to the Yale game away. Why, it was his own fault. "Great that your Negress can attend!"

"Nicholas!" my mother said.

"And who's the other?" he said.

Everyone counting tickets.

"Friend of Kate's," I said. No need to bring in the dancer.

"Friend of Kate's," Mom repeated with relief.

I was in a raft heading down the Niagara River, deafening roar ahead, no way to steer to the banks. Dad tried hard to seem he didn't care one way or the other about the game, but he cared, all right. The game was the reason he'd come home. He and Mom were cozy through the long Friday night of cocktails and promises. After we'd eaten, the old man showed us how the recording machine worked, a complicated threading of tape around rollers and heads, chunky steel microphone on a stand. We took turns recording our voices—weird to hear your own—and then we sang a Beatles song, "Yesterday," which Dad had always loved abjectly, playing it over and over again, none of us too tuneful. Mom kissed his neck, kissed each of his fingers: martinis.

Dad pushed the buttons on the Wollensak. "Got it for a steal," he said.

4

Kate's college at Yale was a medieval cloister, except that the girls emerging from the portico wore blue jeans and peace signs. There wasn't a bra in the bunch, not that I was looking. My absurd entourage and I had picked up Emily at the enormous carriage house her family occupied on the grounds of the manicured and extensive estate her parents managed, the home of the ambassador to France and former Secretary of State Arnold Walton Wadsworth.

Some date: Emily erect in the sumptuous back seat of the High Side Bentley between my chattering Mom and mysterious Sylphide. Linsey and I were up front with the taciturn chauffeur, poor guy with a bandage across the bridge of his nose where my dad had popped him. Visions of Sylphide's little breasts in Georges' louche piano hands leapt into my mind as they had all morning. And here she was, dressed like anyone else going to a football game, deflecting my Mom's conversational gambits, asking Emily about her teachers, about her plans, about her stretches, her shoes. Emily only murmured in reply. Linsey plucked at his nose, wiped his hands on me. The chauffeur hummed, clearly unhappy to have me in his car.

"I'll go up," I said, but my door had been remotely locked, no way to escape.

"No, no," Mom said. "You stay here and entertain the dance committee!"

Dr. Chun—that was the chauffeur's name—was already opening her door.

Emily helped Mom get the trailing edge of her big, borrowed, thoroughly absurd fur coat out the door behind her. I looked back and shrugged. Sylphide didn't seem to mind my gang, but only shrugged back, disconcertingly direct eye contact. Just when I would have turned away, she made binoculars with her long hands, put them to her eyes, wriggled a forefinger as if to focus.

Whoa.

Mom had only been gone a minute when she reappeared in the college portico with Kate. Oh, sister! She'd always been tall and blond, but a kind of luster had come over her. She was no longer lanky and pale, no longer too thin, twenty pounds heavier at least than when I'd last seen her back in August, all filled out and muscular, shining with health. She'd been playing tennis for three and four hours daily—her legs were as tanned as in high summer, her face bright with sun. She scanned the yard happily, pleased hostess, looking for the Malibu wagon and Dad, no doubt, but the Blue 'Bu wasn't there. You saw her scan past the Bentley two or three times—some rich kid's parents—and then you saw her actually register us. Instantly she turned on Mom, stomped her foot, threw her hands in the air, shouted something indistinct.

"Uh-oh," Emily said.

"Kape!" said Linsey, growing upset.

The chauffeur muttered something about the time, put his arm out to keep Linsey in his seat. I tried the door handle again: my first electric locks, like I was in a trap.

Kate's dormmates pooled around her, carefully excluding Mom, who made placating gestures, reached to touch Kate's shoulder. An Asian girl— Ling-Ling Po?—actually pushed Mom away. "Fucking *assholes!*" Kate cried, slapping Mom's hand. Then she repeated it, poor Mom, her own favorite phrase thrown back in her face. Kate suddenly turned and, pushing past her pals, raced heedless through the quad and off across campus.

"Can you open this?" I said to Dr. Chun. "Open this door."

Ling-Ling Po stood in Mom's way.

The chauffeur was impassive, holding Linsey back.

"The *door,*" I said.

"Lizano, let's let her go," said Sylphide.

My mother made a movement toward following Kate, thought better of it—she would have had to knock Ling-Ling on her butt—then stood still as a trophy, undone.

DR. CHUN PARKED the Bentley in a space marked RESERVED in a row of other fancy cars at the edge of the parking lot closest to the Yale Bowl, a gorgeous old stone stadium. I was about to point out the parking restriction when I realized that one of cops on duty was directing us to a spot: everything had been taken care of.

Dr. Chun hopped out efficiently, opened my mother's door, waited. But Mom was frozen.

"Perhaps I should be going back to try to speak with her," Sylphide said at length, very gently. "Dr. Chun could be taking me back. I'm thinking we miscalculated, you and I."

My mother threw a sigh, brightened as best she could. "It's no one's fault," she said, meaning that it was her own fault, the closest she got to apology, ever.

Gradually we climbed out of the car, dazed survivors suddenly deposited in a parking lot. Our space was in the no-man's land between Yale fans and Princeton fans; there was a lot of good-natured banter and taunting back and forth across this DMZ, pennants waving, air horns tooting, little boys going out for passes across the blacktop, little girls jumping cheers, Frisbees flying, also half a hundred flags, crew cuts, flattops, effortlessly American. It wasn't a place you were going to see peace signs or smell pot burning. Hamburgers on charcoal, that's what I smelled, hot dogs, toasting buns, ketchup, mustard, apple pie, humiliation.

I pulled my hair out of my collar and let it blow in the breeze. I preferred no one look at me, take in my size and think, Jock. Emily was the only brown-skinned person in sight. And with Dr. Chun one of the only Orientals, as I would have put it back then. He got to work pulling an elaborate stainless-steel barbecue out of the Bentley's boot. It unfolded in ingenious layers, produced its own legs, refused to stand straight. I went to Dr. Chun's aid, and together we got all the latches right. With nothing else to focus on, the women watched us closely. There was a table, damask tablecloths, matching cushions for the chairs.

We were attracting considerable attention. Several of the women in the crowd had recognized Sylphide: you could see her name on their lips. Oblivious, the great dancer breathed in the air, breathed it out again, someone who knew how to contain her emotion. For Linsey, she pointed out a clown on stilts, a Princeton tiger costume, a bikini girl on roller skates selling pennants. "Sylphide!" someone called, but to no reaction. Emily followed the great ballerina's lead, breathed the air, pointed out her own sights, the Goodyear Blimp coming into view, a television perched on the hood of a car. By the look on her face you'd think it was *her* name the voices called out. I didn't dare look at Sylphide, stood between her and Emily, close as I could to both.

A stray football wobbled through the sky directly at us. I reached just in front of the great ballerina's face at the last second as if casually, grabbed the ball out of the air with one hand. I could have been a tight end, fingers like that! The man who'd thrown it—a Yale freshman, beanie and all, waved comically, cried "Here!" And I fired a pass those thirty yards straight as a string, a bullet that drilled his chest and knocked him down, all to the screaming laughter of his friends. He leapt up triumphantly, ran through the crowd as through defenders, made his own kind of touchdown by running up on the hood of a VW bug.

"Such a beautiful, efficient core," Sylphide said to my mother. And to Emily: "See how the football is carrying his anger forward." She held my eye. She had a way of turning her shoulders at you.

"I'm not angry," I said slowly.

"Well, you didn't *kill* the poor guy," Emily said.

"Should I call Daddy?" My mother suddenly said. "Daddy could call Kate."

"Sylphide!" that same voice called.

None of us reacted, but only the dancer didn't hear.

Dr. Chun found coolers full of food, two thermoses of martinis, fancy glasses, which he passed around, an olive each.

"I'm not old enough," Emily said eagerly.

"Let us not stand on convention," Sylphide said.

Dr. Chun poured, full glasses for everyone but his employer, who accepted only a few precious drops.

In the close distance a cherry bomb went off, making us all jump, then a whole pack of firecrackers, the explosions followed by screaming and hilarity. Dr. Chun quaked visibly. A fight song rose up somewhere.

"Our team," Sylphide said, a toast.

"Our team," said my mother. I refilled her glass with my own: the drink tasted like gasoline to me.

"Trouble," said Linsey, or something like, a lot of *t*s and *l*s.

A SPECIAL USHER gripped our special tickets and guided us through a mossy, dripping tunnel and then back out to the periphery of the playing field. When we hit the sunlight, Linsey wailed like a spanked baby. And it *was* like being born, the sky above us blue, the concrete stadium rising on all sides, every molecule around us vibrating with sound—thousands of people laughing, shouting, clapping, stomping. Fortified with gin, my mother took the lead, the usher trotting to keep up, and we crunched along the cinder track to a row of elegant, portable field boxes, each with its own gate and its own little stairway, two rows of three plush theater seats each, the whole section raised directly behind the Princeton bench. Mom administered the seating plan as if we were a dinner party, sat the great dancer beside her, top row, sat me in front between Linsey and Emily. That left an empty seat beside Mom, an instant rebuke—she kept patting it, stroking the velvet nap.

Emily said, "When do they let the lions in?"

Sylphide liked that, laughed and hiccuped daintily, playing drunk—she'd had no more martini than I.

Precisely then, through the great mouth of the stadium, the Eli marching band roared in, all brass and piccolos, the bass drums vibrating the very cement, drum major kicking up his legs. Even Emily grinned, leapt to her feet. Shortly, the Yale players poured in—cheers and shouts and boat horns blaring. After them, the Princeton team rushed in, too, but to a sound like wind, which was the whole place *hissing*. Coach Keshevsky hobbled after them in his signature rumpled suit, pulled up at the fifty-yard line directly in front of us, ignored the catcalls aimed at him from all around. He looked like a granite precipice with a hat.

Sudden silence in the stadium, the band easing into "The Star Spangled Banner." My heart welled when groups of students all over the stadium booed. Vietnam, of course, and President Nixon's late decision to increase troop strength to some 500,000 men, regular guys only slightly older than I.

Just before kickoff, Coach Keshevsky looked back, found me in the box, gave a short salute, eyed the people with me briefly, countenance unchanging. At halftime, a water boy brought a note scratched on a slip of old cardboard:

HOCHMEYER. JOIN US LOCKER ROOM AFTER GAME. KESHEVSKY.

And the contest was brilliant, at least in terms of offense, touchdown after touchdown, one of the highest-scoring games in college history, as it happened, Princeton winning 79 to 75, the lead having swung back and forth until the last seconds, when Matt Morrisey, my hero quarterback, threw the winning bomb. Even Emily could understand the drama in that, stood and cheered despite herself.

"It's a dance," Sylphide repeated, pleased at the revelation.

"If dancers tried to brain each other," Emily shouted.

"But dancers do," Sylphide shouted back.

Linsey and my mother had had their own hilarious time, finishing off a tall thermos of martinis between them and cheering at all the wrong moments. At game's end they stood tottering like old friends and hooted with the small Princeton contingent, drawing stares from the crowd around us.

Emily draped a hand on my shoulder.

"Mutts," Linsey said. Helmets, he meant, dedicated old equipment man.

He and I left the females to get back to the Bentley on their own, crossed the middle of the field unchallenged—such were the times—to visit the Princeton locker room. My future team was in high spirits, of course, shouting and snapping towels, various stages of undress, odor of mildew and old socks and victorious sweat, a sudden Princeton cheer, pumping fists, the win like a drug. Linsey hooted, collected helmets and pads. Coach Keshevsky was as impassive as ever, but the win shone bright in his eyes as he took my two hands, leaned to me.

"Tell me that wasn't Sylphide," he said.

EMILY GREETED US by the Bentley, where Dr. Chun had everything packed and ready to go. "Your mother is *smashed*," she announced, quite drunk herself. She turned her shoulders to us, I noticed, held herself very erect. "She's ranting about Kate. Sylphide's talking her down, though. Don't worry. Oh, David, David, Sylphide is wonderful."

Linsey blew a gigantic fart, and so we all moved a few steps toward the car. Emily leaned at me, leaned more, but I didn't manage to put my arm around her, or whatever it was she wanted. Dr. Chun opened the passenger door for Linsey, who dithered. Emily took my hand, didn't care who saw, squeezed emphatically. "This is the most perfect day," she said, and abruptly spun and hugged my neck, let me go brusquely, fell into me. I kissed at her mouth and missed, kissed again as she leaned further, our lips pressed tight together through a long beat. And that was it: our first kiss.

"How was the locker room?" she said to my mouth. "All the victors having sex?"

We laughed at that, millimeters apart, and then I tried again, ducking in just as Emily did, our teeth clacking together. She cocked her head and we tried yet again, the thing suddenly working: we were sharing a kiss, a long, plain kiss, sharing a kiss through several bars of the fight songs and loud laments erupting all around us, kissing, Emily and I, a long, plain kiss.

ON THE MERRITT Parkway in the increasing dark I studied every ornate bridge, every brutal abutment. Mom had crashed immediately, Linsey, too, his breath at my neck where I wished Emily's would be. But Emily was talking with Sylphide.

Who said, "I am knowing who your teachers are, dear. They do talk about their better students." Her accent, often barely noticeable, had grown thicker with weariness. "Come dancing for me one afternoon," she said.

I turned as subtly as I could. The two dancers were snuggled face to face on the big seat. By way of answer, Emily imitated her father, Sergeant Bright—crisp, polished English over subtle Afro-American and military accents: "I'm to *finish* school and go *on* to conservatory and when I am *done* with that and I have *reached* my majority I can *start* to think about a pro*fess*ional life in *dance* if *such* a life still holds *interest*."

"Oh, fathers," said Sylphide. "What could be more simple?"

"Well, it's my mother." Emily turned all Korean: "Dancer? Why dancer? Isn't it better to be doctor in audience? That way you can enjoy dance! So much less to suffer!"

They laughed, whispered more intimately. I felt I was losing them both.

But very soon we were in Emily's driveway. Very soon Dr. Chun was opening her door for her. Very soon again she was shaking my hand for her parents' benefit (their heads visible in an upstairs window), meaningful pressure in her fingers, a new light in her eyes.

AT OUR HOUSE Mom climbed out with Dr. Chun's help, deflated and miserable, her betrayal of Katy like a stone tied around her neck. Dr. Chun walked her to our front door—she needed his arm. I climbed out of the Bentley only slowly. Linsey was still snoring (impossible to wake him up, I knew; Dr. Chun would have to carry him when they got home). I walked around the beautiful car's sculpted, massive hood, leaned in the open rear door to say good-bye to Sylphide. She muttered something about Emily.

"Pardon?" I said leaning closer.

She leaned closer, too. I felt the heat of her, smelled jasmine. Repeating, she said, "Emily, she's a star."

"I think so, too," I said.

"So I am teaching you to kiss." And abruptly she leaned and put her lips on mine. She pressed hard and plain a moment as Emily had, then something different: she actually kissed me, kissed me twice, three times, put a hand on my neck, drew me even closer, pulled me off balance, hungry sounds, kissed me a fourth time and a fifth, touched my teeth with her tongue, a kind of request, showed me some things about tongues, finally caught my lip in her own teeth, pulled away.

"*Whoa,*" I said.

Linsey grunted in his sleep.

"First lesson," Sylphide said all sultry. "Not being made of wood." And after another long and soulful kiss, timed perfectly to beat the return of Dr. Chun (or more likely it was *his* discreet timing), she shooed me out of the Bentley.

Undressing that night I found a little smooth stone in the back pocket of my blue jeans. I didn't remember the dancer's hand on my butt, but then again I did. A beautiful polished stone, flat and speckled, vague shape of a heart, just an inch or so across, weighty, cool, very smooth, greenish, heavy with meaning unclear.

ONE FIVE A.M. not a week later, Dad woke me. "You've got to get Crazy May on the phone," he said, clearly panicked. Crazy May was his affectionate name for Kate. The original May had been one of my father's seven aunts, a woman who'd ended life a suicide, as had my father's father. And Dad practically pulled me down the stairs, gave me no time to clear my head, dialed the phone, thrust it at me. Katy was his girl, and he couldn't live without her, couldn't forgive Mom and me for pushing her away: "Gotta get her, Son."

What a surprise when Katy-cakes answered.

Her tone was false: "Oh, *David*, it's been so *long*. Where have you guys *been*? I call and *call*." You could make claims like that in the era before answering machines, but I knew from her voice that she hadn't tried, not once.

I said, "What are you doing up at five-thirty?"

"Tennis, Captain. How about you?"

"Dad got me up."

"Good old Dad. Is he the best you can do for a conscience?"

With Dad listening I couldn't take that on, had to skip ahead several moves: "I'm sorry about the Princeton game. I wasn't thinking."

Almost warmly: "Well, no, Mom was thinking for you."

"Kate, Katy, what is it between you and Sylphide?"

Dad waved his hands: Jesus, don't ask that!

And he was right: Kate hung up, bang in my ear.

For my father's benefit, and to prove him wrong, if only to himself, I kept going, pretended to converse the full three minutes, an apostrophe full of the kind of lies that make up the story every family tells itself. Dad listened closely, nodded his head whenever I offered a positive note, starting with how sad Sylphide had seemed about the encounter at Yale, and how sad Katy herself must be about the whole thing, the "whole thing" being her falling out with the dancer, which I said must of course have been precipitated by Dabney's death, and that I didn't mean to excuse Sylphide for what must have been just *terrible* treatment of Katy, but hadn't all that been about the dancer's being in mourning? In shock? At any rate, whatever had happened between them surely wasn't Katy's fault.

My father nodded vigorously.

So I added some more about how sorry Mom was about being so insensitive, so *intrusive* (Katy's favorite descriptor for the old lady), how sorry I was to be an accomplice. The sands of time were running out, so after pretending to listen a moment, I added a final, more cheerful note: my coming year at Princeton! We'd both be college kids!

Dad pointed urgently at the timer.

Happy to oblige, I said good-bye to no one, put down the receiver quietly, and pushed past Dad to get my filthy self in the shower, where I stood till the hot ran out. Afterwards, I dressed in a fury, made a violent breakfast, a full dozen eggs well scrambled. Mom and Dad and I ate in silence, looking three directions at once: our theories of Katy didn't quite mesh.

Then it was time to walk with Dad to the bus stop. Because, embarrassingly, ever since the Blue 'Bu had been stolen, he'd been getting on the school bus with me, eccentric man, riding as far as the Post Road, walking from there to the station. Who had money for taxis? He didn't have friends to drive him around like Mom did! He was a hit on the bus, playing high school kid for laughs. He called it father-son time, as if it were the most normal thing in the world, walked along with me to the end of our street, waited there at my bus stop in the fall sunshine, talking investments: "Open-optioned, pre-treaty Carter-Jackson third-world cash markets," for example, arcane stuff at a mile a minute, apparently practicing for his day working phones in the office, possibly making it all up.

And talking Kate: "I wish she'd find a major. She says maybe philosophy, but I don't believe her. Ancient Greek? What are you going to do with that?"

"When do you ever talk to Kate?"

"Whenever I fucking want, Chief."

Dad did not normally curse. I could feel something quaking inside him;

the very air between us seemed to vibrate with his emotion. I thought of that wrong-way train ride. *Ask* Daddy *what's going on.* He'd been coming home from work angry and mussed, unlike him, making big drinks, gargling them down (he'd been a teetotaler in younger years), accusing my mother of *pitying* him, of all things, strange battles. "You think I'm too much of a *sad sack* to make a *living* for this family?" Mom had broken Kate's heart, is how Dad put it, had put Kate in a compromising position. She'd set Kate up! I'd piped up during a severe altercation, taking the blame for the Princeton–Yale day (and meaning it: it was indeed all my fault, and what could be plainer?), saying that he was right, that Kate had been treated unfairly. Dad had turned on me, redoubled rage, pressed his chest against my belly, grabbed at my biceps, looked up at my chin, said, "*Kate?* What did you do to deserve *Kate!* I could fill one of Kate's oldest, smelliest sneakers with ten thousand of you and still have room for her *foot!*"

In a teenage word: weird.

After a long, sun-shot pause at the bus stop, maybe thinking I was changing the subject, I said, "What really happened to that briefcase of yours?"

You could practically see the insults making their way up from his bashed adrenals, through his throat, to his lips. But he held back, held back in the very sweet breeze, tapped his foot to a stop, rolled his neck. "I lost the briefcase on the train," he said firmly.

The bus came. I sat in the front seat Dad and I had been claiming, but he kept going, all the way to the back, sat with Fritzy Blatz the motorcycle kid (who was off his wheels and on parole, thus the bus). Weird again. He didn't say a word to me as he disembarked on the Post Road, nothing but a friendly thanks to Mr. Davis, our driver. And then he trundled south toward the station, a triumphant look on his face. His posture gave him away though: hunched and beaten.

SATURDAY — A FOOTBALL DAY, so what—I got on a train to New Haven, not a word to my folks. I sprinted through that broken little city, found my way to Katy's college, quizzed everyone I saw, finally got the word: Kate had been staying with Professor Cross, Jack Cross himself, the author of *Everyday Joy*, a book I knew well from sardonic discussions with Kelly Fenimore (who'd reviewed it for the school paper), a classic of hippie thought, or, more charitably, an application of world philosophy to contemporary life, and such a huge bestseller that even Johnny Carson made fun of it on the *Tonight Show*. I'd actually read parts of it—Mom had bought it years before—a whole chapter on ecstasy, which was largely about sex and which I'd managed despite arcane language to jerk off to. Easy enough to find his offices, get his home address from a secretary: Drixel Point Road in Madison, just a few exits east on the Turnpike, a decommissioned church out on Long Island Sound.

Two rides hitchhiking and then a four- or five-mile sprint out to Drixel Point, the secretary's crude map in hand. I stood at the old church doors a long time cooling off, finally knocked, knocked louder. Shortly a tallish, well-tanned gentleman in a towel answered the door, his hair dripping, chest sunken and overly hairy, great handsome sculpture of a nose, which he turned up at me.

"Well," he said, unswayed by my smile, his thoughts on his face: Who the fuck was this? Boyfriend? Seeker? Reporter for the *Yale Bulldog*?

Then Katy appeared, wrapped in a thick leopard-print robe, looking bewildered, very tan and taut, hair in damp strings. "It's my brother," she said.

Her professor put a hand on her shoulder, claiming her. They'd just gotten out of the shower, I realized. Everyday joy, all right. I was shocked and proud and titillated in equal measure. Professor Cross gave me a frank look. "Come in," he said.

I waited in the living room while they got dressed upstairs. This took a long time, the two of them discussing what to do about me: he said have me to dinner, she said no, rustle of robes and towels, noises of emotional kissing, maybe more going on. The stairwell was big and open and the sound just carried right down. I didn't completely mind hearing the talk, since the truth was useful, but didn't want to embarrass them or myself. I got up quietly and walked through the blue-and-white beautiful kitchen and out onto the rocks over the inlet, a battlement of distorted cedars, the tide coming into the river in bright sunlight. I saw a striped bass jump, then another, saw a big trawler coming in, the drawbridge opening to allow it, horns and whistles, Sylphide's kiss, Emily's, the passage of time, something close to an hour, all chilly without my coat.

Kate found me out there. She was flushed and mottled and freshly screwed in a blue, pale turtleneck and very much more beautiful than I recalled, hair more strawberry than I recalled, more reddish, even, with streaks darker, almost auburn, eyebrows dark, too, like Dad's I realized, busy eyebrows as she inspected my face in turn, finding Mom, no doubt: "You're forgiven."

"Thanks Kate."

"I know who engineered the whole thing. And I know it wasn't you."

"At least Emily Bright was along."

"You're dating Emily!"

"You made quite an impression."

Glimmer of a smile: "No doubt. How's Mrs. double-martini handling the racial issue?"

"Is there a racial issue?"

Kate's eyebrows rose.

"Okay," I said. "Dad calls her Negress. Mom's okay about her, I think."

"Mom's okay about nothing," Katy said.

We just looked at the ocean. The breeze was picking up, the tide turning. I said, "So . . ."

"So how did Tee-Tee like the game?"

"She said it was a dance."

"Everything's a dance to her, Captain."

And that was it for talk. Luckily there was a huge freighter out there to observe, luckily a dozen sailboats. What a beautiful place the professor had. I said so, maybe a touch clumsily.

Anyway, Kate took offense. "I'm always in a secret," she said. She sat on the ground suddenly, stopped herself crying almost before she'd begun, put a finger to her nose, blew snot onto the lawn one nostril at a time, true tennis player. Bluntly she said, "Oh, David. One time years ago? Dabney tied my shoe. He bent down and tied my shoe in London. My Adidas clay shoes, you know, three green stripes."

I put my hand on her back and watched the water and heard seagulls somewhere up in the sky behind us and sometime in the last four years the most famous rocker on earth had bent down and tied my sister's shoe. I understood the intimacy of that gesture, but somehow it didn't go with the tears and didn't seem much of a secret, what with Jack Cross a hundred yards away no doubt feeling pretty good. Now the tide was roaring in, filling the river's mouth, purple and red and yellow seaweed billowing in the current, mythic tresses.

And then suddenly, thick-headed jock, I figured out what anyone outside of me and Mom would have known years back, what Dad must have figured out at some mysterious point, what in hindsight seemed like the most obvious thing in the world, duh: my sister and Dabney Stryker-Stewart had been *lovers*.

INDOORS A LITTLE later, the famous Jack Cross and my big sister gave me a tour. Vast living room, partly sunken, once the church sanctuary, tall windows in rows on both sides, spectacular sunlight. The kitchen had been the choir loft, with new windows that saw the water and the twisted cedars we'd been standing among. And so forth, room by room, just magnificent, huge stone basement full of old tools, Jack's hobby next to boats. I was feeling suspicious of him, suspicious of everything in his house, like it was all just an elaborate seduction machine, well greased. He had a little office off the dining room, glowing marble sculpture in there (bright white, nude goddess), state-of-the-art IBM Selectric typewriter. He had a photo of himself younger with what looked like a Buddhist monk, the two of them trying not to grin. Three guest bedrooms upstairs had been Sunday school classrooms, very spare, almost no windows, nothing on the walls. The bathroom still had four sinks, four toilets, room for a whole seminar's worth of Yale girls to hose down before sex with Jack Cross. The enormous master bath had been a classroom, too, towel heaters, deep Jacuzzi, fixtures black, fittings gold. The master bedroom had been the chapel, stained glass surrounding an oval window to the Sound, rumpled round bed the size of a playground. Jack had probably already made a million on his book, and a million meant something in those days.

"Look," Kate said.

I turned and at first didn't see it in its grandeur, but suddenly there it was: on the wall opposite the sea in an ornate frame hung a big painting, an exquisite orange view of a garden through a tall, mullioned window, light more real than light itself, visionary vernal palette, something imminent in the scene, something about to take place, a party perhaps, something consequential, transcendent.

"Bonnard," Jack said grimly.

"It's mine," Katy said, reading my face. " 'The Afternoon Meal.' Dabney bought it for me, and it's mine."

Dad's boot prints in the High Side parlor!

"Where are the small paintings?" I said, maybe more accusingly than I wanted.

"What do you know about small paintings?" Kate shot back.

"You gave them to Daddy," I said, everything coming suddenly clear.

"They were Picassos," she said. "And they were mine, too. We had to pay my tuition."

"Please, let's not lie to absolutely everyone," Jack said sharply. When he turned to me, I knew there was much more to the man than I'd thought, much more to his relationship with Katy than I'd thought. He'd already devoted himself to her: "We pay her tuition, Kate and I. Those paintings she gave your father were worth any number of dozens of Yale tuitions. The man came begging. Katy lent a hand."

"Okay," Kate said, something lifting off her. "Oh, David. I just wanted my painting back from the High Side. This one right here. I didn't care about the others. Dad helped me, and I helped him. I wouldn't call it begging."

"The painting is hers," Jack said, poor guy, caught between love and ethics. "I have the paperwork. Though the method of reacquisition may have left something to be desired."

LATER, JACK LOANED me one of his cars, a black Volvo that had belonged to his deceased wife, slightly older model, but with fewer than eight thousand miles on it. Kate saw me off, showed me how to run the seat all the way back so I'd fit.

"The paintings are mine," she said.

"Okay," I said.

"Dad just helped me."

"Okay," I said again.

"Sylphide doesn't think so, but they're mine."

"Okay. I believe you. Kate, I believe you."

"And don't tell Jack, but . . ."

"Uh-oh, Katy. Don't even tell me."

"I think Daddy may have taken something else. A little gold bust. It wasn't mine. I just made the mistake of pointing it out. On a table in the foyer there. Okay, it was Sylphide's. It's of one of her famous dancers. I didn't *see* him take it. But that coat with the huge pockets? I just have the feeling. A souvenir. Heavy as shit."

"Good old Dad," I said.

She couldn't suppress a mirthful grin, the first I'd seen in ages. "His coat was clonking against everything. He was leaning to one side, I swear."

I grinned, too, said, "It's good to see you happy."

"Happy," she said.

She pecked my cheek and I wore that little kiss all the way home to Westport in the nice new car.

5

I asked Emily to the Rocks for Friday lunch, a pretty daring suggestion, the Rocks being off school property and officially off-limits, deep in a private forest. Just my having told Kate that Emily and I were an item made me bolder.

A perfect afternoon, as it happened, balmy, dry. We hurried through the parking lot and down the infamous path into the trees, a ten-minute walk, the drums of the Friday pep rally behind us. I carried the big basket she'd brought—she'd gagged at the thought of my bologna sandwiches. She was silent so I filled the woods with my voice, bits and pieces of the story of my visit with Kate, but not the big news: Kate and Dabney!

We spread the tablecloth I'd brought on the biggest, flattest boulder. Inside her basket was a deft wooden chest, and inside that, glimmering cloth bags and precious bottles and tiny thermoslike jars, all kinds of fragrant leaves, curious noodles in a pungent broth, gelatinous beads in various sizes, a big block of rice molded in a wooden bowl, finally a selection of sauces and unfamiliar vegetables.

"Daikon," Emily said, and poked something piquant in my mouth with her chopsticks. "Ginger sauce. Pak choi. Lemon grass. Glass noodle. Kimchi."

Each bite a revelation. Each revelation a little too spicy for me. My family didn't use garlic or anything hotter than a radish—not so you could taste it, anyway—and never an herb except parsley on boiled potatoes or a dash of oregano in spaghetti sauce. I gulped water from the canteen I'd brought.

Emily laughed, fed me more. Some kind of tart cauliflower. "My Auntie Oh in Seoul used my pantyhose to strain pickles. She pretended it was a mistake."

"You had pantyhose?"

"Not after that. And there's Auntie Bo, and Auntie Tik. They steal my shoes. I have to bring three or four pairs each year!"

Each year in October were the big Korean holidays, everyone traveling home to honor ancestors. Emily put a bite in my mouth, clearly pleased by my interest in her family. There had been two brothers on her mother's side, both lost in the Korean civil war, the Noodle-Loving Boys, as they were called. There were endless other relatives as well, stepaunts and step-grandmothers, cousins from a month old to seventy-seven years. Emily's grandpa, the reigning patriarch, was ninety, still sharp and loquacious. He'd outlived three much younger wives, was preparing to wed a teenager named Bo-Kyung Kim. Nothing so scandalous, though, as Emily's mom marrying the American sergeant.

The last bites were squid, which I had always thought of as bait. I licked them and pressed them with my tongue, couldn't soften them.

"I'm full," Emily said. There were times she looked Afro-American and this was one of them, her pretty, wide nose, her full, exotic lips, whatever trick of sunlight and passing cloud shading her skin darker. Her teeth were unbelievably white. Her neck was slender, slender. Her eyes were upon me, dark and Korean, possessive.

"Me too," I said, far from it. How could people subsist on so little? We packed everything up, tidied it all back into the chest and that into its basket.

A breeze rattled the dead oak leaves above, and a shower of them fell around us, drifting quickly down and clattering on the ground. I took Emily's hand, all very dry and simple. When I turned to her it was as if I had actually put words to my desire, she blushed so hard. She looked down, seemed to be staring at my pants.

She picked up on something I'd told her on the walk: "They'd been in the shower together?"

"They came to the door in towels."

"And you won't tell your *parents*?"

"Why would I tell my parents?"

"She wanted you to know!"

"Nah. She didn't even know I was coming."

"He's her teacher!"

"He's very nice. Nice and solid."

Her voice went husky. "And they went back upstairs and . . ."

"I think so, yes."

"In the *afternoon*?"

"It was still morning, really."

She thought about that a minute. A chilly breeze started up, grew stronger, chillier. She said, "Okay. I know all about how you and Jinnie went steady. And all about that girl in seventh grade, Mary Louise who moved to San Diego. Anyone else? Did you have any girlfriends when I was at conservatory?"

"Sara Slaughter," I said. "For about maybe a month."

"I heard rumors."

"We didn't get along very well."

"How far did you go with her?"

"About an inch," I said.

She dropped my hand and caught her knees, leaned back, gazed up at the sky, seemed to float up and off the rock. Dreamily, she said, "I asked my dad if I could have another date with you." Then more businesslike: "I mean, if you ever were to inquire, like a real date, at night. He said yes, sort of, but he has to meet you this time, and he has to talk to your father first and then make the decision. He didn't like it that that chauffeur guy came to the door the other day and not you. But mainly it was that my mother hates Chinese."

"Would you like to go out this weekend? I won't bring Dr. Chun."

"He's a doctor?"

"Tell your mom that! Banished by Mao!"

She said something in what I took to be Korean, looked briefly like her mother—very cross—then returned to her own face and the discussion at hand: "How far did you go with Jinnie?"

"More than an inch."

Emily leaned closer, said, "How far?"

"You know. We liked to make out. In their rumpus room."

"All the way, rumpus?"

"Not quite all the way, rumpus."

"But what?"

"Touching and stuff."

"Touching like where?" Her voice had gone past husky, something lower yet.

I muttered, "Places."

Emily put her lips to mine, and I wasn't wooden but kissed her, once, twice, put my hand on her neck, kissed her again, put my tongue to her teeth, took her lip between my own teeth, arousing myself fiercely, guilty image of Georges and those bushels of peaches falling to his tongue, also my kissing lesson, whoa.

Emily panted. I had not heard her pant before. "I'm not jealous," she said, sounding as if she were. She sighed and rocked back to me, kissed me too hard, letting her lips part. She pulled her hands from mine, put her arms around me. I did the same, my arms around her, and we held this single hard kiss—wooden, I had to admit, but good wood—held it till she pulled away, dove her face into my shoulder. She whispered something, tried again too quietly, then again so I could hear:

"I'm sexually excited when we kiss."

And though it seemed too clinical to describe my own state, I said I was sexually excited, too, using those words.

She struggled out of her big down comforter of a coat, snuggled into mine, her face over my shoulder. She said, "Is it very uncomfortable for boys?"

I said, "No, no."

She said, "I used to think being sexually excited meant I was in love."

Which was as close as we got to saying anything more on the subject. She kissed me again, opened her mouth too wide, surprisingly awkward, touched her tongue to mine experimentally. Abruptly then she lay down on my coat on the rock, pulled me alongside her, tugged her big parka over us. I had a hard-on like a steeple, as my lost friend Jimpie Johnson had been fond of saying.

"Touch me places," she breathed.

I put a hand on her breast, pressing the coarse weave of her sweater against her, found the bump of her nipple, nice.

"It's my birthday," she murmured.

"And you don't say a word?"

"I'm a Scorpio," she said hotly, meaning I knew not what. She put a hand on my chest, pressed as if to push me away, but she was not pushing me away. At length she sighed, threw a leg over mine, pressed into me. I couldn't stop the images of Sylphide and Georges, of Katy and Jack. I reached down in the course of that everlasting kiss, not wooden, pulled Emily's skirt up inch by inch, then in a handful, put my palm over the front of her underpants—hot cloth, grassy feel of pubic hair beneath—pressed gently at a sinking spot as the cloth grew damp.

"That's good," Emily said, her hips beginning to dance without her, really writhing. She said, "Go harder."

Her own hand found my belt, pulled at it ineffectually as she began to gasp. And then, suddenly, it was as if she had fallen asleep. The pressure from her lips slackened, her hand fell from my buckle, her leg slipped off of mine in a way that forced my hand away from the layer of thin, soaked cloth.

Recess was over.

AFTER DINNER THE night he was supposed to call Emily's house, I heard my father talking in the living room. I crept halfway down the stairs as I'd done with Katy so many times. But Pop wasn't talking to Sergeant Bright.

He was talking to his boss, begging. "Why would you send those guys to interview *me*?" He listened long, said, "I don't like you threatening me. . . . Well, you're scaring me. . . . Yes, I'm on my home phone. . . . No, no, Mr. Perdhomme, I gotta say no. . . . No, no, wait a minute, past tense. I *owed* . . . I know exactly how much, and those paintings . . . I get it. I get you have to disavow me. . . . But don't tell me you don't remember those paintings. And the other stuff? . . . Okay, that was a gift, fine, I'll accept that, a very valuable gift, give me credit, but not the paintings, those were payout. You and I both know. I'm still saying it, though—why did they interview *me*? Those fuckers were in my office, Mr. Perdhomme. You sent them to my *office*. Yes, my home phone. . . . I don't want to take the fall here. . . . Well, that's what it sounds like you're saying. . . . I know how deep I'm in. . . . I know that. . . . Yes, worse things than taking a fall, I know. . . . Okay, now you're scaring me again. . . . Crazy, yes I know he is. . . . I told you I'll fucking try."

My ineffectual dad, negotiating who knows what. Apparently he hadn't been paid in quite a while. In the end he was plain groveling. He stopped talking in mid-sentence, only slowly hung up, sat staring. I'd never seen him so bleak, an image that has stayed with me: finally the quintessential Dad. I shambled on down the stairs as if I were just coming down, stepped up behind him, hugged his shoulders. He threw my arms off, suddenly irritable, the microphone from the Wollensak in his hand with the receiver, a tape running on the big machine.

"Who're you recording?" I said gently.

He had to think, rubbed his eyes to buy time, offered a feeble lie: "Oh, the Chevy dealer, what's his name. We can't drive a goddamn *Volvo* everyplace." My mother, at least, still believed the Volvo was a loan from Katy's suitemate.

"So why are you recording the Chevy dealer?"

He turned to look at me square, went on the offensive: "Mommy says the school called. Mr. Demeter, whoever. The principal. You were in a fight?"

"A fight?"

"Some kid reported you."

"What? It wasn't Mark Nussbaum, was it?"

"Here's her note—you look."

It was Mark Nussbaum, all right.

"He hit *me*, Dad. Grazed me, I mean. A sucker punch. And he forced himself on Emily, that's the real issue. And he's jealous and devious. Me, I turned the other cheek."

"Okay, Mr. Christ. Listen, I'm all for smashing the kid. Teach him a lesson. You're both supposed to see Demeter tomorrow. It's right there on the note. Emily, too, it looks like. Your mother and I are proud of you for protecting the Negro race."

"Very funny, Dad. And I know you were you talking to Mr. Perdhomme."

"Bah. I don't give Perdhomme the time of day, son. Why so fixated on Mr. Perdhomme?"

"It's just that you were going to call Emily's dad."

"Oh, son, meant to tell you. I tried over there. They hung up on me twice. The Oriental lady, her mom. 'Emiree can'tah!' I guess she thought I was you. Aw. I know how you feel. But you'll be back in the saddle after this Nussbaum thing blows over."

Leaving me, he went to his desk in the living room, started cleaning it energetically, noisily crumpling papers and tossing them into the fireplace, groaning, muttering. In the kitchen I made popcorn, brought him a bowl to no reaction, carried the rest upstairs to my desk. Nussbaum? I would make short work of him in front of Mr. Demeter. And Emily would back me up. And her father would warm to me. I was a warrior in all things, would win this battle, too.

I stared at my French homework for an hour, gave up. I was onto a secret: Dad was in desperate need of money. I had an idea, a way to make some, and quickly. Flush with my inspiration, I wrote a neat note to our neighbor:

> Tenke, hello. Not like Katy's job, but I would like to ask if there is any work for me over there? I can help mow and I fix things very well and paint or shovel snow, things like that, really anything at all. I don't have a car, so working so close to home would work out well for me. After school and on weekends. Not expensive.

Nothing more than a job application when you thought about it. Sealing it in an envelope made it safer. I tucked it in my shirt, slipped downstairs and out the back door (Dad preoccupied at the fireplace, putting a match to his trash pile), silently jogged over to the High Side, slipped my missive under the great doors. Sylphide's kisses, Emily's, my head swirling with confusion: these women. A few minutes later I was home in my own backyard, lurking—I could see that Dad had moved into the kitchen, and I didn't want to have to explain myself. But then, oddest thing, he slid the patio door open, hurried out into the night carrying a big manila envelope. He didn't look around, certainly didn't see me, hurried down to our rowboat, crossed the pond with efficient strokes, trundled up the long hill to the High Side.

We were both back in our rooms when Mom got home from her tennis match. I could hear Dad murmuring, heard the tone of her answers: they were talking about money. The situation was extreme. But Mom had lost the usual advantage because of her mistake with Kate: she could hardly call him out for his money troubles after what she'd done. They were going to have to cooperate.

Late, I heard them making love, closed my door tight.

THE NEXT MORNING, Emily wasn't in school. I went to the principal's office at the appointed time, no sign of Nussbaum, either. I told Mr. Demeter exactly what had happened between Mark and me. He nodded fondly, no love lost on my brash classmate, nothing but trust for me. He said, "Of course, David. And since it's his complaint, and with your permission, we can let it drop. He's got enough trouble at home, believe me."

"I agree, sir. And I can take care of myself, sir. But the person with the real complaint is Emily Bright." I rushed into his confidence: "He forced himself on her."

"Sexually, you mean."

"I guess, yes."

"Well, that's a horse of a different color, David. That's serious stuff. I'll have to have a word with our man."

Whoa. "I'm not so sure about that, sir."

"Worried about Emily's honor, are we? Trust me, I'll treat the matter delicately."

The next day, I waited till I was late for homeroom, then till I had *missed* homeroom (and had to go to Mr. Demeter's office for a blue slip, he kindly as ever), but Emily didn't turn up. It wasn't like I could phone her, not in those days, when phone calls were practically dates. Then, oddly, she was in math class, something different about her. Clothes, for one thing—she looked like a church girl, all in yellow with bows in her hair. Aloof, for another: she didn't so much as raise her hooded eyes to greet me. I hooked my feet in the rungs of her chair, lifted her off the ground, but she didn't even turn, made herself heavy. At the bell she hurried out of the room, pointedly avoiding me.

She didn't turn up at the Rocks (I'd made big plans for the Rocks, had a blanket in my gym bag), and then she wasn't in the senior parking lot after school. Wednesday she was even more elusive. I spotted her near her locker after lunch, but she skipped math altogether. It was Thursday before I finally cornered her against the retaining wall, having spied her at the bus line. She couldn't hold my eye, and I noticed again that she was wearing someone else's clothes, a cable-knit sweater, white Dacron pants you could only call slacks, hideous. Plus her hair was out, carefully brushed, long down to her elbows, glossy black. She'd even been forbidden her signature braid! In place of her sandals, sensible pumps and Pedi-Sox. And, the ultimate indignity, there she was waiting for the bus: her BMW had been taken away.

"I'm grounded," she said flatly, and would say no more.

WHEN I GOT home there was a note taped to the front door, definitely not Desmond's writing, no scent of jasmine, embossed HIGH SIDE, a maid's handwriting perhaps, anyway, feminine: "Sylphide would like you to know she's in Europe these coming weeks. Meantime, your note about work has been placed on the desk of her manager, Conrad Pant, and a copy forwarded."

That was one efficient household.

6

What had happened to our nice, normal family? Kate at college, swell, but living with her professor and a near-priceless Bonnard liberated from the home of the greatest dancer on earth. Mom, well, she'd been in the dark about all that, still moped about her treatment over a silly football game, spent her time with ladies who had better things to do: tennis and martinis. Dad was still taking the bus with me, still liked to give me a hard time, though he was the one sneaking off to the High Side with his big manila envelopes, no one home over there but the watchman and a skeleton staff: Sylphide and her retinue and her retinue's retinue were overseas.

I've long since lost the photo I'd clipped from the *Times*, but the image remains fixed in my memory: the ballerina poised and pleasant, Linsey wide-eyed just behind her, Georges Whiteside slouching in the background, Queen Elizabeth II beaming—a posthumous knighthood for Dabney Stryker-Stewart. I started to call my sister Lady Kate, though not to her face, and not around my folks, not aloud at all.

RANDOMLY ON A Monday night after Dabney's elevation, the lights came back on at the High Side. I mean all of the lights. By the next afternoon, exotic cars were parked helter-skelter like boats off their moorings, in the driveways, on the lawn, wherever they'd been left. Huge trucks pulled in and out of the service road unloading mysterious crates and pallets back by the garages. The Bentley came and went, came and went, ferrying arrivals from the train station. I heard guitars tuning up, a loud P.A. system being tested. My mother perked her ears as I did.

"We'll be invited for the party," she said.

I was hard on her: "Yes, you and me and Kate."

"Certainly we won't tell Kate!"

And of course there were things Kate and I wouldn't tell Mom.

And things Kate wasn't telling anyone.

Mr. Demeter, our noble principal, came to the door of my history class that Wednesday, interrupting Miss Butterman so that Dr. Chun could present me with a letter—that gorgeous note paper, the intoxicating scent of jasmine, Desmond the butler's handwriting, his sense of humor, too, no attempt to sound like the ballerina, small words:

GET YER HUNKY BUTT OVER HERE

I was being summoned. Always one for the arts, Mr. Demeter formally excused Linsey and me, and Dr. Chun drove us to the High Side. Desmond at the door gazed up into my eyes.

I took advantage: "So. You knew all about Dabney and Kate."

"Sir, I know only that you are expected in the ballroom immediately."

"What about my dad's shoes?"

His gaze fell to my belly. "The shoes didn't match, sir. Very close, sir. As it turned out, sir. But not a match. And I know nothing about any stolen paintings. So don't ask me about that, sir."

"Sir yourself," I said. "Who said anything about paintings?"

He said, "I, sir. It was I who said it. May I just . . . Sir, may I punch you in the stomach?"

I lifted my T-shirt for him, and he took a shot, bam.

"Ouch," I said, to please him.

"Like cement," he said.

I raised the shirt a little higher. "Kate and Dabney," I said.

"The poolhouse," he said. "That was their domain. The old carriage house."

"And my father," I said. "Did my father know?"

He gazed at my belly. "I've made you pink," he said.

"Did Nicholas know?"

"No sir, no. A great effort, in fact, was mounted that he should not."

"Does he know now?"

"You will have to ask him."

I dropped my shirt. A harried man wearing a black beret burst into the

foyer as if from another dimension—there were a lot of doors leading in
and out of there, several under the stairway.

"Perhaps sometime you and I could box," Desmond said. "You might
be surprised at my prowess."

"Ha," I said.

Desmond hurried: "Your father was banned. By Sylphide. He isn't welcome here and has not been since Mr. Stryker-Stewart's death."

The beret man was Conrad Pant. His handshake was a slice of pressed
turkey, limp and cold. Desmond introduced me as Sylphide's new executive assistant. I mouthed the title back to him. He didn't seem to be
kidding. Pant looked up at me with huge disdain, bid me follow, led me
at warp speed to the Chlorine Baron's old ballroom, which I'd seen only
in my imagination—Kate's stories—a startling, ornate cavern the size of
a school gym but with mirrors and barres installed on two long walls,
chandeliers hanging from gilded plaster escutcheons, high-arched doorways, no windows, stage lights on a retractable rigging of pipes and cables, a convertible theater. My guide looked me over once more, sneered
and stormed off, leaving me in the midst of a careless understory of music
stands, instrument cases, duffel bags—people, too, all haphazard, apparently on some kind of break: dancers stretching, musicians chatting and
running licks, a dark-skinned techie in dreads measuring the floor and
laying out precise lines in black gaffer's tape.

I kept wondering: How did Dad's actual shoes not match his actual
footprints in the actual High Side parlor? Had he been there with Kate
or not?

Shortly, Georges slipped in without a look in anyone's direction, sat
at the biggest piano, slumped and stared lugubriously, his satyr's earring
glinting in the light tests. One of the female dancers—a plump woman
with a strange, long face—showed the others a step on flat feet, and then
they all tried it, laughing. Vlad Markusak came in from the patio—the
Cavalier himself, dressed in tights that showed his bozzer quite plainly,
no shirt, no shoes.

A suite of teenage girls flounced into the hall from the double doors at
the back, all in tights and bare feet after the day's classes. They saw Vlad
and flew to gather around him. He bussed their cheeks, both sides, each
girl, lifting them up at the waists to his height, enormous strength, perfect

control. I thought of the driveway full of cars. Hard to imagine any of
these people getting on a train or driving—more likely they had drifted
in on currents of air like spiders casting silk.

Suddenly Conrad was back, vast shift in attitude. Clearly he'd been
yelled at. "It's Lizard, then," he said, all transparent. "Let me apologize for
my earlier greeting. You just seemed so young. Like a newborn calf, no
offense. A wet, enormous, staring, stupid, mucous-covered newborn calf,
for which image I apologize. Here's what's going on: Sylphide is forming
a new company, ongoing auditions, old friends, lots of the folks you see
here, plenty of new young dancers. Youth the watchword, eh? She's determined to mount Dabney's benefit, the one he always waxed on about,
dance performances in the form of rock concerts, untold millions for
Children of War. All right? Of course she's going to ruin her reputation
and mine in the process, but there you go."

"A mucous-covered wet calf," I said, impressed.

"You and I, we're going to get along fine," Conrad said.

Children of War was Dabney's foundation, everyone knew, a big part
of why he'd been knighted, funded by the robust proceeds of his most
remarkable album, *Children of War,* every song a hit, all those kids'
voices. He himself had traveled to places like Borneo and Laos and
Colombia—and of course Vietnam—always at great personal risk, supposedly, went wherever the wars were, free concerts, meetings with world
leaders, visits to schools and hospitals, the fierce media focus he brought
to bear like sunshine.

Pant said, "The lady's got commitments from all of Dabney's old
friends, and we're gathering new commitments every day, concerts
around the world. Listen to this: Eric Clapton, Pete Townshend, Grace
Slick, Bob Dylan, Jimmy Page, all the Beatles but McCartney, Mick
Jagger. They all want to be involved, which means everyone else wants to
be, a whole new audience for Sylphide and her dancers, of course." Apparently her plan for the New York engagement ("I have stopped arguing,"
Conrad said) was to go up against every Christmas event—*Nutcracker*
and Rockettes and *Messiah,* all that stuff rock fans didn't care about, all
the stuff ballet fans did, and sell out a week or ten days of shows, every
night different.

"Whoa," I said.

"And as Sylphide's executive assistant, you are going to help make it happen."

"I don't know what to say."

"Good. Don't say anything. What we need now is a theater. Two thousand seats give or take." He handed me a neatly typed sheet of addresses, phone numbers. "You're going to call these people, explain what we're doing, drop all the names I've been dropping, and make appointments. Be snooty, lord it up. You're somebody, now. You're Dabney Stryker-Stewart and Sylphide put together, with all their clout behind you. Tenke said she'd be down in a minute to show you to a phone."

I fingered the smooth stone in my pocket, lurked and watched the action, considered my father's shoes.

WHEN SYLPHIDE FINALLY appeared, she flew right at me, grabbed me by the hand, full speed to the kitchen, where several cooks were at work in front of the famous Victor range. I thought I'd be getting a snack, but no: she pulled me into the pantry, of all places, vortexed me up a spiral staircase into a storage loft, lots of empty boxes. She slid a secret panel aside as if it were nothing strange, pulled me into a dark passageway and to another panel, which she slid aside with a flood of light: a sudden, sumptuous dressing room, no windows, no obvious doors, just rows of hangers heavy with costumes, ceiling so low I couldn't stand straight.

"My office," she said. And indeed under piles of clothes and torn envelopes and note cards and books and polished rocks and seashells there was a huge old oaken eminence, like a dance floor with drawers. She pushed some papers aside so I could sit, tossed a bralike thing to a waiting chair, gave me a shove.

I felt a strong sensation of falling toward her, when in fact I was falling away, sat on the desk. "How was London?" I said to save myself.

She put long fingers to my lips, stood between my legs, hands on my thighs, continued to hold my eye. "London was lovely," she said, leaning close, then closer, levitating somehow (going up on her toes no doubt), kissed my forehead, kissed my mouth. Before I could respond, something came visibly over her, some air of gravity. She backed away, became a businessperson, calm and articulate: "Now, let us get to work. Conrad has filled you in, *ja*? You have got the list? I am finding the phone."

She drifted to a buried dresser, stripped out of her sweatpants and leotard. Naked, she found a sheer kind of frock in a drawer, held it up to herself, slowly put it on. Trick of the light, you could still see her body. She seemed muscular to me, not perfectly attractive. The phone was on the floor. She dug it out, bending from the waist. I watched every movement from the very edge of my vision, every inch of her legs.

"I should not kiss you so," she said abstracted.

"It's okay," I said.

"Good boys cannot live in my world."

"Good boys could try."

"Just something to keep in mind: Good boys *cannot*."

"So Georges is not a good boy?"

That got her attention. She stood and faced me, said, "He is teaching me some little yummy somethings. But he is a troll, not a good boy at all. He should be living under a wooden bridge in a swamp somewhere nasty, with fog and mold and Spanish moss."

"He's incredible, really. At piano, I mean."

"Oh, he is incredible, *ja*. Dabney was being very, very fond of him." She poked her chin at me, a pointed thing. A lick of pink fire had risen up from the collar of her frock into her neck—I wanted to put my hand there, or anywhere. She found a slight pair of underpants in her drawer, pulled them on under the shift with no particular modesty, someone used to dressing in front of others.

She caught me looking. "Oh, Lizard," she said. "I have not had a normal life. I am emotionally stump-ted."

"Stunted?"

"*Ja-ja*, that's so."

I gathered my thoughts, a vision of her through binoculars, said, "I don't think I know what that means, emotionally stunted. Or anyway, it doesn't sound true. I mean, you seem pretty grown-up to me."

"Did you want to know something? Georges is my first lover. And you, you are the first man I ever kissed."

"Just that thing in your car? That's what you're talking about?"

"And just now, ungrateful you. The first, *ja*. I can't stop thinking of it."

"That one little kiss?"

"Two of them, now," she said. "Don't be making fun of me." She cleared her high dresser off, perched upon it with a simple hop, her head almost touching the ceiling. Her hair came past her shoulders, seemed a little dirty. I'd never seen it out. She could easily be a classmate, maybe someone who didn't know about shampoo. She said, "You don't believe me."

"Well, no. What about Dabney? What about Georges?"

"I never developed. I am dancing all the time. All the time. Dancing is the only reality, the only thing I do. Others kiss me, *ja*. They kiss me all the time. That is not what I am saying. I am saying that *I* kissed *you*." The blush on her neck and clavicle had fallen back into her neckline. She raised a leg, impossibly placed her foot flat on the dresser beside her, matter of factly hugging her knee to her cheek—that's how long her legs were, proportionally speaking. I loved the way her thigh fit into her hip, the way the crease worked, the sight of her underpants. She caught me looking again, just kept going: "Dabney, he was a miner's kid, and then he was a miner himself. Love was about battling and getting an upper hand. A man worked very hard all day and then he drank and when he wanted some cunt he pulled off your pants. Sorry, is that not a nice word? Okay, cunt. I won't say it. You worship your woman, you build a shrine, *ja*? You are using all your strength carrying the beloved up there and after a time you are being exhausted and so you leave her up there, you never come back to claim her. That was Dabney and Sylphide. Do you know how we met?"

Everyone knew how they met: rhetorical question.

"He saw a photo in the *Times* of London. I am not even nineteen. He pulled on a few ropes and sat in the front row at my Royal Ballet debut. I did not know him. I did not know to be star-struck. After the performance, there he is in my dressing room. Everyone rushing in to touch him like I'm not there."

"And you just ignored him!"

"I have heard that rumor, too. But not true. If everyone wanted him, I would have him. And this part you have not heard, because it has not been told: we are having dinner at his hotel, and then up to his room, no resistance from me. But in his bed I am surprised by what he seems to intend. I have been sheltered, Lizard. I am perfectly pleased to be touched, kissed, naked in his hands, fucked if he wants, all of it, it's not like I do not know what it all is, but I cannot begin to comply. I mean physically. There is a medical word for it, but I forget it. I closed up tight! He is knocking away, and pushing and prodding, but you know, he cannot even get started. I am crying. I cry and cry not to make him happy. I am not understanding. It is funny, *ja*? You smile? I thought he would hate me, but he did not care. He is liking my innocence. He finds some way around it, gets his satisfaction. We married the next week. I was grateful to him. But grateful is not love, I have come to learn."

I picked up the huge phone, put it on my lap, picked Conrad's list of theaters out of my shirt pocket, gazed at the names and numbers almost longingly.

Sylphide said, "Kate doesn't brag of him?"

Suddenly we had landed on my sister. Was that why I was there? I felt protective: "Far from it. Total secrecy. I just found out like, last *week*."

"I was finding out the night he died. Those little tennis skirts of hers, *oik*! You know his song 'Love Fifteen.' That is how old, she! And then two years more it went on! He is writing this for her! And she's the one being furious with me!" Sylphide turned her head just so, cocked her shoulders so, crossed her ankles, put herself forward in some ineffable way, the sexual body no longer on display, a dancer in its place.

"That was the only time he try with me. That one night in that beautiful hotel. He had all the girls in the world. I was the one he couldn't. And before Dabney there was only Vasily Bustonovich Bustonov, my *impresario*. I was twelve, *ja*? I knew nothing. I loved him very much, so far as I knew. He is taking me from my home with the blessing of my parents . . . ."

"They were farmers in Boda. An island."

"They were not farmers. That error, over and over again endlessly. But it was an island, and quite severe, two hours of daylight in winter. My father was being a grain broker." She told the proper story, not like what I'd heard: her mother had grown up in a house of drunkards, had known the dancer's father from childhood, was not a mail-order bride. The mother had, in fact, been a dancer in her youth, had run off and lived in Russia, well into her thirties. Bustonov had been the mother's mentor, and was her correspondent in Sylphide's youth, likely a lover, but certainly not Sylphide's actual father, per rumor.

"And Bustonov brought you to the Kirov School for training. In Moscow, which was still in a shambles from the war. You met Vlad Markusak there. He defected years later in Boston in order to dance with you again."

"I see you have been making a study of me. But low marks: it is all being much more complicated than you want to believe!"

"And you got in trouble in Moscow, trying to protect your friends. Or Bustonov tried to keep you from your friends and you rebelled. But whatever, he took you to Bournonville's company in Denmark. He had a diplomatic passport. You took the name Sylphide."

"Well, and you are ready for the exam, I see. Yes, to Denmark. But Bournonville? He died in 1864 or something like this. He only started the company I was in: Danish Royal Ballet. Very proper, classical ballet. Vasily very proud of me, very protective. I was given to understand that he was my lover."

"Given to understand?"

"He is saying we are lovers, and so I believe him, *ja?* But in fact we did not make love. Our only intimacy was conversation, very good talk. I was calling him Uncle in public, lived with him in Copenhagen. We are not sleeping in the same room, not even that. His sexual needs are nothing to me, only a few kisses on my forehead when I am lying down to bed. He draw my baths, he help me dress; I have no sense of shame in my body, none at all. He likes me to do my barre exercises in his bedroom while he does something or other under the quilts. I never inquire about it, never understand it in any explicit way till Dabney explains. I just mistook it all for love. And what else did I need?"

Dance.

Dance provided all the physical expression she needed, every bit of it across the entire range from plain exercise to the sexual, as she understood it then. And I wasn't to misunderstand her: Bustonov was quite fascinating. She would have said she loved him. "He kiss me on the mouth only once, a lot of warm spittle, how I was seeing it, a disgusting event."

She was my age by then, having already had five years with the man, who had turned sixty, and just the one kiss. Which was itself part of a very nasty scene. He'd grown jealous of Tenke's dance partners. He had demanded that she quit. He wept and begged and raged and made promises. "I left him forever the next morning. A boat to Newcastle, a train to London, all the money he was having in his purse.

"Then Dabney. Then Georges. And that is all. So thank you for my first kiss. I love you for my first kiss."

I looked this way, she looked that, and the dressing room was just a hot stillness, one minute, two minutes, three. I couldn't think of a thing to say, wasn't at all sure what she was implying, didn't believe she was only confiding. Also, had she just said she loved me? She made no motion to get off her dresser. I stayed put on her desk, the heavy phone in my lap. Was I supposed to make a move?

"Make your telephone calls," she said after a long wait. She slipped off her perch and onto her famous feet, the frock rising up in the process to show her naked thighs, her tiny underpants complete, her bellybutton then, which I was almost surprised to see she owned. She straightened the garment, wrapped herself in a silken robe, crossed in front of me unhappily, jasmine zephyr, pushed at the bottom of yet another innocuous wall panel, which opened to reveal her boudoir—the very room I'd seen her and Georges in, the very bed, the very windows back behind it, a tree fort somewhere out there.

I MADE CALLS till after six, left a lot of messages at the theaters on Conrad's list, got busy signals, felt deflated, depressed even, finally a receptionist who was indifferent till I said I worked for Sylphide. Her boss would call in the morning! She called me Mr. Hochmeyer, then, let her voice grow breathy, whoa. Then more busy signals and long-ringing phones and perfunctory answering services. Restless I stood and paced with my neck bent under the low ceiling, paced up and down all the rows of dry-cleaned clothes and costumes, whole deep shelves of accessories: wings, halos, hats, tails, feathers, scarves, wristlets, anklets, silver corsets, golden girdles, leather thongs, pants and panties and pantaloons, jewelry fake and jewelry real, all full of meaning, no doubt. I'd have to skip school in the morning. I'd skip school and come straight back to the High Side, where a man like myself was needed.

I thought to leave a note for my dancer, for it seemed with kisses she had given herself to me. Flowery phrases crossed my mind but there was no pencil anywhere, no pen, not a typewriter. At Sylphide's dresser I touched her bra-thing, thought of how she'd undressed right there in front of me, that boundless physical aplomb. Which was married, I suddenly saw, to her surprising sexual insecurity. I brought the slight garment to my face: jasmine, sweat, warm cotton. On impulse I stuffed it into my pants pocket. In its place on the dresser I left her the pretty, speckled stone. Definitely the shape of a heart. That would have to do for a note.

Downstairs the High Side was entirely empty, dark and silent, not even Desmond to be found, not so much as a chambermaid coughing in the wings. Abandoned, I left my list of calls and phone messages on the butler's little dais for Conrad, let myself out, made my way down the lawns and to the pond, rowed home from my first day of work, dazzled, confused, exhilarated, spent, but supremely ready for whatever crazy thing was going to come next.

PART TWO

Firfisle

7

Eighteen-some years later, trading on a fairly undistinguished Miami Dolphins career and hometown fame, I opened a bistro back north in Westport. I'd returned from Miami to the family home, which against Kate's better instincts we had never sold but rented. And as it happened the place had come empty just at my most aimless moment in the desultory years after my retirement from the NFL.

(But more about all that later.)

On a particular morning in the autumn of 1994, Restaurant Firfisle's fifth year (yes, I named the place Firfisle, and yes, I was still stuck on the dancer), our mushroom man brought in a prodigious selection of fresh forest mushrooms: porcini, king oyster, yellow and blue chanterelles, all these great textures and shades. With the night's menu still in question, our famous and colorful chef, Etienne LaRoque, simply commanded me to make mushroom sausages—an item I'd never made and never heard of—offering nothing but a quick idea of how I might proceed. From his head to my work station: sauté both coarse and fine-chopped mixed wild mushrooms and tiny wedges of green cherry tomato from our garden in olive oil and butter, equal-equal, add finely rubbed sage, add garden basil and more than you'd think of our fiery Thai chilies, plenty of salt, a little onion, a little shallot, a handful or two per pot of milled rice as a binder. Then press the mixture into cold glass bowls and cure all afternoon in the walk-in, stuff just before service into the handsome, somewhat elastic soy skins our impulsive chef had found someplace.

He grilled only one to test, just an hour before the first orders came in, skin of the balls, as he would put it, his confidence in his own mastery not misplaced: gorgeous sausages, fat and firm, speckled and textural, juicy, jazzy, subtlest mushroom flavors. He'd made green-tomato fries for the side, fresh pasta for the base, a silky leek cream to finish: beautiful.

I recall the invention of that dish vividly, not because of the muscular mushroom textures of the sausage, and not because of the compliments all night (regulars sticking their heads in the kitchen to enthuse, wait staff beaming), not even because it became a seasonal bestseller that no one in any other kitchen anywhere could imitate, but because it's what Mr. Perdhomme ordered when he came in.

Yes, that Mr. Perdhomme. My father's boss.

I'd seen the name on the reservations list, which as any evening got going I liked to check for friends, regulars, celebrities, critics. I brooded— Perdhomme!—grew grumpy, stalked the stations of the kitchen giving orders. But probably there were lots of people with that name. Why should this Perdhomme be mine? I checked the book again. Whoever it was had requested our one best table, a nice, square four-top in the biggest of the beachside windows, dinner timed for an autumn sunset: inside information.

I peeped out of the kitchen at 5:50, peeped at 5:55, peeped at 6:00. His guest and he arrived just after that, it seemed, because when I peeped out again at 6:05 they were there, definitely they, two devils who'd figured large in my imagination for over twenty years, my father's old boss, all right, same old air of command, in his early seventies perhaps, erect and polished. And accompanied by the man my father in surprise had called Kaiser—really he, indisputably he, the very Kaiser, my parents' killer, a perfectly nice-looking man in a very expensive suit.

My heart pumped scattered thoughts through my head; I felt the strain on every vein and artery along the way. Because here was proof, no more allegations—Kaiser and Mr. P. were connected. But their appearance together at my restaurant wasn't a mistake, and it wasn't a confession, either. Instead, it seemed a calculated threat: *We know where to find you.* Dolus Investments had been in the news—they were tangled in the savings and loan scandals, congressional and criminal probes in progress. Perhaps they feared old crimes coming to light, old witnesses.

Whatever, they got the best treatment they had ever gotten or would ever get at a restaurant. I told the staff that Kaiser was a critic, the old guy maybe his boyfriend—they did seem a couple—and as the evening progressed everyone paid subtle, graceful attention. Back in the kitchen, I personally plated their orders, personally arranged the brilliant green-tomato fries, personally lined the mushroom sausages side-by-side-by-side, personally drizzled the leek cream, a gorgeous dish.

In the end, the Kaiser guy paid in cash. Later, the staff would complain about his cheapness—shouldn't reviewers tip like anyone else? Mr. Perdhomme was an ungodly long time in the bathroom. I took the opportunity to slip out to the parking lot, quickly found Olulenu (chief of valet, was the joke, Darfur refugee, was the truth, a state department placement in Bridgeport, big machete scar from his forehead to his chin, slightly walleyed from the injury). I slipped him what was in my pocket, four twenties, no amount too high, said, "Follow the Jaguar. All night if needed. Tell me where they go."

"Yes," he said.

I watched then from the kitchen window, a long wait. But finally Mr. Perdhomme fell into the low-slung car. Kaiser closed his door, looking like any rich guy's younger friend. Maybe just a coincidence, I told myself, two old dudes checking out a hot restaurant on their way back from a leaf-peeping trip, no idea at all how close they'd come to me.

Olulenu followed them out of the lot in his girlfriend's sputtering Rabbit.

Not even an hour, and he was back. I dropped the plate I was working on, intercepted him, too anxious to act as I'd planned, like it was all a lark. He stared up at me with the one eye first, then the other, his face shining black, a person who did not ask questions, a person who just did his job.

"They drove northwards," he said. "Bloody slow. And north again up on the Weston Road, there. Took them a left on one eerie old road. And then, sir, a right. Stone towers, sir. A duppie castle, sir! I hastened back."

"The High Side," I said.

"*Fuckery*," said Olulenu, offering a handshake in which he skillfully passed me back my eighty dollars.

8

I don't know why I'm so dismissive of my National Football League years. Regret, perhaps, a kind of mourning, what might have been. Though when you think about it, the whole thing is pretty impressive, a history few can claim. I guess I just don't actually think about it much. But I promised to fill those years in. So:

After my solid career at Princeton, and after a particularly big senior year (record running yardage, record scoring in the league, positive winning percentage), I reluctantly entered the NFL draft, where I was a seventh-round pick of the Miami Dolphins. My initial salary wasn't stratospheric but more than my father had ever made, about standard for rookies at the time: $42,500.

The kind of thing you call your folks about, but of course I couldn't do that: my folks were dead. Instead I stood in the hallway of my dorm, gloomy March afternoon, and called Kate.

"Dickhead," she said.

By then I didn't expect much more from her: "Kate, it's a big deal."

"You can talk to Jack."

It took a while for him to come to the phone—maybe she just threw it down for him to find—me there in my regular student housing, not a guy to join any fraternities or secret societies or even to live off campus—but when he finally answered he was generous. He had no clue about professional football or the NFL draft; still he was warm and excited for me, apologetic about Kate. "She's climbing out of it," he said, the usual optimism. Climbing out of her tailspin after college, he meant.

And he said, "She's playing tennis again. Wants to get on the tour. A rough road, David, as you know. But by god, she's finding her way, four

years since she touched a racket." A year or so after the deaths of our parents she'd quit the Yale team, but not before she'd made a scene or two,
flinging herself on the clay of a tournament court her very last game and
crying into it after *winning*, no tears of joy, her face and her whites completely orange by the time they picked her up. "She's back up to weight,
she's beating the club pro. I mean drubbing him, little cocky bastard, nice
to see. She's going to Forest Hills unseeded next month, if all goes well."

"I was insensitive," I said.

But Jack didn't catch any irony: "You have every right to your excitement, David. And she can't wait to see you play. We can't wait."

"Well, you'll have to wait, I guess. I'm just going to be a scrub, and only
if I make the spring cut."

"You'll make the cut, David."

I made the cut, all right, didn't call with the news.

THAT JUNE, WITHOUT Kate's particular blessing, I rented out the family house and furnishings and drove to Miami, same old Volvo wagon
Jack had loaned and then gifted years before, taking only what would fit.
A beautiful city, I quickly decided, scruffy and a little mean, with shark's
teeth among the shells on the beaches and good Cuban music clubs back
in the neighborhoods, black beans and rice. Which I mention because I
was more excited about the shark's teeth and beans and music than about
football, or anyway quite numb about football, nothing new, a vacuum
of feeling that Coach Keshevsky had tried to fill repeatedly, talks in his
office, talks at his home, talks in the bleachers at Big Brothers/Big Sisters boxing matches in Trenton: "You're an all-time great, David. If only
you'd love the game. You must love it more than life itself!" He also liked
to point out that there were some five million kids playing high-school
football, some fifty-five thousand playing NCAA college ball, but only
some twelve hundred in the NFL, only about two hundred draftees each
year, of which at most ten were quarterbacks. I'd barely made it, was my
only observation.

On the Dolphins I was third quarterback behind the superstar Bob Griese and the remarkable Don Strock, both of them single-minded lovers
of football—life itself, you bet—never quite my friends, though frequent

hosts on their deep-sea fishing boats off-season and in their handsome houses. I worked very hard at football, arrived early for practice every Wednesday through Friday, got to the airport two hours early on Saturday mornings, or got to the team's (secret) Miami hotel on Saturday afternoons, first player there.

I played nearly every game those first few years, it's worth remembering, if only to set and hold the ball for Garo Yepremian, our brilliant All-American Armenian-Cypriot place kicker. I was cycled in for particular running plays, too, short yardage mostly, fourth and one. Don Shula, of course, was head coach, a guy who always had time for me, who called me in nearly weekly my first couple of years. "Son, you were great."

Great? I felt I'd done nothing, game after game.

"You're part of the master plan, mister. You're right in the middle of it. Big picture. Future payoffs. Work your way up. Pay your dues."

He'd put me in his beautiful creaking leather chair at the big desk in his chilly office at the stadium, rub my shoulders absently. "It's a mental game," he'd say, kneading away. "And you are great at it. One of the very best. A mental game. But try telling your body that! Body says, follow me!" And having separated mind and body, he'd enumerate my flaws, which were all in the area of attention, focus, concentration, edge, the dumb body taking over and leaving mind behind. "Mental, mental. A mental game."

Coach Shula seemed to know an awful lot about me that I hadn't told him, asked the team for silence in the locker room on or near every October 30, "In memory of a great dad and mom." I'd play like a monster next couple of games, get to play whole quarters, even an entire second half once when Strock puked from the flu, a good half, too: three touchdowns (the first a faked field goal), nearly 200 yards passing, over 200 rushing, big spread in the *Miami Herald* in the armchair edition next day. And several of the other teams in the league developed the "Lizard Defense" against my goal-line work: the backfield standing as tall as they could behind their frontline, a nice idea, though they forgot I could pass, always left me a receiver.

The professional game is much faster than the college version, much more painful both physically and emotionally, far more intense, more cerebral, too, as Shula never stopped saying, less fun, never a moment to rest, twice as many games to pump up for, always the game coming at you, the coaches, your teammates, the opposing players, all of it bearing down, very much more a business than college ball (which is a business, too, just not your own). Your NFL contract states that you are *paid to practice*. The games, they're just supposed to be gravy.

I memorized playbooks and signals and patterns like an understudy learning the big role; at practice I played the part of opposing quarterback and took the blows in blitz-formation trials. I threw the ball in pattern drills, too, nailed the receivers (many of whom I'd idolized from my junior high school years forward), passes as hard as I could make them, which was very hard most days, drew complaints. But Coach only grinned and said to throw harder. I was surrounded by men as hungry as I, hungrier, and all of them more dedicated. I was no longer the fastest man on the field, and no longer tallest, no longer smartest either, not even most tragic (that honor went to Cleveland Morris, whose entire family had famously died in a hotel fire at his sister's wedding). And I was not the best quarterback, though I could put on a pretty good show.

Those were winning years, the Dolphins' golden era, and really, it was more than I ever thought I deserved: two Super Bowl rings, muscular pay raises year after year, plenty of attention, expiation for the sin of quitting on my father, I mean quitting football way back when, quitting the game when the game was our only bond.

KATE CLAIMED IN later years to have never finished at Yale, but she does have a degree—I've seen the diploma. It must have come in the mail, or maybe Jack picked it up: she refused to attend her graduation. What she didn't finish was tennis, so maybe that's the confusion. Anyway, I was privy to almost nothing in her life at that time, and anything I did know was because of Jack, who called every Tuesday and filled me in. Kate would seldom take the phone, and the times she did she was overexcited, often incoherent. Jack tended to leave out the bad news, talked a lot about tennis. Her game was erratic when she resumed playing after Yale, but she was more powerful than ever when she was on, and eventually she got seeded on the women's tour, peaking at number eighteen or so—eighteen in the world, I mean, very serious. She had a serve no one could hit; she was strong and car-crash fast. She was beautiful, too, sneer and all, and that made her a natural for certain kinds of endorsements, the tough girl, the rebel, the babe: Virginia Slims, Victoria's Secret, cervical caps and spermicidal jellies ("I whack 'em with my racket" was her joke). There's no way not to count her a success.

But Kate could do strange things under pressure, especially when ahead, impulsive acts that got her disqualified from matches, like leaping over the net and hitting her own lob back to her own empty court. How do you score that? She spanked a line judge with her bare hand, bent him over, pulled down his shorts, and walloped him, film that made the evening news. Really, everyone loved her—easy when you didn't know her. She lasted three seasons before the final blowup. I still don't know all the details, just that her team's plane had to make an emergency landing at Heathrow, where she was met by security and jailed, later hospitalized, her first full-blown breakdown, something in the bipolar range, certain doctors said; schizoid tendencies, said others. This was before people began to realize how serious the symptoms of post-traumatic stress syndrome might be, and how delayed, not that I'm offering a diagnosis.

Back in the states, months of misdirected rehab, and then, with her usual furious energy, she started on a graduate degree in social work, left after a partial semester, her usual paranoid complaints. No matter—Jack had a grander vision, the two of them traveling to Egypt then camel-trekking through all of North Africa to Morocco, where they lived in some splendor for an entire expatriate sabbatical year. There were weekly letters from Jack, occasional notes and gifts from her (a fez!). Home again, she got it into her head to begin a career, though she had no particular career in mind. So several years of assorted jobs, from Christmas-tree farmhand to furniture salesperson, from executive assistant at an alternative energy company to philosophy-bookstore clerk (where she may have had an affair with the hunchbacked owner), from day-care manager to tennis-camp coach. I'm filling all this in from later stories she'd tell when the mood struck her, wildly funny stories, and dark ones, very dark. Whatever steam she managed to build up at each job, she got fired from all of them.

I felt powerfully that I could have prevented her pain, equally powerfully knew that I could not, walked around with my head split thinking about her. I loved her, adored her, but was antsy in her presence, too much of Dad there. She and Jack visited me in Florida a number of times in the off-season, and generally we went somewhere else for the week or two they'd allotted—the Keys, the Everglades, the Gulf Coast. But all I ever wanted was to get back to my workout schedule, all the stuff Coach Shula put in front of me as I worked to become franchise quarterback. Our visits were drawn-out disjunctions moderated by Jack and punctuated by diving on the reefs at Pennecamp, say, or paddling canoes on the Seminole Trail through lost mangrove thickets, athletic adventures our best bet.

I LIVED SPARTAN, never bought a house, instead rented a series of fairly nice but plain apartments in one or another of the new towers on South Beach. I bought a table, two chairs, a single bed, a cheap television, one large bookshelf, and wherever those things were was my home, walls painted real-estate linen-white, no art, just the big and then bigger windows looking out high and then higher over the ocean, the increasingly dazzling heights from balconies, always a Gulfstream tumult out there, great ships passing day and night, the water a Kate's-eye blue, Sylphide's-eye green near the beach.

For a while there were women. In fact, and unhappily, I was featured in the *Miami Herald*'s "Ten Most Eligible Bachelors" article, posed for photos with my shirt off and butt showing, stupid, bales of letters, temptation I never entertained.

But I dated here and there (the league issued endless memos on conduct, recommended written consent from any sex partners, definitely a mood killer over dinner), women the team wives introduced me to. I had only one real girlfriend in those years, the sister of a teammate, an excitable Detroit girl named Honey (she was sweet and she stuck, she said). And don't get me wrong: I enjoyed Honey's sense of humor, loved her bad habits (red wine and soap operas and screaming fits around policemen), enjoyed her rousingly inventive sexuality, also something I hope it's fair to call her African-American sensibility, a certain kind of heat and light, a skeptical charm, incisive judgment about absolutely everything, no dithering, never. She was a great cook, and after the initial year or so of intense and frequent sex our intimacy was about eating, anything to do with food—buying it together, searching out recipes together, bringing home ideas from our many trips (she was a Ford Motor spokesperson, always on the road for trade shows). She got plump, then plumper yet, very sexy in my eyes, but lost her job with Ford: she couldn't fit in those narrow spokesmodel gowns anymore.

I liked her very much, all but loved her, a familiar refrain. And I didn't want to marry her when in her estimation the time came, and that led to a very messy breakup—she stuck, all right—and eventually bad blood between me and my teammate her brother, who, as it turned out, was as sticky as she. I ended up having to pay her off, rent for the many accrued months I'd stayed over at her house, was the logic, half the price of her car (I'd used it extensively, okay), tuition for the back-to-school plans that I and all my cooking was seen to have necessitated, a large reward for emotional distress, but I didn't want to go to court to bring an end to it all, didn't want to be featured as a cad in the *Miami Herald*, found it easy to write a final check.

I was even more careful after that, focused on football, my strong feeling that my time was coming in love as in sport, always alone, alone even in a huddle, even in the pig-pile after my first participation in a Super Bowl victory, even after each of my seventeen career rushing touchdowns, 100,000 fans shouting the name they'd learned to call me, lingering on the z in Lizard such that the busy air of Miami buzzed.

As for love, I remained in my mind devoted to Sylphide. I followed her growing career as choreographer and director, kept a little scrapbook, examined the men in the background of newspaper photos, sent letters to theaters and dance companies around the world just ahead of her, received notecards in return: Desmond's pretty handwriting, kind words, breezy news, jasmine, finally clippings from a British magazine, neatly folded and tucked into an envelope, no note necessary: five-page photo spread from the dancer's shipboard wedding to Percy Haverstock, one of the world's first billionaires, room for two hundred guests on his yacht, the bride radiant in pink T-shirt and blue jeans.

BOB GRIESE BEGAN to struggle, missing routine passes, blowing crucial plays. After we missed the playoffs in 1977, Don Shula's interest in me intensified subtly. That spring, while the other guys were with their families or girlfriends or hobbies or simply healing from the season, I worked on, a couple of days a week with the offensive coordinator, Chick Johnsson. Other days it was just Strock and me, no one saying much about the future. I ate nearly every Sunday dinner at Coach's house. And though he put his hands on my shoulders and offered advice, I felt too old to open up as I had for Coach Keshevsky. I'd had all the fathers I could handle.

Just before the 1978 season, Chick took me aside and suggested I might be playing a lot more in the coming year, perhaps a lot, lot more, maybe starting. My breath quickened—I wanted it more than I'd thought. The possible change in my fortunes was only intimated, but Chick had an articulated message for me, too, which he wouldn't say was from Shula: "Lizard. Word to the wise: get to know the defensive guys better, get to the know the defensive coaches, too—we're all one team." I had an especially bad rap with the defensive backfield, apparently.

"You're the Princeton guy," Chick said. "That's how these gobs see you." He found my eye again: "You gotta lose that Princeton guy."

"I hear you," I said.

"You hear me what?"

"I'll lose the Princeton guy."

Chick hooked me up with Lionel "the Lion" Smith and Carter Jeffries (superstars the fans among you will know), and soon I was attending their famous barbecues, drinking the way they famously drank, famous fishing trips on their famous yachts. Before long we were boon companions if not great friends, and before long again my reputation among my teammates was apparently repaired. Chick even went so far as to congratulate me.

Trouble was, the guy I couldn't lose hadn't gone to Princeton. The guy I couldn't lose hadn't gone to college at all. The gob I couldn't lose I'd already lost.

It had to have been Coach Shula's idea for me to get some family down to visit during the season, another attempt to humanize me for the boys, no doubt, though he'd been talking in our conferences a lot about my isolation: sports psychology was all the rage. Anyway, he and I had a dinner date with the team owners, a scary pair of elderly businessman brothers, serious phrases about my bright future, misgivings couched as jokes. The subject of comp tickets came up to much hilarity. I was the only player on the team who'd never used my tickets! Ha-ha! The great savings to the team was appreciated! However, well, wasn't that just a little odd?

So that's why I invited Kate and Jack down for a November home game. Jack said no at first, but Kate had gotten hold of the idea and became obsessed with seeing me in a game, of seeing me in my home, traced the idea across a Milky Way of possibility, decided they had to come, that she'd only live if they came.

She arrived two days early, no notice, ding-dong at my door ten p.m. having breezed past the lobby guys in her swinging little sundress, no luggage, nothing in hand but a clutch and a pack of travel tissues. Even her guilt was supercharged: she mocked Jack, insulted Jack, claimed they'd gotten a divorce, claimed she'd come to live with me.

"I don't even have an extra bed," I said.

"1-800-Mattress," she said. "It's twenty-four fucking hours!" And then she got on my phone and called them, ordered up a Sealy king.

Why not?

I took the phone when she was done and called Jack, poor guy. He had no idea where she'd gone, no idea she *was* gone, pictured her at the gym, merely late home. "Inquire about her meds," he said, not a word of small talk. "Easier said than done, I know. Doubtful she's brought them. What's your pharmacy down there? We'll get Doctor Naughton to call it in. And no alcohol."

Kate heard what I was up to, pulled my phone out by its cord, yanked it out of my hands, threw it off the balcony, and that was the end of that.

She found my tequila in the cabinet over the sink, one try.

"Jack says . . ."

"It'll calm me," she said. "Believe me, it's needed. I mean, look at me for Christ's sake!"

I made weak margaritas and we drank them fast looking out over the ocean, twenty-five stories up, crashing loud and windy after the passage of one or another of the great hurricanes, probably Hurricane Kate.

I made stronger margaritas and we drank them more slowly, leaning over the railing out in the wind, her sundress blowing round her legs, snapping, my phone kind of funny lying down there in the courtyard. The alcohol did cut her intensity, made her warmer, none of that chilly Mom stuff. She remembered to hug me hello. I was very, very glad to see her, as it turned out. More margaritas. The night swung past, the wind off the ocean tossing her hair in her face as she talked and talked, so smart, so funny. She might have been sixteen again, full of stories. She'd gotten kicked off the circuit, once and for all. I'd seen something about her status in the sports pages, but these things weren't so public then, and I hadn't heard the story, which she made hilarious, an altercation with the net umpire, and then with the president of the Lawn Tennis Association. "I called her Mrs. Modess!" She'd bought a puppy, found it evil, returned it to the breeder, who turned out to be evil as well. "He was the father of those dogs, I'm telling you." I brought out food, but she wouldn't eat. She made us more drinks, very strong. She was thin, she was energized, she leaned into her words like the guest on a marathon talk show. "I've been working on the case," she said suddenly. "Do you remember Detective Turkle?"

"Detective Turkle," I said cautiously. "Of course." He was the very sweet man who ushered me around after the shootings, took my statements in such a sympathetic way, drove me to the morgue, recognized my shock, testified in court, warm and kind and exact.

"He's got access to the evidence locker. All the shit's still there! There's a sweater. There's a whole bunch of stuff. He knows everything about the case. He's given me stuff."

"Kate."

"And that little cop is sexy as hell, David, Jesus. Small, but perfectly formed."

"Kate. Does Jack know about this? Does Jack know anything about this at all?"

"Jack? David, you dumb shit. I'm not allowed to talk about any of this stuff in front of him." And, voice of one weary Yale professor, she intoned, "'We're to accept and abide by the decision of the jury and the judge in all cases pertaining to the matter at hand.'"

"Kate. There may be good reason for that."

"Anyway, David, shut up, Turkle came *through*—I have the list. From the shooter's car. The rental car. Abandoned in the New Canaan train station parking lot. No fingerprints on it anywhere. And did any of this come out in court?"

"Yes."

"Only the gun, David. Don't be a moron. Here's the list. You can have it. I have it memorized: one Smith and Wesson forty-five-caliber semiautomatic handgun, no fingerprints; one pack Big Red gum unopened, no fingerprints; Playtex rubber gloves size large yellow, no fingerprints interior or exterior; roll of Bounty paper towels, eleven used and crumpled; one bottle Windex, no fingerprints; fourteen pounds shattered window glass, no fingerprints; and of course your famous flower pot, David, your fingerprints. None of which ever got mentioned in court. Am I right? None of it!"

"Because it wasn't relevant."

"Relevant, ha. Listen to this, last item on the list, still in the box, David, slightly soiled, no fingerprints, tell me this isn't relevant: one pair brand-spanking-new Chippewa Work Mate boots, size nine."

"Well, ha. Dad's were worn to the elevator inserts."

"Exactly. Dad's were ancient."

"So what does this have to do with anything?"

"They were trying to *frame* him."

"In his own death?"

"No, David. Don't you see? In *Dabney's* death!"

"Dabney's death? Dad? Who would try to frame him for that?"

"Who do you think?"

"Oh, Kate."

She gave me the gentlest look, like it was I who needed the placating. "You're blind when it comes to her, brother."

"It was an accident, Kate. Dabney crashed into the bridge abutment up there in Greenwich. He was all alone."

"David, David. So naïve."

She wanted a walk on the beach, so two in the morning we headed out, plenty of others walking, too, and lying in the sand and even jogging. We walked hours, up and down the beach from one inlet to the next, my sister ten steps ahead of me most of the way, dropping back only to repeat Turkle's list, which (painful to admit) had caught my interest.

It was dawn before I could get her back up to my place. And there she made yet more margaritas, fine by me. Our conversation took a gentler turn, the usual stuff people talk about, my dating disasters, her home decorating, quite a bit of football, tequila flowing freely. You shouldn't buy the half-gallons.

The doorbell rang, shocking us. We looked at each other like convicts caught in a riverbed, the shackles still binding us together: *Jack!*

But no, it wasn't Jack, just two incompetent young men delivering her mattress, a monstrous thing. It was nine in the morning and we were smashed. The dudes hefted it in and set it up, highly amused by Kate, who danced for them, pulled off her shirt comically, wobbled her breasts, drummed on her belly. You bet they set that bed up. I dressed in panic and rushed to the stadium, nothing for it, late for Thursday practice, un-brushed, unrested, unsettled, more than half drunk, my worst day ever on the field.

Kate was off to shop. Linens! Comforter! Pillows! Duvet!

JACK ARRIVED ON their scheduled flight Friday, looking like photos you see of hostages after extended hijackings, two suitcases, his and hers. I'd never before seen him chewing his fingers like that, never seen the bags under his eyes, never understood the price he paid, day in and day out. I'd failed to get Kate's meds, I'd let her drink, I'd taken her to glitzy restaurants, I'd let her stay up all night two nights, I'd entertained her crime scenarios, I'd gone through two days of practice with almost no sleep, come home to shopping bags and the same discussion, like it had never stopped, each item on Turkle's list of evidence analyzed and reana-lyzed, every word Freddy the bodyguard had said to me, every word any-one said in court. She was having the sweater combed for hairs: Turkle had access to the newest technology, and nothing was hotter than DNA evidence, soon to be legal in the courts, though where that would get us Kate couldn't quite say, especially with the sweater and its hairs removed from police custody.

Didn't matter—I'd grown excited, too.

Jack gathered her in, surprisingly sheepish girl, plunked her in a cab, whisked her to their hotel—she'd have to start her meds protocol all over again, which could only be done gradually after these hiatuses. Coach was footing the bill for their visit complete, his own pocket and insistence: my emotional health, ha.

At dinner that night, no preamble, Kate announced that she'd decided to become a scientist. Rapid speech, she outlined her plans to go for her doctorate in genetics. "Dad always wanted it," she said.

Not in my memory. I looked around the restaurant to avoid catching Jack's eye. I allowed myself a Bloody Mary, didn't drink it, didn't even look at it when it came, big salad of vegetables sticking out of the outsized glass, sickening to see: Dad's last drink.

Jack patted her hand. "Let's ask David about the big game," he said.

"Pittsburgh Steelers," I said.

"CpG islands," Kate said seriously. "Codons, plasmid vectors, eukaryotic DNA—I've been learning it all—phage lambda cohesive end sites, phosphodiester bonds, zoo blots."

Jack looked mournful over dessert, put a hand through his thick hair, which had gotten shot with gray. "It's not your fault," he said, Kate in the ladies' room an awfully long time, perhaps decoding a gene spool in there. "Really, it started a couple of weeks ago. Genetics this and genetics that. And the horror is, she's fully capable! In another life, she'd be a scientist. You should see the books we suddenly own. I can't keep up with her."

"It's always been this way," I said. "The illness takes over, but it can't stop her from being smart."

"Lately, David, I find it very difficult to separate the illness and the personality. Maybe they're the same. In any case. I need help. She wears me down. She wears *herself* down. There are parts missing. Not everything comes back after these bouts. This thing about your parents? Detective Turkle all of a sudden? It's not benign. It's not a hobby. She took him to Mexico, I've just learned. When I was at the conference in Milwaukee. They spent the week in Mexico. She and Turkle. He had no idea she was attached."

"Oh, no."

"David, he's bought her an engagement ring."

ON GAME DAY Jack and Kate sat in the end zone with my teammates' friends and families, the "Dolphinators," great bright faces full of pride. Kate wore a fresh pink sundress, and while Jack smoked a tremulous briar she told everyone around her that she was a genetic chemist, that she was on the verge of finding the answer, or so I was told later by more than one impressed teammate.

I prepped for the game in my usual way, all but superstitious: Sunday paper, huge carbo breakfast with the other quarterbacks over the playbook, stretches alone or with a trainer, a long walk during free time down to the harbor, the cries of gulls, the stench of low-tide mud, then over to the stadium, full game-day stretches, playbook review with the offensive coordinator, playbook review with the defensive coordinator, more playbook review on my own, two coffees, whirlpool, pads, quick snack of peanut butter and jelly, team meeting, more peanut butter and jelly. I kneeled for the team prayer—something I usually skipped—and forgot Kate, felt only the genius of the coaches, how all of our energy had been beautifully orchestrated through the practice week, culminating as we sprinted out onto the field in juggernaut formation, the long weekly climb to the top of the mountain together, great vistas before us. This was a late-season game, a chance to clinch both the division and conference titles at home, playoffs in sight.

Garo kicked three field goals, all in the east end zone, as it happened, and so I got to perform for my sister, no different than I'd felt in peewee league, no different than in high school, receive the hike, set it up, boom. After the plays I'd find her up there in the cheering throng, always chatting, chatting with whomever was beside her, behind her, on the bench in front. It was a very close game all the way through to the last minutes, when we found ourselves three points behind, fourth down on the one-yard line, routine field goal to tie, only a couple minutes left to play.

Coach Shula called a B-ninety, and after that it was all poker faces, the B-ninety being a fake field goal we'd practiced endlessly but seldom attempted in a game. Four times, in fact. On three occasions I'd made the yard we needed, on the fourth (my very first season), I'd burst through for a touchdown. That touchdown ran through my head vividly. And in my head I saw myself making another, and saw Katy leaping to her feet, we win! Very simple: you take the hike as always, Garo fakes a kick as you pull the ball away, then you stand and run left behind the entire team blocking, only thirty-six inches progress required, an arm's-length, a touchdown in all our heads, careful body language: this is only a kick, see you in overtime. With his call Coach Shula had put all of his faith in me, all the team's faith, all the fans' faith, just as he said he would. Get that touchdown and we go to the playoffs. Fail, and the long road continues for everyone.

And so in a light Florida mist, very muggy afternoon, Garo took his preparatory three steps left, his one step right, kicked the dirt just as he always did, raised his arm just as always, dropped it fast. The snap was perfect, a spiral right into my hands. And as Garo rushed past me to block all comers I straightened the ball, poked it tip down into the grass and held it for the kick that wasn't going to come. By the time I realized my lapse—football a mental game, all right—I was already under a great pile of defenders, and the game was lost.

CHICK JOHNSSON LET me know that the Miami Dolphins would pay for any kind of therapist I wanted, at any price, gave me a list of people specializing in sports, offered to make the call for me. And over the subsequent months I saw hypnotists, art therapists, two psychiatrists, a Chinese herbs guy, an osteopath renowned for mystical cures, finally a smart psychotherapist, the first guy I ever heard mention the phrase *post-traumatic shock*. He just let me talk, and let me cry, and I believe it was he who recommended bodywork, as he called it, believing (as the osteopath had) that the body stored disaster. So to the acupuncturist, the masseuse, the chiropractor, the witch with the wax candles and incense. Maybe they were only doses of love.

One willowy bodywork expert pulled at my arms—so good—pulled at my head, passed her long hands an inch over my flesh smoothing my energy fields (or something along those lines—I never quite got the explanation). She pulled at my legs, she pulled at my toes, my ten fingers, my ears, wonderful, rousing, always the gentle scent of almond oil. Her hair was very long and dyed deep black to contrast her very pale skin, pale blue eyes, and in them a pained wisdom, a wayward whiff of judgment, too. She put her hands on you the moment you entered her inner sanctum, touched you even as you pulled off your shirt, even undid your belt and drew it through its loops as you lay back on her table, like preparing for sex. So it seemed natural one humid July afternoon when she crossed the line I'd been unconsciously pushing at and started kissing my belly (which at the time was like armor, but with nerve endings). She was unapologetic, very straightforward and natural, kissing my belly and then my chest and my neck and my face, some new treatment, you'd think from her demeanor, which was serious and really quite professional, hard to explain. She bid me rise and kissed the rest of me thoroughly, too, down to my toes and then back up, turning me this way and that to be sure that every stretch of my skin had felt her lips. Under her kimono she was only herself, and had always said giving was as therapeutic as getting, so I kissed her as she had kissed me. We made love on a pile of her plush towels and meditation cushions without rearranging them, using the office as it was, she reminded me, not as we wished it would be, the next patient eyeing me carefully as I floated out through the waiting room.

BENEDIKTA PEKKILAK CRABTREE. Her business card said B. Crabtree. Finnish by heritage, and though she was taller and thinner and less robust and more conventionally pretty, something about her reminded me of Sylphide, a certain emotional remove, an even more northern chill. Benedikta was distant in another important way in that she was married (to Crabtree), and *happily,* if an unfaithful kind of happiness is not too hard to understand, and in the end I guess I didn't mind that she had an "existing condition," as she referred to her husband. Her long-view unavailability made her possible for me, she liked to say. I saw her for months and then years, near daily appointments in the off-season, as

many as possible in fall, one of her prime two-hour slots in the late afternoon. She was free for occasional chats over breakfast but for sex only
at my appointment times. And it was never only sex, but all the other
elements of bodywork, the stuff that formed her regular practice, never
quite tender.

Benedikta was my library, a new book in my hands every week, poetry
and novels, politics and science, cultural criticism and a certain kind of
hopeful memoir, also a lot of biographies of great men, since she worried
I had no role model past the age my father had died, which was forty-four
and coming at me swiftly, not that I realized it then. She wanted me to
re-create my philosophy courses at Princeton for her, and I did what I
could, boxes of books, assignments, oral exams, Heidegger, Alcibiades,
Kant ("Out of the crooked timber of man no straight thing has ever been
made").

Because another part of her healing protocol was talk.

The third part was touch, which we had down, spending whole hours
gauging the sensations of one instep upon another, one hand placed on
a buttock, etc. From this sort of thing she reached her climaxes, which
were thoroughgoing, very long, a kind of ratcheting and clenching of her
limbs, ratcheting and clenching under my touch, my tongue; and then
release, often sobs.

The fourth, overarching part of her protocol was the not-touch, amazing, a definite sense of strange powers as she stroked and patted the air
over my face, or kidney, say, or calf.

I all but fell in love with her, getting to be a pattern, the closest I'd gotten since high school to that kind of plunge. And she all but fell in love
with me, a pattern, yes. The shallowness of her gaze was no character flaw
but was the inexplicable Crabtree, standing in my way. As for me, I was
not receptive to her deepest love, so she told me. Something blocked me,
something that had to do with my parents and their deaths, she thought,
and not with Sylphide, as I always tried to claim, and not with Emily,
my backup position, though Benedikta was correct when she observed
(her hand just over the nape of my neck) that somehow I'd managed to
tangle my memories of those four people in a hopeless knot. Kate was
the answer, she thought. Though not in a way she could articulate, just

something she could feel when her hands hovered in the air over my heart, hot flawed prescience: "You have a twin."

We often ended our sessions angrily, frostily. We were at least that close. Once, writing out the usual check (one hundred ten dollars was a lot, late seventies!), I called her a prostitute. She drew herself up, all her tiny-breasted naked pride, all her black-hair-swinging-lank pride, and with her face untouched by any emotion but her customary honesty, said, "You only say that because you pay me."

After that for a month or two I campaigned for her divorce from Crab-tree, for us to marry. "Your aura isn't evolved enough for a soul merger," she said, her one kind of joke. But seriously, even with the benefit of her teachings and other ministrations, she didn't think I'd make it to her level in this life. Her husband was much more thoroughly enlightened, she let it be known, bitter tones as we made love on her worktable. "It's just that he doesn't turn me on."

"That doesn't seem so enlightened," I breathed.

We were this close, both of us, holding on to the edge of orgasm, some-thing she'd taught me, could easily go on for hours.

Lying across me another afternoon, she let her black hair cover and un-cover my face and very, very slowly said, "You say Kate collected oddballs. You make her out to be mysterious. But you seem to collect oddballs, too, or make all your people into oddballs. Anyway you go on and on about all your people and their extraordinary lives and extraordinary quali-ties, everyone so beautiful. Probably you even make me seem strange and beautiful when you talk about me, yes? The more beautiful, the more wonderful, the more elegant, the more I think you're covering up your own sort of ordinary and mundane grief. Which it's time to abandon."

Later, I got dressed and wrote her a check.

I DIDN'T GET up to Connecticut at all in the weeks and months after Kate's visit. Jack kept the breezy letters coming for a while, the weekly phone calls, but the next fall they slowed, then stopped. It occurred to me to call him, to check in, but I did not, even knowing what must be hap-pening. We played in New York—I didn't call. We played in Boston—I did not. Even Philadelphia. How far is that? An easy train ride.

So it wasn't a shock when an anonymous someone sent a small *New Haven Register* clipping via the front office: Kate had driven the newest of Jack's Volvos down a boat ramp at some park east of New Haven and straight out into Long Island Sound—the car floated twenty minutes before she got a window open—then, help not arriving, she *swam* nearly a mile to New Haven, climbing out of the icy water near the summer theater down there, her illness like a furnace to keep her warm. Dripping and naked, she traipsed all the way through the city to her old residence hall, where she was found calmly sitting in her former entranceway, found and gathered in by several kind young Yale women offering blankets and towels.

Jack had asked for help, and I hadn't come through. Guilt's alchemy left me feeling nothing but fury, fury at Kate, fury at whomever had sent the news item, fury at the girls of Yale, fury at the huge new mattress stuffed into my bedroom (five-hundred-dollar sheets), fury even at Jack, who was blameless. He'd used his connections and modest wealth and probably every ounce of his pride and gotten my sister placed in a great in-patient program in Boston.

MY NEXT DINNER with Coach and the owners was postponed, postponed, and then never mentioned again. The official interest in my family and my personal life faded. Coach Shula didn't have me up to the office. No more hands on the shoulders. No more confidence building. No more queries after my happiness. The season went on, ten wins, four losses, not bad but no playoff berth, which, of course, eleven and three would have brought. I suited up with the rest, disconnected from them. The months passed, the off-season unfolded, winter in Florida, spring, a lot of rain.

Then, in summer training camp, Bob Griese tore ligaments in his knee. Don Strock took over as the season opened, which meant I was second in line, called on to run a play or two in nearly every game of 1978 and 1979, full quarters in eight games in those seasons, successful quarters, too, including my patented brand of head-on touchdown runs, slowly erasing the memory of my lapse. By 1980 Bob Griese's injuries had taken their toll. Career effectively over, he stepped off the team and toward the Hall of Fame and a stellar career as a sportscaster. Anyway, I saw an opening in the forest where the tree had come down, raced toward the sunlight, saw myself succeeding Strock, who couldn't go on forever.

But in the next year's draft the team picked up a new phenom, LSU helmsman David Woodley. He and Strock alternated starts from his first game: soon the fans were calling them Woodstrock. Strock didn't last long, just as everyone had predicted, and 1982 was my big year, second behind Woodley, a lot of action, scraps of fame, full respect, dinners with Coach, Woodley fading, once again the light ahead of me. But in 1983 Dan Marino came on board, and he'd prove to be one of the greatest quarterbacks in the history of the game.

9

Around that time, Carter Jeffries and Lionel Smith let it be known that they were looking to open an upscale soul-food restaurant in the old city, part of a revitalization scheme the city council of Miami had cooked up, all kinds of tax breaks and rent incentives, an endless flow of cruise-ship customers by contract, not to mention a home base for Carter's flashy party scene. They only needed a little more money and someone to take the reins—a minor financial partner who'd take a major managerial role. They'd be the famous football players, the public face of the place; all that was needed was some poor sap to run the place, or make that a rich sap. I wasn't tempted.

But then one night in the middle of the season I sat up in the enormous bed Kate had bought, her silk sheets rustling, her down comforter sliding to the floor.

Why not?

It wasn't like my last years with the Dolphins were going to keep me very busy, and on my new month-to-month contract (including humiliating pay cut), who knew when the end would come, except soon? My experience cooking with Honey had touched something in me, real pleasure in the handling and transformation of food. Carter just laughed when I told him all that after team meeting one Monday, showing those famous gold inlays. "I suppose she made you *Black*, too!"

I knew nothing about restaurants, even less about business, and nothing about soul food, true, but none of that mattered, or so I argued: all of that stuff could be learned. With me they'd have a tall and memorable presence in the house, David "Lizard" Hochmeyer himself, still Miami's tenth most eligible bachelor.

OUR TIMING WAS excellent, as it turned out, downtown enjoying a resurgence, and soul food a long turn as the fad of the moment. Our enterprise, called Soul Train, was a bustling success from opening night forward. Carter signed autographs and hosted big, free-for-all sports discussions at the bar. Lionel acted as dining-room manager, seating his adoring fans, sprinting out dinners in front of the wait staff, a lot of fun for everyone.

But within a few months of constant crush, the flaws in the restaurant came clear: the kitchen set-up was clumsy, the head chef a nasty lush, the wait staff quirky in a bad way. Two reviewers called the menu stereotypical. One went so far as to say our food was "coarse, gross, loaded with sugar and fat and salt and starch, mistaking volume for quality, fine enough food for the defensive line, maybe."

Ouch.

Business began to fall off.

Carter knew a real chef, one Etienne LaRoque, an old college acquaintance of his. We flew him in from Mobile, where he ran a health-food kitchen of some kind, not very promising. Carter had warned us about all the tattoos—didn't matter, I was shocked anyway. The guy was covered, even his scalp, even his face, the Virgin Mary benevolent on his *forehead,* her soulful eyes gazing out over his own.

At Carter's seaside mansion, in his private kitchen, Etienne prepared meals for us through two long days. He was a whirlwind, from the butcher's shop to the fish dock to the farm sheds to Carter's kitchen.

"So it's soul food," the interviewee said, first lunch.

"Soul food sure enough," said Carter.

Dish by dish it came out, a perfectly timed progression: red beans and rice and fresh pickles and cornbread and actual chitterlings and thick pork chops, mashed potatoes and gravy, collard greens with pig's feet, sweet potato pie with a ginger-pecan crust. We'd brought in our best waiter and the poor guy shuttled back and forth to the pool and the beach with tastes all afternoon, Etienne alone in the kitchen making dinner for twenty but sending out little leek tarts and strange squid sticks and samples of sweet teas, kale-pesto corn fritters, knuckle-jelly "caviar," an endless stream of riffs on our theme, more and more formal as we came off the beach and dressed and our guests began to arrive: four teammates (more than half a ton in aggregate), also their very lovely wives (barely a quarter ton), also Miami mayor Hector Hernandez and his toothy daughters, also three local chefs we'd gotten to know, also special guests of my own: Benedikta and her husband, the redoubtable Crabtree, not the first time I'd met him, but the first time I'd ever seen her at night. Out of her office she seemed tall and severe, less glamorous despite the dressing up, not the woman I knew.

I helped the waiter serve a potato-and-fatback soup, taking my tastes when I could, unbelievably clean and flavorful given the humble ingredients. Crabtree, a guy who liked to talk, had the mayor's ear, a guy who didn't like to listen. Benedikta closely monitored their conversation. She wanted to bring spiritual healing to government, muttered the appropriate chants under her breath. I hoped she was impressed with me. Etienne had meanwhile gone Cajun, blackening thick cuts from redfish filets (this is before that prep was well known), smoke like a forest fire filling the kitchen, sudden, thrilling food emerging from the conflagration, actual *applause* when Etienne came out to see what we thought. During the first wine break (Etienne's small-plate pairings, a peppery ceviche with a surprising French blush, Vietnamese stuffed baby cabbages with a Malbec of all things, then seven fresh salsas with seven fast whites to put to a vote, then—*what?*—a flight of miniature knishes and blinis with three Polish noodle soups, very small servings, quick visits in his spotless apron for commentary, shots of vodka.

"But is this considered soul food?" the mayor said.

Etienne looked him up and down: "It's all soul food when I make it, baby."

His rich Jamaican accent morphed as he cooked and visited and joked into a Creole patois, then into a Detroit homeboy street rap, then into stiff-lipped Andover Prep, then just plain earnest New Jersey suburban (his actual heritage), and back to Jamaican.

Benedikta excused herself, wandered onto the deck and then out to the beach, disappeared. I exited through the kitchen, made my way round the dune. She looked more herself in the moonlight, more her own height with the heels kicked off.

"Obviously hire him," she said.

I put my arm around her, tried to draw her in.

"You're thinking our sexual relationship will transfer from my professional space to yours." Hard to tell when she was kidding.

I said, "No, no. This is the beach."

"And you thought perhaps under moonlight we could move our relationship a little toward the romantic and away from the clinical. Well, David. I do like the moonlight. I do like the sea air. I do like you. I like the tension right now, as well. I'd like, actually, to be pressed down in the sand and ravished. But in fact I prefer a therapeutic tension. You have an appointment Monday, I believe."

I said, "You are in fact a strange woman."

She swayed for my benefit, said, "I am in fact drunk. Also, sweetie, I don't want a bunch of sand in my panties." With that she let me kiss her, a nice companionable smooch, not very promising.

"How's that for therapeutic tension?" I said.

"I'll bill you," she said.

"For one kiss?"

"I'll bill you the whole dinner, darling—we're going on four hours."

She kissed me a little more, found a brief moment of passion. I gathered her long dress in my hands fold by fold, eventually found the skin of her legs.

"Sorry, no," she said. "Crabtree will taste you later."

"He's so sensitive?"

She ignored me, looked out to sea. She said, "Also, I'm puzzling over things here. I see you trying to erase yourself, all your accomplishments, all your sorrows, trying to slip into a new world where you can be a kid again, a figurative kid, learning new things, around new people, lessons from adults, a new school. Right—you're the new kid, you're going to be the new kid. And nothing that happened back in the old neighborhood will matter anymore."

"You're losing me."

"I predict. I refuse to play parent. Carter—he's your dad, I'm going to say, your proto-father. And this new one, with the tattoos, with the woman on his face and in his body, he's to be your mom."

"They'll never live up to Nick and Barb."

"You aren't funny."

I gathered her in again.

After a while, she said, "You are growing invisible."

"I'm right here."

"But some other creature is taking your place."

The waves came in set by set and there were freighters at anchor out there, long strings of lights. By separate routes and staggered timing, we found that Etienne had seated everyone in the living room and was actually giving a *talk,* explaining the points he'd been making about service and métier, as he called it, also a few notes on pricing. Afterwards, all of us comfortable there, he served a kind of alcoholic espresso pudding, whoa.

I didn't mind the idea of a new family. I looked at Etienne with thoroughgoing interest.

"A restaurant needs a great name," he said as we ate.

"Soul Train," Lionel answered. Maybe Lionel could be my uncle.

"Your tattoos," Crabtree said as we ate, total non sequitur, unable till then to ask whatever question he'd had in mind. Talk about an erased man.

Etienne pulled his shirt off to show that he was covered, Mother Mary continuing down his chest and into his trousers, whirligigs and creatures and stray words, little portraits, numerous flowers, a lot of vines. I felt suddenly that my future was in his hands. And more, that he held the key to the past.

Etienne pretended to unbutton his trousers: more to show, ha-ha.

With that, the mayor and his daughters applauded, stood on cue, shook all our hands, and quickly left. More slowly, more applause, lots of hugs and encomiums, our teammates thanked us, thanked Etienne, and staggered out on the arms of their wives. I gave the waiter the pair of hundred-dollar bills Carter had slipped me to tip him. The visiting chefs left in deep conversation: there was a new master in their midst.

Carter hustled Lionel and me back to the spotless kitchen for the briefest possible conference. When had Etienne had time to clean? Three thumbs up. Our man entered with the last dishes in his hands.

"Floridiana," he announced, the name all but visibly coming to him at just that moment.

"Soul Train," Lionel said forcefully.

"Floridiana," Carter preached, his comical best: "Gives us some *latitude*, and not just *attitude*. And try it on your *tongue-uh*. Floridiana! It's music, it's location, it's the *ocean-uh*, it's the farm, it's the colored people, but baby, it's everybody *else-uh*, too."

He raised his hands, I raised mine. We regarded Lionel till he raised his reluctant hands in the air.

"You got the *spirit*," Carter said more seriously. "And Etienne here gets his name: Floridiana-uh!" Then he made the offer: six-figure salary, profit sharing after a year, full bennies immediately, the works. Etienne looked touched, went all dramatic, plain homeboy New Jersey accent: "I want to. I would love to. It's just that there's something I have to confess. Something Floridiana must know before it hires me. Might even be a deal breaker. I'm sorry, gentlemen, to have waited. There just wasn't the opportunity. I'm happy Floridiana likes my food. I'm *happy* you like it. Those pork chops? Those were fun to make! They were fun, right?"

We clambered to reassure him, dark possibilities flashing through our besotted brains. We knew about the drug arrests. That part of his life, we'd been assured, was more than ten years gone. And obviously, he was gay, not exactly unusual in Miami. In fact, he'd put it plainly. Tattoos, fine. Had he killed someone in prison? What language did you use to withdraw an offer?

Our man played the moment to maximum effect, held the silence to its breaking point, looked at each of us in turn, divulged his secret, great comedy from a great comedian: "Gentlemen, I'm vegetarian."

"*Fucker!*" Carter shouted after a beat.

UNANNOUNCED, I FLEW north to see my sister at McLean up in Boston—an intense and well-kept place with a kindly vibe, corridors full of brisk staff and apologetic patients roaming. I waited over an hour to learn that my sister had been moved into a residential house on the outskirts of the campus, a pretty clapboard place where the inmates cooked their own meals, did their own cleaning, formed a kind of family, worked to help themselves toward long-term recovery.

My touchstone, my living history, my heart, Lady Kate opted not to see me that first afternoon—stupid of me to just show up at reception—but the nurse said she'd invited me back for the next afternoon's "open family period."

I felt the need of support, waited in line at the pay phone in the nurse's station, one of those old wooden booths, dialed Benedikta.

"You missed your session," she said when I repeated my name. "And you didn't call to cancel."

"I suddenly had a couple of days."

"You can't save her."

"I can't abandon her, either," I said.

"Said the one who was actually, in fact, abandoned."

"You almost sound hurt."

"Oh, Lizard, I am I think."

"Can we reschedule for Friday?"

"I will give you the morning. You'll be tight after flying."

"Thank you, B."

"You had a chance you know," she said. "You had a chance to break away from them. To make yourself new."

"I think that's just what's happening."

"You can't make yourself new in quicksand, David."

The man at the window knocked.

Repressed tears got into my voice. I said, "I've lied to her half my life."

"Friday, then," Benedikta said a little coldly.

"Friday," I said. Then, clinically as I could: "I'll have missed you."

"Okay," she said more warmly. "I'll have missed you too. Careful, then."

I kept it cool. "Yes, careful."

"I love you, David." She'd never said that before, nor anything close.

"You're manipulating me," I said.

She thought about that, said, "It's my job."

I MET JACK in Mystic, Connecticut, for dinner. We toured one of the old whaling vessels, remarkable, admired the deck prisms that had brought light to the sailors working below, not much to say, but tangible warmth between us.

"Where does your devotion come from?" I asked him over lobster rolls, long conversation about Kate's latest treatment, the new drug regimen, the guarded prognosis, all the damage her body had been through, her weariness after years of illness. After all she'd put him through, I meant, how did he hang in?

"I love her, Lizard. It's simple as that."

"That's not very simple," I said.

Next afternoon I found her playing Ping-Pong with a fellow patient, a thick-waisted Japanese-looking man with castlike bandages still on his forearms. The two of them gave no quarter, slammed that ball back and forth. It took maybe a half hour for Kate to get to twenty-one. Muted victory dance in slippers. She still liked to win.

"Hi David," she said grinning.

"Hi yourself."

The grin faded, triumph fleeting. "I have some energy again. Really a lot of energy. Appropriate energy."

"I see—you two used the whole room for that game. It's brilliant."

"He lets me win."

"No way," said her opponent. "I was trying my best." He had a crush on her, you could see, also that he really had let her win.

Her face was bloated, the rest of her diminished, an older and more fragile person than I'd expected, terribly skinny, no sunshine in her, meds and oversleep. The raised lip expressed more fear than contempt, and maybe that had always been true. Hard to keep her gaze, which was disconcertingly steady. I guess I didn't like the flatness of her eyes, which had gone gray, the ocean of her meeting the sky of her in an indistinct horizon on a cloudy, windless day.

I said, "Everything good?"

She looked to her Ping-Pong partner.

"You're very strong," he said encouragingly. He wasn't going to leave us to ourselves.

She said, "I'm using myself up. You know? Just burning up the fuel. This stuff they've put me on makes mud puddles in my head."

"Better than landslides," the Ping-Pong guy said likeably.

Kate ignored him. "I'd want to learn to play the guitar. I would love that. Certain songs are in my head when I see you, David. 'Fire and Rain,' for example. I imagine I could play that. I want to have a business. It would be nice to sell something."

"Jack sure loves you," I said.

"Everyone loves Katy," her partner said.

"Like furniture. I would love to be able to make and sell furniture. Jack and I visited a shop when I had a weekend pass where they make these perfect, stable chairs. Shaker something-or-other. Design something-or-other. They have a school attached to it, or an apprenticeship program of some kind. I'd build boxes and then things to put in boxes."

"You were always good with tools."

"Kate has been through so much," the Ping-Pong guy said.

"I imagine you have, too," I said.

"All self-inflicted," he said.

"You love me," Kate said, not quite a statement, not quite a question.

"Of course I love you," I said. "I love you, Katydid."

"What happened?" Kate said. "I mean, what the fuck?"

"I guess we know the answer to that," I said.

"I guess we don't," she said.

"There are things I need to tell you," I said.

"You'd better tell yourself first," she said.

"That's a lot of pressure to put on Kate," her friend said. "Maybe a better way to say it would be, Now I'm going to listen to you."

Kate had looked away, wouldn't look back, nothing more to say.

"You're a nice man," I said to the friend.

"That's a lot of pressure to put on me," he said.

Soon an attendant came in, indicated it was time for me to go, took my arm like I was a ward, escorted me all the way back to my car and practically put me in it.

"There's so much I haven't told her," I said sorrowfully.

"This shit's no picnic," the attendant said. He wanted me gone, didn't want to have to listen to the visitors' stories, too.

▢ ▢ ▢

ETIENNE CAME ON board at Floridiana immediately, stepped into our soul kitchen two weeks after his interview and served his first meal that very night, our regular menu with our regular provisions, and yet everything looked better, tasted better, sold better. Same number of guests as the night previous, double the gross.

After that, small changes every day, new workstations installed, fresh suppliers, individual meetings with staff, a new attitude overcoming everyone, a new culture of song—Etienne always singing—joy in the work. The regular customers didn't know what hit them, it came so gradually, but slowly the place was made over in Etienne's image. Best of all, he didn't mind my cooking beside him, seemed to take pleasure in handing me insurmountable tasks. The two of us were first in, last out every day, both of us married to the work and therefore to each other, in a way, long discussions over morning prep quickly becoming personal. He never offered advice, just wanted to hear my story, or so it seemed, so much so that I didn't notice he never talked much about himself and his own struggles, if any.

He was fascinated by Kate, considered her driving into Long Island Sound a sensible response to all that beset her. In his view, she'd swum naked as a newborn to Yale in order to return to the moment of our parents' deaths. She was attuned to them, that's all, aware of their needs in the other world, which left her weird for ours. "Those deaths must be avenged to put her right."

"What kind of gentle gay psychology is that?"

"That's voodoo gentle gay psychology, boss, with skulls."

After a few months, the restaurant roaring along once again, I set Etienne and Kate up talking on the phone once a week, thinking he'd like her, also that he'd be as good for her as he'd come to be for me, and maybe she for him. She had become a vegetarian at McLean—you got better food that way—and this opportunistic strategy had turned into a passion. Her campaign was to get Floridiana to stop serving meat—any kind of meat—because after all there were a million other things to serve, things that didn't have eyes and didn't feel fear, whose deaths wouldn't load bad karma upon us.

"But meat *feels* good," Etienne liked to respond. Even ribbing her, he was the one person who could make her laugh. And before long, contradictions upon contradictions, he was putting vegetarian items on the Floridiana menu, as passionate as she, just subtler. He never used the word *vegetarian* for example, mixed and matched fantastical Caribbean fruits and flowers with familiar grains and vegetables, a multiplicity of beans, varietal rices in traditional African spices and herbs. Dish by dish, week by week, he began bumping meat plates off the regular Floridiana menu.

"Poor people never got much meat," he explained in a short segment on *60 Minutes* highlighting the Afro-American chefs of America (as if they weren't just chefs), for which, he said, he played Black. "That's what soul food all *about,* bein' poor. Rice and peas, greens and knuckles. Corn meal and potato flour, pig's ears and tripe, any leafy thing at hand, anything the rich folk won't touch, Mister Wallace."

YET REVENUES, WHICH had spiked after Etienne took over, began to falter. Covers were up (numbers of guests eating, I mean), a good thing, but expenses were up as well. The new dishes were maybe too brilliant, the new restaurant maybe too good, the new customers maybe too, I don't know, plain *odd*—despite brilliant reviews, better service, sexier atmosphere, the old regulars started going elsewhere, plenty of choices around Miami when it came to meat. Which was Etienne's point, of course. You forged a clientele, not just a cuisine, a clientele that couldn't find your product anywhere else on the planet.

I had another always-a-bridesmaid season with the Dolphins, less play than any year previous, less money, too, and was very happy to get back to the restaurant after The Team was shockingly bumped from the playoffs.

And so I was there the night a huge reservation, some kind of wedding party, walked out when they saw the chef's sheet for the night—I mean thirty-five people who'd come for meat. Of course the bride was some cousin of Lionel's mother's niece, and word got back to him, and from him to Carter, and, Lionel at his side, Carter was upon us the very next night, wrath of God.

"I wanna see barbecue back on the menu *to-fucking-night,*" he shouted around the kitchen during prep, fresh off a plane from Dubai. Etienne rolled his head on his neck, *Yes sir, sure sir,* very dead serious, not a single look in my direction.

Lionel tried to soften things, sweet guy, always more articulate: "And, yo, E.T., if we could eliminate the roots-and-fruits."

"I'll tell you what we're going to eliminate," Carter said, big finger in Etienne's chest.

Then my partners took me outside and Carter threatened me, too: if I didn't manage the place the way they'd envisioned, whether profits shrank or rose they'd push me right back out on the street and no amount of lawsuit would get me my investment money back, not one dime.

I looked to Lionel. "I'm with Carter," he said simply.

KATE WAS RELEASED from McLean in early March that year, required to go back up to Boston weekly for group meetings. I flew to Connecticut to stand at her wedding to Jack, a nice civil ceremony, purely functional, Jack doing the right thing, Kate quite subdued, I thought, a new generation of meds flooding through her. My gift to them was a honeymoon at such time as they were ready to take it. I could barely stand to be in their house—nothing to do with them. It was that painting, that gorgeous painting high on the wall over their bed.

I made a second visit a month later, and as the honeymoon didn't look imminent, I bought her a guitar, maybe a little fancier than required, a beautiful Martin D-26 with pretty abalone-shell inlays up and down the neck. She didn't make fun of me over the expense as she might have in the old days but actually went through ads in the local paper and immediately signed up for lessons, trying harder than I'd seen her try in a long time, all irony having abandoned her.

Jack promised they'd visit, no conviction in his voice.

Kate, meanwhile, kept up her phone calls with E.T., talked with him some days for hours, his infinite capacity for empathy, speaker phone murmuring while he prepped in the mornings, neither of them minding if I listened in, Kate strumming chords for him as she learned the guitar, inseparable strangers, those two.

Jack was reluctant to bring Kate down to Florida, of course. But in April he relented, really had to—her medical team thought she needed independence. And their family therapist thought Jack needed some himself. He hadn't written a thing in two years, for example, hadn't traveled to a single conference, wasn't buoying himself toward retirement.

She traveled alone, arrived with her guitar and a proper bag, disappeared into my room, no interest in seeing the sights, no sense that she'd displaced me, that I was back in my single futon in the living room, not much talk or interaction at all, just Kate and her guitar and several basic chords, enough to play versions of quite a few old songs behind the closed door. Her singing voice was thin and high, no great talent hiding there, but very moving in its thinness, the saddest possible songs. I delivered her meds night and morning and witnessed her downing them as per Jack's requirement. She didn't fuss about it, just ate the pills like they were glass shards, went back to her music.

Then one evening the woman emerged, Kate unbowed, a notch or two too thin, skin sallow, but pretty summer dress and bright lipstick, high heels.

"We never go out," she said.

INVITE THE PAST, and the past will come: the very next day I got a note from Emily Bright, letting me know she was in town. She'd been following my career. She'd seen Floridiana in a magazine article, seen my name. She'd watched a number of Dolphins games over the years, had gotten glimpses of me. I called her hotel strategically at ten a.m. and reached her just rising.

I'd been following her, too. She had her own dance company, and it had been a great success, as successful as a contemporary dance organization could get in those days of the waning importance of the art, nothing of the sort Sylphide had achieved.

"We've got a weekend down here," she said.

"I'd like to see you dance again," I said.

"And I would like to see this restaurant you've opened."

"Come be my guest."

"I'll leave a ticket for the show. When?"

"Kate's staying with me," I said.

"Kate your sister?"

"Yes, Kate. She's been ill, but she's on the mend. Tomorrow maybe? Tomorrow evening would be good."

"It's at eight. Two tickets then, is that what you're saying?"

"Yes, two. And we can have dinner after at the restaurant."

"Dinner, yes. With Kate."

"And Emily? If we could avoid any talk of Sylphide?"

"But she's my mainstay. I was really hoping. So many stories."

"No, I know. I mean, in some ways she's my mainstay, too. I mean, she is. She's my mainstay. Not that I hear from her much. It's Kate. There are things I haven't told Kate."

"Ah. Still with the old family games?"

"No, it's. It's her illness. I don't want to stress her."

"I'd have thought she'd know all by now. Not that I know much. Just that our lady likes you."

"Emily. Is this going to work, or not?"

"Not a peep, David. I'm not your mother, after all."

I couldn't think what to say.

Emily said, "I'm sorry. I'm sorry I said that. I'm not who I used to be, honestly. That's a crack from the past."

"Do you hear from her much, from Sylphide?"

"Not so much lately, not with the new husband. He's caught her fancy, I guess. He's very rich. They have, like, a ship. David, I have to go. Rehearsal in five minutes. I just thought. I'd like it if. We had some time to just talk, the two of us. I feel like there's a lot to say. I feel full of things to say."

"Maybe say one thing now?"

"I've just been thinking. We were the two. We were the ones who were different. With special talents, you know. None of our own doing. These capable bodies. Anyway. She picked us out. Sylphide picked both of us out. It was all choreography."

I COULDN'T SLEEP, began to picture a steamy reunion, Kate home to my place, Emily and I to her hotel, which would be silken and sumptuous. We'd seen one another a few times through my Princeton years, more and less stilted visits as her career got launched in New York, dancing for

Sylphide, the *Children of War* show I'd helped put together. Kate knew nothing of any of this. As far as Kate knew, Emily and I hadn't spoken since high school, Sylphide and me the same. But it was more than that. Really a lot more than that. I wished Kate were capable of hearing it, but her friend at McLean had been right: this was the time for listening. I remembered the Rock at Staples High, Emily's particular scent. We'd been falling in love when the murders fell instead, and the cataclysm had struck her nearly as hard as it had struck me. We had that in common, too, two kids on a rock with our hormones pumping, two kids unaffected by all that was to come, last chance.

That next morning, Etienne liked what he saw, reached to pat my head as I stared out the windows: "Boss, keep cooking, cook while you daydream. Tonight your food will taste like *memory*."

Without a word about it, we conspired to make the night meatless. This was to be in honor of Emily. She'd have the meal we wanted to make for her, the dishes we'd been enjoined from cooking by Carter and Lionel. The kinds of things her mother had once put in her lunchbox.

THE DANCE PERFORMANCE that night was my first glimpse of Emily's internationally acclaimed choreography, even stranger than I expected, a youngish girl in the company all but naked for example, pouring actual water from an actual jug on top of three or four other dancers who just looked cold and uncomfortable to me, like dancing goose bumps. And after that, of course, the stage was wet, and the poor kids were slipping around, in danger of falling. Oh, and no music, just recorded noises. Emily in bare feet appeared late in the piece wearing a kind of metal headdress, strands of tinsel her only clothing (the lithe figure gone to hardest possible muscle), stomping and splashing around the stage.

Kate felt crowded by all the people, didn't like sitting in our perfect seats at the very center of the auditorium: too far from the aisles. She gripped my hand as if we were in a rocket taking off, sat at stiff attention, unclear to me what she was thinking. Me, too, truth be told, stiff attention, not so good for the people behind us, like a seat behind columns. I guess I'd expected an aftershock, damaged overpasses coming down to make way for modern freeways of romance, but what I felt was deep

sorrow, nothing really to do with Emily. The lights went low and the cur-
tain came up, and the years washed over me. Something similar or worse
must have been happening to Kate: she left at the height of the standing
ovation, hurried down the aisle and over all those toes in nice shoes and
out into the night.

I swam upstream through the departing, glowing crowd, handed over
flowers in the dressing room, kiss-kissed Emily's flushed cheeks briefly.
She barked orders at the crew back there, cursed at the dancers—they
were on their way to Texas, a long drive for the bus-and-truck people,
who had to leave a full day before their star: Emily would fly alone in the
morning. Everyone seemed terrified of their boss, rushing with chins
down. She'd shaved her head, a pretty skull hard as bronze, everything
about her more metallic than I recalled, like her costume had stuck to her.
Her gaze was more forlorn than ferocious; our feelings weren't far apart.

"Can't wait for dinner," she said, as if food were the issue, false cheer.
"I've been craving that Floridiana barbecue, maybe ribs. Twenty minutes?"
And back to her dressing room to change, shouting orders all the way.

Kate had apparently walked home, anyway, she wasn't at the car.

And Emily wasn't vegetarian anymore. I called Etienne from the lobby
of the theater. "Woman loves barbecue," I told him. "Woman loves ribs."

"Oh, we got plenty ribs in the walk-in, bro."

"You've been cooking for her all day," I said.

"I've been cooking for Emily all my life."

I drove Emily over there.

"Okay," she said. "Very serious question. Is this the same fucking
Volvo?"

Obviously not. But it was good for a laugh.

And that was it for talk. What had always seemed stern in her now
seemed merely frozen. She stared forward, no doubt processing the Miami run of her show. "Processing": I was starting to think like B. Crabtree.
I drove, trying to bring back the Emily of the Rock. But she'd departed.
All the conversation I'd imagined had simply disappeared. In its place,
memory pressing on memory. My dad waiting at the bus stop with me.
My mother's face reacting to him, that cross face she'd make. She'd put a
lot of pressure on the guy. That was something I hadn't thought of before,

all the pressure she put on him to be anything but what he was. Then again, what was he?

"You remember my parents?" I said.

"They were nice," she said. "Complicated. I hardly ever saw them. Your mom at that Yale game. And then."

"I don't mean to bring it up. Not like that. Just curious. How are your folks?"

"Same as ever. All the same. Still wondering what I'll do when I grow up. David. Just say it. What happened to Kate?"

"I guess she walked home. She's a big walker."

"I mean."

"Oh. Sorry. Mental health issues. She's had a hard time. A really hard time."

"She always seemed so together to me."

"I guess no one's really together."

"Have you had a hard time?"

"At times. At times, yes."

"I was so, so in love with you, David."

Definitely past tense. I steered the car through traffic, thinking about that, tried to lighten things up a little: "Did we ever say that?"

She thought a long time, four blocks of lights. "We did," she said. "We said it later. In your room at Princeton. We said it a lot, actually."

"If Kate turns up."

"Not a word, don't worry."

"She doesn't actually know about any of it. I mean after."

"After your folks you mean."

"Yeah. That's exactly what I mean."

"I felt so guilty."

"Tell me about it."

"I mean, we'd just been in their bed."

"It was nice," I said.

We pulled up at the restaurant. There was Carter's brand-new purple Rolls Royce convertible, his jersey number painted on its doors. Great— the one night he picks to visit. I showed Emily the kitchen, pointed out the details of the view from the dining room. She loosened up very slightly:

she could see her hotel from there, admired the lights of the wedding-cake cruise ships off in the harbor.

Carter was out in the hostess station. His gaze when it fell upon me was hostile. Something must have transpired between him and E.T., something perhaps about the food my friend had been cooking on my request, the food Emily didn't want, something maybe about all the queers in the bar drinking persimmon-and-agave Mojitos.

"May I present Emily Bright," I said, just as my mother had taught me.

They looked at one another a long time, these two people with shaved heads.

"Join us for dinner," I said to Carter.

"Yes, join us," Emily said, ducking her eyes from his in a way I remembered clearly.

"Believe I *will*," said Carter, suddenly tender.

Emily looked up from the brand new carpet, slow smile.

Carter, too.

The other beautiful princess was home on my deck catatonic. I had to carry her inside, not a word between us, guide her to the beautiful bed she'd bought, put her between the pretty covers: she could sleep in her clothes for that one night (her last in Miami as it turned out), she could sleep in her glass slippers, return in her dreams to the scene of the crime.

I LEFT FOOTBALL that January, after one last great year with Miami, including one complete game at the helm (Marino down with a vicious flu), a huge win against a strong Chicago Bears lineup, 315 yards passing, 200 rushing, seven touchdowns. This was glory my dad would have loved and Mom couldn't have pretended not to notice, the subsequent Super Bowl big fun, too, though I didn't play, just one of the guys pacing up and down behind the bench, shouting and ready to go in if called upon.

Something in the restaurant shifted after my retirement from the NFL: for the first time E.T. could see me as serious. I was no longer a just a football player with a sideline. No, now the two of us were all restaurant, all the time.

In new spare hours, I entered the one-year graduate restaurant program at the perhaps somewhat less than renowned Miami University Hotel

School. I learned sauces. I learned reductions. I learned butchering and that meat was king, also salt. I learned accounting and marketing. By November I was a proud member of the class, rushing back to Etienne with knowledge to share.

One morning he brought me a newspaper item, propped it at my station. Just a little AP squib with a beautiful photo: The internationally renowned choreographer Sylphide, 42, had separated from her husband, Percy Haverstock, "the Bell-Curve Billionaire." He'd been caught in an elaborate sting on a trip home to Australia: hotel room, seven underage girls, two kilograms of cocaine. The dancer stood to reap a multi-hundred-million-dollar settlement, the highest in history: there'd been no prenuptial agreement, and apparently criminals did poorly in Australian divorce courts.

"Don't get your hopes up," Etienne had written in the margin. But there were long nights to get through and of course I did get my hopes up, elaborate fantasies: Lizard dancing beside Sylphide, the only man tall enough for her new ballet, whatever it might be, ha. And of course, one thing would lead to another.

Meanwhile, the ongoing physical renovations at Floridiana reached the kitchen. Lionel and Carter (whom Etienne had started calling Ma and Pa) shut us down for three glorious weeks, gave us both a paid vacation. E.T. and I did something we'd talked about for a year, flew to visit his first mentor's restaurant in France, traveled to Italy to sit at the feet of several masters, studied beans of all things, also lentils, studied plant-based sauces, mushroom hunting, looked at kitchen gardens, ate huge meals, twenty-one heavenly days, long conversations about dream restaurants we might open one day, brothers on the road. He got a new tattoo somewhere in Marseilles when I wasn't looking: a lizard on the blank spot on his calf, the place he'd always said was reserved for true love.

MA AND PA were in the kitchen one August morning when I got in. I knew Carter had just come back from New York, a visit with Emily. She hadn't told him, and so I didn't, that that she and I had once been lovers. I'd pretty well gathered that they were lovers, not much of a leap given the spread in *People* magazine, the rights to which Carter had actually sold to benefit the Police Athletic League.

"Time to talk," Carter said.

"We're letting Etienne go," Lionel said more gently.

And suddenly, I figured it out: *Sergeant Bright.* That was the attraction! I laughed with discovery despite myself: the beauty and the beast, both bald!

"Quit the giggles," Carter said, and I stuffed it.

"We need to move past the current clientele," Lionel said.

It wasn't hard to say: "If Etienne goes, I go."

"We would like a friendly parting," Lionel said. It was he who'd stopped in after hours the Friday night previous to find the bar in full swing: buncha homos, Etienne's already vast network of new friends.

"So we will friendly say good-bye," Carter added.

That day was my last. Etienne, too, all done. He got three months severance, very generous. I was to be bought out based on a bank appraisal, hoped at least to double my original stake, though the recent construction would no doubt limit the payout. Etienne, superstitious but cheerful still, lowered the lights, emptied the seeds of several dried peppers onto a dish, stirred them with the joss stick on his necklace, read the signs, licked his fingers, announced his decision: he would go back to Mobile, Alabama. His ailing mother had been moved back there after his father's death in New Jersey, back to her old hometown. And then he simply bought himself an airline ticket and left.

I sat by the pool at my condo three days, four, trying not to think. I called my sister, really needed to talk with her, got their new housekeeper, who informed me that Kate and Jack had at long last gone off to the sunny Balearic Islands of Spain for their honeymoon. I had the team travel agent estimate the cost of such a trip, rounded it up, and sent them a check with a cheery note. I tried in that season of bruises not to feel hurt by their secrecy. A honeymoon was a private thing, after all, as was Kate's recovery, apparently.

I DIDN'T HAVE a joss stick, but took it as clear augury when the tenant who'd been in the old family home in Westport for over ten years called:

he and his wife had finally gotten their U.S. citizenship and had found a house of their own to buy, would close six weeks hence, mid-October. At first I felt panicked by the news, but then thought, Hochmeyer Haven, why not? The place that made Kate's stomach turn had always given me a kind of security, an unspoken feeling that somewhere I had a home, that I wasn't entirely untethered.

Or maybe I thought I could drift back in time and change it all: I would cut my hair at seventeen, play the complete senior year as per boyhood plan, win the season for coach and father, fail to meet Sylphide, never get interested in Emily, meet the love of my life at Princeton, someone frisky and solid named Cookie or Weezie, a subtle beauty with no interest in dance, a business major, more than likely, invite our four parents up for football games, a regular career of wholesome dates and good grades, better luck in the pro draft, a team I could actually start for, marry the college sweetheart, two children leaping from her loins, a girl, a boy. And after my big career I'd announce games on NBC and model fancy underwear, never so much as peek into a restaurant kitchen. Or, while we were using the Way-Back Machine, I could recede a little further, to a particular morning during high-school days, and padlock Dad's briefcase to the cast-iron porch railing, or further yet, and keep Kate from taking a job at the High Side so she'd never meet Dabney.

My condo in Miami sold immediately, nice profit, such were the times. I closed it up, loaded the latest Volvo wagon and spent one final night in Kate's stripped bed. Next morning, my last scheduled bodywork session with Benedikta, who acted as if I were just one more long-term client coming to termination. And maybe I was. Anyway, our clothes securely fastened, we assessed where I'd come in three years of treatment—a long, long way in her estimation, less in mine—and I wrote her a check, shook her hand good-bye, her boundaries suddenly like blast walls around a third-world embassy. In the parking lot I leaned my head on the Volvo steering wheel till once again thoughts began to enter my brain.

And then it was the long road to Connecticut, mile by mile, afternoon by evening by night by morning and repeat, six diners, two motels. The old family house when I finally arrived felt very different after Florida. Dry, for one thing. Dusty, for another. Also drafty, very cold.

Alone for a couple of winter months in the little place, I kept myself busy painting the walls and fixing the plumbing and scrubbing madly, brought down all the old possessions from the attic where I'd stuffed them. Within a week I was sleeping in my old bed under my old model planes on their old threads and thumbtacks, and Mom's blender was back in place in the kitchen. I hung all the old prints of paintings, all the old photos, placed the grandfather clock, filled the kitchen cabinets with the kind of stuff I recalled: plenty canned goods, a year's supply of paper towels. For a while I slept a lot, didn't know what to do with myself when awake. But gradually my mood improved, my spirits rising along with the length of the days.

You really had to get on to the next thing, and what better place to start than home?

10

Kate and Jack returned from Ibiza—a three-month honeymoon!—and were my only contacts with the world, weekly dinners at their house, the two of them on some new plane that seemed to involve even more constant sex than before, or anyway more showers. Jack returned my honeymoon check after I asked why it hadn't been deposited. Pulling me out into their driveway, as angry as I've ever seen him, he said, "You can get us something concrete. A piece of furniture, if you like. Something real. Something we can use. We need outdoor stuff. Nothing symbolic. Kate doesn't do well with symbolic."

I didn't understand, not a glimmer, and said so.

And Jack, terse and unyielding, said, "David, you don't need to understand."

I brought them a teak deck set. I bought them an enormous, striped umbrella. I bought them a barbecue kettle. I cooked for them out there. I never brought or mentioned alcohol of any kind. I avoided the symbolic, didn't talk in abstractions, still puzzled as to the problem. Jack slowly softened up, let me sail with them on his boat, a Concordia yawl called *Deep Song,* which he claimed he'd named for Kate before he ever met her, romantic guy.

Come fall, I cooked for them in their house. I cooked for them a lot. I bought them a couch and sat with them upon it as fall came in, no football. But I was forbidden alone time with Kate. Not expressly. It just didn't happen—Jack was always there, and I mean always.

I stayed in Westport, always alone, supposedly developing a business plan, some sort of consulting. Maybe something to do with wine, which I knew well by then, and furnished for myself without limits. A restaurant

seemed out of the question—with wine, at least, someone else had done
all the hardest work. Across the pond the High Side was dark. Dad's rowboat was still on the shore. I sometimes got in it under moonlight, rowed
back and forth. I ran, ten and fifteen miles a day. My physique was the
one thing I still had from the former life. I joined a very expensive gym,
where occasionally people recognized me, made inane conversation. I
didn't mind. Inane was fine with me. I could work out endlessly, discuss
Miami football endlessly.

Etienne called monthly. I'd invested twenty thousand dollars of my
savings with him, and he'd started a proto-vegan restaurant called Health
Spot back in Mobile, a clientele of weight lifters and elderly women, all
while his mother lay sick in her tiny house. Month five, she died. Month
six, he met a man and fell in love, first time in years. RuAngela, no last
name, who, like all of E.T.'s serious boyfriends, was a masculine cross-
dresser, five-o'clock shadow, sassy skirts. Month seven, and RuAngela
was running the Health Spot dining room, doing the books. Month
eight, and they'd made their rent out of revenues for the first time. No
dividends as yet. Month nine, they had a fire-code violation and had to
spend some money, or there would have been a disbursement for me.
Might have been nice, too, as I'd gotten no payment from Lionel and
Carter on Floridiana. Month ten, and a call from RuAngela, whom I'd
come to love and trust: could I invest just a couple thousand more? Like
twenty thousand more?

Of course I could, of course. It was only money, and more was coming
once Floridiana got settled. Also, Etienne was my only real friend.

I MISSED THE Cuban beat, the bikinis on the street. In Westport, I wasn't
going to let myself be anyone's most eligible bachelor, made no attempt
to meet women. Our old neighbor, Mrs. Paumgartner, had passed away
a few years back, and in her place was a Catholic priest who seemed to
be shacking up with his housekeeper, an immensity who walked in front
of their kitchen windows in her bra and big panties, gave him hugs and
squeezes out in the driveway. Westport was completing the generations-
long conversion from fishing and farming village to suburb, a place where
most of the money was made elsewhere, where beautiful housewives had

nothing whatever to do, the old cow-path streets jammed with aggressive drivers in gigantic tanks flipping you the finger for driving too slowly. I'd forgotten the sea smell, the huge estates along the water. I avoided the road that went by Staples High, hated the sight of the train station. I avoided old acquaintances. I was still the kid whose parents had been murdered, though on any given day I could forget.

The town thought of itself as artsy, but it was too expensive for any real art scene. The restaurants were meat and potatoes, attached to threadbare inns. The one exception was Che Guevera's Attic, lively and alcoholic, the Mexican food an unfortunate afterthought, and where but Westport would Che Guevara be imagined to have had any sort of attic?

One night as summer was fading the old rotary phone in the kitchen rang. It was Etienne, crying so hard that RuAngela had to get on. They'd lost the Health Spot. I guess I don't mind saying that I thought of my money first, managed not to blurt anything about it. "I'm sorry," I said instead.

"I saw it coming, Mr. Hochmeyer, saw it coming a mile away, tried to protect him, you know, but it got so bad I just pulled the plug. If we'd paid bills one more month, we would have lost everything. My house, Mr. Hochmeyer, it's mortgaged to the roof tiles, all so these people could eat the *best food they ever ate.*"

ONE DAY IN late September that year I took a long run, all the way down to Compo Beach, a rare public strand, stone breakwater and tennis courts, not much to explore there except memory, and no one around, couple of furtive teenagers at a picnic table, sweet aroma of pot in the air. Even their boom-box music took me back: Led Zeppelin. I wanted to tell them that I'd met Jimmy Page, sat at a table with Robert Plant. I wanted to tell them the famous dancer Emily Bright had sat right there on that very bench, and not so many years before—perhaps about the time they were born, think of that.

Jogging homeward along the water I spotted a large rectangular building for sale, an undistinguished wooden structure all alone on the shore side of the road, shuttered and forlorn.

Slowly, I realized it was Trompetta's, which had been a pretty good little Italian restaurant in its day, nothing but a dive by the time I was in high school, one of Dad's hangouts, at least before it was shut down by the state.

I forced the broken back door, looked around inside, just a big empty space, a few of the old restaurant chairs in there, graffiti on the walls.

The next morning I called the agent listed on the broken sign.

"Yes, of course," he said. "Let me find some paperwork here for you. That's waterfront. No certificate, and that's reflected in the price. You cannot live there. No one can ever live there. Food service only. Uh, so, you cannot have a beach or boat club, no dockage. Town water and septic, that's good, one good thing. You cannot have takeaway food. It's table service only. So like, no clam shacks. No live music. No dancing. Though you can have alcohol. Ten p.m. closing, midnight weekends. Parking lot dimensions are fixed. Signage fixed. Price is six."

"Six what?"

"Six hundred thousand."

I'd learned from E.T. that silence was the best negotiating tool, and I let one stand. The place had been for sale seven years.

He didn't hold out long: "But here in this situation I'm gonna say make the lowest lowball offer you can imagine—Chase Manhattan's not gonna be insulted. Couple hundred thousand, it's yours."

Long silence.

The salesman sighed heavily. "They'll carry your mortgage," he said. "I'll bet they'll take sixty grand. I'll bet they'll take two down. Even less. What do they care?"

And in my mind, at least, Restaurant Firfisle was born.

11

Etienne was terrified in my house the first few nights, slept on the pull-out in the living room, claimed later to have made peace with the ghosts upstairs, who he didn't think were my folks but much younger people, a beautiful young pair. And with that understanding he and RuAngela made the move. Party mode, we toured the restaurants of Fairfield County, three and four a day, little of note, then into New York City, only an hour away on the commuter train, days on end. Mornings, Etienne and I cooked and experimented, crowded into the little kitchen at Hochmeyer Haven. We laid out menu schemes, excitement growing along with what in a dance company would be called repertory. RuAngela modeled various gowns and make-up protocols, always dressing for work, but she also drew up charts, gradually put the Restaurant Firfisle concept on paper—she had a great brain for numbers, projections, percentages. In my vivid dream, salt waves washed up against the Trompetta family's seawall throwing spray at our restaurant's newly installed windows, our delighted guests eating and laughing, kitchen clanking and steaming like a fine old engine.

Back on earth, RuAngela worked up a lowball bid for the building and I duly submitted it: $40,500, not a chance they'd bite, but RuAngela was firm.

AFTER A COUPLE of weeks with no word from the Trompetta's people, I drove my new partners up to see Kate and Jack in Madison. The restaurant was to be kept secret—I had Jack in mind as a possible investor, if it came to that, but we'd need to have our burner knobs all in a row before he heard or suspected anything, a perfect business plan that is, which might or might not mean our being up and running and already showing our success—we'd have to see about that. I had money enough to get the doors open, and the cash from Ma and Pa at Floridiana was on its way, no doubt, plenty to see us through. And so the story was that my friends were just visiting: not a word about living with me, not a word about real estate.

We arrived with a big box of produce. Kate hugged Etienne in the doorway, patted his face, hugged him more, touched the tattoos again. He clearly couldn't believe how truly gorgeous she was, tested the hem of her absurdly short skirt as if to see if she was real, put his finger to the flaw of her lip, a kind of blessing. Meanwhile RuAngela in a sensible tweed skort and spangled blouse took Jack's hands in hers, introduced herself, laid it on thick: "Your house! A church! You bought it from fucking Jesus Christ Himself!"

He recoiled, the subtlest thing, but something you didn't miss. Certainly RuAngela didn't miss it. She turned to hug Kate, gave Kate a long look. Jack took the chance to clutch me, pretend to kiss my cheek, whisper in my ear: "Let's wrap this up before dinner. Before your sister extends any invitations. Three o'clock, okay?"

"Jack, fine."

"And nothing about detectives, none of that."

"It won't come from me."

"She's been a little wired, David." He puffed a breath, about to say something more, but RuAngela took his arm, tugged him into the living room, plunked him on the plump couch. *"Everyday Joy!"* she said, as if it were his secret name.

"You've read it?" he said warily.

"Honey, I've read it twice, who hasn't? Etienne and I have done all the trust exercises—wonderful—every one. You changed the way we *talk* to one another." And so on: I hadn't thought about it, but singing at bedtime was a Jack suggestion in *Joyful Couples,* which was his newest book, and might explain my housemates' little nightly arias in reedy voices, harmony both figurative and real, pretty nice. Taking both of Jack's hands in hers, RuAngela carried on, perfectly sincere: she knew the books chapter and verse, really knew them. And Jack was pleased; you could actually see him relax, see him falling for her, looking in her shirt, our queen of illusions.

"Let's cook," Etienne said.

He and Ru-Ru and I had stopped early morning at two farms she'd been courting and taken away everything we needed for a lunchtime frittata, excellent eggs from chickens we'd had to shoo off the car, potatoes straight from the furrow, rainbow selection of peppers, a big purple cabbage, baby squashes, and herbs by the handfuls. Etienne had brought his knives along, of course, and handed me the biggest as Kate led us into the kitchen.

Immediately she lowered her voice: "David, I've been thinking about Dad's briefcase."

"A beautiful home," E.T. said loudly, instant conspirator.

And Kate murmured: "I think I know where it is. I mean, I think I've worked out where it must be, given all the variables here."

I said, "Kate, we're not supposed to talk about this subject."

"David, I'm not saying anything about 'this subject,' just the fucking briefcase, okay?"

"Kate, Daddy left that briefcase on a train."

"Oh, *bullshit,* David. You *know* that's not true."

"Gorgeous kitchen," said E.T.

"It's true," I said.

Kate hissed, "When did you ever believe Dad? I have the key. He gave me the key. The key to the briefcase."

I couldn't suppress my interest: "Okay, and where is this key?"

"The windows!" Etienne exclaimed. "The harbor out there!"

"Right here." She tugged a necklace up from inside her shirt. "I've been wearing it all these years."

Oh, sure. I knew it well. Her necklace. I'd assumed Jack had given it to her, just a little golden key on a delicate golden chain. She'd never said a word about it. RuAngela had Jack laughing in the next room, really busting a gut, a miracle. They were getting to their feet, soon to join us in the kitchen. "But wait," I whispered. "That briefcase had a combination lock. A little row of numbers you turned, remember? Like four little wheels. We played with it all the time."

She did remember, of course she did. "But David. Daddy gave me a *key,* this key. He came all the way up on the train to deliver it. He was supposed to be at work."

"And where did he say the briefcase was?"

"He didn't say. He said he'd let me know. And then, of course, they got him."

An image came to me, our Dad sneaking down the lawn to the pond, that big manila envelope in hand. Jack was telling RuAngela something about the Bonnard. Urgent Kate pulled the necklace over her head, stuffed it into my hand, pretended to give me a kiss, laughed falsely, hissed in my ear: "David. Will you please look for the briefcase? We have to find Daddy's briefcase, all right?"

I kept the key for two weeks or so, long enough for her to settle down, I hoped, then sent it back in a nice little box, her one real memento of the old man.

LIKE THE PAIR of worried parents they were becoming, Etienne and Ru-Angela had begun to irritate me, always asking if there weren't some kind of club I could join or some kind of class I could take to meet women, maybe a victims-of-violence support group. Something like Kate had had at McLean and still attended weekly, a major undertaking for Jack, as my sister had lost her license permanently, not that he ever complained, not once. RuAngela invited single women for dinner most weekends, ostensibly as tasters for the developing menu—the hygienist from her new dentist's office, the lady from the dress shop, the woman who ran the animal shelter, her Vietnamese manicurist—all of them really nice people, all of them very available, all of them answering to RuAngela's fertility-goddess taste in women. Not that I wasn't tempted, it's just that I wasn't particularly in the market, wasn't in the market at all.

Meanwhile, Etienne's confidence had fled. He was anxious, lots of hand wringing, quick to tears, quick to embarrassment and guilt over his dependency on me and over the Health Spot crash, which had really roughed him up, catastrophes looming everywhere he looked. RuAngela was the positive one at our house, spent large portions of every afternoon on her face and clothing, plucking hairs from here and there, working on her wigs, getting ready for the night's adventures, even if only a walk outside.

"Am I beautiful?" she asked me once.

I knew what she meant—beautiful to a heterosexual man. I just said, "Yes, yes, my God, are you kidding?" And there was truth in that—she turned men's heads all right, that body of hers, always the high-high heels on a person already tall, narrow pretty calves, bubble-butt (padded, but still). And her skin was beautiful indeed, her cleavage smooth and brown as a 74 percent cacao mousse, hormonally induced breasts lovely to contemplate, never a bra, confusing appeal. I didn't tell her the next thing, that her manly jaw, her heavy five-o'clock shadow, her deep voice, the knowledge of the existence of fully functional male equipment tucked down in there somewhere definitely got in my way, sexually speaking. I mean, she peed standing next to me in the backyard like any old dude. She didn't talk about sex-change operations, either. She was already what she was and wanted to be. Which among other things was a good friend to me.

The letter from Lionel and Carter's legal team when it finally came threw me into a funk, but not RuAngela: she immediately began a campaign of guilt and shame, playing momma. Supposedly the independent audit had shown Restaurant Floridiana operating at a deficit for the entire five years of its existence, pure fuckery. My buyout share—which was to have been the startup cash for Firfisle—was *zero*. I wasn't one to sue, not over a lost cause like that. RuAngela wrote a letter of protest for me to sign, and then she dressed me down. Self-respect, that was the word. She got Lionel on the phone, carried on so dramatically that a settlement offer arrived the next day by FedEx, and later a check, mid five figures, exact recoup of my investment.

Which is how the Firfisle Express got through Christmas and New Year's (1989, the year the Berlin Wall would fall), even past Valentine's day. We had a month of menus planned and tested, suppliers lined up, knives honed. RuAngela began interviewing wait staff and kitchen people. We just needed our building. So, Ru wrote another letter to Chase, the bank that held the old Trompetta property, and *lowered* our offer: $35,500. I felt the whole thing slipping through our fingers, felt the stupidity of having got stuck on one building.

"You watch," RuAngela said.

□ □ □

I **RAN INTO** Miss Butterman at the town library, where I was checking out a new pile of world cookbooks. She looked no different than she'd looked in history class, same wry look in her eye, same wig of short hair. "Have you recovered?" she said warmly.

I shook my head even saying "Yes," managed a rueful smile.

"No, you can't," she said, more cheerfully than not. And then she caught me up on a number of my classmates, a lot of corporate jobs among them, a lot of births and marriages and divorces and deaths, smallest details. She complimented me on some specific touchdowns from my Miami career.

"Oh, and Linsey's been ill," she said to finish. And then, confidentially: "His stepmother writes me. Sylphide, you know."

"Yes," I said, making it sound as if I were as privy to the star's secrets as she, though I'd only read it in the papers: "A heart attack."

"David, I think our fine-feathered friend would like a note from you. He's in New York there on Sutton Place. He can't do the world travel any more. But they keep such good people around him. And he's able to go to his school still. He has a girlfriend."

Home, I wrote the note, all right, just a few sentences for someone to read to him. I had an absurd stack of old Dolphins promo shots—me smiling in my shoulder pads—clipped the note to one, sent it off. Of course I had the thought that Sylphide might see it, might cast her green gaze upon my face and feel a flood of warmth and appreciation, a woman just rising from divorce.

I **SCRAMBLED UP** from a power nap when the phone rang one March afternoon, raced to answer, only slowly waking. Formal voice on the other end, much static. It took me several sentences to realize that it was not the Trompetta's people but good old Desmond, Sylphide's very butler, phoning me from Chile, where the dancer and her company were in the midst of a two-week engagement. Gradually, I deciphered that Linsey's health had taken a bad turn, no warning at all. His heart, of course. Dr. Chun and two of Linsey's trainers had taken him to Doctors Hospital, not far from Sutton Place. But the bad news was that he was probably not going to make it.

"He loved your photo," Desmond said. "He's been sleeping with it under his pillow. He's rather ruined it."

The sadness welled up in me as Desmond went on: the dancer needed a favor. Sylphide's foundation jet had been grounded due to sudden political trouble in Chile. There were very few commercial flights going anywhere, and it might take days, though Conrad Pant, her manager, was trying to arrange a military helicopter to get them to Buenos Aires. Could I get into the city? Be by Linsey's side? Just in case? "We'd rather he didn't die alone," Desmond said.

"Put her on?" I said.

"She can't," said Desmond. "Not just now."

"Enough discretion," I said.

"She's not taking it well, sir. She's not taking it well at all. Devastated, sir. Please, please go to him. Sutton Place at your disposal, of course." Desmond in tears!

At Doctors Hospital my name was already on the limited visitors list, and I was shown into a private room on a high floor of that very nice facility. Linsey lay there with his eyes open. He saw me, knew me, reached up for me, held on to me as I went to kiss him. And I held on to him, careful of all the tubes in his nose and mouth and chest. He smelled of pee as in the old days, every muscle flaccid. A monitor beeped. The TV was loud. I turned it off with the remote at Linsey's hand. The little stinker had no idea what was happening to him. He seemed very weary but quizzical as ever.

"Mommy," he managed.

"She's coming," I told him.

The night was very long. A nurse rolled in a big gray kidney-dialysis recliner, slipped me a blanket, and fitfully I slept. In the morning someone brought a tray of food, but there was no reason for it: Linsey couldn't eat with all that gear in his face.

"Fat bottom," I said, one of his hits from history class, a reference to Miss Butterman.

Barest smile, and he closed his eyes, struggling to breathe.

"He's going," said the stoical nurse who answered my buzz.

But it was two more hours, then three, his breathing slower and then slower yet. Late in the afternoon, Linsey Stryker-Stewart opened his eyes one more time.

"Hey, Wizard," he said clearly.

WE MOURNERS BARELY fit into the huge High Side ballroom, Queen Anne chairs and wooden rental chairs arranged as if for a major recital. I sat between Etienne and RuAngela, and they held my two hands, crossed. Miss Butterman gave the eulogy, quavering tones, great charm, claimed that our Linsey was the best student she'd had in all her years of teaching, never late, no backtalk, the most cheerful person she'd ever met. Then she listed some of his insults, to laughter. Linsey's girlfriend, Toot, a middle-aged classmate of his at their special school, got up and said, "Linsey is very nice to everyone. Very quiet in the night. I like him. Well, good-bye."

Sylphide sat in the front row, plain gray dress, Desmond stiff at her side. Georges Whiteside was far from her at the big Falcone concert piano and played several Dabney songs with great feeling, the melodies that, mixed and tumbled, Linsey had continually hummed, what Kate had once called his theme song. When it was my turn I thanked everyone for coming, said something about how Linsey and I had gone to high school together, and that I loved him. I added that Kate had loved him, too, and that she wished she could attend, though the second part was not true. Or, at any rate, she wouldn't come to the phone when I'd called to tell Jack.

Sylphide didn't speak publicly, but greeted people in the receiving line warmly, clearly exhausted—they'd barely got in the night before. There'd been no chance to visit with her. I'd never clearly seen her as the boy's mother, not at all, but for nearly twenty years she'd been all he had, when you thought about it, all he'd ever known. (According to that week's *People* magazine—which RuAngela bought, knowing I would secretly treasure it—his actual mother was one of the Rattner family's neighbors back in Newscastle, perhaps a drug connection for the rotten Rattner boys, Dabney and Brady, a known addict, according to the article, much Dabney's senior. She and Dabney had married when he was sixteen and she was pregnant, which was done in those days in that place. They led a drunken existence, pregnancy no obstacle. And then she left after the baby was born, never to be heard from again.)

We all ate petit fours and drank champagne, as Sylphide told us they'd always done on Linsey's birthdays.

Dr. Chun, old stalwart, had stayed outside with the Bentley. I brought him a couple of the little cakes and a cup of coffee, had to pull open his door to hand the stuff to him. He was a good one to yank himself together instantly, but I could see he'd been crying. He said something unintelligible, then tried the word again, a mouthful for a guy who'd grown up in Beijing: "Sorrow."

Late there was only Miss Butterman's old Ford Fiesta in the High Side driveway—she'd gotten a little potted and found a ride home with Emily's old friend Dwight Leonard, whom she'd flunked in Medieval History. In the High Side, only Sylphide and her staff. She and I sat on the great stone steps in the grand foyer as Desmond and two young women cleared the parlor, precise teamwork, no talk among them. They'd all loved Linsey, despite what he'd put them through.

"Linsey was a good boy," said Sylphide.

The Calder mobile floated very lightly above us, faint wind from the movement of our bodies. I saw she'd had her hair done, cut square to her shoulders, a little overcombed, little black hat pinned on top. The staff finished up their chores, filed upstairs to their rooms, palpably pleased to be home in the countryside. The foyer grew dark. Sylphide was at my side, fragrant with jasmine. Maybe it was all the black and gray that made her seem smaller than I remembered. Her arms were very pale.

She said, "I am feeling so irresponsible."

My heart welled. I said, "You didn't know he'd take a turn. You didn't know there'd be a coup d'état or whatever it was going on down there."

At length she said, "So, about you. Who were your friends tonight?"

Explaining Etienne and RuAngela led to the whole story: end of football, move back home, Kate so deeply troubled, the idea of the restaurant, my lowball bid on Trompetta's. I thanked her for the name: Restaurant Firfisle.

She liked that very much. "Firfisle," she repeated.

"Tenke," I replied too tenderly—she'd only been saying the name of a potential business.

The mobile slowly rotated, seemed to hover, turned back on itself. Upstairs someone had won the card game, muted hilarity. The dark in the foyer deepened. Perhaps outside some clouds were moving in.

"Time for you to row home," she said gently.

I tried to recall if I'd seen her weep before, realized she'd always only been a tower of strength, all her troubles notwithstanding. At first it was just a little sniffling, but then she really collapsed into it. I touched her shoulder, and as the tears came harder, pulled her into my arms, choking sobs like a little kid's, the feeling the world would never be right again. I pulled her up into my lap, just like that, nothing to it, and rocked her, rocked her, what seemed like hours.

THE NEXT AFTERNOON, the Realtor called. Our revised offer on the Trompetta's property had been accepted—$35,500, *whoa*. The bank wanted to close immediately, two-week-maximum grace period. RuAngela thought April Fool's day auspicious, and so we scheduled our meeting. And quickly then there was no going back: we owned the Trompetta's building. The three of us spent a whole day there, walked the seawall, poked around the decaying premises, pictured the place full and hopping. Shifting tides, it was Etienne who exuded all the confidence now—his general anxiety had lifted with the one bit of luck. My own excitement was tempered by an equal measure of fear, but my fear was tempered by what could only be called delusions of grandeur: we'd have a great restaurant up and running in record time, one of the best restaurants in the history of the world, pronto.

RuAngela had long since calculated startup costs. Rather than tap my full savings, I went to Dwight Leonard, who was now an officer at Westport Trust (WE KNOW YOU!), and on scant collateral and little evidence of worth was granted a large loan, 8 percent interest, a bargain at the time. Quickly, we pulled all the contractors we could find on board, promised them bonuses in exchange for speed.

We could open without the parking lot paved, we could open without a sign, we could open without a liquor license, if necessary. But we couldn't open without a kitchen, without at least a skeleton staff, and not without that fire system. So merrily (shades of Nicholas Hochmeyer), I dipped into my savings, made a loan to Firfisle-the-restaurant from Firfisle-the-man, a legal technicality that would protect me personally from the bankruptcy I had started to see coming.

END OF SEPTEMBER, 1989, and I was in the gorgeous kitchen shaping up at Restaurant Firfisle, helping the new fire-suppression contractor run the pipe for the foam system, getting to be a damn good plumber. RuAngela was likewise out in the dining room painting, always in a dress, our Ru-Ru, though she hadn't shaved for some weeks, her rally beard, as she called it—oh, the delicious weirdness of her! One of the cement guys working on the foundation could say, "Nice dress, buddy," to RuAngela, and she'd just bat her eyes.

E.T. engaged every single human being we crossed paths with, fed anyone who was there at lunchtime, anyone who worked late, offered a Sunday brunch to anyone who put in the extra day, nearly always vegetarian (100 percent converts among those who worked day after day, carnivores shrugging and asking for more). RuAngela, and E.T., the ultimate asset. Even out and about the two of them made friends very easily—everyone wants an exotic acquaintance.

And Etienne and RuAngela took care of me, held me to a day off each week, during which I hardly knew what to do, just stopped cold, thinking of the restaurant every minute, practically mooning. So I wasn't thrilled by our big plan to take time off before we opened. A week for them to get back down to Mobile and collect belongings, a subsequent week for me to do what?

"Stay at a B and B," RuAngela kept saying.

Groan.

And E.T. would exhort: "Go find an island, lie on the beach!"

Anyway, I was in the kitchen pulling down on a huge wrench, tensioning the last leg of the fire system while the contractor put the last foam-head in place inside the cooking hood. E.T. was sautéing something while working the phone, interviewing local growers and foragers. The pipe turned slowly, the foam-head coming *squeak-squeak* into position. A bowed gentleman in a blue suit came into my peripheral vision, inspector no doubt. The contractor ignored him, so I did too. And the man watched as we completed the work.

But it was Dr. Chun! Ho! Stiffest hug in the history of the world! Pat-pat on the frail shoulders. All business, eyes averted, he handed me one of Sylphide's big envelopes, the gold piping, the jasmine scent. The fire-suppression contractor looked at me sidewise: still a lot of work to be done, Prince Charming.

But it was my shop.

Dr. Chun was impatient—Knicks home game, early start. "Just a minute," I said, and found a scrap of lumber the size of a note card, why not? I drew a frilly border around its edges with a red grease pencil, drew a heart, then wrote in the center, nice block letters: ECLIPSE? Sylphide had always liked men who acted like men. Dr. Chun took my wooden epistle from me with only the trace of a grin, and that was our good-bye.

In the walk-in I opened Sylphide's envelope. Maybe she'd meet me in Japan, Turkmenistan, Madagascar, Antarctica; I'd heard the beaches were spectacular. I'd be philosophical about the loss of the restaurant. She'd be philosophical about Percy Haverstock and his bad habits. We'd find our way into our new love gradually. But in the envelope, not so much as a note. Just a tidal flush of disappointment in the form of an outsize check for an outsize amount: $100,000. It was made out by machine to Firfisle Restaurant Corp., written on an account called Tenke Thorvald Foundation for the Arts, signed with impressive formality by the director of the foundation, one Conrad Pant. I had the impulse to rip it into a 100,000 pieces. Along with the check was nothing more rousing than a form letter:

This check represents a one-time grant from the Tenke Thorvald Foundation for Fine Arts. Your organization has attracted our notice as deserving of support due to the quality of your artistic vision. Funds are unrestricted and may be used as you desire, starting immediately. Please make no effort to contact the foundation or Ms. Thorvald—your continued excellent work is all the thanks we need.

LATER THAT WEEK, in the insane flurry of finishing up, Jack called. Kate wasn't doing well, and he was worn out, needed a few hours to himself, errands to do, the boat to put up, and she in such a state that he was afraid to leave her alone. I'd never heard him so baldly desperate, poor guy: "Just don't entertain any of her delusions, okay? You've got to promise me. None of this business about Barbara and Nicholas and Dabney and Danbury, please. Promise me that. I know you're susceptible too. She'll push it on you, believe me. It's all she ever talks about. Do something physical. She likes to take a walk. It quiets her spirit. But she won't walk with me, and won't go without me."

I took the next afternoon off, drove up there. Jack answered the door the way I'd first seen him, wet and wrapped in a towel, might have been forty again, though of course he was close to sixty by then. "We've made up," he said simply. He looked pretty relaxed, not what I expected. Shortly he was back, dressed for his errands in pressed jeans and flannels, worn Topsider shoes. "Kate'll be down. She's still in the shower. Just, please, I know it's not your fault and I know it's not easy, but please don't entertain or encourage any of that crap. Talk about cooking. Have her help you make lunch. We shopped just this morning. I shopped, I mean. She sat in the car. But we've fixed it. Crested another hill. Sorry no wine in there. Talk about those friends of yours. Anything but you-know-what."

"RuAngela sends her best."

And Jack actually laughed, made the first joke I'd heard from him in months: "I've never wanted a man so much."

"Everyone loves RuAngela."

Kate sang a loud phrase upstairs.

Jack said, "Nothing. About. Turkle." He put a finger to his lips: *shhh.* And then flew out the door and to his glimmering new Volvo and away in a cloud of safety.

Kate singing upstairs, something indistinct, cheerful as Jack, it seemed.

In the kitchen, piles of new groceries. I dug through, imagining a pretty elaborate late lunch after a very long walk, that kind of appetite. I pared a couple of carrots. I peeled onions. What would it be? Something simple.

Eventually Kate came down, hugged me, kissed me, had a look at me at arm's length, smooched me again.

I said, "Let's put something on the stove before our walk, yes?"

"Lentil stew," she said. "We got stuff at the market this morning. Or Jack did. I sat in the car."

"Just as he said."

"Because he won't let me talk about my evidence, biggest fight ever."

"Well. It seems like you softened him up some."

"Enough to get you here. And I know he made you promise not to let me, but you're going to like it."

I cored brussels sprouts, pulled them apart into leaves—very nice in a spicy stew. "No, Katydid, I'm not going to like it."

"Oh, well. You cook, I'll show you some things, and then you can tell me who's right."

"Kate. I think we know who's right."

" 'The trial was definitive,' " Kate said, channeling Jack. " 'That has to be our mantra. We can't just keep it going forever, Katherine dear! A respected court has ruled on the case.' "

There. Just like that, she'd pulled me in. I said, "Respected court, my ass."

And Jack was no more. Kate got the wickedest look, the look of the girl on the stairs at fourteen, that boy in her room, Dabney not yet in her sights, the scar on her lip pronounced. She said, "He let me take things. Anything I wanted. He had the authority to close the case and discard everything—they can do that after x number of years, once it's been ad-judicated and any appeals are in. They're switching to electronic every-thing, so all the old shit must go! I've got boxes and boxes of *stuff*. All the paperwork, or some of it. And the sweater, and . . ."

"Kate. Who are we talking about? Who let you take things?"

"We're talking about a friend of mine. Who's a friend of yours, too."

"Detective Turkle?"

"You said the forbidden words, not me!" Triumph. "I'll be right back."

I got the darkest feeling then, alone there with the work, the feeling that I was cooking for Mom and Dad, that they'd attend this meal, that they'd want to know I'd done well, that I knew what I was doing with this crazy restaurant thing. Dad, of course, would approve of the money I'd skinned off the dancer, Mom of the way I'd followed all the rules. There'd be plenty to talk about, and yet nothing—we'd never bring up Kate's illness, not a peep; we'd never even say the two of them were dead.

I splashed a generous half-cup of Jack's elegant olive oil in his big, unused Dutch oven, put the heat too high, cut the rest of the mirepoix energetically. I was still an athlete—my folks would recognize me. They'd want to know whom I'd married, that I'd avoided the "Negress." They'd play with their grandchildren, the ones they didn't have, and wouldn't ever.

Onion into the hot oil, ten minutes. The food would shield me, and not in some vague way—this was literal, working on the far side of the granite island in the kitchen so I could face the door, see them when they came in. They wouldn't be like zombies, nothing like that, they'd only be themselves, Dad so careless (he'd throw his coat over Jack's priceless vase), Mom so judgmental (who can live in a church!). They'd want to know what a Princeton degree was doing hidden in their closet, what two homosexuals were doing in their room back at home, *Negro* homosexuals. I slipped off my Super Bowl rings, put them in my pockets, separate pockets so they wouldn't clank together and give themselves away.

A little frantically I rinsed a cup of red lentils, then a half cup more, left them to a brief soak in salted water: always make a lot when you're expecting guests. Add the mirepoix to the onions, develop those flavors. This was my game, untainted. My folks forever in my restaurant. Mom, a tour of the gardens. Dad, a special drink in the walk-in with the men. The guard oiling the snap on his holster, oiling it again, testing it, pulling the gun, lightning draw.

Tomatoes chopped fine, two whole bulbs garlic, one handful raisins, couple tablespoons raw rice to bind, cumin ground in the coffee beaner, a nice bay leaf crumbled fine so no one would choke, couple of grinds pepper, a bouquet garni, which I couldn't wait to explain to Mom: basil tied up, stems and all, one sprig rosemary, pull it before service. Thick pinches of salt. Taste, like blood. And finally, Dad and Mom, a cup of vermouth, the last alcohol in the professor's house, aged under the sink fifteen years at least, or call it nineteen: same vintage as your deaths.

I HAVE A memory of going upstairs at that juncture to look at the Bonnard, a clear image of the extraordinary light of the thing, the shadowy male figure behind the woman standing ready at a large table set for dinner in the garden, but this can't be right—I wouldn't have left the meal prep at that point, for one thing, and for another, right about that time, primarily for insurance reasons, Jack had arranged a permanent loan to the Metropolitan Museum of Art.

Kate was nowhere to be found.

The stew needed some body. Back of the fridge I found a packet of baby portobellos, washed them luxuriantly, sliced them very thin, pretty shapes to anchor the stew.

Kate reappeared in her hiking boots, an armful of legal-size file folders, cobwebs in her hair: original documents from our parents' case and the cases around them, all the legal proceedings, all the failed prosecutions, no one ever convicted in the multiple homicides, a lot of mistrials. Her theory hadn't changed: Dabney's death and our parents' had been related somehow. The "somehow" came down to an increasingly paranoid view of Sylphide, that this world-class ballerina had done something awful, arranged to have Dabney killed. Really? Her own beloved husband? And having rubbed him out, the world's most accomplished dancer had ordered our parents killed, too.

"But, Katy, why?"

"To punish me."

"For what?"

"Don't be stupid!" Katy cried.

"For Dabney?"

"Of course for that. He was about to leave her! For me!"

"Maybe so." Better soften that: "Probably so, I mean definitely." Go for the logic: "But, Kate, it was a car accident."

"A car, David, but not an accident. And not 'maybe' or 'probably definitely,' either—why do you think he was giving me those beautiful paintings?"

"So you could give them to Dad?"

"Don't be a fucking prick."

"And, really, Kate, what about Perdhomme?"

She shouted, "What about him?"

"Perdhomme," I said more sharply than I meant. "Him and Kaiser."

Kate trotted back upstairs. The stew, honestly, I could throw it away. I cored a few Brussels sprouts, dropped them in a leaf at a time, calming myself. Nice color, a little texture.

She returned shortly with another precarious pile of folders, produced a stapled sheaf of documents—knew exactly where in the profusion to find it, pressed it into my hands.

"Perdhomme was strongly implicated," I said not looking. "Whereas Sylphide, not at all. Kaiser, Kaiser was right there. This far away from me."

"Perdhomme and the hit man, is that all you ever think about?"

"Just that they were involved," I said. "It's the plain truth."

"I haven't worked all that out. But Perdhomme did well in court, right?"

"He prevailed, if that's what you mean, in our case and in all of them."

"All of them what?"

"There were other Dolus execs killed, remember? And that lawyer, what's his name."

"Dick Fortin, in case you think I forgot. Okay, brother. You want to know what I think? I think Perdhomme was just pulled in to deflect attention from the real killer, everyone knowing he'd get off."

"And it wasn't just Fortin. There was that milquetoasty guy in Chicago."

"Pervis."

"Who was a Dolus executive, Kate."

"So?"

"And the two guys in the hotel in New York?"

She glowered at me. "Insufficient evidence. And your man prevailed in the civil suit, too."

"Don't call him my man!" The civil suit was a famous disaster, brought at great expense by the several grieving families (though not ours— too broke) who in the end had been ordered to pay Perdhomme's legal costs. Cold.

She said, "You're the one who keeps bringing him up."

"And that assistant D.A."

"I adored that guy. A great investigator."

"He liked you, too, Kate. He liked you a lot. And he died falling off a roof at a party in SoHo."

"People have accidents."

"During the trial? The day after he'd told Turkle he was going to meet an informant? Someone from Dolus?"

"Which you didn't believe at the time. I was the one who fucking told you, don't forget."

"But Katy, at the time, we didn't know what we know now. And at the time you certainly believed it! Who could think you'd deflect attention by implicating the head of a major corporation?"

Her lip drew up almost sinister, that scar. "Someone even more major, that's who."

I said, "Jack's going to hate me. Talking to you about this. The stew can simmer. Let's walk. Let's get outside. Take me out to the beach."

"You're just as excited as I am."

I shook my head: No, no, not me. And then I flipped through the pages she'd handed over, a police report, it looked like, formally addressed to that weasel of a D.A. in Danbury, sick memories of the cinderblock court-room. Mom and Dad were at the door. I felt their presence at the door. Kate knew what she was doing, knew how to draw me in against thin resistance.

"Kate."

"'Kate.'"

"Don't mimic me. This isn't even our parents' case."

"Keep looking." She flipped the pages for me, pointed to a specific paragraph near the end of the blunt and grotesquely graphic report:

Mr. Stryker-Stewart's death must be treated as suspicious. Grand Jury inquiry warranted in this officer's opinion. Deceased found in wooded area .43 miles from site of collision. Presence of a second party neither established nor disproved. Actions of second party neither established nor disproved. Further investigation warranted and recommended.

And so on. A further page under a different letterhead had a dissenting opinion written by an officer of the Connecticut State Police, but that wasn't why the hair of my neck stood up. The hair of my neck stood up because until that moment I hadn't realized that Dabney's death had been ruled suspicious by anyone official, ever. I'd always thought the rumors were just that, the conjecture of distraught fans. There'd never been any kind of official inquiry, no grand jury, nothing. Whole books had been written on the subject of Dabney's death, and all but the most sensational dismissed foul play.

Kate handed me papers as if making a case: there had indeed been strong sets of footprints leading from the highway to where Dabney had finally died, two sets in, one set out. These had been explained away in the press and in subsequent testimony as the prints of a potential Good Samaritan who'd gotten spooked when he found a body, or more so when he recognized who it was, maybe a smart person who knew no more could be done and that his own life would be turned upside down. And anyway, what kind of murderer drags a body all over the place for no reason?

"No reason?" Kate said, though I'd said nothing at all. "No reason?" But that was it: she didn't provide one. She was flushed and growing pinker, already dressed in jeans and a thick sweatshirt for our hike. I thought how her healing had always come: two steps forward, one step back.

"Why don't we go?" I said. "I'm feeling spooked. I'm feeling sick, if you want to know the truth."

But she trotted back upstairs.

So, I washed the knives and cutting boards I'd used, tasted my stew, added some pepper flakes, a crumble of thyme. The pot was beginning to bubble. I brought the heat down, still feeling the front door was going to open, madness in the air.

"Dabney had company," Kate called down the stairs. Her own mood was lifting. "Why, I don't know, David. But someone left these footprints and it wasn't someone friendly and somewhere there has to be a report. I've been trying to get the report. Chuck couldn't find one, and I have yet to find it. But I'm still looking. When Jack lets me, that is. Or when he's not looking."

That was supposed to be funny, but I didn't laugh. "Who's Chuck?"

"Chuck *Turkle*, you idiot!" In a while she trotted down again carrying yet another envelope, this one huge. "There was a sweater in the Mustang that was not Dabney's. A *sweater*, David. Bloodied. A sweater that no one ever saw. They put a *sweater* in evidence, and it never came up in court!"

"Kate," I called. "Why don't we drop it for tonight? And please don't call me an idiot, okay? I'm more tender than you seem to think."

"I notice you still never swear." She opened the envelope, pulled out a loud yellow sweater, size small, badly stained at the hem. "Never so much as a fuck or a shit."

"Kate!"

She whispered: "David, do you remember Dad's work boots?"

"Of course, yes. I think about them all the time. In fact, they're in the basement at Westport. Still in their place under the metal workbench."

"Didn't Freddy try to take them from him? Dabney's guy, remember?"

"He took 'em all right. And then he gave 'em back." I had to resist Kate's intensity, her really overwhelming logic, bent as it was. The whole story just confused me, had always confused me, but any show of confusion on my part would just make her more determined. That sweater—it made me want to puke.

She said, "And why would he take them and just give them back? Were they trying to frame him?"

"Kate," I said. The lentil stew had begun to bubble, my focal point, the pure alchemy of the kitchen. Something thumped at the front door, something pushing at the front door. I began to pant, felt my heart pounding. I stirred the pot, turned the burner all the way down, gave a quick taste, quick dose of reality, delicious. I said, "We'd better settle down."

Kate had no interest in the cooking. "No," she said instantly. "I'm absolutely not going to settle down. Answer the fucking question."

Very gently, I said, "I guess there were footprints in the parlor."

"Yes, fucking footprints. And there were more in the woods! Why don't you ever swear? What the fuck is that all about?"

Their phone rang, old-fashioned bells, loud. I leapt like I'd been poked with a branding iron. Kate pointed, oblivious of my emotion—I was to pick up. She never touched a phone anymore; that was just the way it was. Face pounding hot, I gave a big, cheerful hello, half expecting Dad's booming laugh.

Jack saw right through me: "Oh, no, David," he said.

"We're under control," I said.

THE AFTERNOON WAS cool, leaves blowing in a sweet breeze off the Sound, but the sun very bright and hot in our faces, nice, the afternoon slipping slantwise into evening, sunset only a couple of hours off, that first day you know summer is done. Kate led me up the rocky shore path, high tide and lots of slippery sea grass and wrack to traverse, tangled piles of driftwood, parts of fishing boats, lost pilings bristling with unlikely spikes. I collected some of the seaweed and then fat mussels from a rock submerged in a crystal pool, stuffed a plastic bag that happened to blow up against my legs at just the right moment.

"Sam Goody!" Kate said alarmed.

It took a minute for me understand that she was referring to the logo on the bag. Sam Goody, the record shop. It still had a branch in Grand Central Station—Dad had brought home all our Beatles records from there. I said something about all that, then realized what I was saying, where I was going, didn't mention all the Dabney albums. Dad had brought them home, too, starting before the prince of British rock had even purchased the High Side. Kate and I had worn the grooves right off them, playing the hits over and over and over again, every note memorized.

"It's just a bag," I said.

"I don't believe in *signs*," Kate said. After a couple more steps, she continued more thoughtfully: "I was always first to have the music." And then silence. Of course her thoughts had followed the same trajectory as mine.

We clambered along at Kate's ambitious clip, two or three miles toward the big state park, Hammonassett Beach, walking an adjacent stretch of rare undeveloped shoreline, tangled oak and pitch pine forest alternating with low marshes, small openings of sandy beach, no conversation, just Kate's increasingly frenetic energy, the two of us marching faster and faster. After a half hour we came to an inlet, maybe thirty feet across, deep blue water, not a house or other structure in sight, tide still coming in.

We climbed down on the tide-stripped rocks of the breakwater, sat at water's edge, dipped our feet in. The water was ankle-aching cold, terrible, so it took me by surprise when Kate pulled off her sweatshirt, then her peasant shirt and jeans, all she was wearing, and just dove in. She swam a fast, neat crawl to the other side, the current putting a strong curve in her progress, pulled herself up on the great sand delta a hundred yards away, a dangerous nymph, one of those Rhone River undines that pull you under, tangle you in their hair. But didn't she look fine over there! Fit and tawny and if anything too thin. For a drowning man, Jack had it pretty good, I thought. Except for the evidentiary obsession, of course. And of course a caretaker shouldn't stare, a brother even more so. I poked around in the exposed rocks after more to eat, found a crevice full of small but good-looking oysters, collected a couple dozen. My panic, I noted, had passed.

Across the way, Kate was peaceably ambling, flipping up shells with her toes, inspecting finds. She might have been eighteen at that distance. Or even ten: there wasn't a hair on her body, another of her symptoms— obsessive shaving. I studied the current in the inlet, no longer worried I'd have to dive in after her. A striped bass cruised by in the clear water, and me without a rod and reel. Bait mackerel battled the current in large schools, menhaden flashing. A succession of crabs walked by on the rocks, just under water. There was a great, satisfying stench of salt and sea. The tide came full, the current went slack, everything paused, pent, five minutes, ten, started back again the other way, slowly gathering momentum, heartening. I felt a portal had opened, that a wind blew through my brain. I'd been mourning the loss of everything: Floridiana, the Dolphins, years of my life. Barb and Nick, yes, the unsayable names, coming clearly to the foreground.

How strange to find a serene moment in the company of Crazy May.

And of course, senser of fine thoughts, here she came, perfect stroke, everything timed so she emerged like the crabs at my feet, her skin taut with the cold of the water. She lay on the warm rock on her back, hands behind her head, eyes emphatically closed. Any naked body is interesting. Probably twenty years since I'd seen hers, some nude beach somewhere. She wore that key on a chain between her cold-gathered breasts, the one Dad had supposedly given her, a key for a briefcase that had a combination lock. I almost smiled. Certainly that would not be unlike him. Never a word about my having sent the key back to her, mysterious Kate.

Her figure hadn't changed at all. Her shoulders were broad and muscled. Her belly was narrow and flat, her shape narrow, too, narrow through the hips, slightly masculine, her thighs more powerful than you'd notice in a skirt. In every sinew the memory of tennis. I looked away, kept my eyes on the horizon, a shimmering, numinous day.

Her feet began to kick, heels jamming into the rock. She drummed her fingers under her head, making it bop; she wriggled her hips; she drew up her knees, up and down, up and down, a kind of kinetic storm. Suddenly she said, "We have to comb our memories, David. It's just as simple as that. Any little thing could be the answer. We have to *get* these fuckers. And when we do, you'll see."

"I'll see what?"

"You'll just *see*." She drummed and bopped and kicked, repeated the whole imperative word for word, then: "Comb, comb, comb our memories."

Enough. I put a hand on her shoulder, just a little pressure, like keeping a boat from floating away from its mooring as the tide rushed seaward. Very slowly she settled down, very slowly all those hard-won muscles came to rest, very slowly her flesh molded to the warm rock, and finally she lay still in the sun.

"We're all we have," she said.

"There's so much you haven't told me," I said, hungry to communicate, trying to reverse the polarity of my confession at McLean.

She thought about that a while, took a breath like sighing, said, "But there's nothing you can do about my secrets, fucker. It's yours you have to worry about."

Soon she slept.

After an hour, the sun losing its force, my belly rumbling, sack of mussels and oysters and seaweed waiting, I shook her a little, then shook her harder. She sat up fast, an almost panicked look around. "Dad?" she said.

I wasn't taking that on.

We watched the ocean. We watched the sky. As if languorously, she slipped back into her three garments. We breathed the air. She touched my arm.

"Don't open a restaurant," she said.

PART THREE

Children of War

12

Nicholas Bernhardt Hochmeyer. "The only," he used to say, instead of "Junior." He'd abandoned that suffix in high school after his own father's suicide by drowning, history that seemed to hang in the shadows around him. I'm considerably older now than he ever got to be, and want to believe that his anger has worn out, that it can't live on without him.

I look for the good in the man. He never bullied me, for example. He could spend all day playing catch, nailed a plywood target to the back of the garage for me to hit with a football when I wasn't more than six, did a play-by-play as I threw, gave me prizes for ten bull's-eyes in a row, later a hundred. He put on his Chippewa work boots and flannel shirt and built me a fort with free materials from the dump and from a collapsed barn up the road (no permission, not him)—big glass panels, corrugated steel roofing, old studs and siding, fancy doors—and then he sat in there with me playing cards at a tiny table till fall came and it just got too cold. He taught me to play poker so I wouldn't get taken advantage of like he did when *he* was in the service. World War II and he was a grunt walking drunk through France after the liberation, never near a single bullet, got there after the real work was done, kisses for candy bars. He advised me not to register for the draft, to just sidestep the whole Vietnam thing, and that's what I did, with no thought that it might be terrible advice but in the end no repercussions. He was right when he was wrong, and wrong when he was right; he couldn't win and he couldn't lose. He smelled good night and day. He didn't drive well, very poorly, in fact, but he knew it and never broke a rule of the road. Handsome forever, with that strong chin and forged face, the charming light in his eye, at least when he wasn't miserable.

My mother kept her distance, surrounded herself with a sense of mystery, anyway she wasn't a big one for hugs or self-revelation, not with her kids, not with anybody. Barbara Makepeace Barton, of Grand Rapids, Michigan, where Dad had gone to attend a friend's wedding. She had a reckless side, loved a martini, loved two martinis, liked a naked swim. She would have found Nick pleasingly cocky, insecurity recognizing its own—beauty, too. Anyway, they were married not long after they met and Katy was born not long after they were married and Mom was glad she'd moved east—exurban Connecticut never stopped seeming upscale to her. She had cultural pretensions, too, took Katy and me to pops concerts, all the museums in New York, to Sturbridge Village, flower shows, Shakespeare festivals, lectures at the library, but never really followed up in any way: these things were good for you, like oats. You ate them and you were done.

Dad hated all that stuff (including oats), hated being anywhere the public gathered. But he shared Mom's vision of the good life. He brought her champagne, extravagant bouquets, headshots of tennis stars with autographs possibly real. He bought steaks the size of tires, used four bags of charcoal to grill them. Hula hoops, color TV, convertible VW Bug, we were the first to have them all, though the VW didn't last, disappeared in some kind of squabble with the bank. He taught us to swim in Long Island Sound at a secluded beach with imported white sand and elegant rafts, part of an estate he claimed was a friend's, ours alone till a certain year (I'd been maybe ten), when a gardener and the Westport Police escorted us back to our car, which he'd parked brazenly in the stone mansion's massive portico.

Like my Mom's father, I was close to a foot taller than Dad, taller from the age of twelve, a state of affairs he didn't comment on, though you knew he hated looking up at a seventh grader as much as he hated looking up at his father-in-law, always finding ways to make himself taller: big boots, high hair, a barstool at the head of the kitchen table, a perch on the curb in a crowd or on the next step up no matter where.

Mom was more comfortable socially, loved parties, increasingly went alone, a source of friction between her and Dad. She was crafty, careful, held love and even the smallest secrets close to her chest, big ones, too (none of us ever did learn where she bought those black-dark chocolate chips, or why she refused to speak to her sister Ellen, or who the man was who telephoned one Sunday night). Dad was more open than Mom, even inappropriate (we knew about every gal he found desirable and why, knew he couldn't stand his brothers, ditto). He was much warmer than Mom, too, despite some tricky corners. Mom never tired of reminding us of his childhood nickname: Sneaky.

Her nickname if she'd had one would have been Ambitious. Yale, Princeton, that was Mom's vision, and she told Kate and me from kindergarten where we'd be going to college. She loved sports, had excelled herself, and that was going to be our way in, just as it had been her way into the Westport Country Club, a place we never could have afforded nor would have been accepted otherwise. She was the ringer in the tennis tournaments, trophy after trophy in the club lounge, and the ladies were very fond of her.

My parents' mothers had both died young, and I never met either grandmother. Even photos or stories were rare: we Hochmeyers avoided painful subjects. Her dad—a guy I saw once or twice a year—was like her: competent, loyal, murder on the tennis court, maybe a little disappointed in life. His expectations must have been hard for Mom to live up to. And my father did not meet expectations. Dad's own father was mean and unsuccessful and a suicide as I have said, drowned himself with the aid of a cinder block and chain when my father was fourteen, something Dad mentioned to me just once in a black mood and that otherwise we just simply never talked about, something he'd had to overcome, and silently. You have to wonder how that death shaped him, and how in turn it shaped us all, genetics aside.

SO MUCH KATE hadn't told me: suicide attempts, for example, four. First at Yale, nothing I ever heard about. The damage, whatever it had been, was why she'd quit tennis for a few years. Then, after her return to the game, there was that time she was pulled off a plane at Heathrow in handcuffs for trying to open the cabin door and leap. The phrase *critical depressurization* is in the official report, which I've only recently seen. Next was the drive into Long Island Sound and subsequent swim, which I'd only found out about via that anonymous news clipping, and never took up with her, and not with Jack. And then she'd dived off their sailboat, *Deep Song*, Jack running full with the wind. It had taken him almost twenty minutes to get back around and fish her out of the frigid water, her metabolism as crazy as she was, full breaststroke the whole time, not so much as a case of exposure. Their "honeymoon" was actually a kind of homemade rehab, thus Jack's bizarre reaction when I tried to pay for the trip. Much later, recently in fact, here in a new century, I asked him why they hadn't told me. "For your own protection," Jack said, though of course they'd been protecting themselves.

Or was that me, keeping my distance, protecting myself?

Because there was so much I hadn't told Kate: that Mom and I had gone to the dancer's for tea, for example. That Sylphide had kissed me in her Bentley. That I'd seen the world's greatest ballerina not only naked, but having sex. Through Dabney's binoculars. That Sylphide had subsequently been my boss, kissed me as I sat on her desk in a secret dressing room off her boudoir. That I dearly thought we were developing a relationship. That in fact we were, no less perverse than Kate's with Dabney.

I combed my memory, all right, saw myself emerging from Sylphide's secret dressing room after my first assignment, the High Side empty, everyone off on some adventure that didn't include me.

Home that night, my parents safely asleep in their bedroom, I found Sylphide's soft bra-thing in my pocket, held it to my lips, lay on my bed sniffing jasmine and parsing every word she'd said to me. Had I really been her first kiss? Could it be true that Dabney hadn't ever really slept with her? Georges was definitely a troll, but that gave me no comfort: he was Sylphide's troll. Maybe I was going to be her giant, complete the fairy story. The bra-thing was so, so soft. The jasmine arousing. Memory of kisses, first this one, then that. Memory of her hardened body as she pulled off her sweats, her tights, my slight repulsion at all the muscles, the call of the little underpants. The thought came to me that with Kate at college and Emily off in Korea I was free to go back for more, calculated I could skip a little school in the coming days and weeks, maybe a lot of school. The dancer needed me. She needed me in the way Dabney had needed my sister, a need my sister had hidden from me. In fact, my sister had hidden herself from me altogether.

Our secrets gave us power.

And then they took our power away.

From whom had we learned that?

THE HIGH SIDE was quiet when I got there the next morning, quiet
except for Desmond, who acted as if he didn't understand when I asked
where everyone had been the night before. He'd gotten instructions to
set me up in a little office back behind the parlor, another big phone, gorgeous polished desk, an amended list of theaters neatly typed, longhand
note from Conrad. I was to make APPOINTMENTS, not leave MESSAGES:
"Don't take no. You are DABNEY. You are SYLPHIDE."

Desmond handed me another note, one of Sylphide's signature envelopes, neatly addressed to Emily Bright. He said, "If you could deliver this
at school. Madame has had an impressive report on your girlfriend from
Brandi DeAngelis at the conservatory."

Whoa.

Desmond stood too long behind my chair in case I might need something, came back too many times with tea and cakes and a pillow for
my back. I closed the door finally, shut him out, put the envelope in my
jacket pocket—Emily would have to acknowledge me now whether she
liked it or not—put myself to work, dialed the phone. Soon I was talking
to theater owners, office hours in the executive suites, all these important people excited by the prospect of *Children of War*. A subtle feeling
of power washed over me. I was Sylphide's executive assistant, and Kate
didn't know. I was Dabney, just as Conrad had said. I stopped making
calls, didn't have to: the phone rang every time I hung it up. My list of
appointments grew longer. I stopped periodically to recopy it, sixteen
theaters at our disposal, all previous engagements to be cancelled: the
dancer's name was gold.

About noon there was a knock at the office door. Not Desmond, but
the woman herself. I felt suddenly shy. But she didn't want to talk, not a
word about any speckled stone, nothing about her missing garment. She
perched on the arm of my plush chair, which was of course hers, looked
at my list.

"You are being my eyes and ears," she said finally.

"Thanks," I said.

"I mean when you and Conrad are visiting theaters. I am not trusting his taste."

She left abruptly. I took more calls. Desmond brought lunch, rubbed my shoulders a little, snippy to be spurned. "Don't bug me," I told him, playing Mr. Powerful. The phone rang, rang some more.

Sylphide was back, sweaty from the morning class, morning for her, anyway, bare feet and sweatpants. "I'm afraid I'm telling you too much yesterday afternoon," she said, sitting on the desk so I couldn't avoid her eye.

"No, no," I said.

"Life is dancing, all the time. Dancing only. That is all I was trying to express to you. Dancing is the highest physical expression. And in that way of talking, Vlad Markusak is my only lover. Sex was never anything like so wonderful as that. Though maybe it gets better?"

"You're going to say too much again."

She never found me funny. We both looked out the window—chicka-dees, tufted titmice—there must have been a feeder just out of view. She put a hand atop my head. That famous photo, she and Vlad caught at a restaurant by a photographer for *Paris Match,* a very deep-looking kiss. I mentioned it.

"Public relations," she said. "Vlad is queer one hundred fifteen percent."

The phone rang. I answered businesslike, handled the inquiry. Absently, inches from my face, Sylphide clipped one of her nipples between two fingers, scissored it through the scant cloth of her workout top, a kind of cotton leotard, which was under a little bit of a sweater. When my call was done I forced my gaze to the dancer's pocked face. Her profile was so sculpted, so intelligent, like a shell alone on a vast beach. Chin too pointed, cheeks too high, brow too flat, altogether however a woman of surpassing beauty, as the critics liked to say. Finally her distracted eyes found mine again, that rare green so close I could see the dark-brown line drawn around the rim of each large iris.

"What did you mean by the binoculars?" I asked boldly.

"They are very fine, *ja?* Dabney always said so." She smiled slowly, seemed suddenly to notice what her fingers had been doing, quit with the nipple, pulled the little sweater thing tighter around her shoulders.

She looked at me such a long time, like maybe a real answer was forming, something direct about the magic she'd used to get me into that tree fort.

I must have looked away, looked at the phone.

"You want to make calls," she said.

"Conrad wants me to. Or asked me to. Told me to."

"And do you work for Conrad?"

"No, I work for you. A theater for you."

"I am working on a dance," she said. "But Vlad is in Houston. Always in demand, our Mr. Markusak. I'm needing a stand-in. Someone tall." She slid off the arm of my chair, floated to the open door, disappeared. I understood that I was to follow, trailed her through the parlor with its missing Bonnard and Picassos and into the foyer and up the grand stone stairs to her suite, glimpse of the famous bed, then leftwards through another little parlor and then a tiny kitchen, through a tiny maidservant's room with single bed tightly made, finally through a long room with a lap pool, a luxury I'd never heard of, a single long lane in crystal blue, then out the far door into a large dance studio with its own piano and mirrors and barres and perfect shiny wood floor, pretty view out across the side yard I'd just been looking at, the endless High Side grounds.

She tried a few stretches at the barre, her joints popping shockingly, warmed to it. Humming absently, she pulled off her sweatpants, threw off the little sweater, made an elaborate yoga routine in her leotard alone, muscle group by muscle group, the rather worn cotton pulling this way and that and gaping to give glimpses of the most intimate skin if you looked: chest, armpit, crease of the thigh. She was all muscle. I joined her almost unconsciously at first, a half effort, then more so, leaning and bending, reaching and twisting beside her, two athletes, at least that much in common. I sweated in my nice blue school shirt: Dress for success, as Dad always said. And, Quit staring: Mom.

"Dabney helped so many people," she said. Another full minute of stretching, and: "The Children of War Foundation, that was being an expression of his deepest, most injured self." More stretching, deeper stretching, both of us grunting with it. "He was being a child himself, never growing up. He was being a child of World War Two, a child of his parents' domestical war, too. You remember the cover of the *Children of*

War album? The plants blooming in the ruins, *ja?* Overcoming disaster with love. That is how he is talking. That is how he is thinking. That is how I am loving him best." Onto our bellies. Grab the ankles, arch.

She said, "I am seeing a long pas de deux for Vlad and me. Last night I dream it from beginning to end. This morning I sketch it. You will help me block it out, *ja?*"

We sat up. She pointed to my feet. "Like Vlad," she said.

Vlad danced barefoot.

I kicked off my sneakers, yanked off my socks, stood where she pointed, ready to be a dancer. She stood wearily, took a place in front of me, inspected me closely.

"Fifth position, please."

"I don't even know one through four."

She took this as a joke, didn't like it, kicked at my instep, surprising force, knocked my feet into something like the form she was looking for. "Bend at your knees just a little, won't you, lazy?"

I bent my legs like squatting, my feet impossibly tangled.

The dancer pushed behind my knees, pressed the small of my back, tangled me further. "*Ja-ja.* Exactly," she said. "Very nice. Flatfooted is fine. Vlad is, um, *status,* and I am being the implacable force. You know *status?*"

"Static?"

"Or anyway, quiet and still." She gazed at me critically, suddenly pulled my shirttails out of my blue jeans. Not enough. "Vlad will want his shirt off, I imagine." She tugged my shirt up.

I smelled the jasmine, first time that day. Her sweat, and something piquant from the deeps.

"Don't move your feet!" she barked.

I laughed, held my awkward crouch, let her pull my shirt over my head. She took it from my hands, folded it nicely, placed it with her sweats. "And your trousers. Take 'em off? Vlad is being in tights, of course."

"Nah," I said.

But Sylphide plucked at the button of my Levi's, and I went along with her vision, fell out of whatever position I was in, dropped my jeans (playing Vlad, who wouldn't hesitate for a second), kicked them aside, stood in my BVDs—new BVDs, happily, bought by my hallowed mom not a week before, plain white. The dancer bent to retrieve the blue jeans, folded them as she had folded the shirt, retrieved my sneakers, balled my socks, collected her own sweats and tiny sweater, folded them, too, stacked all our items together, lined my huge shoes up alongside the pile, flexed and muscle-walked her way to a large drafting table, long legs on such a little person, her belly sculpted, that day's breasts too matter-of-fact to be as compelling as those of the previous day, her own fingerprints in powder on her calves, the whole effect not especially feminine, suddenly, nothing sexy about her in fact, nothing nymphlike either, half her game *illusion,* I realized yet again. She leaned over some notebooks on the table, leafed through the pages of a huge drawing pad, pencil scrawls, great sweeping marks, little symbols. When she regarded me again it was a pillar she was seeing, something solid, a fluted column, or anyway it wasn't me. Slowly (all those muscles dedicated to grace!), she floated my direction poised on the balls of her feet, then on her bare toes, making her legs longer yet. "*Ease,*" she said. "Make it look *easeful.*" All but naked, she looked like a shot-putter—how had I ever found her sexy? She kicked at my feet again. "Perfect," she said, looking up at me. "I discover I am wishing Vlad was so big. You are something to *climb.* He will just have to dance tall."

I smiled easefully, great effort.

"Do not grin," she said. "You are not being Yorick's skull, you are being a pillar in a garden and the day is fair, *ja?* You are a boulder in the forest. You are being solid, whatever you are, and you are being what you are. A menhir, *ja?* You know that word? Some stone thing left after civilization is dying. You have great mass. Your weight presses into the ground, you are rooted in bedrock. Sturdy, you are, everything solid."

Somehow that helped. I felt my feet sinking into earth, felt the rock under there, felt the air on my legs. Sylphide danced toward me, is the only way to put it, something different in her stride that made what had been walking into dancing, *increased* toward me, to get it just right, a growing, skirling thing, some sort of vine, one of the plants that bloomed after war. She patted at her belly, which was a plate. "Put your hand right here when I am ascending." She sank to the wooden floor behind me, only very slowly let the floorboards produce her. She grew from my feet, one tendril climbing the back of my one naked leg, another tendril climbing the front more stiffly, then more tendrils, quite a few more, certainly more than a person should have hands to imitate, tendrils climbing in and around my thighs and up my back, climbing between my legs and up my front, and, after the tendrils had passed, her trunk rose, the vine itself, a kind of tropism, gravity-defying, impossible to see how she managed it all from my vantage point as pillar or menhir. When she was at full height, tendrils snaking around my neck and my face and up into my hair, climbing above my Doric capital—Doric was the simplest one, as I recalled—up there at the height of the eminence I had become and catching breezes, she began to hum some ancient song. Then she rose some more, left the floor, turned to face the same way I was facing while yet clinging to me, physically impossible. But no. Numbers, she was saying numbers, counting. I put my hand on her belly as she had instructed, kept my feet flat and properly aligned, my crouch as correct as I could manage, three-four.

"Perfect," she said, rare praise, "not bad timing," and then made a preternatural forward lean, still humming, tendrils seeking, a couple of grunts, her feet on mine, or on my shins at times, even on my knees, a pulsing up and down, a slow rising from the roots, then falling, a drooping, too little rain perhaps, then new weather and a rising, tendrils encircling me impossibly.

Okay, forget vine and pillar, implacable force and the sweep of time, forget tangled flat-foot stance, or fifth position, or whatever it was: the woman's muscular and extremely solid butt was sliding in worn cotton from my mid thigh to my lower belly, sliding back again, the smoothest movement imaginable pressed implacably against me, hands reaching behind me, one leg wrapping my thigh. I was not Italian marble; I wasn't some boulder in a field; though I didn't move I *was* moved, and suddenly: the muscles of my *corporus cavernosa* relaxed, allowing blood to flow into the spongy spaces therein, with the entirely involuntary result that my penis stirred, began to rise. Meanwhile, my testicles climbed their own vines. The implacable little fanny seemed to know it, too, pressed harder into me, found a snaking path, a tendril at my backside pulling me closer. I lightened my touch on her belly, tried to give her butt some slack, tried mortified to *think* my way out of arousal: garbage truck, hot-day road

crew spreading tar, math formulas, insects, marble, granite, feldspar, all
to no avail.

She stopped the dance abruptly. Stepped away from me. "Well," she
said.

The heat moved up my rigid chest to my face, not stone. I just stood as
Vlad, wavering on my big, burning feet, gave a tiny shrug.

Not chilly, not warm, but looking directly at the insistent form in my
briefs, the dancer said, "Unintended effects."

She spun around behind me, rose on her toes so her voice was in my
neck: "You'd best move past this phase so we can work. Just move past
desire. Acknowledge it, move past it. Here." She drew her hands down
the jumping muscles of my torso, tugged on the waistband of my shorts,
pulled them down incrementally. I stayed a pillar. "Like this," she said.
And her hand found one of my own hands, placed it on my first-class
erection, then found the other, this expert arranging hands as she'd arranged feet. "Go on," she murmured. She guided my movement, abruptly
abandoned me to myself. "Don't stop," said the voice in my ear, more
breathless. Her hands found their way up my chest. And because she
was behind me and because her voice was in my neck and because in a
way it had happened before many times (that album cover), I could manage it, my underpants around my bent knees, my pose unchanged. A
tendril grew through my legs from behind, the timing I must say pretty
altogether thoroughly exquisite. I shuddered out of position, lost my
mooring on the bedrock, stumbled hard, spurting. My dancer held me a
second then spun and ran and used the whole floor in an exaggerated and
rather comical series of leaps, amazing air (I'd never seen anything like
it up close), grabbed one of the dozen nice towels hanging on the barre,
spun back, wiped the floor with a flourish, wiped me roughly, and finally
pulled my shorts up for me, snapped the band at my waist.

"Desire," she said, as in *no big deal.*

I reached for her.

She let me hold her very briefly, her lips near mine as I bent to her, but
then she slithered out of my hands.

"I got what I am needing," she said, perfectly professional. She meant
for the dance.

I watched her grab her things and breeze out of the room, stood there a minute half mortified, half exultant, also half naked. I dressed shaking my head and shivering, laughing out loud, then groaning in embarrassment. Some pillar I'd turned out to be. I had to get back to the office downstairs. Conrad was going to kill me. Desmond would know where I'd been.

I skipped past the lap pool and through her private salon and out her private door and down the grand stone stairs of the very public foyer and to the office behind the no-Bonnard parlor and back to the ringing, ringing phone, big and fulsome and desirable and calm, a kid who'd found the very center of the cosmos.

At the end of the day, Sylphide nowhere to be found, I rowed happily across the pond, trotted up the lawn and to the kitchen doors, found Dad and Mom sitting down to dinner, felt I loved them more than humanly possible, loved the food she was serving, loved the air in our house, loved even the tension, Dad all distracted, painful private thoughts, loved the thoughts, too, whatever they might be, loved the pain: it was his pain, and the pain was him, and might have something to do with Kate. I loved Kate, loved Kate abjectly, loved even her absence, loved having a new secret from her, a secret from them all.

Momentarily the black cars would pull into our cul de sac, momentarily the FBI guys would pull their guns, momentarily they'd take the old man away.

13

The morning after the arrest, Mom insisted I go to school: we weren't going to let things fall apart. I didn't protest. I'd already skipped enough that week, didn't want to break any more rules, never again. Mr. Davis on the bus asked where Dad was. "Arrested," I said, and the sweet old fellow laughed: pretty good joke.

School was surreal, the hallways dressed in black streamers and pumpkin cutouts, paper skeletons and ghosts. Mom had played it tough that morning, chain-smoked cigarettes though she'd long since quit, ate nothing. Her day in Danbury would consist of looking for legal representation for Dad and then for us—I noticed that distinction, the implication that we had legal interests separate from his. When the Bridgeport paper thumped on our doorstep she rushed out to get it, but there was nothing in there about Nicholas Hochmeyer: good news of its own kind, even if it was going to be temporary.

When she was done searching the columns she offered me orange juice, asked how late I'd stay over at the High Side that night, all very businesslike, at least until she broke: "Good thing you've got work, darling, whatever it is. Because your *fucking* father didn't leave a *fucking* cent in this *fucking* house, not a *fucking* cent in the *fucking* bank. There's only the money in my *fucking* purse. Like eight *fucking* dollars." Her eyes filled, but she didn't cry.

No one had called Kate, I kept realizing. But Kate couldn't stay shielded for long. I climbed to my room, found my bag of quarters, brought them down to Mom. Businesslike again, she counted me back one dollar: lunch money. I was frightened but oddly giddy, worried about Dad but unaccountably ebullient, terrified for Bar-Bar, way afraid of what Kate would say—I knew I'd have to be the one to break the news—but weirdly thrilled by all of it, our disaster like some elixir I'd drunk.

Emily was missing from the morning crush, nowhere to be found. I scrawled an inane quick note on the back of Sylphide's invitation, wanting to be sure Emily knew who the messenger was, slipped it through the vent in her locker. She wasn't in math class. She didn't seem to be in French, either, big Lizard peering through the narrow window of her classroom door. At the buses Dwight said he'd seen her, all right: her parents had picked her up after lunch in the ambassador's limo. "They're on their way to Korea, Liz, just like every fall. It's like Ancestor's Day or whatever it's called. They burn money so the dead folks can go out and get a decent meal."

"She's already gone?"

"She's gone, Liz."

Not so much as a farewell to the likes of me. As I slogged aboard the bus to go home, Mr. Davis said, "I thought you was kidding," and slipped me a rolled *New York Post,* afternoon edition, a slow Thursday in Newspaperland, no doubt. Anyway, the cover story was the scandal at Dolus Investments, big studio photos of two executives who'd been found dead in a Times Square hotel, apparent suicides. Another had been found shot in his driveway, familiar name, a guy from accounting my father had always hated, a do-gooder. On the inner pages were a dozen faces in two rows of studio headshots: the bad guys. And hapless Dad was among them.

OFF THE BUS, I rushed home, desperate to get back to Sylphide's, loud drums over there, like something carried on African wind. I hurried to eat something, found a terse note from Mom:

> Precious. Talked Daddy noontime. Heading for Danbury. Arraignment tomorrow a.m. Will spend the night. You are in charge of yourself. Mrs. Paumgartner next door in case. Please call Kate. You don't have to tell her every little thing. Food in fridge, xo.

I scrawled *High Side* on the back of an envelope, also *Tried Katy,* though this was not true. Mr. Kerklin had recently taught us the second law of thermodynamics, and here was proof: things actually *do* fall apart.

AT SYLPHIDE'S THE cars were back, Cadillacs and Mercedes Benzes and Porsches and Jags. Also a Ferrari 512-S, one of only three hundred ever made, I knew, worth more than my family's house by several times. "We're surprised to see *you*," Desmond shouted, opening the great doors, loud drums back in the ballroom. And behind him in the foyer, a return to bedlam: carpenters and soundmen, dancers and costumers, a half-dozen young women getting dressed, two of them stark naked right there in the wind of the doorway. Perfect gentleman, I didn't stare.

"Who's we?" I shouted back, sounding like my father.

"We here at the High Side," Desmond said.

"Show must go on," I said.

"She says you're needed at home. She offers her support and her sorrow and releases you."

I said, "There's no one at home."

"I'm to turn you away. Apologies." He handed me one of the familiar envelopes, gold piping, something in there. I stuffed it in my back pocket. The next arrivals were at the door, a pair of ladies in perfume and fancy suits, another group of people behind them. Desmond, grandly formal, offered the dancer's warm greetings. Lizard, for the moment forgotten, took the opportunity to slip inside.

In the ballroom, the gut-punching boom of tom-toms came amplified out of stacked speaker towers stenciled STUDIO INSTRUMENT RENTALS. Why on earth did the drums need mikes? All but hidden inside a double battlement of tom-toms and snares and bass drums and stainless-steel stands and large brass cymbals was a big man playing them hard, sticks flying, long hair straggling down in reddish curls, an engine of sweat. I edged right up to the platform and it was like the drums were inside me, loudest thing I'd ever felt. "Ginger Baker!" someone shouted. I recognized him then, the drummer from Cream, whoa. His hands were a blur. He'd been friends with Dabney, everyone knew; Eric Clapton and Jack Bruce and Ginger, they'd all been friends with Dabney.

Georges emerged from one of the many doors at the back of the room, clambered up onto the makeshift stage, a guy with talents and fame I couldn't touch, a certain noble carriage, like some minor baron from days gone by. He made his way back to a Hammond B-3 set up high on a double platform, gradually took his place—drums throbbing, cymbals crashing—pulled stops, touched a key or two, struck a tentative chord. When at last I turned I saw that the ballroom had filled with people: designers and seamstresses and techies and maids and photographers, all sorts of assistants and dancers, even a nervous knot of High Side gardeners. Roadies were loading in even more speaker cabinets through big doors swung open like the place was an airplane hangar, the side yard out there. A stiff photographer was setting up reflectors, his assistant looking stressed under the ungainly equipment. The girls who'd been naked in the foyer came in dressed, did stretches. And then more dancers, men and women, many of them older than Sylphide, it occurred to me. And there was Conrad Pant, wearing an ascot now, and always the beret, chatting up the tweed ladies I'd seen arriving, the three of them pinching champagne flutes.

More people arrived, then more again, serious faces, a lot of nice clothes, a lot of intense discussions, everyone carrying briefcases, duffel bags, someone dragging in a very tall stepladder from god knew where. A lady with gels for the lights climbed up there, turned everything pink, then amber. The roadies pulled cables, set mikes, taped off a makeshift stage on the floor between the batteries of speakers, all carefully measured by a guy in green overalls who shooed me back out of the way. I found a chair, turned it backwards the way the dancers did, sat with my chin on my hands the way they did. Mr. Baker played all the while, ungodly noise, everyone's feet tapping, heads bopping: you couldn't help yourself. More dancers trotted in, all shirtless in tights, men, women, all half naked, so what? To me, a pillar, desire was but a trifle. They made their way back past four guys in suits poring over forms, guys with guitars, ladies with violins, two men rolling their bass fiddles in front of them, a whole chamber orchestra, it looked like: clarinets, oboes, a harp.

The lights went down, came back up unevenly, went down again, a test. The room hushed anyway. I felt contemptuous—what did all these people think we were waiting for, the Second Coming? Ginger Baker stopped his banging abruptly, middle of a phrase. He blinked and looked out at the room. He noticed Georges, then, and the two laughed to see one another, shouted one another's names. Georges hopped down from his organ; awkwardly the two men hugged over floor toms and clashing cymbals. More people hurried in. Guy with a notebook. Lady with a basket. More dancers, a crowd of them, youngish girls in pink. Someone closed the great doors. Something *was* going to happen. Why had no one told me? Freddy the goon emerged from the back. He and a bigger man—the other goon!—gently cleared everyone off the marked stage. I moved again, found a corner where I wouldn't be blocking anyone's view, stood there grumpily. My father was a fucking asshole, you really had to agree with Mom.

The lights came down to dark.

SUDDENLY MOVEMENT, AND then Sylphide, no more vine but some kind of nymph or nixie, racing around from behind the drums, leaping into the clearing, a sudden enchanted forest, gauzy mist of veils and skirts, flat shoes, comedic sweep around the stage, an imp peering out at all of us. Like everyone else in the room, I felt there was a special glance for me. And like everyone else, I felt my troubles fly, felt the dancer's joy as my own, felt great love.

From somewhere among the speaker cabinets Vlad Markusak suddenly appeared, bare-chested, barefoot, racing. Sylphide reached one corner of the stage precisely as Vlad reached the opposite, both of them stopping in expectation as if by coincidence, and exactly then a spotlight opened on Ginger Baker, who tucked into an incantatory roll on those toms, soon graced by a high wail from Georges's loud Hammond, spotlight a little off the mark, his head flung back, arms stretched to reach double keyboards.

The shirtless chorus raced onstage in a black-legged flurry and surrounded Vlad, captured him, carried him toward Sylphide. He seemed simply to float on all that bare skin, writhed in all those bare arms, mayhem. The drums tumbled, the cymbals rang, rimshots like guns going off, bass kicks, subtle roll of tom-toms, irresistible beat, complex rhythms the dancers caught perfectly, darkly, carrying Vlad, the Hammond growing darker, too. Suddenly, they fell backward—dropping Vlad slam on his belly as Sylphide fell, too—fell backward and landed dramatically on their naked shoulder blades, the music rumbling to quiet. Slowly then, Vlad and Sylphide floated to their feet, danced in tandem in and among the other dancers, leaps and lifts and arabesques. Before long the drums picked up again, the organ, too, soaring notes, the shirtless chorus rolling and rising, sweeping over the stage. At the pinnacle of all the noise and action Sylphide was lofted—unclear how—and stood miraculously on dozens of fingertips, looked bemused, bedazzled. The dancers shifted under her somehow, and she was gone, just disappeared. Vlad gave a huge, hearty laugh, and as the drums battled on (Mr. Baker leaning into his work), all the other motion came to pieces, individual dancers suddenly visible again, just graceful people making their own movements, people with their own lives separate from the choreography, people with parents, people with lovers, people with problems, movements more and more provisional, the greater piece unfinished.

No one clapped. No one moved. The silence was weird, just the sound of Vlad shuffling off the stage. Conrad Pant turned to the champagne ladies. Georges stood and stretched. "Mate," he said to Ginger Baker, who shrugged happily. The gardeners turned and left looking skeptical. The maids followed them out. A few of the chorus dancers reappeared. Vlad's deep voice, advice.

Sylphide reappeared, entirely herself, frankly sweating in her leotard, little towel to wipe at her face, accepted kisses on both cheeks from the champagne ladies. She beamed, she glowed, she laughed out loud at whatever they were saying, more than mere compliments, it looked like. Georges and Mr. Baker struggled down off their platforms, joined the little group, Georges immediately engaging them, something serious about the music. Vlad sauntered over to them, dry as a shed snakeskin. Sylphide put her hand on Georges's shoulder, adjusted the toe of a shoe. His hand went absently to her bottom, squeeze-squeeze, even as he made some crucial point with the other.

The rest is blurred in memory—I still feel like it came from me, as if the anger and panic and loneliness of my day suddenly materialized in the form of a stocky fellow in a black suit. He blew in through the big doors from the side yard, a shadow, really, hurrying toward Sylphide and Vlad and Conrad Pant and the foundation ladies as they made their way in a huddle toward the nice breeze streaming in.

The guy didn't hesitate, pushed into the group, grabbed Sylphide by the arm, jerked it up behind her and cranked. She let out a cry. "Message from a friend," he said distinctly. He pushed her to the ground, still holding her, put a foot on her back, twisted that arm hard, dragged her several feet pulling on it. Everyone around froze in horror, even backed away. Not me, not this time: I knocked several chairs over, five big steps and I was there, pushed him, caught his little hand, crushed his knuckles with a sound I could feel, jerked his arm up as he had jerked Sylphide's, broke bones in there, too. I would have finished subduing him very easily if he hadn't sprayed me with something, sprayed me straight in the face. I bellowed, went blind, and vomited.

I WOKE PANICKED and all alone in the attic at home, five in the morning. I'd barricaded myself up there, giddiness having given way to fear. My eyes still itched powerfully. Downstairs, I made an elaborate breakfast, couldn't eat it. I put on the TV, looking for news, found nothing but test patterns and *The Modern Farmer*, left it on for company. Mom hadn't come home and hadn't called; my note was untouched. I bounded up to their room and stared at their empty bed, all I had of them. I tight-tucked the sheets and plumped the pillows and pulled the quilt up nicely, folded it back the way Mom liked. Dad had left dirty socks on the floor, Mom her nightgown on the old rocking chair. I collected it all for the laundry. I was hungry for order. In the pink dawn I went into a full-scale cleaning fit (a kid in shock, I realize now), raced through the house picking up, straightening, washing dishes, vacuuming, dusting, trying to put things right.

They'd taken Sylphide off in an ambulance. Conrad had called the police, broken Freddy's golden rule and in the process proved it: the police really weren't up to the job. Sylphide's assailant had gotten away clean. Conrad berated Freddy: *How the fuck?* But Freddy had been sprayed, too. The police came just after the ambulance—several cars of unimpressive men. "Jealous boyfriend?" one of the sergeants asked. The other asked all friendly if there was any marijuana in the house, if they could have permission to search.

"You're on the wrong track, fellas," Freddy told them, pawing at his eyes still.

I held a wet towel over mine, courtesy of Desmond. The foundation ladies, the real power in the room, tried to give their stories, but the cops weren't particularly interested. They'd seen worse, was the implication— these weren't life-threatening injuries. No sympathy at all, mostly just suspicion, like they'd come upon a hotbed of foreign intrigue. They didn't lock down the house, didn't look around outside, nothing. Sylphide cried inconsolably but silently, eerily. It wasn't her shoulder she wept for, either, but her very life as a dancer, we all knew that. The medics lay her down, checked her pupils, her pulse, strapped her arm. Georges was at her side, held her good hand, patted it. And he and Conrad followed the ambulance to the hospital.

I hung around, thought I should provide some assistance somehow to someone, even though my eyes were still pouring tears from the mace, or whatever it was. But Desmond just told me to go. At the pond I discovered the rowboat missing, had to cross the brook on foot through cattails. On our side, muddy to my knees, I found the boat pulled up high on the grass. The guy who'd attacked Sylphide must have used it, then run up our lawn. Which meant that whoever it was knew the boat would be there. I sprinted to the house. Our big rotary lawnmower had been thrown through the patio sliders, rested upside down on the kitchen floor in a pile of shattered safety glass, gasoline dripping. I didn't have a single thought of danger but raced into the mess, my one thought to get the guy. I wouldn't let go this time—he could pluck my eyes out with his fingers. But the front door stood open, cool air pouring in. I trotted out to our cul-de-sac, then out to the main road, nothing. Tire tracks on the edge of our lawn, inconclusive: lots of people parked right there, our neighbor's guests and maintenance men, teenagers. Back inside, I turned the lights on to discover that the locked cover on Dad's old rolltop desk had been pried open, and the deep, deep drawers pried open, too, all of them pulled out and dumped in drifts of paper: old bills, cancelled checks, useless brochures, legal-size documents, dunning notices from every imaginable creditor (including Yale), drawings I'd made when I was five, notes Kate had written, clipped articles, file folders by the score, all methodically emptied out onto the couch and the carpet. No way to know if anything was missing, or what it might be.

I knew better than to call the police. Instead, I cleaned up, threw the damaged lawn mower back out into the lawn, swept up beads of glass, wiped up the gasoline. Fine with me if the guy returned: if the guy returned, I would kill him with my hands.

But later, after a half hour sweating it out in bed, I'd dressed again and climbed up to the attic, closed the hatch door, lined up the family bowling balls as weapons, slept fitfully with my baseball bat in hand.

At dawn, obsessively putting the kitchen right, I heard the *Bridgeport News* hit the front stoop. I dropped the piece of plywood I'd been inexpertly fitting to the smashed patio door, raced to get the paper. Because of the local angle, they had an involved story about Dolus Investments—four columns of the front page—mostly about the accountant gunned down in his Fairfield yard. But Nicholas Hochmeyer had his place in the paper, too, a three-column photo of him climbing out of the FBI car in Danbury with a coat over his head like any thug. Money laundering, securities fraud, embezzlement, extortion, mail fraud, felony theft, felony currency manipulation, all of them tied up with conspiracy charges as well, including racketeering and accessory to murder, whoa.

The actual murder indictment was another guy, someone in the Chicago office, Pervis Z. Oliver, 38, no one I'd ever heard of. There was a side article about Dolus's ties to organized crime, as well: nothing definite. Mr. Perdhomme wasn't indicted for anything, painted himself as a dupe, but the paper had printed a large photo of him, this gentle-looking bald guy smiling sadly in a suit and striped tie. Caption: VICTIM OR ARCHITECT? I knew how my old man would answer that question.

The median potential sentence for Dad's alleged crimes was *twenty-five years,* which the paper thought likely, given all the evidence.

I ransacked the rest of the pages, but the attack on Sylphide hadn't made it in. I tuned the kitchen radio to the all-news station, couldn't sit still: President Nixon, Cambodia, another moon shot. Nothing about Sylphide, happily, not a word. I called the Bridgeport Hospital. No information could be given over the phone. Not so much as an acknowledgement that she was there. I dressed for school, started for the bus stop. Suddenly I missed my father, missed him terribly, realized standing there at the end of our little street that there was no way I could get on the bus: by now all of Staples High would know everything.

SITTING ON MY parents' narrow bed mid-morning, I called Jack Cross's office again. And after a single ring—unwanted miracle—he answered. "Well, David," he said warmly enough.

"I need to find Katy," I said.

"She's got tennis till ten, I think. What's up? You sound upset."

And then I *was* upset.

Jack was quiet as I cried, just, "Okay," and "I'm right here," very tenderly, the first moment I loved him. When I'd subsided a little, he said, "What's going on, David?"

I told him the story, as simply as I could, the Dad story only, looking out the good patio door toward the High Side. My job with Sylphide, the attack on Sylphide, that was too much, of course, too much for Katy. Dad in prison, definitely enough. While I was talking, Jack found the item in the *New Haven Register*. He read it aloud, quite shocking, all that murder and manipulation.

"I'll find a way to tell Kate," he said. "And then I think you should come up here."

No way.

Suddenly I remembered the envelope from Sylphide. Jack talked logic as I tore it open: the lump in there was the speckled stone, of course. I smoothed it and smoothed it and smoothed it as Jack went on. When he finally hung up I dug once again through all the papers on Dad's desk. What was missing? New mail in a rubber band. Just more bills, all of them overdue. A notice from Westport Savings and Trust announced that our mortgage had lapsed, three missed payments: we had ten days to come up with two hundred eighty-six dollars, a fairly large figure in my experience, ten more days to pay it again, ten more days for a third payment to catch up and avoid dispossession. Nearly a thousand dollars due in a month, a vast sum.

I dialed Jack's office again: busy.

He was talking to Kate, of course.

I smoothed the speckled heart, smoothed it, smoothed it.

MOM CALLED FROM a phone booth at the courthouse in Danbury. Dad would go state's evidence. She explained what that meant. He was largely innocent, she said. "'Largely,'" she repeated, obviously quoting him. She sounded actually kind of upbeat, laid out all the legal maneuvers their lawyer had planned, the public defender. Guy named McBee, fat as a house, she said. There was no money for better. There was no money at all.

She said, "You remember how Dad said the Blue 'Bu was stolen? Well, it wasn't stolen. He *sold* it."

"He sold the Blue 'Bu?"

"Sold it to pay some bills, so he says. There's a lot he's going to have to explain. We're all going to have to be pretty brave, honey. We're all going to have to be pretty goddamn forgiving." She did not sound forgiving, she did not sound brave. She'd been staying at a crappy motel, constant meetings with lawyers and judges and jailors, had seen Dad twice for all of fifteen minutes, Dad at his cowed worst.

I kept meaning to tell her about the smashed window, the lawnmower, the action at Sylphide's, but the opening never quite came, the information too ambiguous, and maybe not for her. Anyway, suddenly she had to go: the public defender had just appeared, and she only had ten minutes with him, fifteen if she were lucky.

"Mom, just quick, the mortgage, it's lapsing." I pulled out the notice, read it one more time. "What should I do?"

"No, honey, the mortgage isn't lapsing. I gave Daddy checks for that."

"Lapsing," I said.

Silence. Then, "Honey, do you have any money in your savings account?"

Yes, I did, enough to cover two of the payments, money I'd made shoveling snow and mowing lawns from age twelve, some of it from the mowing at Sylphide's.

I thought suddenly of something I'd learned as a quarterback: praise for the team in tough circumstances. "Mom. I just want to say what a good job you're doing. You sound so calm."

She gave a short laugh and said, "That's how you win at tennis, David."

14

The High Side was in full roar by noon the next day, music and trucks rumbling and occasional shouts clearly audible, Mr. Baker pounding his drums, guitars accompanying, maybe someone singing, the driveway full of cars, also one of those very fancy tour buses, craziness, like no one cared what had happened to the dancer, shades of the days after Dabney's death, the party going forward. I'd fallen asleep on our living-room floor, only to be awakened by the phone ringing.

I plunged to answer, but it wasn't Mom.

"Mr. Demeter?"

Our kindly principal cleared his throat, said, "Taking a another day off?"

"Well, yes. Things are a bit rough here, sir."

"Roger that, David. We've seen the news items. Just wanted you to know you have our support."

"Thank you, sir."

"Now David. Anything you want to tell me about your friend Nussbaum? Mark Nussbaum?"

"No. I mean, not since he didn't show up to our meeting with you."

"Where were you yesterday afternoon, son?"

"Sir? I was at the High Side. Sylphide's place? I'm working there part-time."

"The High Side. You were there between what hours, exactly?"

"Exactly, sir? Um, I took the bus home, and then I went right over there, like three o'clock. And I got home late, like maybe ten or eleven. Working, sir."

"So you were there at about five, between, say, five and six?"

"Yes, sir. What's going on?"

"And are there people over there that can attest to that?"

"Yes, sir. Of course sir."

"David, wonderful. Imagine my relief. Because Mark Nussbaum was dragged out of his car yesterday behind the science labs, driven out to the beach and severely beaten. This was early evening, after a double detention for the matter to which you just referred. He's in guarded condition at Norwalk Hospital. They may have fractured his skull. Both hands broken, both arms, teeth broken, bruised spine. It's very serious."

"I'm sorry, sir."

"And because, as before, Mr. Nussbaum has placed the blame on you. Which he's done in the past, of course. I told the investigators just that. So you'll do well to get a note from someone over there at the High Side. Maybe multiple signatures?"

"Sir, there was an incident at the High Side. Right about that time. The police came. They took my name. They took everyone's name."

"Then we can check with the police."

"Do you have to? The police aren't very good at this stuff."

"Again, I know you are protecting Emily Bright's honor, and I appreciate that. Quietly, David. We'll do this very quietly. You've done nothing wrong, so your name should not be dragged through this and won't be, nor Emily's. I believe you implicitly, but I'm afraid there are others who may not. Nussbaum's parents are very powerful attorneys, and naturally they are quite concerned, quite concerned."

"Just what I need," I said.

"No, now, never mind. I'll run interference for you, son. It's best for everyone involved, including the students and faculty of Staples High, and probably Mark, as well, to get this cleared up as quietly as possible. In progress, son. Meanwhile, please give my best to your mother and your dad, and my best wishes in these difficult times. And let's get you back to classes as soon as possible."

Nice guy.

FREDDY GAVE ME a long, appraising look from the front doors at the High Side, said nothing: we were all feeling guilty. He wouldn't let me pass: the house was shut down. Finally Desmond appeared carrying a tray with a glass of water and a pill bottle. He said, "Mr. Hochmeyer," very professional tones, didn't invite me in. He just went about his business, climbed the great stairs.

"How's Tenke?" I called after him.

"Come again, sir?"

"Sylphide, how is she?"

"She's resting upstairs."

"Did they find the guy?"

Confidential, said his posture—he'd never discuss anything about his employer without express instructions. More clipped even than usual: "I'll tell her you are here."

"We'll find him," Freddy muttered, still standing in my way.

I kept mum about the damage at my own house. Freddy was still the goon, as far as I was concerned, and a failed one at that: when there was actual trouble, he hadn't protected the great ballerina.

Shortly Desmond was back: "Sylphide will see you."

Freddy looked surprised, let me pass.

I bustled after Desmond up the scooped stone stairs. Desmond knocked gently at the heavy door to Sylphide's suite, opened it, let me in, let grief cross his features. "You may go in. No more pills, no matter what she says." He turned on heel.

"Wait," I said. "The guy trashed my house. The guy who did this to her. They went through my father's desk. I mean, obviously there's some connection."

Desmond turned back to me, gave me a long look up and down. "And you think your father isn't it?"

SYLPHIDE WAS DEEP in her bed, shoulder encased in ice packs, silk sheets pulled up to her chin and folded nicely, Desmond's work. "Lizard," she said fondly. Her teeth were bright white, tilted very slightly sidewise as if by strong currents, something I hadn't noticed before. The layered muscles stood out on her good arm, a few freckles. Her eyes were darker than I remembered, her face more relaxed, prettier for that, add acne scars for character, that tall nose for nobility: the woman never looked the same to me twice.

Gently, I said, "Happy Halloween."

And she said softly, "What do you mean?"

Even more softly: "Skeletons and pumpkins, trick-or-treat, all that?"

"Oh, *fie fahn*," she said slowly, letting her eyes droop closed. "A great crowd of children are coming as ghosts last year and terrify poor Dr. Chun." Her head was propped too high in pillows. I took one away, and she let her neck fall back—gratefully, I thought. She said: "He is exploding my shoulder, everything about it: muscles and tendons and rotator cuff. The nerve is pinched in my neck. The hand is numb. These pills, they do not work. I'm all black and blue and green and yellow under here, swollen."

A great drum roll from downstairs, background noise, well muffled by the walls of that lair, the heavy door.

I said, "You'll dance again."

She murmured something fondly.

I leaned close to hear, asked her to say it again.

"Oh, you," she breathed. "You're so very stupid."

She wriggled slightly, adjusted the ice pack on her shoulder. Her eyes fluttered open. Her good shoulder was bare and parian pale, delicate passage of blue veins. Her lips parted slightly. She seemed to search for my thoughts, then let her eyes close again, took measured breaths, her shoulders rising and falling in the silk of her sheets just slightly. "These *useless* pills," she said, vexed. She brought her good hand up and out from under the sheets, inadvertently exposing a pretty, pallid breast. I tucked the sheet back up. She reached to me, patted my cheek, let her hand drop, patted my shoulder, squeezed my bicep, ran her hand down my forearm, found my fingers, twined them in hers.

"Warm," she said, and strong as ever pulled my hand to her cheek and to her forehead, seeming to ask me to stroke her, so I did, working my fingers into her hair. "Oh," she said. Her eyes fluttered, her jaw twitched, her breath grew ragged.

I slipped the speckled stone heart into her palm.

She closed her fingers upon it tight. "Oh, Dab," she murmured. "Oh, Dabney, darling."

❑ ❑ ❑

AT HOME, THE rain came suddenly and very hard, cold drops like hail almost, they were so big. I started in cleaning again, wanted that house spotless. I'd hurt Sylphide's attacker—broken his arm (I'd felt it go), crushed his hand—so he must have been at our house before he went to get Sylphide. A bucket, a sponge, the top edge of every baseboard, nutty behavior. But if I could clean things up, I'd be in control.

Finally the phone rang. I leapt to answer.

"David, hello. It's your mother." She sounded almost cheerful. "Honey, there's really no time to talk right now but I want to let you know that they'll release Daddy after court on Friday, good news. Your sister and this professor of hers will pick you up nine o'clock that morning and chauffeur you. There's to be a hearing, okay? A formality, but fatso the public defender thinks the appearance of a loving family will be an asset—and then we're all going to go get a nice lunch and try to sort through some of the issues here. Your father won't be able to come home for a while, but."

My father had gone state's evidence and was to be sequestered under guard in a secret location, was the gist of the rest. Mom was calling from a pay phone in the courthouse, about to enter a meeting with the federal prosecutor. So that explained the businesslike tone, the brusque good-bye.

Not a word from Kate.

Early dusk under the dense overcast, the hard rain soothing. I made myself dinner from sparse leavings: can of beans over rice, chunks of onion, heavy dusting of chili powder, first class. I scrubbed the counters after, washed the skillet and pan and dish I'd used, rinsed the bean can doubly. I had felt for a moment what to be loved by the dancer would be like, and the tumble of it suffused me. To have been mistaken for Dabney even momentarily was somehow promising, even suggestive, not as discouraging as you'd think.

Cheerful as Mom, that kind of will, I sat down to do homework, no trouble guessing the calculus assignment: chapters ten and eleven in our ponderous book. Mr. Demeter expected me at school Monday, and maybe I could talk to him, clear my name in the matter of Mark Nussbaum, for whom I felt nothing but pity.

After an hour I wandered upstairs and retrieved my private Sylphide gallery, a photo from *Life,* another from the *Times,* two from *Newsweek,* the very moving photos from *Rolling Stone* (never a ballerina on the cover before or since), finally, the art from Dabney's *Dancer,* that naked butt. I sorted through them all, but one of the photos in the *Rolling Stone* spread moved me particularly. I brought it out to my small desk, just a shot of Sylphide from the waist up looking back at the camera over her shoulder, that frank, vast gaze, her hair falling out of its bun, leotard strap off her shoulder, dangling. That fragile shoulder! To love her as Georges loved her would be very simple. But I wanted to practice purity and so concentrated only on her face. I wanted to love her chastely and not use her as others did or even to so much as think of her or any dancer that way. All that purity left me feeling beautifully light, warm in my chest. I lay on the bed and studied that face, found myself overwashed with a rarefied desire that was not lust, fell hard asleep.

HEAVY BALLS OF rain still crashing down—that's all it was, and branches in the wind—but then there it came again. I leapt awake and off my bed, grabbed my baseball bat, slipped along the carpeted hallway and down the stairs, peered between balusters to inspect the remaining patio door, nothing but reflection—I'd left the kitchen lights on. Still the tapping came, more insistent. I slapped at the two-way light switch, the kitchen went half-dark, and suddenly out there past the perfectly polished glass was a *person.* I gave a little shout of surprise: Emily Bright.

She staggered in as I slid the door open, left a wet trail. Her shoes—just little dance flats—were covered in thick mud; she was mud to the knees, mud in the ends of her thick braid. She swayed there regarding me, let a sheepish smile take hold, leaked sudden tears.

"Whoa," I said.

She said, "I've done something really nuts."

"I'll get a towel," I said. Mom kept beach towels in the laundry room. I retrieved four, handed one to Emily, who put it immediately to her hair. I wiped the floor, laid out a towel for her to stand on, helped her out of her shoes. She put a hand on my shoulder, dripped on me. All I could think of was getting her clothes in the wash. I stood to suggest she get a hot shower, borrow some of Katy's old clothes—stood up right in her face,

and she just suddenly kissed me, pressed her lips to mine, kept it coming, gasps and sobs, not wooden. In there somewhere the phone began to
ring, rang twenty, thirty times. A kind of disgust overwhelmed me, the
extravagant sighs and her pointed tongue, but then in a rush the feeling
passed and suddenly I was in my mother's kitchen kissing the girl I loved,
kissing her just as hungrily as she'd been kissing me, letting the phone
ring, first time in my life, just letting it ring, knowing full well that whatever it was it was probably important, probably Mom.

"I jumped out of the car," Emily said suddenly, tugging at my shirt.
"I just opened the back door and jumped out and ran into the woods." I
pulled at her shirt, too, pulled it over her head, just a light shirt, a shirt for
an airplane ride to a warmer place. She looked like Emily again, someone
I recognized again, her features adding up. She pressed her breasts naked
against my chest and pulled at my belt—disquieting expertise—shoved
my pants down as far as she could, put her hands on me, this sudden heat.
So I put both hands in the back of her unlikely Capri pants—they were
ruined anyway—and pushed them down off her butt, just popping the
buttons in front, pushed them down, soaked panties and all—she'd been
in the rain for hours.

"On the way to Kennedy," she said.

I got my shirt the rest of the way off and tripped over my pants, sat my
naked butt unintentionally on the mud and gravel she'd brought in. I
said, "You jumped out of the car?"

"I just opened my door at a light and jumped out."

We both laughed. Suddenly it all seemed pretty funny.

She didn't wait for me to get my difficult shoes off but fell on me naked
and crawled to my mouth and kissed me more, our foreheads banging—
we were no less clumsy than ever—our brows knocking, our tongues
counting teeth, her hair falling out of its braid thick and black and soaked,
the smell of vanilla and rain, her hips pushing at me, her cold toes pushing my pants down as far as they'd go with the stupid shoes in the way
and then her legs straddling me and her hand on my hard-on, way too
skillfully putting it to herself, her soaked self, all but drinking it in, and
she fucked me, that's the only way to put it, with every bit of an athlete's
attention and focus, muscle, too. Huskily, rapidly the words tumbled

from her, like she couldn't stop talking, all the things she'd planned to say: "I jumped out of the car at the tollbooth in probably Greenwich and just took off."

"Whoa," I said, trying to get my hips flat on the linoleum floor—the girl was cracking my pelvis.

"And I lied to you," she said, pushing herself on me, around me, her eyes full of lights, pushing her pubis on me uncomfortably till finally I got my hips square enough to push back, push up, arching myself up with every muscle, pushing up and into her maybe all of three times till I felt everything building and humming and massing at the gates.

"I lied to you," she said again emphatically. "I lied, I lied a lot."

I tried to pull out—yes, you lied, so what—tried to disengage, knew everything about babies being made, but Emily wouldn't have any of it, clutched me with her legs, kissed me with her hot mouth, kissed me and clenched me and I let go, like nothing I'd ever felt or anticipated, let go in silent waves and lingering spasms, nothing like alone, nothing like with Jinnie and her dry little hand, more so even than with Sylphide, those triumphant leaps she'd made around her studio.

"I *felt* that," Emily said.

My first time, not hers.

WEARING MY FLANNEL shirt and nothing else after a shower, Emily made a noodle soup from the dregs in our kitchen: one frozen chicken leg, odd vegetable butts from the drawers in the fridge, a shake or two from all those jars and jars of untouched herbs and spices in the pantry, finally a decade-old can of coconut milk. Just add spaghetti, which we had in abundance. And the Noodle-Loving Boys had nothing on me.

Afterwards she went through her purse, found a little bag of pot, tucked some fat pinches into a tiny pipe from a hidden pocket, lit the bowl with a miniature Zippo she stored in there as well. It's not like I didn't know: her crowd at school had always had the whiff of dope about them. I refused a puff, refused another.

"You need *something*," she said. She went to the liquor cabinet, Mom's A&P brand Vodka. In the kitchen she made tea and honey, added the last teaspoons of coconut milk, a couple of spices, let it all steep a while, total focus on the task, her legs long and brown and recently parted, her hair still damp, back in its loose braid. At length she poured her concoction over ice, two big tumblers, and added an equal amount of vodka. She might have been in her own house, the way she led me into the living room, set our drinks up on coasters, put on a record, Brazilian jazz of my father's, his best moods, one hand on his belly, the other out to the side, make-believe samba, Mom drifting in to make it real, all love and smiles. My girl drifted away into the music, sipped at her drink. She leaned into me, kissed my chest.

"Mark saved my letters," she started.

"Letters, so what," I said, but I already knew what was coming. I'd been thinking about saying something about the little creep getting pounded, not now.

"He gave them to Mr. Demeter. Did you hear? You heard. Mark got beat up. By like grown-ups, weird. I'm worse than grounded. The letters were pretty, I guess, dirty."

"You mean, like . . ."

"Like really dirty. Like everything we did. I pretended like I'm so innocent, but really I'm not. Okay? Okay, I said it. I just wanted you to like me. Because I like you."

I sipped my drink, found it delicious, sweet, direct contrast to the conversation, heavy bite of alcohol, whoa. I said, "You didn't have to worry about that. That's in the past."

"He would strangle me and pull my hair. He's very crazy. I liked it, okay?"

"All right," I said. "That's fine. This is getting to be quite an apology."

"It's not an apology. It's an explanation. Demeter called my father. It's like a hundred letters. We did stuff all summer, Mark and me. I wrote him a letter every single day because they turned him on. And now we all have to have a conference. Mark and me and his parents and mine and Demeter and Mrs. Haggerty and maybe more, maybe the police. There's some drug stuff in there. And a time we broke into the field house at the polo club."

"Emily. And you're not making this up?"

"I wish. He thought you set him up. These guys? They said, 'A message from a friend.' And they basically kidnapped him right from school."

"Message from a friend?"

"Probably some drug thing, that's what I think. Mother and Daddy are freaking. I mean, all that, and then your father. Mother showed me *The New York Times* yesterday. Holy shit. It's like a crime wave around here. I'm never to see you again."

We drank our drinks. The Brazilians played on. We listened to two whole songs, quite separate on the couch. I'd told my dad about Mark. I was pretty sure I'd told him. How Mark had popped me in the jaw. Message from a friend!

Dad?

Emily said, "Okay, and it gets worse. After the thing with your father in the paper, and after this morning, my mother announces that I better pack a second suitcase, because she and I are going to *stay in Seoul*. We are moving to Seoul! She went *nuts*, David. She blames it all on the United States. Also on my dad and his 'Black-Negro' ways. She's full of racist stuff, I'm telling you. And he's not standing up for me. She runs him like a factory. David, they were going to make me stay. I might have never come home."

Emily rose to get her little pipe, had a puff or two more. I felt my disgust return. She was no victim. She was bad as Mark, maybe worse.

"The other thing is that I love you," she said.

"You do?"

"I really do."

I pulled her up to my face, kissed her mouth. I could taste the pot. She kissed me back, kind of the old way, and then she really kissed me. We held on tight. I wanted to say I loved her, too, couldn't get it out.

"I'm in big trouble," she said. "I'm in really big trouble."

"So am I," I said.

She kissed my chest, kissed my belly, took me straining in her mouth. Whoa. She knew when to stop, too, called the moment perfectly. "Go in me now," she said, arranging herself so I could, my second time. She made noises like I hadn't heard before. I kept thinking of Mark. Should I strangle her and bite her and pull her hair? I was quick, I was gentle, managed to last a few strokes longer than the first try. We lay a while in my contentment, the samba record repeating for the third time.

"I'm not really done," she said after a while.

"Okay?"

"I mean, you know. Like I did for you." She wriggled, positioned herself, pushed at my shoulders, made it plain what she was saying. It wasn't like I hadn't heard of such a thing, even knew the Latin. I slid down, couch cushions falling all over the floor, my first view that intimate of anyone, the most beautiful vista I'd ever encountered. I gave a few tentative kisses, fell enthusiastically to my task, the root and salt fragrance of her. She pulled away some, said, "Just easy, is how that works." I slowed things down, relaxed into it, something going right, going very right, a kind of violence building—she pushed herself on me, the rhythm breaking, something going right for sure, really going right, gathered herself and gathered herself and gathered herself and then abruptly let go, let go in several waves, squeezed me and my fingers and face away from her suddenly with her legs and a giggle unlike her.

"I DON'T NEED sleep," Emily said. I'd finally got her to climb the stairs with me.

"I'm more of a sleep person," I said.

I pushed the door open to my room and we staggered in together.

"Oh," she said.

All my photos of Sylphide, spread out on my covers!

Emily looked me square in the eye, awaited an explanation.

"I just like her," I said.

"You like her a lot."

"I like her a lot," I said, "yes. Plus, I'm working over there."

"It's okay," she said. "So long as you like me."

"It's very different," I said. "How I feel about you."

"Very different," she said. "Like, unattainable versus a blow job in the living room with a nice cold drink in your hand after you've already been laid on the kitchen floor?"

"Maybe something along those lines, yes." I gathered the gallery in a loose stack, put it on a high shelf in my closet, really wished the girl hadn't seen them.

She said, "I got her note, by the way. In my locker, thanks. She wants me to come dance for her, do an audition. *Sylphide,* David. So like, I'm going to go live in Korea? Are you kidding me?"

"So that's why you're here?"

"Oh, David. Yes." Kisses, her hands on me.

DAWN, AND WE still hadn't slept more than an hour, tangled up naked in my sheets under airplanes. Emily was pumping me for information: "But, I mean, what's she really like?"

"She's nice. She's hurt her shoulder, you know. There was, well, she had an accident."

"An accident?"

I skipped ahead: "Her real name is Tenke Tangstad. She named herself Sylphide when she was maybe your age."

"No, much younger."

"Well, right, you'd know all this. It's the name of some second-rate ballet."

"Second-rate? *La Sylphide?*"

"That's what Kate said, second rate."

"Well, we all know about Kate. I mean all about Kate and Sylphide."

"I guess." What we didn't all know about was Lizard and Sylphide. Increasingly guilty, I felt I was balancing my way along the top edge of an endless two-way mirror, Emily on the dark side, the great ballerina seeing all. But Emily and I hadn't really been together till now, and Sylphide and I would never be, and as for honesty, some things were just best left unsaid. Overnight I'd caught up to Kate, sexually speaking. And learned a little Korean: my *jaji* was raw, Emily's *boji*, too. My airplanes turned on their threads.

A matter of subtlest movements and then raw or not Emily and I were making love again, less urgently, more companionably, like a conversation. In fact, she was talking, a series of languid, distant, disconnected sentences like sighs: "I saw it just like two years ago . . . . With Carla Fracci as the sylph and Erik Bruhn as James, amazing . . . . We've been studying it at conservatory, too . . . . It began the era of the romantic modern ballet . . . . Natural and ethereal settings, flowing dresses, satin toe shoes, ballerinas en pointe, partner lifts . . ." She climbed upon me, and the talk stopped, all right, deep kisses, whoa, till we'd climbed the mountain via the dozen ravines and seen the brilliant glaciers on the other side, a nice long climb up, a quick trot down among the wildflowers.

Flopping off me, she said, "But the big thing was it had a story—like, a really involved plot, which they didn't used to have."

"*La Sylphide*, we're talking about."

"Yes. *La Sylphide*, David, what did you think?"

And as the sky pinkened in the east she laid it out for me: Olden Scotland. A young man about to be married. He falls asleep and dreams of a comely sylph, a gorgeous forest setting. She falls for him, crosses over to this world from the dream world, a very dangerous proposition, apparently. Something about a magic blanket, a lot of other sylphs, a suitor for his fiancé, a jealous witch, Emily laying it out in detail. Late in the ballet, our hero ends up in the dream world, the world of the sylph, not good.

CARS IN THE High Side driveway again, if not so many as on the day of the attack.

Desmond unlocked the door when we got there. "Mr. Hochmeyer," he said.

"This is my friend Emily," I said.

"Miss Bright," Desmond said, already apprised.

Music in the ballroom, just a piano: Georges. I didn't want to share Emily with Sylphide, and I didn't want to share Sylphide with Emily. But it seemed either wittingly or not they'd used me to get to one another. I brooded, some mood—direct counter to Emily's bright nerves. Scenes of our many encounters in the night played in my head, didn't cheer me, not exactly. I wanted to be home again, home in my bed again, making love again, possessing Emily solely, didn't want to see Sylphide, didn't trust my emotions. Emily had been compassionate about the great ballerina and her injury, but there was the glint of ambition in her eye as well: Sylphide was out of the way.

And Kate didn't know a thing about any of it, and no way to ever tell her, another dark spot in my vision. In the ballroom the action had been pared down; still, it was even clearer that the show would go on. Vlad was instructing three male dancers. Sylphide herself, shoulder still wrapped with ice, arm in a blue sling, was talking in the far corner of the ballroom to a guy with a guitar. I tugged Emily over.

"Just in time," the great dancer said, gave us both kisses on our cheeks, no surprise at all that Emily was along, like the date had long been planned. She didn't introduce us to the guitar guy, a face I recognized but couldn't place. You could see the painkillers in her posture and sleepy eyelids, pain, too, a lot of pain, too much to ignore. Jimmy Page, that's who it was. From Led Zeppelin. He touched Sylphide's good shoulder as they said their good-byes. He walked off pulling a pack of cigs from his shirt pocket, nodded at the two new guards at the huge hangar doors, one of whom accompanied him to his limo, an extended Morris Mini-Minor painted in zebra stripes.

"Emily Bright," the great dancer said.

"Hi," said Emily.

"We are going to start class in ten minutes or fifteen. I am keeping you for the day, if okay? *Ja?* We want to see you dance. Lizard, sweet boy, you are going into town to inspect theaters. Be very tough with Conrad. We are wanting the perfect venue, not the first you see, but the perfect. Use your judgment, not his. Tell me what you find."

Emily stepped further from me, further.

CONRAD DROPPED NAMES like atom bombs, demanded contract concessions that made me sweat, insulted the food and drink we were invariably offered, but no one seemed to mind—they were very, very hungry for Sylphide and *Children of War.* I kept my mouth shut, tagged along. Conrad had warned me not to smile, not to blink, just to look around as if I smelled something rotten no matter how nice the place. The only theater I liked was the Shoebox. I sniffed and sneered, but no one was paying much attention to me. Conrad seemed to prefer a more traditional stage, hated the Shoebox, what seemed like technicalities to me: stage doors in an alley, center aisle in the orchestra, Greenwich Village location. In the Bentley between venues I tried to get him to talk about the attack on Sylphide, but it didn't seem to interest him.

I was too young to recognize discretion.

"My parents," I said, needing to talk, but he waved me off with a hand. He had notes to take, didn't need anyone's problems but his own. I tried to picture Dad in a jail cell. He'd be miserable, cocky, too; he'd try to sell the guards investments. He'd be fine, the more I thought about it. He'd be in his element.

Mom, on the other hand, would be nothing but pissed. Her idea of hell was a motel of any kind. Her idea of hell would be paying for a cheap dinner from a bag of quarters. She wouldn't sleep, she'd find a bar, she'd drink martinis, she'd start smoking again, there'd be a man telephoning some Sunday night soon.

It was ten before Conrad and I got back to the High Side, an expensive but lousy Times Square dinner in our bellies. I was exhausted, though my thoughts had clarified considerably: I couldn't wait to see Emily, Emily was my girl, Emily forever.

Sylphide met Conrad and me in the parlor, let Conrad describe the theaters he liked, a couple of functional large houses in midtown. When he was through with an animated spiel, practicality after practicality, Sylphide turned to me: "What do you think, Lizano?" Her face was pale from a day of pain, her ice pack melted and sagging off her shoulder. She belonged in bed. It was like football, I realized: you weren't supposed to give in to injury.

"Well," I said.

"Don't say Shoebox," Conrad said.

"Shoebox," I said. "In the Village."

No reaction from Sylphide, nothing. She just moved onto her next subject, a checklist before bed: "Emily is having a great day. She is so very natural, so very human, a lot of tense angles, and that braid flying around." She settled her arm in its sling, shuddered privately. "Marvelous physique, of course, and comic timing, *ja?* But needing to build her technique. Conrad, we will set her up with Neville. She don't know how to isolate that tall-girl torso. *Doesn't* know. An hour before class each day?"

"So she'll get an audition?" I said.

"She's been hired," Conrad said.

"*Children of War,*" said Sylphide, just business: time for her to go to bed.

It was time for me to repossess my girl, too. I said, "I'd better get Emily home. Across the way, I mean. And back for class tomorrow? Around ten?"

Desmond approached, took Sylphide's good arm, turned her toward the stairs.

She said, "No, Firfisle, no. I'm sorry. But Emily will stay here. Already she sleeps. We work her so very hard today. Not so hard as you work her last night! She need rest. Also some privacy. If she is going to be dancing with us, I mean. She is needing a home, her own. Away from those parents, and away from you, who has his own troubles."

ON OUR LAWN I turned to look back, saw Conrad's little car pull out of the driveway over there, saw Sylphide's light blink out. I watched the darkness that was left, watched a long while in the chilly night. In the morning was Dad's court date, hateful, more time away from my dancers. I'd been thinking of Emily's skin all day, tasting her, living in her kisses, looking forward to more. I'd been thinking of Sylphide's ability to become a vine, to turn me to stone, then water, then wind. I felt something had been taken from me, that both women had used me. I skulked, hoping maybe Emily would make another break. But no.

Late, lonely, I plunged my hands into my pants pockets, found my house key—I was keeping the doors locked, all right—and found the speckled heart, Sylphide's heart, as I slowly realized, smooth as secret skin.

How did she do these things?

15

The BLT I ordered at Restaurant Les Jardins is clearer in memory than anything else from that fateful morning. Oh, and the Bloody Mary. The combination seemed to disagree with me, or anyway, the taste of bacon and vodka was with me all the rest of the day. I have cared very little for bacon since, less for tomato juice. But there was a delicate serving of coleslaw, too, colored with beet slivers, and I ate the cabbage strand by strand as Kate fulminated, a perfect, impressive uniformity of knife cuts, unexpected herbs, and raisins. Who put raisins in coleslaw? Delicious.

Kate was rough on Mom, nothing new, and Mom was rough on Dad, ditto, but something had changed: there was no irony in any of it. Dad was cavalier, and that was new for him. Jack was perfection, calibrated his role so delicately that I almost forgot he was there. Outside a tall window I spotted trellised tomatoes and pole beans reaching for the sky from the very top of stick teepees, an abundance of beans in a green rainbow of colors, the very beans in our drinks. On the hill a cabbage patch, many heads cut, many to go, like so many medicine balls just waiting for the fitness coach to give a command. I decided Les Jardins was the most wonderful place I'd ever been. The lobster bisque? First time I was ever moved to use the word *divine*. The BLT, a simple thing, was made like a sculpture, the bread sliced from a yellowy, rich homemade loaf and toasted just crisp. They didn't trust themselves with the mayonnaise but put it in porcelain ramekins, tiniest little spreading knife, nothing precious about it, pure function and solicitude.

Jack had a way of reeling Kate in—I imagine Mom noted it as I did, something surely we would have talked about later, if there'd been a later. The guy knew when to get my sister out of there. Her hug for me was very brief, none for Mom. For Dad, a long embrace and an earful of secrets, enough to make him giggle: what were they up to? He put something in her hand, I thought. I've always thought.

I loved having Mom and Dad alone, then. I didn't much notice the guard, who was inspecting his fingernails closely, standing off by the waitress station, his weapon unused all these years, holster falling a little too far behind his back and under his jacket to be accessible, snap rusted so that one hand would not be enough to open it. Not that I considered that. Dad offered a soliloquy on the subject of the Staples High Wreckers football season, unclear what he was getting at, though he did seem to think they'd be doing a lot better if I were there. I think it was I that ordered the cake, or maybe Dad—Mom wouldn't ever.

"Hochmeyer belongs at the helm down there," Dad repeated.

Mom clacked her tongue, a noise to put a stop to all nonsense.

Add chocolate to the flavors of the day, the tastes and smells that bring it back. We all split that enormous, moist, all-but-glimmering piece of cake, supposedly reluctant Mom edging out the competition and eating most, three busy forks.

Outside, the beauty of the day. The solicitous guard opened the restaurant door for Mom, then held it for Dad, too, who was drunk, I realize now, who was staggering. That piercing, clear October light slantwise, and a car coming down the stately gravel drive, nothing more sinister than that.

MEMORY RETURNS IN Mom's kitchen with the image of her stout old Waring blender, glass pitcher on a throne. Also a knock at the door: Mrs. Paumgartner, Mom's great tennis friend and our closest neighbor. She was helpful in that I comforted her while she wailed and wept, and this gave me something to do. Dad was upstairs, I felt deeply, maybe polishing his wingtips. He was always polishing his wingtips because they were old and the leather was cracking and shoes made the man. He disliked Jean-Anne pretty violently. You'd never get him downstairs in a million years when she was over.

Mom was at tennis, was how I felt.

Something I had to do for Dad, something I had to do immediately. I left Mrs. Paum on the living room couch clutching a kitchen towel and pounded up the stairs, sat on Mom's and Dad's bed, dialed Coach Powers. He wouldn't know about my folks; nobody would know, not yet. I offered it as an announcement, not a request: "Coach Powers, I'm going to come back and finish the season with you."

"Hochmeyer," he said, noncommittal.

"You guys are four and three on the season, right?" Dad had just told me that at lunch, and the next bit, too, nearly verbatim: "Not so bad. But if you can beat Stamford Catholic, Bridgeport, and New Canaan, last three games, you're on to the state finals."

"I don't know, Hoch. Quitter like you." I heard the wavering, a certain greed, his need to win trumping his need to dominate me.

"State finals," I said, very firm. I wanted that championship for Dad. Dad could not face eternity as a loser.

Powers pretended to think, gave a couple of strangulated coughs, trying to compose a paragraph no doubt, a face-saving paragraph of terms and conditions.

"So I'll see you tomorrow," I said and hung up, bang.

Mrs. Paum's thready voice calling up the stairs: "David?"

"I'm here."

"Oh, David, I'm so frightened!"

GRANDPA ARRIVED EFFICIENTLY at seven-thirty, limo from LaGuardia Airport, quick flight from Detroit. Mrs. Paum had seen to it that I got into the shower, and had dispatched my clothing to the washing machine, later for the garbage: we'd only slowly realized I was covered in blood, yet another of the unbelievable things of the afternoon Kate had missed. And was still missing.

Mrs. Paum looked like a midget shaking my grandfather's hand, one of those moments when I realized how big I must look to everyone else. Grandpa had an angry air about him, but regardless managed a smile, a muscular handshake. We didn't say anything about the disaster, just sat down at the cramped kitchen table to eat.

I needed to throw a football if I was going to play the next afternoon. The old duffel bag was still in the garage. I excused myself—fresh air, I said—and dug it out, two dozen well-used pigskins that Dad had some-how procured from the NFL when I was all of eleven and already six feet tall. The plywood target he'd made was still bolted to the back of the tool shed, and I stood at increasing distances, drilled the bull's eye, *thump, thump, thump*. I hadn't lost any accuracy during my abdication, might have lost a little feel. So I threw on the run, threw falling backwards, gathered the strewn balls, threw diving, threw bombs from the goal line, little shovel passes, bull's-eye every time, my hair streaming in my face, no matter, every shot for Dad.

Grandpa and Mrs. Paum were in the kitchen. That was their way to deal with traumatic shock: play cards. I heard them laughing, threw the ball harder, put myself through familiar drills. Then I heard Grandpa on the phone, giving people the business. He was trying to find Kate, would find her or be damned.

I'd been out there maybe two hours in the deepening chill and dusk when a car pulled into our cul-de-sac. It was just a regular car, but it made a circle in the dead-end, pulled into the deep shadows under Mrs. Kellogg's overgrown hemlock trees, put its lights out. Then nothing. Maybe Chip Kellogg, college kid, with a girl? I tossed the football a few times, loud booms against the back of the garage, watched the vehicle warily. The driver's door opened. A guy got out. Freddy. He looked all around.

I bent and picked out the next football, gripped it, threw a sudden hard string, caught him in the neck. He staggered, found me too late as I charged. I put him on the ground before he could even react, yanked his right hand up behind him, pulled his gun out of the back of his pants, tossed it away.

"Nice," he gasped.

I drew his arm up tighter.

"I'm sorry for your loss," he said breathing hard. "Desmond saw it on the news. Your folks. We are all very sorry, and upset. Mrs. Stryker-Stewart is beside herself." He did not sound upset, not even very put out by my grip on him, everything the same to him, just a groan to give away his pain: "She is also concerned for your safety, so I am going to park right over there all night and just keep an eye."

"Who keeps an eye on you?"

"Mr. Hochmeyer. Lizard. I'm sorry about what happened the other day with your dad. That was a misunderstanding. By now you know we're friends. Mrs. Stryker-Stewart sent me. The second we heard the news. I'm here, and I'll be right over there in that car all night."

"Where are his shoes, Freddy?"

"Your dad was a good guy."

I let up on my grip. "The shoes," I said.

"Better than the shoes," Freddy said. "I'll find out who did this murder and who provided the cash, and we will take them both out. I'm right over there in my car if you need me. Now you get back to your people and be their strength."

I felt a rush of gratitude, blurted: "The guy's name was Kaiser. Who shot them. My dad said his name. It was *Kaiser.*"

"Noted," said Freddy, definite flicker in his steady gaze.

MRS. PAUMGARTNER WAS driving Grandpa up to Danbury to view Mom, and no one expected me to go through that again. Not a word about Dad from Grandpa, like it was only Mom up there to be identified. Well, winning the game at Catholic would be for Dad, for Dad alone, his one consolation. The murders had made the Saturday headlines, all right, large photo of the portico at Restaurant Les Jardins, sketchy article, just a little about the shooting, most of the rest about the Dolus Investments indictments, speculation that there might be some kind of connection, duh. Mrs. Paum came over and made breakfast, platter of eggs, a pound of (yet more) bacon, big men. The phone rang over and over again. Mrs. Paum answered, like she was our secretary. Mom's friends, mostly. Two reporters I'd never speak to. But no Kate. Freddy's car was there when I looked, and it was there when I looked again, and then it was gone: the police had finally arrived, those same FBI men in the same black cars, asking the same questions Detective Turkle had asked me the day before, then lingering to talk to Grandpa, finally offering to drive him up to the morgue in Danbury so Mrs. Paum could stay with me.

The second they were gone, I told her I was leaving, too, had a game. And though she protested violently I suited up, cleats to helmet. She tried reasoning with me as I squeezed behind the wheel of the Volvo Jack had loaned us, probably kept reasoning as I drove away. Out on Flory Ridge Road a car came racing up behind me, assumed a certain distance behind me, shot of adrenaline, but then I saw that it was Freddy. He followed me all the way to Stamford Catholic, half an hour or so. My mind was dense and blank and very dark. I parked in a remote lot, Freddy right behind me, hurried through the back gate in the formidable fence, hustled through the crowd thronged there, made my way to the visitors bench, not more than a minute before kickoff.

Coach Powers gawked, then sobered, hurried over to me. "I heard the news, Lizard, Jesus."

"Jesus yourself," I said.

"Son, you can't play."

"I have to play, Coach."

"There'll be time for that, Lizard. What'll people think, I put you in? I'm sorry. I'm sorry this has happened. Horrible, awful. You don't belong here."

"For my dad," I said. "You put me in."

He put his The-Tough-Get-Going face on, hurried away. My teammates followed his lead, left me to myself behind the bench. I said nothing, glowered at anyone who chanced to look at me.

Kickoff.

I lingered, tugging at the hair hanging out of the back of my helmet. Fielding got sacked twice, then fumbled: Catholic touchdown. Next series, he got the team to midfield, where our boy Greenie Stumpatico punted nicely. Then Catholic scored on a long pass. And that's how it went to halftime, a drubbing, Staples High down 42–3.

As the Wreckers took the visitor's locker room I hulked off in my helmet and pads through the spectators milling and sat in the Volvo, Freddy impassive in his car like any old stranger in the next parking space. I didn't want to talk to him, and I certainly didn't want to listen to Coach Powers pontificate. After halftime, I took my place behind the bench as we kicked off: return for Catholic touchdown, extra point, kickoff to our one-yard line, where Jimpie couldn't get a handle on the ball till too late, pig pile, nearly a touchback.

"Lizard," Coach Powers said.

I stepped up neither fast nor slow.

"The old plays," he said. "Twelve, fourteen, three, four." Then shouted: "Hoch is going in. The old playbook, everybody."

Wes Fielding clapped his hands—nothing to lose in this game—urged me on. I breathed and felt huge. In the huddle—no eye contact—I called Coach's first number, but after the perfectly executed hike I didn't run the play, not even close, but let the field flow left, faked the pass everyone expected, and then took off, spun and charged through the Catholic linesmen, easily evading grasping hands, easily racing everyone downfield, ninety-nine-point-nine yard touchdown. I didn't really hear the shouts from our side of the little stadium, didn't really care about beating Catholic. I just wanted to do the thing for Dad, who had lived for my powers, and maybe to do it for Mom, okay, who simply liked an athlete, especially an athlete who won. Kate was in there, too, somewhere, like a little spinning top you wanted to grab, just grab it so it would stop, stop long enough to hold.

I took my place behind the bench. The opposing coach came racing across the field in protest: was I on the official roster for the day's game? The refs gathered around. Coach must have felt pretty smug: yes, Hochmeyer was on the official roster. He'd inked me in on the basis of my phone call, so much for pride: he'd known he'd play me from the moment he heard my voice.

Next series I called another of the old plays, but I wasn't going to hand the ball to Jimpie Johnson, no way, instead motioned to Eric Unbattle (great hands, but unfairly disrespected by Powers for his small size). Catholic didn't even notice the small kid hustling downfield, and I hit him past all the defenders: touchdown. The next series was longer, Catholic having made some adjustments. I called all the Jimpie plays but simply withheld the ball from him, let him stagger past me unmet, several beautiful fakes in effect, the entire defensive line swinging after my ex-friend while Unbattle took the real handoffs and made short gains. "Why do we need a fucking huddle?" Jimpie hissed.

"Let's just win the game," I said.

After one of four third-quarter touchdowns I stayed out on the field, made myself part of the line for the kickoff, tackled the all-star return man two steps into his run. And stayed for the defensive plays: I couldn't let Catholic rack up touchdowns. I was big, fast, tricky, but in that game I was possessed, too, a reptile, all right, got in on every tackle, caught punts, ran them for thirty, forty, fifty yards, never took the sidelines. Eric Unbattle ended the game with the hundred-year school touchdown-reception record, I forget how many, a fantastical, come-from-behind rout that brought Staples High even in the standings with Catholic, theretofore touted as the best team in the league.

Game won, I bolted, drove myself home to Westport, Freddy close behind. In my room, the reptile gave way to Lizard, and Lizard gave way to David, then Davy, who wept: defense, offense, there you go, Daddy.

THE DOUBLE FUNERAL was Monday morning, no delays as there was no question about the cause of death, no trouble with the medical examiner's office up in Danbury. We had our corpses on time, Dad's in a plain pine box, Mom's in a plush silver chariot.

Grandpa walked head high into the church, still angry with the world. I'd played a football game, and as if that weren't bad enough, Sunday morning early he'd found Kate and me passed out on the living-room floor, TV squealing. She'd only got in late Saturday, Jack decorously dropping her before going off to their hotel. We'd slept the day away while Grandpa did all the heavy lifting—phone calls, visitors, church bulletin to write, obituary to submit to the local papers, half a column about Mom, very few words about Dad, and anyway plenty about both of them on the front pages. He was unhappy that Kate had a professor for a boyfriend. He was unhappy that we didn't have a family car. He was unhappy that his daughter had ever married Nick. He was unhappy with the coroner. He was unhappy with the FBI. He was unhappy with Mrs. Paum, who wept uncontrollably when not saying sunny, revolting things about life everlasting.

I let Grandpa's rage sink into me: I could have stopped Kaiser, could have leapt on him the minute he climbed from his car. Also Emily's skin, her mouth on me, our showers together, the two of us on every bed in the house, a guy debauching himself on his parents' last night, bad guilt. Not a word from her since. Playing the football game, too, a mistake, some misplaced urge to violence. And Kate had disappeared, gone off with Jack to his hotel, a shower no doubt.

On the church steps, Aunt Ellen's mood was dark. *"Murdered,"* she said, when I went to hug her.

"You always said Nicholas was trouble," Grandpa said, not lightly.

In the church I sat beside him in the first pew. Aunt Ellen sat away from us as if leaving room for someone. The place filled up behind us. I took sly looks back over my shoulder. Dad had not a single mourner of his own there, not that I could see, certainly no one he worked with. Not even his brothers—both of whom lived in California, as far away from home as possible. Uncle Shelton had called late the night before and waxed on mournfully: "David, terrible. Terrible. Always on the wrong side of the luck, your father." A cough, or tears. "Once he stole a huge sapphire ring from Trift's Jewelers—is that still there in Westport on Main Street?—*stole* this display ring for his girl at the time, who was Betty Clearmont, said he'd saved up and bought it for her. So Betty about swoons, you know, and suddenly they're hot and heavy, and after a week or so of the googly pants she takes the ring into Trift's to be sized. Trift about threw an embolism. Our old man nearly broke your father's arms, I'll tell you, shaking him. No love lost there! Night in jail, day in court. And then the kid was washing sidewalks downtown for six months in lieu of jail time. And of course, it's him who ends up staying in Westport. David, I'm too ill to travel. Long story. You'll have to give your Mom and Dad my best sendoff. And I'm going to mail you a formal letter. I'm going to forgive your dad's debt to me. It's about six figures by now. I'll put the exact amount in the letter and forgive it, okay? I loved your Dad, David. But he was a pill, if I may use the mildest word possible. No need for you to live with his debts."

Uncle Pete didn't even call, but eventually a letter came from him, too, identical wording to Uncle Shelton's—those decent men colluding—except more money involved, debts I'd never heard anything about. My anger revolved back around to my father, and awake in the night I'd found myself hating him as Grandpa did, all my tears for Mom, who'd been my tender beloved and soul-mate and one true friend.

Reverend Glass entered, came to us in the pew, took Grandpa's hand, patted it lovingly, irritating the old man, I could tell.

Gentle smile and professional warmth, here was the good Reverend who had never given up on me as I struggled with confirmation class and finally bailed out. "There is no tragedy that is not also a lesson," he said very slowly.

Grandpa grunted: he'd once kicked a preacher in the balls, famous family story, a stranger who'd come to his door and called him a sinner.

Reverend Glass took my hand. "I'm always here, David. You're going to need to talk. We'd love to see you in church."

I promised he'd see me, knew he wouldn't, felt angry at him, too: these holy men, eliciting lies daily.

At the last possible second, Kate arrived in a burst of cold wind and leaves from outdoors, but elegantly dressed, new little skirt-suit in charcoal-gray tweed, appropriate sober demeanor. Jack escorted her to the front pew, hurried to find his own seat far from Grandpa. Katy settled in between Aunt Ellen and me. And, oh, how Ellen's face lit up: Katy was her favorite. Reverend Glass took my sister's hand, smiled at her indulgently, said nothing—Kate he'd given up on long ago.

No sign of Emily Bright.

We'd made love in my parents' shower, on their bed, on every piece of their hard-won furniture, terrible. And we would have made love the very night before they died, the very morning, if Sylphide hadn't stolen Emily, no comfort there.

That same October sun slanted through the sanctuary windows. Reverend Glass took the lectern. Kate hugged my neck, a sudden, surprising gesture, very near a chokehold. Grandpa put his hand on my knee, even more surprising, leaned into me. Aunt Ellen slid closer to Kate, all of us connected, an arbitrary unit, myself suddenly at the center, being strong for them as Freddy had advised. Behind us in the church, row after row of Mommy's friends, groups of Kate's friends, a few kids I knew from school, a large contingent of our teachers, people we all knew from town, the pharmacist, the post-office guy, the lady from the flower shop. And okay, one mourner for Dad: Mr. Davis, our school-bus driver.

I'd been right to play the football game, right to go help the team clobber Catholic, right to go behind Grandpa's back. Because touchdowns were the only genuine memorial Dad was going to get. And, in fact, the back rows of the church were taken up with the whole team, cheap suits and muscle-bound solemnity, Jimpie sitting with Jinnie, Jinnie weeping copiously: she'd really liked my dad, told him to his face he was a *piece of work,* didn't seem to mind when he squeezed her plump bottom.

So, make that two for Dad.

Three if you counted Freddy, who stood in the vestibule with the deacons, watching closely.

Reverend Glass gave a stolid eulogy, carefully offering it in Katy's and my names—neither of us was up to saying anything—an actually very thorough rendition of my parents' lives right up to the fatal brunch in Danbury, not leaving out a struggle or two, but leaving out the fact that they'd been shot. I gazed off through the bubbly-glass windows at the perfect day outside, the colorful shrubbery. We stood for another hymn, and as soon as the last organ tone died out a wail came up, a long hooting, the pounding of heavy orthopedic shoes. And suddenly Linsey was upon us, hugging Katy and me to him, waterfall of tears: he understood death, all right. Katy gave me a sharp look, but I gave it right back: I'd invited no one. Back through the pews there was a ripple of response, fond chuckles, teenage snickers, explanations and scoldings that crescendoed only slowly into fond laughter. Back by Freddy I spotted Sylphide, and just behind her, Emily, Emily at last. The attention in the room subtly shifted back there. The great Sylphide!

Kate, quaking with fresh emotion, got Linsey to sit between her and Aunt Ellen—Linsey hadn't forgotten Kate in the faintest—got him to settle down, her great gift of loving him, and the service went on, another mourner in Dad's column.

OVER DESSERT AT Sizzler, which was Grandpa's favorite, Jack laid out a plan. I could go live with him and Kate. Grandpa laid out a counterplan that would take me to Michigan. He'd spent the afternoon sputtering and fuming at Dad's rolltop desk, unpacking the cubbyholes I'd stuffed so hurriedly after they'd been rifled by our mysterious visitor. From what Grandpa could tell there was no estate left, less than zero. All the bank accounts were empty, the house remortgaged six times over, six different banks, dunning notices unopened, threatening letters unopened. I didn't mention Dad's debts to his brothers: Grandpa was disdainful enough.

"When a child's parents transfer in his senior year, he often stays on," said Mrs. Paumgartner brightly. "It's not uncommon. Perhaps Mr. Demeter would be amenable? David could stay here. I'd keep an eye. We'd all keep an eye."

"This isn't a transfer," said Grandpa, sloshy with cheap Sizzler wine, red in the face, furious.

"Plus, there's the thing about football," I said slowly.

"Football?" said Kate. And then the old ESP: "You mean *nookie*."

Mrs. Paum fell into tears again: such nasty language.

Grandpa slammed the table: "Your brother saw fit to play a game Saturday."

"I did it for Dad," I said.

"Even worse," Grandpa roared.

"The rest is for Mom," I said, no real idea what I meant.

"Home is where the heart is," said Mrs. Paum helpfully.

"Next he'll be dancing ballet," said Kate.

GRANDPA COULDN'T BEAR to sleep in his late daughter's room one more night, took up Mrs. Paum on her offer of her guestroom. Freddy kept his vigil under the hemlock trees. I didn't point him out to Kate, who would not have been pleased. She'd disappeared after Jack left for their hotel, a private quarrel over whether she'd stay with me or go with him. Late, after some hours alone with inane television, I found her in the attic, where she'd always gone to get away from everyone, and where once upon a time we'd played. Our great-grandmother's trunk was open and all the play clothes strewn about, Kate draped in the ermine cape that had always been our prize.

She said nothing, just put the old stovepipe hat on my head. I sat beside her.

"Oh, David," she whispered after a while. "What have I done?"

"You've done nothing," I said.

"We're orphans," she said.

I hadn't thought of that, but certainly pondered it then, the power of words, Katy pulling an old silk ascot around my neck and tying it, little kids again, playing aristocrats.

"It's Perdhomme," I said firmly. We'd had a battle over dessert. Like me, Grandpa thought the killer an associate of Dad's, someone who wanted to shut him up. The FBI thought so, too, and he was never going to budge from an opinion so well grounded.

"No, it was me," Kate said. "Really. It's my fault. I was in such a hurry to get to my tournament. And even after I heard, I didn't want to leave—I wanted to beat that bitch from Penn so bad. Have you ever heard anything so selfish?"

"You wanted to do it for Mom."

"No, for *me*. Oh, David. If I'd only stayed at the restaurant!"

"But, Kate. We had no way of knowing."

"There's a way, all right. At the cemetery today I figured it all out. It's *Linsey*. He's the center of everything, David. Does Mr. Perdhomme know Linsey? No. Does the FBI know Linsey? No. It was that day. Sophomore year. No one picked Linsey up at school. So I took him home on the bus. Dabney answered the door, very simple. He was still holding his Strat, David, and him with his impossibly skinny chest all bare. The staff had all gone off with Sylphide and no one had thought of Linsey. Whose fault is that? It was not my fault. I mean, it was Dabney Stryker-Stewart standing there, David. Do you know how *lonely* he was?"

She went on in a rush, I in my top hat trying to slow her down, trying to quiz her, trying to get her to make sense, but she didn't make sense, and she wouldn't slow down, Linsey at the center of it, Dad always hanging out trying to sell investments, Dabney's brother, Brady, egging Dad on, her story quite confused, a lot of vague male pronouns, Brady Rattner flirting with her when Dabney was on the road, Brady sleeping with her or not—unclear—something about Freddy kicking Brady's ass, breaking Brady's arm or leg or jaw, and then it was Sylphide. Sylphide was behind it all, Linsey at the center of it her dupe, Dad hanging around, Brady warning her about Sylphide, Dabney's crash no accident, Freddy again, Freddy throwing Dad down the High Side stairs, Kate and Dabney alone for a month in France, Linsey at the center of that, too, somehow. Dabney wanting to marry her, make it all correct, buying paintings at Sotheby's to fund their elopement on the day she'd turn eighteen, Brady actually very nice, not like Sylphide thought: that was a trick to keep Dabney close.

"But you were sleeping with Brady, too?"

"I don't know, David. I'm not like that. No. I loved Dabney, David. Dabney of course. And when Sylphide found out she ruined him."

"But how did she find out?"

"Brady, of course."

"Did Dad know? Did Dad know about you and Dabney? And Brady?"

"You already asked me that."

"Just did he know?"

"Not till Dabney was dead. Then everyone knew."

"And you feel Sylphide was involved in all this?"

"I feel? You fucker. She hated having them around, hated it."

"Hated having whom around?"

"Dad. And Brady. And all those other idiots and all their girls."

"But why would Sylphide want to hurt Dad?"

"It's Linsey. David, I'm telling you. Don't be so fucking stupid. It's Linsey, Linsey. He's at the center of it. And all you want to talk about is Mr. Perdhomme, who's just, like, Dad's nice old *boss*. And meanwhile, I see Sylphide owns Emily, now. You'd better think about that, bro. Perdhomme was just Dad's *boss*. While Sylphide owns your girlfriend! And we're fucking *orphans*. And what about *Brady*?"

"Kate, this makes no sense."

"Why does it have to make sense, David? Who is sense going to serve? I'll tell you who—Sylphide. And maybe some of your sick-fuck football friends, and Mommy!"

I let it out then, all the tears I'd been withholding, totally confused, great-grandfather's top hat on my head, Kate patting my back profoundly, a river of tears, an ocean, couldn't stop, couldn't stem the thing, not for Kate, who hadn't yet shed a tear, snot in my ascot. The worst thing was that in a way, despite her incoherence, my sister was right, perfectly right: nothing made sense. Nothing made sense at all and there was no sense in trying to think anything through, and there was no one who could help, no right question to ask.

❑ ❑ ❑

JACK COLLECTED KATE the next afternoon. I waited a decent time, three-handed hearts with Grandpa and Mrs. Paum, the full hundred points, then the minute they left to go to her house, trotted out the kitchen doors.

At the High Side, Desmond answered my knock. "Devastated," he said, and pulled me to him, brief hug, his face pressed to my solar plexus, welcome warmth.

I said, "She's here?"

"Whichever you mean, both here," said Desmond. "The lady is sleeping—she's exhausted. All these goings on. Your parents! It's incomprehensible."

"I just want to see Emily."

"She's exhausted, too, dancing with Vlad all day. She made a point of telling me she wanted to see you, however. I'm to show you upstairs."

On the narrow back steps, he just kept talking: "The police do nothing, and we're left to connect the increasingly obvious dots between your household and ours. While meanwhile it's Freddy who's on the trail of that maniac. Madame's shoulder, David! It's a crime against the *world*! And this boy, this friend of Emily's! Both his hands crushed, his face smashed, a miracle he's survived."

"Mark *Nussbaum*?"

"I believe that's the name, yes. Pulled out of his car after school and stomped, if I may use Emily's word. She was interviewed by the school authorities today."

"Whoa."

"She says he is something of a blackguard. Any number of enemies, that young man. But never mind." We continued up the stairs, another winding flight even narrower than the first.

I couldn't quite formulate the question I wanted to ask, tried anyway. "Desmond," I said, "you were on duty all the time. You live upstairs. Would you say my dad was over here a lot?"

No hesitation: "Too often for Mr. Stryker-Stewart. And the butt of many a drunken joke, if I may say so. But I, I liked Nicholas. He always had a kind word. He spoke to me of my financial investments as an equal, and I appreciated that. His hair was always so well combed. A handsome, charming, agreeable man. With a prize of a perfect daughter, I might add, or Mr. Stryker-Stewart would never have put up with him, all that talk about investments!"

"Does the name Perdhomme mean anything to you?"

"The head of Dolus?"

"My father's boss."

"Ah. Of course. I have a small account with Dolus. Small but thriving. Thanks to Nicholas. Something else to remember him for."

"Does Brady Rattner still come around?"

"Brady? No sir. Of course not, sir. No, no. Brady was banned long ago, Lizard. Brady is a pariah."

"Along with my dad."

"On a different plane altogether, sir," he said crisply. "Though Brady did seem to have an influence on Nicholas. And they did spend an inordinate amount of time together. Out in the poolhouse, thank goodness. I seldom saw them. I mean, thank goodness as regards Brady, not your father, who was a fine man indeed."

We climbed yet another narrow flight to a corridor of tidy guest rooms in the eaves of the enormous house, one of them painted pink and white, purple woodwork: Emily's suite. The girl was asleep, fast asleep, curled at the furthest precipice of the high, overstuffed bed. Desmond seemed to have instructions, never did anything without instructions, folded down the covers for me. I stripped to underpants and T-shirt. After folding my shirt and pants and depositing them on the seat of a waiting Queen Anne chair, he turned on heel and left with a crisp good night. I slipped in behind the girl, lay there in a torment, watched her naked shoulder blades flex and fall, flex and fall, put my ear to her back, listened to her fickle heart.

16

More and more, looking back, I admire the way Sylphide handled *Children of War,* the benefit that had been Dabney's great dream. She wasn't able to dance at the Shoebox Theatre with her new troupe—that destroyed shoulder—but she made the show happen, made it happen for Dabney, made it happen for the actual children, too. The original run of three weeks sold out a month in advance, 48,000 tickets at an average of about ten 1970 bucks each (something like a hundred bucks now), and so the engagement was extended to five weeks. And after a mere month and a half of rehearsals, *Children of War* took the stage, Christmas Day, 1970, no night quite like the next, every night screamingly great, the biggest names in rock and roll, the biggest names in dance (Rudolf Nureyev, for example, hobbling after a foot operation but dancing two nights anyway, one of his *Le Corsaire* solos without music, a brilliant squeaking of bare feet in the dead-silent theater), all of it pulling in the precise youthful audience Sylphide had envisioned. Her choreography retained the respect of the dance community, it seemed; anyway, the critics were kind. As for the music, *Children of War* remains a hallmark, of course, up there along with the 1965 Newport Folk Festival, Bill Graham's New Year's Eve concerts at the Fillmore, maybe even Woodstock. The blazing variety, the unplanned jams, the overflow of choreography and dancers, the dynamic happenstance of the music, the accidents of timing, of personality, of recombinant collaboration, all of it rotated through the weeks of the show, improvisation on top of careful preparation on top of plain luck.

John Lennon and Yoko Ono provided the music for Emily's debut, just the one night, her first in the vine-and-pillar dance, which had evolved pretty thoroughly since I'd taken part, had come to be called *Angkor*

Wat. The music was all the way weird, in my first opinion, Yoko Ono singing in a high wail over John's slow-chugging guitar, tabla drums in the background. But somehow it sparked and then combusted, Emily and Vlad effortlessly complementary, needing only a rhythm to make things work, and in wonder you saw the elastic and capacious genius of the thing Sylphide had made.

Emily, everyone remembers, was tremendous, her energy furious, her stage presence electric, every move extravagantly lauded by crowd and critic alike ("Black Panther meets Viet Cong in the form of Rare Beauty," went one typically backhanded effusion, *Detroit Free Press*). Gradually she became the focal point of the show, her various pieces rotating evening by evening, became in fact the one consistent star, something Sylphide must have known would happen, something Sylphide had no doubt engineered: her own replacement. First there was the gushing two-page review by Arlene Croce in *The New Yorker.* Next day, the famous photos of Emily wrapped around Vlad Markusak in the *Times* and then in every other newspaper around the country and around the world, then every magazine, dazzling photographs. Oh, and of course the famous Emily poster in every little girl's and every college boy's room across the nation, different reasons. Sylphide kept herself far in the background, never took the stage but never missed a minute, watched from a side box, flanked nightly by new guests.

I forget how many millions of 1970 dollars went to Dabney's Children of War charities from the Shoebox shows. But that success set off a decades-long avalanche of giving, and the foundation was able to build a solid endowment, all the while taking care of kids in Vietnam, Congo, Bangladesh, Honduras, Argentina, Bosnia, Sri Lanka, and just about every other country in the world. Dabney's vision; Sylphide's brilliant execution.

I wished Kate could have enjoyed it. But she saw it a different way: Dabney being exploited for the furtherance of his ungrateful widow's career.

WHEN I GOT to Princeton the next summer—no longer living life for my father—Keshevsky put me under strict discipline, took me out of scrimmages if I didn't do exactly as he said, gave me written quizzes on the playbook, put me in charge of team laundry my entire freshman year, convinced me to join his Episcopalian church (not that he could make me attend), escorted me to the barbershop (not a buzz cut, but a capitulation nevertheless), assigned me cleanup duties at all the team meals and picnics. He forbade me any personal travel during the season, even to go see Emily (who kept nothing more than a home base in New York, but remained my girl, more or less, and then just less), made me a team player again, made himself the man in my life, pure generosity. As a team the Princeton Tigers did pretty well during my tenure, four winning seasons, good enough for three league championships, the last of the great football years for the Ivy League.

I was a top-end student, too, but amid all those valedictorians with clear life plans I wasn't one of the very best. I had a tendency to moon, always thinking about my mother, whom I missed more terribly as the months and years progressed. I majored in art history, of all things, wrote an honors thesis on Kandinsky, whom Mom had loved, something very academic concerning his connection to contemporary dance, about which I affected to know a few things. Another favorite course was archeology, all that digging in the past, but again for Mom, who'd majored in it, not that it got her anywhere but Westport. I liked psychology, too, for its application to my father's life, my sister's, my own. In the dry tones of the case studies I heard my mother's voice, sure, practical, more than a little judgmental, though trying not. Working against her striver's snobbery, I eschewed the secret societies and the eating clubs. I avoided dates, as well, caressed the speckled heart in my pocket, always feeling the heart: maybe I'd gone a little crazy. Maybe someone would write a case study about me.

As for Sylphide, I knew only what everyone knew. I searched the libraries and bookstores for images, for news of her travels, stared at her many spreads in *Dance* magazine, in *Vogue*, in *Paris Match*, scoffed at the articles, all of them full of mistakes and mythology and plain misinformation, proud that in her face I saw things no one else in the world could see, proud that I'd made the connection that Mom had so wanted for herself.

PART FOUR

Destroying Angel

17

As the restaurant came into focus, Kate and I grew further apart. It's possible I was trying to push her away, but that was not conscious. Jack didn't want her around me, for one thing—we caused one another too much excitement, he said, but he was being polite: excitement was hardly the word. For another thing, I hadn't launched the great worldwide search for Dad's briefcase that my sister had envisioned, and she was plain mad. Also, though she'd made peace with the idea, she really didn't like me opening a restaurant in Westport, felt it exposed us both to something she couldn't quite articulate, pity or scorn, or some sort of combination—those tragic Hochmeyer kids, their loser father.

THE FIRST DAY of my involuntary vacation before Firfisle opened was unseasonably freezing, depressing, Lizard alone at Hochmeyer Haven, Etienne and RuAngela having taken for themselves the room they'd booked for me at some quaint inn in Southport—no refund possible, so why shouldn't they? I much preferred house arrest to a pile of pillows stinking of potpourri.

Major League Baseball playoffs were underway, but I could hardly make sense of the games. I kept turning off the television, feeling I had to get to work. I perambulated, back and forth from the kitchen table to the couch to the car, back and forth, forth and back, TV on, TV off.

Light snow already ended, maybe a half-inch when I'd hoped for a blizzard, still only October. The truth slowly sank in: I was frazzled. Etienne had made me a gallon of some kind of Fusion udon-noodle soup, a complicated pot of flavors with tempura of root vegetables for me to heat and add.

With the prospect of relaxation all my ghosts visited, of course, or anyway called: Kate let the phone ring a good fifty times to get me out of the shower. "I dreamed of waiting tables," she said. "I was very good at it."

"Well," I said warily. "Of course you were."

Then the classic Kate non sequitur: "You want to know the difference between a mental hospital and prison?"

"Okay. But first, your dream. Where did it take place?"

She was not to be deterred: "People in prison? Most of them are guilty as charged. But they think they've done nothing wrong. At McLean? Everyone sick and blameless? They're sure they've done wrong."

"Do you think you've done something wrong?" I said.

"Don't psychoanalyze me," she said.

Quickly, I said, "There's probably a job for you at Firfisle. I mean, there's definitely a job there for you. We're opening in a week and if it takes off, we're going need all kinds of people."

"All kinds of people. I see what you mean. What kind am I?"

"Kate, why are you talking about McLean?"

She hung up, bang.

I opened the rice wine that RuAngela had packed with E.T.'s soup, tried a tiny glass, found it strange, tried to move my thoughts forward from Kate, found my way only as far as Emily, a blessing, as the next stop on that particular train was Barb and Nick Hochmeyer, sitting right there, either side of me at the table. I poured a bigger glass of the wine. RuAngela was right. It was very fine cold. I drank more. Somehow, the soup didn't seem necessary.

Just a couple of weeks to go. The town had approved us, though not unanimously—one of the selectmen had gone to high school with Dad and recalled him at the public hearing as a "one-man crime wave." Luckily, the others weren't in favor of visiting the sins of the father upon the son. Our twenty-one tables had come, a hundred chairs in transit. Ferkie the mushroom man would bring wild fungi on Mondays starting the day I was back. The produce was coming from four farms local, one bigger distributor, also our own garden, which had had a fine first summer.

The pasta flours were coming down from Canada with the pasta chef,

Colodo Doncorlo, a tiny older woman who barely spoke English. No reason we couldn't fit Kate in, if it would help her.

Okay, I was back to Kate. Also, the rice wine was gone. I climbed the stairs unsteadily, performed my ablutions, fell into bed and tried for sleep. Midnight, two o'clock, four o'clock, four-thirty, five, each ghost returning for her hour: Emily, Kate, Mom. And of course Perdhomme and Kaiser, and my completely vincible dad. So sleep didn't come, didn't come, didn't come, something rapping at my bedroom window, dreamcraft no doubt, even as distinct as it was: *tap-tap, tap-da-tap,* impossible rhythm, second floor, must be hail, that kind of night, that trippy, tricky Japanese wine. So to the kitchen for the big glass of water. I ate a banana, then a nice pear, stood staring, listening, eventually pulled out a couple of pounds of dried, mixed-species wild mushrooms Ferkie had provided as samples. I'd sneaked them from the restaurant's incipient pantry days before, didn't want my partners shutting me down too completely. I could rest when I was dead. As my mother used to say.

Ferkie had dried the fungi in a homemade sun-and-wind system of his own invention, and it was true, they were unusually fragrant and whole. My plan was to make a kind of flour out of them, something you could use to make pure-mushroom pastas, perhaps, or mushroom breads. I got the mortar and pestle out, broke the mushrooms down, went to work experimenting with rare powders.

Tap-tap at the patio doors, more sleet, lively images of Emily after she'd ditched her parents on the way to Ancestor's Day in Korea, the way the pants she'd borrowed from Kate's closet fit her: baggy, gaping, plenty of room for a hand. Why contemplate the difference between love and lust? Emily Bright loved me, and love for her was inextricably a physical thing. She lived for the moment, and my moments with her had been fine. I hadn't been as lucky as Kate, hadn't found grown-up romance before the cataclysm.

Tap-tap-tap.

Outside I stood barefoot in the soggy snow, the precipitation having simply stopped, cloud cover breaking into a chill pink dawn, the world still as an egg in a nest. I don't know how long it took me to notice the footprints, someone in misshapen bare feet, nearly a child's prints. No, stocking feet, toes indistinct, the wrinkles of fabric evident, that kind of packing snow, a one-way trail. What creature was this? I ventured out into the night hugging my pajamas around me, followed the elfin prints, leaving my own more monstrous ones, painfully barefoot. Hurrying, I followed the sprite's trail down to the pond and along its partly frozen shore. At the dam end whoever it was had made an incredibly long leap over the boggy, half-frozen brook, a leap I couldn't hope to make, even with a stride like mine. I landed in the icy water running, then sprinting, nearly falling, catching my balance and trotting as fast as I could on the impressionable snow up the great lawns of the High Side, followed the trail to an ornate hatchway cut into one of the large carriage doors of the poolhouse.

This was the only building on the premises I hadn't been allowed to see in the weeks I'd hung around the High Side during the run-up to *Children of War:* "Something must be private," as Sylphide had told me disingenuously. I gathered even then that it was a place Dabney had used, just the look on her face, the fade in her voice. To call it a poolhouse was correct in that it housed the pumps and heaters and equipment for the maintenance of the two enormous old-fashioned pools, but the building was another of the Chlorine Baron's fantasies, a half-size replica of the carriage house at Balmoral, the queen's residence in Scotland, twelve carriage bays with mini-grand doors, two dozen horse stalls just big enough for the legendary teams of miniature horses the bogus Baron had affected. Anyone who'd read the big *Life* magazine story on Dabney in the early sixties knew that. I stood there freezing in the snow a long moment, then—no other choice but frostbite—quietly tried the hatch, found it open.

Inside, something of a barn, slightly warmer than the night. I looked in each stall, each bay, dancing from foot to foot. One of the miniature carriages was still there, a beautifully made thing, tiny lamps, small wheels, gilt frame, leather seats, all kid-size, no one inside. At the back of the building I found a wet sock on the bottom step of a set of otherwise unpromising stairs, climbed them to another door. Which creaked open to reveal a splendid drawing room, everything a little too small, certainly too small for me, decor unchanged from the 1920s. Shivering, I spied another sock in its own puddle under an archway. I ducked through and into an elegant little living room, looked into a scaled-down kitchen, a formal dining room huge even in half-size, pair of soggy blue jeans on the floor in front of an open door. Which led into a hallway along which were several little bedrooms decked out as for the children of royalty: canopy beds, candelabra, bathrooms, sink rooms, toilet rooms. The Chlorine Baron had been a Napoleon, under five feet tall, I'd read, and a famous lover of plumbing, human or porcelain.

A dozen small doors to try. Nothing. At the end of the hall, I spied a tiny pair of green-striped tap-pants, scrunched where they'd been shed in front of an open closet door, shelves of neatly folded sheets and towels, a lot of towels, perhaps hundreds, puzzling shaft of light. I knew enough about the High Side by then to venture in. Of course the back wall was a door. I pushed through into a grand little bedroom, found my snow fairy asleep under a neat sheet and quilt in the oddly small double bed. She breathed emphatically, not quite snoring, curled up on herself like a forest fawn, no pretending. I leaned close, kissed her pocked cheek, forever the smell of jasmine about her. The bed had been made up for two, the pillow beside hers so inviting, the guest-side covers still folded back. Her naked shoulders rose and fell. She snuffled, pulled her hands up in front of her face. The light came from a bathroom, like sunlight through the flung door. I felt my heart in my chest, pushed the ingenious false panel closed, checked the ornate lock on the real door to the room (it was snapped tight), stepped over a wet gray T-shirt and into the bathroom lights, bright and hot and yellow as the sun. I could wait for her to wake.

The bathroom was not one room but several, in the style of the Baron, a kind of porcelain landscape, grottoes and glens. Toiletries were laid out on a bench as if for an expected guest—toothbrush, comb, razor, towels, soap, shampoo and conditioners, everything I needed to get ready for bed. I pulled off my wet trousers, hoped that in my weariness I was reading the situation correctly, stripped out of my shirt and underclothes. The bathtub was a kind of fjord with high walls. The sun, an enormous heat lamp in the ceiling, seemed to go behind a cloud. What if at home I'd slept soundly, hadn't noticed her footprints in the snow? What seemed a fanciful rockslide turned out to be a stile to climb into the tub; what seemed a great carved vine supported by snakes was a railing to hold. Had that been she tapping at my windows? I turned the heads of a pair of matched oxen, and the water came plummeting off several shelves that made waterfalls, quickly growing very hot. She must have been given a ride by Chun, then run home. My own thawing feet felt scalded. I plucked at the oxen, pulled at the wheels of their cart, but the diverter for the shower turned out to be the head of the drover, who, if he looked to the left, released a dozen spouts from the mouths of all the various creatures around him, and rain—an absolute tropical downpour—dozens of nozzles hidden in the clouds painted in the ceiling tiles, quickly warming. The sunlamp came in and out as if clouds were passing. I washed, rinsed luxuriantly. When I turned the water off, the sun reappeared, as if after a storm. I climbed out, wrapped myself in the heavy bathrobe I hadn't noticed till that moment, brushed my hair down over my shoulders with the Baron's golden brush. As I finished scrubbing my teeth, the artificial sun blazed.

Back in the warm bedroom, Sylphide had rolled onto her side, pulling the covers with her—she'd invaded my half of the elfin bed, leaving only an alley of mattress pressed up against the wall. Clean and warm, timid but tumid, too big to be a real lizard, and feeling as though I were following instructions, I slithered up onto the high old bed from its foot, crunch of horsehair beneath me, delicate unfolding of sheet and quilt, gradually assumed my narrow allotment, on the way inspecting her skin from ankles to forehead minutely. Finally her face was at my clavicle, my ear on the pillow that had awaited me, my feet hanging off the other end. Her breath was warm. I passed a hand through the air around her head, passed it closer, stroked her soft hair. She stretched, pushing a muscular leg between my thighs, then further between, lifted her arm across my ribs, continued her untroubled breathing. I put my own arm over her, spanned her night-warmed butt with my hand, slowly pulled her hips into mine, using all my strength to make it easeful, gentle.

But not imperceptible: her green eyes opened, very serious. Who was this?

Well, it was I.

She looked pleased with the results of her plan, not at all surprised to see me. "I am dreaming," she mewled, stretching—each limb, every finger, all her toes, her neck, her back, all the muscle groups, but in that instance working against another body, my own, thorough and languid, in the process pulling herself up and upon me like I was a mountain and she was weather.

"Say my name," I said.

"I am told we have six days," she said, arriving in this world from whatever world it was she lived in, both hands on my chest, legs straddling my hips, back bowed such that our abs brushed, her eyes intent on mine, scent of the same shampoo I'd used in the bucolic bathroom, but faint jasmine, too, and hot pheromones, the storm coming in around us. I felt myself falling into her world, the world she'd once told me I couldn't inhabit.

"My name," I said.

"Six days," she murmured. "That is what I am told."

"Told by whom?" I said.

She said something in Norwegian, *litten* something.

"Translate?"

"Mm. Little folk."

"My name," I said again.

"Firfisle," she said emphatically as she absorbed me, the ethereal made physical, never a body I loved more than that one or a body more completely given, none more completely taken. "Firfisle-mine."

THE CHLORINE BARON'S poolhouse was endlessly fascinating, mysterious, his fantasy all brought up to date via Percy Haverstock's fortune, every little geyser and mudpot working perfectly, miniature everything, room after room, first quality and perfectly restored, from the upholstery to the cuckoo clocks.

"Nice, *ja?* Not so shabby as when it was Dabney's lair. He and his dear friends hanging up on the miniature furniture like swollen lords."

"Hanging out," I corrected despite myself. We were lying on a bearskin that I'd only slowly realized was real. "Kate said Pete Townshend. And Eric Burdon once. And John Lennon all the time."

"Oik, *ja,* the British invasion, all of them. Along with Kate. Very cozy."

"I'm sorry."

"No-no. I knew anything about this."

"You mean nothing?"

"Nothing about this with Kate. Lots of girls out here with those boys, always girls, girls. Your Sylphide is turning her eyes away—I had no interest in their secrets. Kate is with Linsey, that is all I knew, taking perfect care of Linsey. I prized her, Lizano. She never bothers me. I have no idea of her and Dab. The one what bothers me is Brady."

"Dabney's brother?"

"More like a disease."

"The jailbird, right? Brady Rattner? With the beard and the sunglasses and all the motorcycle gear and the huge poof of hair?"

"Oh, that photo, of course. I guess everyone knows it. It's the only one they ever use. That was the legend he makes for himself. But Brady was only in borstal, like reform school, for maybe a half year. He is stealing lumber or something."

"And he was a stunt man, I remember."

"No-no, just more of his rubbish. He drove racecars a while with Dab's money, and then he crashes one on a public way drunk. Several weeks in lockup. That was all. Before Dabney bails him out. By the time he turns up here, he is shaved and haircut and suits like a businessman, very handsome rilly, with his workman swagger. He is happy in his skin, that one. He is sleeping with the upstairs girl, the downstairs girl, the girls from the ballet. And sleeping with Desmond, too, and with our own Vlad. He sniffs around your Katy always. She showed him her backhand at a dinner for President Nixon once. Oik, a real satisfying smash to the face, Brady with his fingers walking up her little skirt there in back of everyone. She is breaking his nose, beautiful, Secret Service guys escorting him out. Another time Dabney is on the road—is with Kate—and here is Brady slipping into *my* bed, just about *has* me before I wake enough to understand. I *bant* him from the house, completely and forever."

"Banned."

"Yes, *bant*. But Dabney is patient with him like with everyone, his little jealous brother, who wants to be business manager. Our worst time together, Dabney and me, very tense time. I don't know how much money we spent on Brady. Always with his schemes. Songs for Dabney to write, foolish business deals. Dabney makes him come apologize to me, so unsincere, you can imagine, hoo, hoo, hoo. I am hating him more than ever after. I double bant him: no more in the house, not ever. And Dabney sick of him, too, by then. So he connects Brady up with your father, two dogs with one leash. Is why I am telling you all this. They got along pretty good, too. Dabney giving them mother-goose chases, days away sometimes. Just so he could have his hours with Kate, I understand now, so your father would not know. I am traveling, traveling, Dabney is traveling. And so it is your poppa and Brady, Brady and your poppa."

"My father was here that much?"

"*Ja*. Right in this poolhouse here. Your father was very polite, something sweet about him, but so desperate. The way he carries himself! Like a bag of laundry! Always begging Dabney to invest. And Dabney lets him manage some large sum of money. Because of Kate, of course. And the money is lost some complicated way. I will never forget it: Freddy is throwing him out, right down the High Side stairs. Your poppa, he isn't fighting back, but Brady, he will not leave—somehow he is in this, too—he is arguing and shouts and tries to punch Dabney and sweet Dab is giving the okay, and so Freddy beats Brady like an egg and thrown him down the stairs after your poppa, those big stone stairs. And you know Nicholas, he's back in five minutes, begging on his knee. And of course, because of Kate, he is forgive. Brady, no. Dr. Chun drives Brady to the hospital—pretty bad, bloody and broken—and Brady never come back. Never saw him again. Poof."

"Your own brother-in-law!"

"My own beast, you mean." She rubbed her shoulder, ran a finger along the worst of the many scars left from failed surgeries. "*Ja*, oik. Bad times." She disentangled herself from me, rose from the bearskin rug, padded naked to one of the several little kitchens, found a big orange there, peeled it busily, broke it, dropped a section on my chest as she passed back by—silhouette in firelight—floated on down the skinny corridor and through the closet into what had become our bedroom. "No more talk," she said. "It is ruining my mood."

THE HEAD OF the High Side housekeepers discreetly dropped off exquisite meals. Maybe a housekeeper had done the same for Kate and Dabney. I kept thinking of them trysting there, thinking of the night the guy crashed his car, my poor sister. The things we didn't know about her. Kate and Sylphide waiting up together for news, Kate come to the dancer's room in tears, maybe Desmond the one with the heart to let her know: Dabney missing, still missing, then found. No need for Kate to confess to any affair—it was plain from the brand of tears: she was in love. And poor Sylphide, the death and the betrayal, all at once.

The dancer and I used the whole suite, all the eight or nine little bedrooms, all the grottoes and virtual hot springs, the waterfall rainforests, the warmed towels in endless supply. We abandoned our clothing within a day and a half, all those little fireplaces blazing. False afternoon by pretend evening her feet came unknotted, her blisters less angry. My sore knees came quiet, my stiff hands loose.

We dropped the subject of my sister, my father. We dropped the subject of Dabney, of his awful brother, all of it. Restaurant Firfisle was not a subject, ceased to exist. Dance was not a subject, football, no. Tenke was a physical person, a great studier of bodies, absently compared the length of our hands, the circumferences of our wrists, the mobility of her joints, mine, not in passing but for hours, even during lovemaking, of which we didn't tire.

I found my pants one night while she slept (I had only the clothes I'd been wearing when I arrived, not that it mattered, washed and folded repeatedly whenever I wasn't looking), retrieved the speckled stone from its place in a front pocket, kept it in my hand through a very long kiss and then through an extended, indolent lovemaking session. When she dozed next, nowhere else to put it, I placed the greenish heart gently in the hollow between her clavicles, the small, smooth stone like a necklace without a chain, admired my work, and fell asleep myself, her belly as a pillow. When I woke she was watching me closely, night or day, who could tell? Not a word about the stone, not another word, more lovemaking, no stone to be found.

One of the last false afternoons I said I didn't want ever to part, and shortly she disappeared—slipped into one of the baths, no other door but the one wide open, and then just didn't come out. When I looked she was missing, vanished. My one wave of anger, which was in fact fear. Then a tiny voice calling. From where? The back of the glacier-themed shower, secret door like moving an iceberg, a hidden room behind, like a bunk-house at a summer camp. I ducked in, puzzled, and from a top bunk she leapt upon me frontally, trusted my hands, held my ribs with her thighs, moist contact.

I walked her around the whole crazy place a half hour, she steering me with her hips, her feet clenching, her mouth at my neck, love bruises to take home with me in the dozens, a carnal tour of the Chlorine Baron's strange legacy, till I fell with her onto a beautiful miniature psychiatrist's couch done in soft leather, pumping at her furiously, not my style, not at all, the one time she didn't giggle when she came, or *went,* as she would put it.

18

Our first trial run at Firfisle was on a Saturday evening in late October, nuts. We'd been inviting contractors for months, set up a full schedule of reservations, all these familiar faces and their families and friends. RuAngela acted as hostess in a sassy pink dress and nail extensions. Our wait staff amounted to two failed soap actors Etienne had found someplace, lovely manners and jocky good looks, no experience, panicky. In the kitchen it was only Etienne and I, also a dour but talented dessert girl who would have to double as salad person, peeving her mightily. No line cooks, as yet: Etienne and I were it, prepping right up against the opening bell. We had no signage and no exterior lights, so RuAngela carved a couple of pumpkins and put them in the street-side windows. And here came the guests, all in a crowd, better than ghosts, but still . . .

Total collapse, a boisterous party with free food, no more than that, everything breaking down. We'd forgotten screws in two of the tables during set-up and they fell over, drinks, flowers and all. The pared-down menu went out in frenzied bursts, my tricky culinary-school ticket system as useless as Etienne had warned. And the toolbox crowd drank a *lot*. Outside, Olulenu parked the cars too tight, forgetting that people wouldn't leave in the order they'd arrived, like working a Rubik's Cube to extricate them.

Some measure of the general confusion was my fault: I couldn't get Sylphide out of my head, a cinema's worth of images, great performances, scene after scene, a very sad ending. I'd awakened the last morning of my vacation and found my dancer missing, found one of the maids cleaning up, a squirrelly older gal called Maria, who crossed herself at the sight of me naked, no English at all, not a trace. She clucked when I tried Spanish—presented my clothing washed and folded, umpteenth time. For the first time in days I dressed, then, increasingly anxious, searched all the secret alcoves, but this was no game: my lover was gone. I let myself out, marched down the muddy lawn bereft and shoeless, leapt the brook. At home I dressed for work, work my one salvation.

Etienne was alone in the restaurant, of course, early as it was. Hugs in the kitchen, happy greetings. It wasn't till noon that I found the speckled stone, a rough heart sitting square in the center of my butcher-block workstation. No way I would have missed it, impossible.

"Not me, bro," Etienne kept saying.

Neither of us had seen a thing, not so much as a shadow.

THE FIRFISLE TEAM regrouped and the next dry run went a couple of light years better, and a lot less eventful. Our guests were people we'd met in the community, people who'd go forth for us, we hoped, like Dwight Leonard, like my dentist, like the priest from Mrs. Paum's house, and a score or so of acquaintances Etienne and RuAngela had made, including the entertainment editor from the local paper, long and skinny and hurried, definitely not an eater.

Eight o'clock and my sister arrived, a mere hour late, Jack on her arm. We'd reserved the best of the window tables for them, moonlight on wavecrests and slow-strobing lighthouse—*all clear, all clear*—and the green and the red running lights of commercial boats and the buoy lights blinking out there and the green light at the end of our cracked seawall, the view as dramatic as I'd dreamed. I stepped out to greet them—more practice, really, the calm chef in the midst of a maelstrom.

"Just gorgeous," Jack said.

"How about a Bloody Mary," said Kate sharply. She looked very thin, or maybe it was the dark velvet dress, purple or black you couldn't tell, her eyes alight, every man in the place focused upon her.

"Maybe a Virgin?" I said.

"It hardly matters," said Kate. "Just stuff it with fucking vegetables."

"Absolutely gorgeous," Jack repeated, looking all around.

"I'll make a salad out of it," I said. Didn't Jack notice Kate's moods anymore? He sat there with the most affable expression, perhaps leaving the heavy hand to me, keep the peace at home.

"A Bloody Mary, David. And just keep 'em coming till it's all one bloody mess."

"Kate," I said gently.

"A shot of gun on the side," she said as if she were just making pleasant puns.

"Jack?"

He shook his head. People go crazy in increments, I thought; perhaps Jack had been lulled along and hadn't noticed. He shook his head some more, put his hand on my wrist. "This time you help me," he said, normal tones.

"I looked up *firfisle*," said Kate. "It took me four hours in that pretty library in Madison. You'd have thought I would have known it was fucking *Norwegian*."

"Kate," Jack said.

"I'll feel better with some food," said Kate, mocking him preemptively.

He pretended not to notice, or maybe didn't notice: "You always feel better when you eat, sweetie."

"My Bloody Mary, *Firfisle*. Or aren't you the fucking bartender?"

"Virgin," said Jack.

"Oh, that'll never happen again," said my sister, suddenly calm. Ru-Angela had slipped up behind me, took over the conversation:

"Katy, where did you *get* that dress?"

"In a dumpster," Kate said, which wasn't true, of course, and which was really funny, at least to Ru-Ru, whose manly laugh is hilarious to everyone, even Kate, even poor Jack, anyway we laughed.

A FEW DAYS later, Halloween, we opened for real and put all our effort into a few brilliant dishes from the abundance around us: Etienne had harvested leeks that morning and braised them, for example, made tarts. Our grumpy dessert girl—Brie was her name, soon to be fired for the attitude—had all the greens she needed and nice tomatoes from under our hoop house, new sharp cheese from the dairy guy, E.T.'s help with a dressing. The final product looking oddly like a dessert, for which I gave her praise: sometimes that's all people want.

Thirty covers, nine tables, very easy, perfect service, our first cash receipts.

I'd taken Kate up to McLean the morning previous. Jack couldn't do it, not again, but got in his Volvo and went to work like any old day. It might have been she'd dosed or even overdosed herself on whatever meds she hadn't been taking for however many weeks up to that point; anyway, she was awfully calm, quiet, abstracted, distant, little remorseful sighs: another failure, as she saw it, hard to take. It's only about a three-hour drive, Madison to Boston, and that's going slow, not a word to say the whole way, though I commented on the sights—the mouth of the Connecticut River at Old Saybrook and Lyme, the submarine base at Groton with a couple of nukes in port, stuff we'd loved spotting when we were kids, the big whaling ships on display at Mystic Seaport, where we had lunch.

Over lobster rolls I said something about Dad, how he'd brought us there when we were little, how he'd gotten in a tussle with a Seaport guard because we were walking up the exit ramp to the ship instead of using the stairs, which of course was Dad all over, one of those formerly funny memories, vivid, so vivid, his white shirt ironed and his face growing dark, *You can't tell Commodore Hochmeyer what to do!* And the wise ancient guard who knew how to shut him down: *Sir, is this the kind of behavior you want to teach these beautiful kids?*

Kate gazed at me a long time, perfectly calm, a flag with no wind: "You think he was so ineffectual. You think he was such a poseur."

"I didn't say that. Though he did try too hard. Socially, you know? And at business. I mean, he tried too hard to impress. He just wanted to please. And that was a strength, too. I mean as a parent he was incredibly warm and kind and loving and present. He'd do anything for us."

"You're like the fucking Mom club. 'Trying too hard to please.' "

I let a couple of breaths go by, spoke calmly as I could: "Her word was for him was *inept*. Remember? I never said it. She expected everything to run on schedule and per plan. But then, that was Mom's strength. She was chilly, I agree. And she pushed him too hard, okay. She could be so critical of him, true. But she was totally practical, forceful, always with the plan and the schedule, not many hugs, but she's the one who made athletes of us, for example. Am I right? She's the one who pushed us toward elite colleges."

Not a ripple: "Oh, 'elite.' Oh, 'for example.'" And then she sang, that mocking kid's thing, two notes, one minor: "*Mom club! Mom club! Mom club!*"

"Kate."

"Like, oh, *Dad,* such a loser. Oh, *Dad,* always with the putrid decisions. Oh, *Dad,* you got me *killed.*"

"Okay, Kate."

"But you know that boyfriend of Emily's?"

"No, Kate. Katydid. I don't know what you're talking about."

"Commodore Hochmeyer wasn't so fucking ineffectual about *that* kid."

"Katy, sister, eat something."

More mocking, a kid imitating her tormentor, real echoes of our father, Jack's famous phrase: "'You'll feel better when you eat.'"

"Exactly."

She picked up her pickle, seemed to swallow it whole, gagged a little, picked up her chips and crunched them in her teeth one by one by one, didn't touch the lobster roll, which I wrapped for the ride back. Plus now the weirdness of having the poolhouse in common, no way to talk about it. I couldn't ask about Brady Rattner, because how would I know? Brady with his hand up her skirt, Dabney buying world-class paintings for her at auction, Dad oblivious, just trying to get someone somewhere somehow to invest the big bucks so he could impress his monstrous boss. So it *was* Dad behind the pounding Mark Nussbaum took?

Whoa.

Shaking off the thought, and trying for something more honest, I said, "I hear Dad was at the High Side all the time."

"Yes?"

"I hear he hung out in the poolhouse. All those fountains and forests and fancy toilets and stuff. Oxcarts to turn on the shower."

"You hear this," she said.

"And he hung with Dabney's brother sometimes, huh?"

"Oxcarts," she said. And then she wouldn't look at me, grabbed her lobster roll back, unwrapped it, ate it in three bites. "So much you haven't told me," she said, but not in a way that made me think she wanted to hear.

"So much," she kept repeating as we got in the car, as we drove. "So much you haven't told me." And then, "Firfisle." Just that, over and over, thirty miles, forty-five, sixty: "Fir-fucking-fisle. So much you haven't said, *Lizard*."

They greet you in the lobby, two big male nurses and a lady psychiatrist, all three of them people Kate seemed to know. You get just a few seconds to say good-bye, hug like a hockey check from Kate, no tears, never any tears from Kate.

Me, I cried in the parking lot an hour.

THOSE FIRST FEW months there were some very quiet nights at the restaurant, including a Tuesday when no one came in, not a single customer, pretty sobering. There was an amateurish, supposedly tongue-in-cheek review in the local paper, that skinny guy we'd fed for free ("Westport's Tragic Son Makes Tofu Touchdown"), but that was it for media attention those lonely weeks and then months (and so irritating that I wrote the editor an ill-advised letter, or rant: I wasn't anybody's son and Restaurant Firfisle would never use tofu or other pre-processed foods in *anything*). On the positive side, the slow pace meant there was plenty of time to invent new dishes. Never have restaurant employees eaten so well.

Spring and the advent of warm weather brought more people down to the waterfront, and with a little more traffic we started attracting more guests, and with some word of mouth attracting more. We had a string of busy Saturdays, and then full weekends, and then, suddenly, starting in June, we were honestly bustling four days a week, then five, then seven, never a lull. By the time Jillian Jeffries, the *Times* food critic, dined unbeknownst with her three tasting friends (two separate evenings and apparently a third evening solo), we were making and serving beautiful food consistently. I had no idea that Jeffries and Sylphide were such great friends, didn't learn that till much later (and not to any chagrin, really, Jillian being a woman of integrity; the dancer had only steered her our way). The adulatory review came out just before Memorial Day (as part of a "Summer in the Country" series of articles), and entirely because RuAngela had always expected and planned for triumph, we were more or less ready for the onslaught that ensued. By July we were booked for the rest of the summer, all the way to September 15, when, incredibly, we started operating in the black.

Somewhere in there, Kate had got out of McLean, a ten-month stay, very serious. She and Jack hadn't let me know she'd been released, and this was hurtful, except that I hadn't been in touch with them, had dropped away completely, Mr. Restaurant Man. Etienne finally made me do it, dialed the phone for me and handed it over. I thought I'd be speaking to Jack, had a whole script written in my head, how busy I'd been, how buried. But it was Kate who answered. She sounded heavily drugged, unnaturally ingratiating, as if her mouth and mind were full of sand.

"Well, that's enough chatter," she said flatly, and flatly hung up. We'd spoken for no more than a minute.

19

Another year passed, Restaurant Firfisle a runaway train, pure excitement, like new love. Emily saw an article about us in *The Miami Herald* and deigned to write, just enough ink to say that she'd seen Sylphide on a recent European tour and had met the great ballerina's sweet new boyfriend, the Swiss financier Daniel Tancredi.

Great.

Sylphide, it seemed, had hooked Emily up with a prestigious performance on German television. After, they'd all gone out to the boyfriend's castle in the countryside for a champagne dinner, and she and Sylphide had stayed up till all hours like girls at a slumber party. Sylphide still thought Emily and I were such a great couple! So did Emily! She'd be home to see her folks one of these days, but I shouldn't hold my breath! She sent love to Etienne. No love for the Lizard, just a quick xo.

And a P.S.: Carter said hello.

SYLPHIDE RETURNED THE following fall to choreograph a new production of her *Madame Curie* for the American Ballet Theater. I saw that in the *Times,* but not until the day after she and her new husband and Vlad Markusak and three society ladies appeared for dinner at the restaurant. I emerged from the kitchen mid-meal, shook everyone's hand, kissed the women's cheeks, my heart pounding, everything else sinking. I resigned myself, welcomed Mr. Tancredi with warm smiles, real smiles. He seemed like a good guy, seventy if he was a day. Daniel, they called him.

The two of them were High Side for the next several months (you were never *at* the High Side, you were simply High Side). They only invited me to the biggest parties, parties too big for me to do anything but shake

Sylphide's hand and lean down to kiss her ear in a receiving line. At a soiree for her foundation I waited almost an hour, got to study her as she posed a couple of risers up on the grand stairway, finally had my moment, kiss-kiss. Anyone watching would have thought she didn't know me, that she only greeted a fading sports figure, the up-and-coming restaurateur, but they couldn't see how I slipped the speckled stone into the bodice of her tight, strapless dress, couldn't feel how she let my fingers linger a moment against her breast, couldn't hear when she whispered my name in my ear, and then a familiar Norwegian phrase, something from our time together, something we'd said over and over again, something a little shy of love, which was how she wanted it: *jeg ar ohso glad i deg*—"I am so very fond of you."

ANOTHER YEAR PASSED, and another, Restaurant Firfisle more an avalanche than a runaway train, a cavalcade of employees and regular customers, contractors making improvements, a thoroughgoing patio under a downpour-proof awning, a dock off the seawall to receive guests arriving on boats, attractive to Jack and Kate, who began to visit monthly, a great relief: my sister was back, calm and rather neutral, effects of new meds, but really herself, Jack back on his game, as well, cruising toward retirement.

I saw in *Sports Illustrated* that Emily Bright and Carter Jeffries had been wed in Miami, photos of their Cadillac procession to Dolphins Stadium, bride and groom standing up out of limo sunroof, double thrust of the knife of regret.

And shortly thereafter, Desmond wrote to say he was ill, an extended battle with HIV. Just a few months later, I spotted his obituary in the local paper, a short column: born and raised in Dorcester, Massachusetts, the rough side of Boston, employed by Sylphide, survived by his mother and eleven siblings.

His sad death explains why the note (I've still got it) is the only one I ever got from Sylphide in her own handwriting, an aspect of her personality I'd never seen, a tiny semi-script full of spelling errors. She'd never done school English, barely done school at all. What's not explained is how the note in its gold-piped envelope got into my front pants pocket one day, to be discovered when I was at work. She certainly wasn't in Westport. *Time* magazine, in fact, reported that she was taking a long-delayed honeymoon month at the Swiss-alpine estates of Daniel Tancredi, after which they'd begin their very public move to London and her directorship of the Royal Ballet.

I waited till I was home at the kitchen table to open the stiff envelope, pulled out the stiffer card. Of course the lump tucked in the fold was the speckled stone. Which fell out and bounced off my lap and onto the floor, skittering. I recovered it, dropped it again, recovered it, clutched it too tightly, dropped it yet again, left it there for what would be several hours, let myself read, my hands trembling:

> Belov'd Reptil: This litten Hart will not be makin You hapy but it is my Hart and Your Hart, too, and is belongin in your Pokket deep. Daniel is gude and also vurry deep, but he is not my Firfisle, no. Firfisle-mine, I Love You. But kinsidder the Worlt I live in. Forever this Hart. Whatsoever else I am, I am Yours.

20

Restaurant Firfisle had been open almost five years the night Mr. Perd-homme came in with his sidekick, the man Dad had called Kaiser, the killer. And just when life had come to seem so, so simple: a restaurateur, his staff, the food, former lovers safely distant, everything present tense, the first periods of weeks on end since the murders that he did not see the blooming petals of blood, that he didn't think of his folks, the black hole in the barrel of that gun. It all came rushing back: Dad's cupidity, Mom's frustration with him, his mounting lies, the pressure she put on him.

Mr. Perdhomme. His coldness as he dared sit in my restaurant and eat my best food. And Kaiser's face in younger then older iterations, his preternatural calm whether shooting people to death or ordering wild-mushroom sausages, the way the two of them, far from remorseful, had put themselves directly in my path, right in my realm, confident they held all the knives.

A kiss Mom had given me when I was nine, a kiss on the forehead after a forgotten disappointment, but the kiss very much alive, the only kiss I can recall her giving me. And Dad, always with the mauling hugs.

The lights stayed on at the High Side those next few days, thousands of chandelier bulbs lighting dozens of windows. Simple facts: Mr. Perd-homme and Kaiser had been Sylphide's guests. And though I hadn't seen her for several years, she'd sent the two of them to Restaurant Firfisle, where, wisely or not, I'd treated them like kings. Irrefutable conclusions, stuff even Jack would have to credit, which I wrote on a guest check that night:

1) Kaiser and Perdhomme know each other.
2) Dad was about to testify about the crimes of Dolus.

3) Perdhomme ordered Dad's death to save his own skin.

4) Kaiser carried it out, and I was there.

5) Sylphide knows both men.

6) Her skin must have needed saving, too.

7) Sylphide has told them where I am.

8) Kate's intuition about her is much better than I want to believe.

9) Perhaps Kate's intuition should be trusted more.

10) Headline in Friday's *Times:* "Dolus Object of Massive New Probe."

11) Perdhomme's old crimes will come to light in such a probe.

12) I was a witness to one of the most violent of these crimes.

13) I am in trouble.

The next morning, a bright Sunday, I seethed and paced, circular rumination like I hadn't committed since I didn't know when, couldn't get it straight in my head what I'd say when I went over there to confront the great ballerina, couldn't get it straight in my head that a couple of decades had passed since the disaster, that I was not a pure and invincible seventeen years old, worked my station at Firfisle in a cloud so ugly that Etienne asked me if I was sick, put his hand to my forehead.

And I'm sorry to say I slapped the hand away, left the restaurant in a typhoon, stayed up all night brooding, planning: I would confront Sylphide in the morning. Monday early I was out on Dad's famous brick patio glowering across the pond.

But I'd blown it. If I'd read the *Times Magazine* when it arrived on Sunday, things might have been different. But, as always, I'd saved the whole thick paper for Monday, my one morning off. Long, adoring article about Sylphide's work in South America, a tour down the spine of the Andes, a series of benefits for Dabney's foundation, still called Children of War. She and her new husband were to leave Monday after a dawn press conference at Bradley Field in Hartford, where the foundation's private jets were based. Gone before I could get my answers.

Old anger returned, stale fear, long-expired fantasies of revenge. And worse yet, fresh trembling. Obviously, I was to be killed. I thought to call my sister, the only possible confidante and advisor, but Jack would murder me before Perdhomme and Kaiser got their chance—I couldn't bring Kate in till I'd come to some plan Jack couldn't dent with his conde-scension. I knew what he'd say: Call the police, call the D.A. in Danbury. He'd even offer to drive me up there.

But I knew that route. If I went to the authorities with this quarter-century-old complaint, nothing would happen. Or, even if some dedi-cated public servant took an interest, all I would succeed in doing would be tipping off Perdhomme, who'd just have to press Kaiser to kill me sooner.

I was on my own.

I dressed in my best old Miami suit, tied a good knot in a narrow tie, combed my hair back with a spot of petroleum jelly, brushed out the ponytail, a tough look on an imposing man, but not good enough as ar-mor went. So, in a box of Dad's things down in the basement I found his sap, a little lead-filled leather truncheon ungentle men of his generation often carried into nightclubs, say, or kept in the glove boxes of their cars. It sagged in my pocket like a spare penis—surely part of the weapon's al-lure for old Nick. At the Westport station, no faltering, none of that Dad stuff, I left my car at a meter, plenty of coins, and got on the train. From Grand Central I marched up Park Avenue, entered the familiar lobby of the Dolus building, marched past the security desk to the executive elevator bank. I would slug Perdhomme across the temple as soon as he recognized me. He'd drop and I'd hit him again, put a knee on his back, jerk his head up sharp to the side, break his neck, something I was plenty strong enough to do. What did consequences mean to me? I'd break his neck and leave him lying there, see to the dancer later.

But of course no elevator came: a keycard was required. And that left me to approach the guard, a scrawny lifer: "Here to see Perdhomme," I said.

"Sir?" the guard said.

And I repeated it: "Perdhomme."

"What company sir?"

"Dolus, of course. This company. What company do you think?"

"Dolus Investments? They left the building in 1971, sir." He went into a drawer in his stand, pulled out an index card. "They are now based in Dallas, Texas, sir. We have an eight-hundred number, sir."

I fondled Dad's sap in my pocket, impotent, useless thing, fell into a period of darkness like I'd never known: his killers had nearly made a killer out of me.

I BEGAN AGAIN to wonder if I was following Kate down the road to decompensation. Perdhomme's visit, the connection to Sylphide, the appearance of Kaiser, it all seemed to have affected my *personality*, like some pure form of stress someone had packed in a pipe and made me smoke. I had violence in my hands, my heart. Etienne thought I had every right to go nuts, treated me gingerly while I obsessed. But these were not magnificent thoughts, quite the opposite. I'd battled for years with Kate over Sylphide's supposed involvement in the murder of our parents, over the connection of those killings to the killing of Dabney Stryker-Stewart. To have Crazy May proved even slightly right required some serious re-wiring of all the processes of my heart and mind.

I had to tell Kate about the visitation. And Jack, too, I had to tell Jack. RuAngela and Etienne were keen on that: no more denial from Jack. We needed to make a plan with him and Kate, get all of us on the same page, the extended family finding a way to bring Perdhomme and Kaiser to justice. Sylphide, too, Etienne kept reminding me (speaking of denial!), my dancer, who'd apparently choreographed more things than I'd ever known.

October again, and that clear, slanting sunlight over the Sound. I got in the kitchen early the second Saturday, tuned the radio to NPR, which I'd be allowed to listen to until the prep crew came in at eleven—their smashy music after that. *Morning Edition* came on, and after a lot of worried talk about the economy, there was an item about the new Tenke Thorvald Dance Company. I listened like an owl in a tree—dead still, that is, turning my head, blinking my eyes—a long interview between Scott Simon and Conrad Pant, who was still Sylphide's manager: the great international treasure and her troupe would be at Lincoln Center for a week in mid-October, huge retrospective celebration of Sylphide's career.

By the time Etienne arrived, I was shattered, pacing the kitchen, try-ing not to be sick. "Kaiser and Perdhomme," I began, but that's not what

I meant to tell him. Try again: "Sylphide, bro. She's coming to town! They're coming to get me."

E.T. nodded soberly, stalwart chef, big cleaver in his fist. No words necessary: We would prevail. Simple superiority. It was time to talk to my sister, all right. No more messing around. He said, "You know how Jack and Kate are always trying to get me on that sailboat?"

"You would do that for me?"

"It's just a sail, Lizard. Proximity, close. Kate contained. And Jack has to listen to every word you say."

"You sound like Olulenu."

"I'll have your back, and I'll back you up. When I'm done leaning over the rail, that is, *bumbaclot*."

"Fuckery," I said.

LONG ISLAND SOUND was sharp with whitecaps, the air over it so dry that I could see the treetops of Long Island itself, seventeen or more miles away, the horizon lifted by shimmering mirages. Etienne had insisted on two life jackets, wore one of my Dolphins jerseys on top, looked like a bird-legged linebacker. Kate hadn't seen his gams before and kept giggling appreciatively—they were shapely and smooth as a teen girl's, also like a comic book, a hundred small and colorful tattoos.

"Your butt is so *fucking* cute," she kept saying, never so cheerful as around E.T., pinching at him as I pushed him onboard from the dinghy, never this cheerful in years, auspicious.

"What a morning," Jack kept saying. And he was right. Gorgeous. Crisp, clear, breezy, promise of a hot afternoon, the last sail of the year, early October: murder weather.

Jack showed E.T. where to sit, where to put his hands, and E.T. held on white-knuckle tight though we weren't yet off the mooring. I sat across from him in the big cockpit, held his knees to keep him from vibrating right out of the vessel. Kate leapt nimbly to the bow and unfurled the jib. It filled with a snap, the whole boat jerking to life.

"We're going?" Etienne cried.

"We're sailing," Jack said calmly. He maneuvered through the tight harbor over a swiftly incoming tide, real expertise. Kate kept busy, quickly unsnapping the mainsail cover, dropping it at our feet for me to fold and stow, stood ready at the sheets. Jack watched her every move fondly, critically. The two of them had been together twenty years, it occurred to me. He was in his late fifties by then, fit and irenic, same as ever except for the graying temples, the increasingly handsome face. E.T. watched Kate more warily: what if she did something *wrong* and everything exploded and we ended up in the drink? I set the jib and trimmed it and trimmed it again to Jack's instructions as we made the end of the large breakwater just opposite their house on Drixel Point.

Deep Song was a 1950s-vintage Concordia yawl, a sweet old wooden vessel painted midnight blue, teak planking, mahogany deck trim, length on deck just under forty feet, fast, elegant. Kate pulled at the lines to unfurl the main, a great flapping of canvas and squealing of pulleys as the sail climbed the mast. Jack pointed out the brails and spars, the handsewn seams, a man in love, a long-term relationship.

"But we have a motor? Just in case?" Etienne asked fervently. "I mean, how do we get back in if the wind's blowing *out*?"

Jack didn't betray any amusement. He said, "We'll tack in. But just in case, Cookie, we have the original Gray motorworks four-cylinder engine." We splashed out of the river and into a freshening wind, the sails and lines suddenly tightening, the boat heeling. "Goat Island," Jack said, and pointed across a perfection of waves backed by blue sky, a pile of rocks out there.

Kate slipped into the cockpit with us, sat close by Jack on the teak bench, her legs stretching toward me. In her tankini she looked like a surf babe stuck in a boat with a radically progressive senator and his bodyguards, ready to leap onto her shortboard and fly. I'd dug out my own old pair of swim trunks and tugged them on at the docks—what Kate did I'd do, though I was already freezing. My own legs, still powerful (as I wouldn't have hesitated to point out), were pale as underground asparagus and covered with goose bumps.

Jack brought *Deep Song* about, threw us tight to the wind. We quartered the swells, booming and shuddering progress. Etienne shrieked in exhilaration, water sheeting over the bow: "That's right, mo-fo, that's right, that's *right!*"

Jack laughed hard—something you didn't see often—and Kate laughed hard—something you didn't always want to see—and Etienne laughed and shrieked and the laughter was funny and made us laugh all the harder and Jack held the tiller and we all shouted and cheered, the boat fleeing into the next trough blind, cresting with a lurch to a view of the world in spray and spindrift, hilarious hiccups and snorts of laughter.

"We'd better all of us get into vests," Jack chortled.

"What!" Etienne shouted, bang into the next trough.

Kate struggled below, handed up orange life jackets, handed up a fleece for me, Jack's wool sweater, a towel for Etienne. We fought our way into the life jackets even as we shot up into the sky, alive.

JACK EASED INTO a sandy cove on a very small island somewhere off Long Island, a beach well configured for wading. Jack had been right—you don't get seasick when you're part of the ocean. Etienne was fine. We had about an hour and a half of tide by Jack's calculation, long enough for a leisurely lunch.

We spread blankets on the fine sand, and deftly Etienne laid out a middle-eastern feast on good paper plates: fol mudamas and kerba-kum, hummus and spiced baked nuts, baby house-pitas and eggplant tapenade, sweet tea, shocking little pickles, candied squash blossoms stuffed with curried rice and onions, pink linen napkins from the restaurant. I'd contributed tiny, spicy mushroom pastries filled with a cranberry chutney. "Eat counterclockwise for fertility," E.T. said. "Clockwise for wealth."

"What does random get you?" my sister said.

"Random for eternal life," our chef said.

Of course we all chose that, just dove in. When we were beyond stuffed he laid out sweets: sticky pistachio squares, chocolate and chilies, a chilled mango soup served in fresh little wooden bowls: nice.

Jack and Kate went off to explore the island, not much to see, a lot of rocks, a lot of trees, the pilings from an old fishing weir. They disappeared over the height of land, a faint path. Kate just looked good: healthy and happy and strong and wise.

"You got your speech?" E.T. said.

"I'll keep it short," I said, and reviewed it in my head: Perdhomme and Kaiser—the actual Kaiser—had dined at Restaurant Firfisle. Kaiser, the killer, a man I'd seen up close but who'd never been sought by the police (the poor court-appointed guard, badly wounded, reported that Dad had said "Hi, sir" to the shooter and not "Kaiser," and the guard's word, being professional, was strongly valued over mine, all his testimony deposed bedside at the hospital in Danbury). There was no physical evidence to connect Perdhomme to any crime, was the D.A.'s lament, no eyewitness to anything but a contract killing that might have been paid by anyone, and professional murderers very hard to trace. My mother? She was merely collateral damage in a war among criminals. I'd played this particular loop of tape in my head a million times, difficult to find the OFF button. But now we had Kaiser. And we had Perdhomme. And we had Kaiser and Perdhomme as a unit: same room together, same table at my restaurant, same car, same destination, High Side.

Etienne took my two hands, looked into my eye. "Remember, no mention of Sylphide. You concentrate on what we *know*. We don't let Kate distract you. We don't let Jackie shut you down."

"And don't call him Jackie, not to his face."

"He call me Cookie, mon! He gonna be Jackie."

Lying back on the blanket in the nice hot sand, trying to relax, I went over it yet again despite myself. Kaiser and Perdhomme, Perdhomme and Kaiser: in court, the defense had taken me apart, played me as the pitiable teenage kid. Dad's phone calls with Perdhomme, my best shot, had been dismissed before I could recount them: hearsay. The tape recordings I'd seen him make were nowhere to be found. Nothing about the High Side was deemed allowable; there was no connection to be made between the High Side and our side. Dad's shoes were just shoes.

The maître d' from Les Jardins was asked by the defense counsel to describe the shooter. "*Très* tall," he said. "Zhoulders *énorme*. Hands, *énorme!* Ze hair? *Très* long. *Comme les dieux mythologique!*" Not the shooter I had seen, not Kaiser, not the shooter I myself had just described to the court, not by a mile. Silence in the gallery.

Perdhomme's attorney pointed at me: "Is this our man?"

The look on the maître d's face—whoa—he'd gotten confused somewhere deep in his traumatized psyche, had plugged *me* into the shooter's role. The gallery, heavily stocked with Dolus ringers, broke into derisive laughter. Everyone knew the tenuous case against Perdhomme had just been blown. And there I was, not saying half of what I knew, represented and closely advised by the same lawyer Dad had been assigned, the corpulent McBee, who we should have known was on the take, rumpled guy like that driving a vintage XKE, laughing privately with the opposition at every recess. It only occurred to me many years later that someone in Dad's legal inner circle had to have told someone in the killer's circle the name of the restaurant Dad had picked for his freedom meal. Who else but McBee? He'd had no questions for Kate, who took the stand for all of three minutes and ranted about Dabney's death, how it was all connected, how innocent civilians were dying in Vietnam, how Dabney had stood against all that, sad heads shaking all around the room: No more questions, Your Honor. She had to be hushed by the judge as she launched into Nixon, and then Sylphide.

Kate liked to say she'd had a feeling of foreboding that day as she took her seat on the team bus to Ithaca. But in fact our parents were dead by the time she boarded. Jack heard late, too—I believe Detective Turkle himself called him, relayed the news businesslike. It wasn't till after five that afternoon that Jack got in his Volvo to bring the disaster to Kate in person. She'd played her first match methodically, picking the top Cornell seed apart in two quick sets. Jack found her at the hotel on campus, where there were dorms for visiting teams, found her in the cafeteria. He took her outside by the arm, relayed the news. And in her confusion she slapped him across the face. That was the story she always told. She slapped Jack with half the team watching out the leaded-glass basement windows of cafeteria in Willard Straight Hall. She got in the car with him to return to Connecticut, but they only made it as far as Binghamton, found a hotel and made love the whole night through, only got back in the car the next noon. And me home cleaning the house, cleaning every little corner, Mrs. Paum washing my clothes, cycle after cycle, trying to get the gore out.

The murder counts against Perdhomme were dismissed. And that effectively ended my role in the proceedings. Officially illusory, Kaiser was never seen or heard from again, though I looked, checking faces wherever I went, right up to the moment he appeared at Firfisle. The forensic audit of Dolus's tangled books and papers and internal memos—two more months—turned up absurdly unambiguous evidence that three people and three people alone had conspired to steal from the company and from its richest customers, that these three had falsified documents of all kinds, bribed judges, congressmen, federal agents, bursars, treasurers, all while trading on angelic Perdhomme's good name, a fancy embezzlement of hundreds of millions of dollars (these would be billions today), which they then sought to cover up with murders. No one cared to ask what would make three bad guys keep such detailed records of their crimes, or store their nefarious memos in their top desk drawers at Dolus headquarters, nor why every little memo was scrupulously typed with fresh ribbon on the same brand of bonded paper, nothing whatsoever recorded in plain handwriting.

Dad, needless to say, was one of the bad guys in this narrative, which the media picked up and ran as the final word on the case, though he himself was dead. As were the others, two equally hapless men, freak accidents. Whatever had really gone on at Dolus, top management was so perfectly insulated that the case stopped cold and the company went on functioning, functioned right up to the great financial collapse of 2009, good riddance.

JACK AND KATE were back. A cool breeze seemed to have followed them down from the height of the little island. "Nothing to see," Kate said. "A very nice rock covered with moss." Her hair was mussed and her neck mottled. No one ever looked more laid than Jack, his hair and backside spangled with moss, eyes all but crossed. We huddled on the blanket, not much time before the tide would turn. I gathered my words, cleared my throat.

But Jack started in before I could, confident of our interest: he'd been writing, he announced, about the poet William Wordsworth's brother John, a sea captain who'd gone down with his ship, family tragedy. The subject required Jack to give a recital of several stanzas of sea poems by both Coleridge and Wordsworth, very entertaining except for the lack of an opening for my own hot subject, and then a disquisition: "The Wordsworths had invested everything in the voyage. It was to be John's great moment. Witnesses onboard said he seized up, didn't order the longboats out, almost as if he had made the choice to die."

"He uses this in class," Kate said, uncharacteristically languorous. "Don't worry, he's working his way to some big question or another."

Jack ignored her, continued: "One of his sailors reported later that he'd seen Captain Wordsworth alive among the other few survivors bobbing in the sea, but captain to the end, he held onto the anchor chain so as to be pulled under. Of course his life would have been worth nothing, losing his ship at that time. All that chivalrous stuff was law of the sea."

"The boat's turning," Kate said.

"We've time," Jack said. And then, "So just to finish." And he started back in with John Wordsworth, audibly hastening.

Etienne began to pack up the remains of our cold feast.

But I hadn't said my piece. And so I grabbed the anchor chain of Jack's parable, held tight, plunged into the depths, interrupting him: "If Captain Wordsworth had been responsible, I mean, I'm not saying he was, not in the way of naval law or anything, but let's say he'd been responsible for the deaths of many of his crew and loss of the boat, what would you think should be his fate?"

"Oh, no question they would have executed him," said Jack, standing, looking out to the mooring, visibly gauging our time. Distracted, he said, "There was a posthumous trial, very involved, ended in a hung jury. And he'd lost the family fortune, if not the family name, which was well buoyed by William the famous poet."

Kate folded the blanket thoughtfully—she knew I was up to something. I stood, said, "But more abstractly. Forgetting Captain John, who is a special case. Let's say some other kind of boat, a more successful kind of boat. We're the family of a crewman who's been commanded to do something everyone knows he just can't manage, and so of course he makes some small error, puts a fatal tear in a sail, something like that, and the captain of the ship, the guy who's really to blame, says to the first

mate, Flog him lifeless!—about our family member, I mean—and the
first mate just calmly gets out the cat-o-nine-tails and goes to work till
the crewman is dead."

"What are we getting at?" Jack said suddenly. "Just spit it out, David,
all right?"

"Captain Perdhomme came into my restaurant."

"Holy fuck," Kate said.

"David," Jack said, quick look to his bride. "Please don't."

"Just listen," said Etienne. "It gets better."

"Worse," I said. "Kaiser was with him. Not a shadow of a doubt. It
was Kaiser, all right. And so that's my question. What should family
members do?"

"David," Jack said.

Kate said, "They just came into the restaurant?" And then in order
to preempt what she knew Jack was going to say: "That couldn't be a
coincidence."

Etienne clapped his hands in excitement.

Jack gripped Kate's hand, looked more than displeased, stared out
at *Deep Song*, no doubt seeing the family ship sinking in whirlpools of
blame, vast reputations to be lost. Reining in his contempt, he said, "What
do we suppose they're after, coming into your restaurant? I mean beyond
a great meal? And how do you suppose they knew you were there?"

"You're not saying you don't *believe* me," I said.

"I'll tell you how they knew," said Kate. And she did her imitation of
Sylphide, a devastating twirl of the hands above the head ending with
splayed fingers around the face.

"Oh, for Christ's sake," Jack said.

BACK ON THE boat we sailed with the wind, spinnaker flying, a
smooth, rolling reach directly homeward, the sun falling fast, none of
the usual triumphal feeling. It seemed up to Jack to say something, and
near Goat Island, he did, quietly, evenly, the rainbow sail bellied out
in front of us, wind at our backs, late sun hot in our faces, words he'd
said many times: "In the eyes of a court, even in the most sympathetic

atmosphere, all we've got to link Perdhomme and the putative Kaiser remains circumstantial. So what if your father's old boss is hanging out with your father's alleged assassin? That's no crime. Guilt by association, they call it. And it won't hold up in court. And neither will an identification twenty-five years down the road, which takes care of the putative Kaiser."

"Putative," I said. "You're calling him putative again. But he's not *putative*, Jack. He was in our restaurant. I *identified* him. The question is what to do about it, Jack. Not whether Kaiser is *putative*."

"Easy," Etienne said.

"We make them *pay*," Kate said.

"Jack, you give me credit. Say it now—Kaiser's not putative."

"Now, let's not get at cross-purposes here," Jack said firmly. "I do give you Kaiser, okay? Kaiser is real, he's really with Perdhomme. Done."

"Thank him," Etienne said.

"Thank you," I said reluctantly.

"You're welcome," said our captain the same. All had been going so well. He said, "And Kate. Everyone. Payback is *their* game. Lubbers like us won't have a chance. If we've got new evidence, we should call the police, go to the D.A. Whatever we think best. But go to the authorities."

"The authorities aren't always up to the job," I said. "The police? They've proved it. The D.A. is worse. You remember."

"It's a new outfit up there, David. It's a whole new court, a whole new system. We go to the D.A. But we'll need better evidence than this single sighting."

Long silence as we sailed with the wind, last warmth of the sun.

Kate climbed up on the foredeck, stared ahead across the water.

"I've ruined the afternoon," I said.

"Nonsense," said Jack. "I'm sorry I was so stiff. You took me by surprise. I do give you credit. I really do. You had to say something."

"Say thanks again," said Etienne.

I felt more thankful this time: "Thanks, Jack. That means a lot."

"Now, gentlemen, let me sail. Our window at low tide this evening is short."

Etienne looked stricken: he didn't like short windows. I felt the same, my sense of safety vanished. The shore held no landmarks for me—time, too, moving separately from my thoughts. And Kate, all separate. So I was surprised when Jack brought us windward again and we entered their inlet, slipped over the sandbar with an audible scrape of the keel. From there it would be a slow drift to mooring in the lee of the bluff.

Kate rejoined us in the cockpit, looking nonplussed, very irritable, a bad sign.

"Jack's apologized," I said. "He says he knows Kaiser is real."

"I know how to get them," Kate said oblivious. "I've been studying up—DNA."

Jack wasn't going to scoff. He said, "We'd need tissue samples. Tissue samples tied to the crime. And tied at this end to Kaiser, whom it is unlikely we'll ever see again."

"Yellow sweater," Kate said. "They found several dozen hairs on there and I have found more. Blood on the sweater. Blood evidence, too, on a pair of rubber gloves. Spittle in a Dr Pepper can. And other stuff, too, pretty much galore, once you have a person to attach it to at this end. It's all sealed and labeled." She looked suddenly like the scientist she'd inhabited briefly, described the forensics process, the developing legal situation. She'd read in the *Times* that two rapists had been convicted decades after their crimes on DNA evidence, an innocent man freed. And she'd seen in one of her genetics magazines that anyone with the cash could bring DNA material to a lab.

"We lure them to the restaurant," Etienne said. "Snick a little spit and curlies."

"Makes some sense," Jack said. "And I'm not saying that grudgingly."

"DNA," Kate said, just the faintest manic glimmer.

"Could work," I said. "But won't the court consider our evidence contaminated? Out of police custody? For how long?"

"Oh, contaminated," Kate said. "We'll put it back."

"Lord," said Jack. "And how do we do that?"

"Chuck will put it back," said my sister firmly. So much for the idea that she'd ended her contact with the detective.

"And then to the D.A.," Jack said, resigned. "Both of you, do you hear me? Straight to the D.A."

"And then to the High Side," said Kate.

"Lord," Jack repeated.

"Look at me," said Etienne, sensing my bubbling emotion. "My first day sailing and no seaweed in my lungs."

21

You'd think I would have harbored a lot of resentment for Emily, but I didn't, not really. Her life had gotten too big for her very quickly, and mine had always been too big for me. That she disappeared when my parents died seemed pretty natural. I'd have liked to have disappeared, too. That she reemerged as the star of *Children of War,* that was fine, too. We'd come through a trauma together, all unspoken, and really, nothing else mattered, except perhaps that Sylphide had picked us both out for whatever the dance was that she was imagining, a dance too big for the stage.

Emily's parents still lived in the carriage house on the Wadsworth estate, still managed the place, a thought that crossed my mind quite a bit my first year back in Westport, then infrequently: Emily must visit them sometimes, right? Last I'd heard from her was the one postcard. And until the return of Perdhomme and Kaiser I had thought of her little, then less.

Awake all night, I caught a quick item on one of these TV gossip shows: Emily and Carter had split. I wrote Emily a note via her dance company headquarters in Miami, letting her know I'd settled back into my parents' house, five years already, time flies, what had she been up to, breezy, like that. I didn't mention Perdhomme. I didn't mention my folks. I didn't mention that our urgent hours together at Hochmeyer Haven had been coming to mind with increasing frequency, memories wrapped in violence. I mean, there I was in the very bed, on the very couch, in the very bathtub, at the very kitchen table. I did suggest that if she found herself home for Thanksgiving or Christmas or really anytime, we might get together and have a coffee.

My phone rang four days later, rang after midnight, Lizard right there reading in the living room she and I had anointed.

"David?"

She was coming home the very next Thursday for a week. She could barely stand the prospect. Her mother wasn't taking Emily's divorce from Carter very well. But maybe Sergeant Bright would moderate things. And her brother the brigadier general would be in town, at least that. She was touring Asia starting very soon, far away at Christmastime and Thanksgiving, so the Brights were making their big holiday event out of the Korean harvest festival. "Chuseok," she reminded me. "Ancestor Days? When all Koreans return to their hometowns to honor their people? It's all about food. Snacks for the dead. I'd love to see you, David. I'll carve out twenty-four hours. But I don't want to see you in that house. I can't believe you're living in that house. I hope that's not harsh. I couldn't even go in that house, I don't think. And I definitely don't want to be staring over at Sylphide's place the whole time. I see her enough as it is. And you know me—I can't handle the competition."

No idea what she knew or didn't know about Sylphide and me, I said, "We were so young."

Emily laughed. Emily really laughed. Emily Bright, the girl who never laughed, a long, burbling giggle like water tumbling through rocks.

ETIENNE AND I had been blown away by the wild mushrooms and fungi in the French and Italian kitchens we'd visited in Europe. Every great restaurant had its mushroom hunter, gorgeous porcinis arriving in baskets stuffed into the back of a nondescript Fiat in Rome or chanterelles and morels recovered at a clandestine roadside drop in Chamonix. Ru-Angela, always with the feelers, had long since found an eccentric fellow in western Massachusetts, a mycologist whose claim to fame was having been fired from the faculty at Harvard, actually a bit of a fungus himself: Ferkie the Mushroom Man. He was full of secrets, wandered the glens and woodlots foraging, kept a basement full of mushroom logs. He'd developed practical drying and freezing techniques: year-round produce. We'd become his exclusive market in our area, and had become friends, as well, several expeditions after delicacies. RuAngela's connection to him had been Jim Riverkeeper, proprietor of the famous Riverkeeper Inn of Lenox, Massachusetts.

Maybe not the getaway Emily had in mind, but such was the timing: Jim and I had long planned a Monday foraging trip and a kitchen visit. Emily arrived at Firfisle by limousine after prep. And here was the thing: her head wasn't shaved bald anymore. That phase had passed. She'd grown out all that glossy, thick, sumptuous black hair and the braid was back, the precious plait. Something had made her happy: I'd never seen her smile quite like that, 1000 watts, very becoming. Etienne laughed to see her and they hugged as if they'd gotten along the first time around. RuAngela reached up to put her hands on Emily's soaring cheekbones.

But that was it for introductions—after a quick tour, we left the restaurant in the hands of staff and got in my decrepit Volvo: north!

THE RIVERKEEPER INN loomed high amid horse pastures, the Colonial homestead of one patriot or another, nice stone buildings dating from before the American Revolution. When we pulled in, Jim popped out the kitchen door, huge man, a solid four hundred pounds but light on his feet, grumpy manner, linen-service kitchen-togs, a real chef's toque cocked on his head.

"I haven't seen so many Black people in one place since I left Boston!" he said. We laughed, but it wasn't clear he was joking.

His wife, Jean, was as big as he, pink and cheery and snugged into a gigantic in-your-face uplift bra, the obvious boss of the place, droll and forceful. "No rest for the wicked," she said, and whisked us off on an overly detailed tour of the stately dining rooms, the antique billiards room, the Prohibition-era basement tavern. We paused in the stained-glass stairwell, like standing in a church, each on our own level, Emily above.

Shortly, E.T. and Jim settled down to inspect the new wood-burning beehive oven, made pizzas on bare brick for a snack before lunch. Not a word between us, Emily and I retrieved our bags from the Volvo, climbed the stairs to the exquisite room she'd picked, twin beds in an alcove on the third floor. "I honestly think we should make love right now," she said.

I was not against the idea.

FERKIE TURNED UP while Emily and I napped and snuggled, or maybe while we made love a second time (old desire insatiable), took no particular notice of us when we joined the group, all but climbed down Jean's fantastical cleavage over our second lunch—complained about the "freaky" pizza Jim and Etienne had invented, leek cream and woven stripes of vegetable: puréed dal for the warp, kale pesto for the woof.

"Mr. Mushroom, you got poor people skills," RuAngela said.

And it was true, Ferkie kept rising up into the conversation like something growing on a stump. Jim and RuAngela bantered with a kind of expertise—old-line cultural insults I didn't quite get, homo vs. hetero insults that I did, tried to incorporate whatever the clueless Ferkie thought to interject, such as "RuAngela, you are obviously a man." You always remembered why he hadn't lasted as a college prof: he was made to be the guy on the water-tank target at the county fair, three throws for a buck.

E.T. took no notice of anyone but pondered, pondered, always something cooking in his head. He roused himself and quietly put together a second small course at lightning speed, five or six unfamiliar types of mushrooms Ferkie had spied at seventy miles per hour roadside on his trip down from a mushroom conference in Canada: distinct textures, individual flavors, various colors, all sorts of culinary possibility, like they'd been auditioned and hired and only awaited their parts. Ferkie brightened at the flavors E.T. had coaxed forth, softened with each bite.

And then, he announced, it was time to forage.

No amount of coaxing could get Etienne out in the woods. He stayed in Jim's kitchen to experiment, and of course RuAngela stayed with him, platform pumps unsuitable for hard hiking.

The rest of us climbed into Ferkie's creaky old Mercedes diesel, and after a series of wrong turns on a maze of back roads behind the inn, drove up an impossible dirt track that ended at a pond-sized puddle in the midst of a vast tract of public land.

Ferkie leapt out, distributed collection bags, and without a word lurched into the dense Berkshire forest, his trajectory like a rocket gone wrong, abrupt swerves and curlicues, all but a rail of smoke out his butt. Emily had no trouble keeping up, even as the terrain grew steep, but Jim and I fell behind, unsettling speed through the underbrush, especially given the several bottles of wine we'd downed with lunch. The two of them stopped over a specimen while Jim and I, puffing, caught up to them. "*Clitopilus prunulus,*" Ferkie told us. "Known as sweetbread mushrooms, easily confused with *Clitocybe dealbata,* which is poisonous, not deadly, but fucking weird, causes sweating and heavy salivation, also tunnel vision."

"You've tried it, of course . . ." Riverkeeper said, ardent hippie hater.

"Just a bite, well cooked. And it was worth it: delicious. Fishy, sticky."

"You suffered *symptoms*?" Emily said.

"Tunnel vision, for sure. And auditory hallucinations. Like mosquitoes and springs popping, and my mother's voice: *Ferkie, Ferkie.* But that turned out to be real. I was still in high school, Buffalo, New York."

We kept marching. Ferkie collected small amounts of this and that inedible for the sake of some paper he was writing, announcing the names: ribbed pluteus, blushing false truffle, candlesnuff fungus. We hiked down into a small, heavily shaded gorge, mushrooms galore, now that I had eyes for them. One grouping was all bright red with white spots.

"Like a roomful of sore throats," said Jim.

"Fly agaric," Ferkie said. He didn't pluck a specimen but lay on the ground and put his tongue to the toadstool, sat there savoring the taste. "These are seriously toxic," he said dreamily. "Tastes like. Like *wind.*"

"So this is how poets die," Jim said.

Ferkie got to his feet, indifferent. He said, "Nah, nothing serious. Not like some. Eat that, you might puke a little. Maybe a little worse if you ate 'em raw."

And like that, dozens of species, till we came upon an enormous log lying covered with pale sheaves: oyster mushrooms, as any chef could see. We filled two large collection bags, then a third, heavy, the excitement of acquisition.

"You assholes pay twenty bucks a pound," Ferkie said.

Oh, Emily's giggle. I couldn't recall her giggling at all.

We struggled back down the mountain to the car—Ferkie knew exactly where it was in the seemingly endless woods—then straight back to a patch of blue chanterelles he'd spotted, striated little trumpets completely hidden from my eye even when he pointed, like ballet costumes.

When Riverkeeper finally saw them, he said, "Now, these, I gotta say, look poisonous."

"There's no poisonous look," Ferkie said. "Some of the most dangerous ones look very tempting. Some of the most delicious look fecal and foul."

Nonchalant, I said, "What are the most dangerous?"

"Oh," Ferkie said. "Right? For a chef, any little tummy ache out there is going to be bad news. Tunnel vision from a bowl of soup, you kidding?"

"Lizard, you could advertise the experience," said Jim.

"But most dangerous around here is definitely *Amanita phalloides*, death cap, it's called, very handsome, big shape, tasty looking, makes you want to take a bite. In fact, people who've survived amanitin poisoning say *phalloides* tastes very, very good. Drops people in the United States every season. Some years dozens. Beautiful things. I could show you hundreds of 'em right around here in a week or two. And a little later in the season, *Amanita ocreata*. Closely related, even stronger, called 'destroying angel,' which I dig, cuz they grow up with these veils like wings."

We collected about half of the blue chanterelles, leaving enough to preserve the patch, made our way out of the woods and to the puddle we'd parked in, climbed in the car triumphant, headed back to the Inn.

Emily and I sat in the back holding bags of the delicate chanterelles in our laps, nice to get out of the misting rain, my head pressed against the ceiling, knees up in my face. Emily put her hand on my leg under the mushrooms, ran it up my jeans very gradually.

Playing it cool, I reached back over my shoulder and snagged one of the mushroom books piled on the dash under the rear window, the fattest one, *Mushrooms Demystified*, by someone named David Arora. The dedication caught my interest immediately:

> I dedicate this book with love to my mother and father, whose admonitions to me as a teen-ager to stay away from mushrooms inspired me to get closer.

Quickly, lest Emily ask what I was doing, I looked up *Amanita phalloides*, then *Amanita ocreata*, having memorized the names, followed notations in the index to an appendix called "Mushroom Toxins," page 892. The first entry concerned certain compounds called amatoxins, and put a spear in my gut:

"Poisoning by amatoxins is extremely serious, with a high fatality rate. It is doubly dangerous because the symptoms are delayed for as many as 24 hours after ingestion of the mushroom, by which time the toxins have been absorbed by the body." And apparently there are various amatoxins, the very worst of which is a group called amanitins, "twenty times more lethal" than other amanita poisons, and they don't get cooked out, don't get destroyed by the human digestive tract. The concentration of these toxins "varies tremendously from individual mushroom to individual mushroom, but an average fatal dose is about two ounces (fresh weight) of *Amanita phalloides*."

I looked out my own window, followed my own train of thought, Emily's hand smoothing my jeans, smoothing, smoothing. And I'd return to that train of thought many late nights subsequent. But of course there was no practical way to poison Kaiser and Mr. Perdhomme. You'd simply get caught, end up in prison.

Emily's smoothing turned to kneading, nice hands, strong person. We'd be back in our lavender sheets before long, and after whatever kind of long second nap we engineered, there'd be dinner, something luscious the genius E.T. had invented for the beehive oven, no doubt, novel uses of oyster mushrooms and blue trumpets. I read:

> Amanitin poisoning usually manifests itself in four stages: (1) a latency period of as many as 24 hours after ingestion, during which time the toxin is actively working on the liver and kidneys, but the victim experiences no discomfort; (2) a period of about one day characterized by violent vomiting, bloody diarrhea, and severe abdominal cramps; (3) a period of about one day during which the victim appears to be recovering (if hospitalized, the patient is sometimes released!); (4) a relapse, during which liver and kidney failure often leads to death.

I pictured Kaiser shitting out his innards, shitting, shitting. A slow and painful death, no known antidote, and no natural defense: kidneys can't eliminate amanitin from the body: "The pancreas, adrenal glands, heart, lungs, muscles, intestines, and brain may be damaged."

Well, it was only a fantasy.

Emily looked over, proffered a long, intelligent, rather solipsistic gaze, a kitty-cat deigning to sit close. "Don't even think about it," she said. I was startled for a blink or so, but of course she wasn't talking about punishing Kaiser and Perdhomme. Her hand grew busier yet under the great blue orchestra of mushrooms in my lap, and suddenly her wet mouth met mine, none of the old awkward bumping, even as I let the fat book of mushrooms fall to the floor.

"Get a room," Jim said happily, the very guy who had provided us with one.

I was sad when the limo came for Emily the next day, sad beyond the moment, sad and not only tired, the whole weight of everything crashing in on me.

Ancestor Days were over.

PART FIVE

Bequest

22

My folks were born in 1929. Crash babies, my father said. Mom's family prospered a while, but by the time her memory woke, they were struggling, had to move to lesser quarters. A teen summer with an aunt on Lake Winnipesaukee convinced her that New England was the height of luxury and romance. She came east to see my father after they'd met at her best friend's wedding, all of twenty-one years old, just done with college. If you did the math, which Kate and I dearly loved to do, Mom was already pregnant by the time she arrived in Westport. What's more, she stayed. Nick wasn't one to do the right thing, but he was happy to marry Barb, the most beautiful and exciting girl he'd ever known, hilarious, athletic, almost as tall as he. The guy had a small stake from his father's death that would devolve to him when he turned twenty-one. He and his betrothed went house hunting in anticipation of the windfall, and for a lark they dressed up and told an agent at one of Westport's premiere Realtors that they were in the market for a fine estate, funds unlimited. Among the wondrous mansions they were shown was a place called the High Side, long empty, but lovingly maintained, and they were given a tour that ended abruptly when the head broker arrived and recognized Dad. Even then the old man had a reputation.

"But I do have a castle in your size," the broker said. And he pointed across the pond.

Dad started at Concept Credit as a file clerk. Mom gave tennis lessons at the club, started her career as a ringer, clobbering everyone in their league, Kate always along. I was born in 1953, my folks only twenty-four years old. The High Side remained unsold till Dabney bought it when I was about four, anyway, I remember the excitement at our house—there were tennis courts over there and Mom pictured herself working on serves with the famous couple. Of course, the call never came.

Dad claimed he had a degree in economics from UCLA, climbed the ladder at Concept, not even fired when he was found out: a new hire in accounting would have been in his class and not only didn't remember him but investigated. Maybe Perdhomme liked a liar; anyway, Dad kept moving up and when the place changed its name to Dolus Investments, Dad was made a vice president, meaningless, but at home we celebrated all the same.

Mom never gave up her dream of the good life. And with Dad, the good life was always right around the corner.

A POSTCARD FROM New Zealand caught RuAngela's attention, and she brought it to me in the kitchen at Firfisle, where once again I was fulminating about Perdhomme. And Kaiser, always Kaiser. Etienne humored me at the edges of my diatribe, but at the center, he was solidly with me: we were going ahead with Kate's DNA plan. The trick was how to get our quarry to the restaurant, and once we got them there, how to get the tissue samples and store them according to the FBI's "Best Practices" manual for forensic genetics. The conversations went from earnest to hilarious to hopeless to enraged, in dizzying bursts. Kate was calling daily with ideas, and even Jack was more or less on board, reading up on the legalities, making fresh contacts at the D.A.'s office in Danbury. But it all seemed unlikely at best, a dangerous tilting at windmills: we were such amateurs, didn't even know enough to know what we needed to know.

"New Zealand," I said, finally flipping the card to see Emily's heavily back-slanted hand, no greeting, no sign-off:

> I'll be in New York for the *gala di diva* and then for a full month after, and I expect you to be my fucking boyfriend the whole fucking time!

Sylphide, by contrast, had communicated nothing at all. Perhaps she thought it unnecessary—the publicity around her grand retrospective was unavoidable, great excitement in the land. I didn't know what I wanted. It's not like we'd had any but the most formal contact in the five years since our poolhouse party, Daniel Tancredi always looming.

Pondering over all that one afternoon, rubbing the stone in my pocket, staring out the high window over my station in the Firfisle kitchen (October light slanting in over the whitecaps of the sound, not a sail in sight, just the familiar lighthouse out there, one container ship tall and distant), I was startled when a knock came at the delivery door, sharp little raps, certainly not Olulenu, who only gave a blunt kick or two.

Dr. Chun. No notice of any kind, not a phone call, not a golden note, not a whiff of jasmine, not so much as a friendly smile. "You come with," he said. "You must."

"Oh, I must?" said I.

I introduced the good doctor to E.T., these two skinny guys who wouldn't shake hands staring at one another. Dr. Chun liked RuAngela, though, practically licked her dress, took her hand and kissed it.

"I refuse to be shanghaied," I said haughty.

"Slow night anyway," E.T. replied deadpan.

"Crucial," Dr. Chun said, a very difficult word his thoughtless employer had stuck him with. He tried again: "Crucial."

I saw Dr. Chun to the door, pushed him out into the bright sunlight. "One hour ride," he begged. "I bring you back. Not late."

I just closed the door in his face.

Etienne stood there, his best Santoku knife poised.

"I think you should go," RuAngela said, quick thinker. "Play along."

"Get some answers," Etienne said.

"Answers to what?" I said, afraid.

"How death feels, mon. They going to take you out."

"Oh, stop," said RuAngela. "This is just the break we need."

THE NEW BUTLER, William, was deferential but not overly friendly, left me to sit alone in a plush parlor by a tumbled pile of coffee-table books. My heart hadn't stopped pounding: once and for all, what had Perdhomme and Kaiser been doing in Westport? My thoughts went *noir:* I'd grill her like a portabella mushroom over wind-fired charcoal, sauce her like a quince in wine. I flipped through an enormous picture book called *The Vision of Sylphide,* each photo more moving than the last, decades of her work as she grew from gamine to dancer to choreographer, her increasingly calm face not always beautiful to the camera, not in any traditional way. The next book in the pile was *The Great Castles of Europe.* Tancredi owned a few old palaces, I knew, was revered for his restorations and conservation, and not only his money. The bottom book was called *Miami Dolphins: The Decade of Greatness,* a couple of photos of me in there, I knew. I'd always wondered who bought books like that, didn't crack it.

Shortly, Tancredi himself appeared. "Old man!" he said. He, of course, was the old man, well into his eighties, older than Dr. Chun and more frail, dressed smartly in yachtsman's blue jacket and Topsiders, bright brown eyes, that aura of power and competence, that sense that he wanted you in his court and knew how to get you there.

He shook my hand, firm grip fading, said, "We see your restaurant business is coming along smashing."

"Smashing," I said. "And going on five years."

"That many," he said, a thoroughly appealing man. He bid me follow, led me to a decorative elevator gate, and then upwards three stories and through a cozy maze of library rooms and offices, finally back to a reading alcove with tall windows overlooking the East River, a city glory of winking lights and coursing estuarine currents and bridges and contrails in the sunset sky. The houseman trotted in behind us, handed me a bourbon on ice, left us to the view.

Still in chef's togs, towel still in the waist of my pants, I said, "This is a magnificent house."

"Oh, turds," Tancredi said, upper-crusty English tones perching atop his indistinct Swiss-German accent. His skin was mottled, his eyes bright and brown behind bifocals, thick white hair combed long back over his skull. His son, a financial writer, had written an op-ed piece for the *Times* about him the previous June: "Best father in the world."

He said, "Dabney Stryker-Stewart bought it, you understand, his uncommon eye, seldom single talents to make a great man. I'd say on a guess he's realized a 10,000 percent return on investment, if only by proxy, given death. Ah, bourbon. I remember bourbon!" He put a long, speckled hand on my arm, pulled my drink up under his nose, sniffed voluptuously. And down to business: "Tenke finds you trustworthy, and aside from myself and one or two of the staff, that is a rare regard. I'm getting older, as you can see, and struggling with bladder cancer, as you cannot, and won't be around for many more full moons."

He gestured toward the huge bank of windows in the dim room. Across the shimmer of Queens sure enough rose a quavering and burgeoning hump of light on the horizon. It took only perhaps three minutes for the full moon to find its way completely into the belabored New York City sky, fat and orange and marked with craters.

"Whoa," I said.

"Nice effect, no? I've used it before, the moon. You simply check the calendar, make your invitations accordingly. Is there such a word as auspicion?"

"There is now. Kind of suspicion mixed with luck?"

"Hm," said Tancredi.

We watched the moon in its splendor rise higher.

At length, my host spoke again, very quietly, more effortfully: "We apologize for short notice. Tenke is fond of surprises, you probably know. She's also superstitious. Silliness, of course. In any case, she's decided she's going to die *with* me, that our fates are intertwined. Ludicrous. Just another perimenopausal storm, no doubt. But still, the superstition, hormonal or otherwise, leads us to practical concerns. What I'm getting at, moon and all, is that we'd like you to be executor of Sylphide's estate."

I just stood there with my eyebrows stuck high, full of the misapprehension that he was telling me that Sylphide was dying, that Sylphide could not be there to see me. If I'd tried to speak it would have been a wail.

Oblivious, Tancredi struggled on: "Her estate is very, very large, I suppose I needn't say. The portion of my own estate that postdates our wedding is to be included. The primary financial beneficiary of the combined will is the Tenke Thorvald Foundation for the Arts, of which you'd become director, handsomely compensated, little to do. After that, the American Ballet Theatre. Also the Royal Ballet of London. A couple of other major outfits. Dabney's foundation is next, Children of War, but you would know all about them. Well, then. Chin up, sir!"

Tancredi dug in his pocket for a handkerchief, handed it to me, fine linen, crisply ironed, too fine to blow one's nose in. But I did, and the old man carried on: "Tenke's Dance Company will be funded with an endowment, as will the Emily Bright Experience. You are acquainted with Emily. A very difficult person, in my estimation, but high marks for form! Finally, you yourself are a beneficiary, to receive the High Side property and furnishings, excluding certain art works. Also funds for its upkeep in perpetuity, including staff. With the catch that it's to be held in trust until you are wed. Yes, till you are married. There's no cash disbursement but you will be paid as executor, and too generously, from my point of view, some sort of percentage of the estate. Your sister is a lesser beneficiary, dating back to Dabney's will and last testament, but she'll receive a considerable sum, as well, and certain paintings in the Stryker-Stewart collection, quite beyond those he bought expressly for her, as well as Dabney's musical instruments and other memorabilia. All quite valuable, as you might imagine."

"I hardly know what to say," I blurted.

No particular judgment in Tancredi's eyes, in fact a flood of warmth: "Oh, that's to be expected. It's we in this case who must know what to say. You heard the part about being wed. Tenke insisted on it, I wasn't for it, more silly girlish stuff from the middle-aged broad. No doubt she's selected your bride, as well." He pressed a button on the arm of his chair and quickly the butler was back, also two nurses.

The butler, William, took charge of me, another elevator ride, two more stories up to an intimate dining room, same view as the library but higher and wider, a large dining table set at the far end for four. I was left to stand, looking out at the risen moon, more whitely familiar, now, less shimmery, smaller, barely a feature in amongst all the bright lights of the far-flung city.

I struggled to recall my mission: Perdhomme, Kaiser, the two of them visiting the High Side, subsequently visiting Restaurant Firfisle, the obvious threat.

Shortly, Sylphide made her entrance, the exhausted Tancredi seated in a wheelchair now, she in a silk shirt and blue jeans and forty-seven, I had to remind myself, pertly erect, cheery, graceful as always, practically glowing, merely herself, utterly detached from any string of years, her hair still blond. She wasn't dying at all—in fact, she filled the room with life. "Lizard," she said. We kiss-kissed cheeks, said pleasantries, took our seats, the houseman opening a noble old bottle of *Châteauneuf-du-Pape*, old-school red wine, offering me the cork, then a taste. Over which I lingered, feeling myself very much onstage. A young woman like a fairy, no presence at all, handed us napkins, another more like a griffin showed her bad teeth in a queer-lipped smile and offered flaky rolls.

"My cook is nervous," Daniel said. "Really quite a wreck. You're much admired." He patted the table emphatically, knock-knock, made me notice a heavy, bejeweled signet ring on his right hand.

I patted the table, too, clonk: Super Bowl rings. I said, "Well, if anyone, it would be our chef, Etienne LaRoque, who'd be the threat to your cook. I'm merely Mr. LaRoque's acolyte when it comes to the kitchen."

"*Oik*, 'merely,'" Sylphide said warmly. Then, "So, Daniel has popped our question? Have you said yes?"

"No," I said, making my decision. "But yes." If she wanted to hand me power, I better well take it. "The answer is yes. Of course it's yes. Superfluous, since you'll live forever, but yes."

"The whole arrangement to be confidential till the second of us is on the other side of the grass," said Tancredi, liking me, knock-knock. "And of course subject to future amendment. We'll give you paperwork to take home to your lawyers—everything's all signed and witnessed on this end. Meanwhile, strictly hush-hush, particularly as regards any of the principals you might have contact with."

"Emily can only stay an hour," Sylphide said, that choreographer's smile.

And William led her in, Emily Bright herself, in a pretty print dress.

"Surprise!" she said.

Shocked, I fell into her embrace.

"I'm just thinking since you are both in town," said Sylphide.

"Nice pajamas," said Emily.

"I was cooking," I said.

"She's speaking tonight," said Tancredi. "At the Ninety-second Street Y."

"Where's that?" I said, but the joke fell flat. The actual questions I had come to ask receded.

William seated us at the square table such that I was across from Emily but close to Sylphide, who hooked her ankle around mine. Dinner was terribly awkward but beautiful under candles in the dark-paneled room, simple portions of pan-grilled flounder, fava beans, fragrant rice, twice the amount for me as for Emily, twice as much for Emily as Sylphide, twice as much for Sylphide as for Tancredi, not too much in any case, a clever wreath of food at the center of each plate, a joy to the eye, a bit bland on the fork: still, I'd have to send compliments to the anxious chef.

I hadn't seen Emily for almost three months. She was dressed for her event, makeup for the cameras. Sylphide was silent, magisterial. Emily, still nervous in the presence of her mentor, nattered on about her tour down under. Sydney had been a bomb, Port Douglas refreshing: diving the Great Barrier Reef, encounter with a stingray. Daniel proposed a long string of toasts till it was time for Emily to go. We all stood. Kiss-kiss, kiss-kiss.

"I'll see you under the warplanes," Emily told me right in front of our hosts, the new no-secrets Emily. "I can't wait to see those bomb-bay doors. Tomorrow afternoon? See you at the restaurant? Put me up a night or two? Ride in together Sunday?"

"Here's to the Westport Air Force," Tancredi said, wry puzzlement.

William guided Emily back through the many rooms to the elevator.

"Okay, whoa," I said.

Sylphide let the tiniest hint of a smile cross her face.

Tancredi excused himself, not another word, leaned back in his conveyance with a terse wave, clearly in pain. His aides wheeled him out efficiently.

"I'm sorry," I said, always apologizing for my tears.

"We're overwhelming you."

"Of course, yes. I mean, why this? Why now?"

"You are someone who is caring about the High Side."

"It's you I've cared about, let's be real. And you aren't going anywhere." She put a cool hand to my cheek. "And Emily Bright," she said.

"And Emily, true. Very subtle, as your husband says. I hear I'm to be wed." I reached for her hand, but it seemed her hair needed fixing.

Her gaze was the same as ever, frank, too steady, the green of her eyes still surprising. She said, "I am wanting to see you both more stable."

Lightly, I said, "That's not up to you, Tenke."

"Apparently it is, Lizano. Anyway, you will both be the richer for it." She rose and floated to the sideboard, retrieved a little gold bust, clearly very heavy, plunked it down in front of me. "You recognize him?" she said.

I didn't.

"He is August Bournonville, of course. The father of the Danish Royal Ballet. The grandfather of modern ballet. The great innovator, *ja?* He is dead a hundred years and more. This is my wedding gift from Dabney, dead twenty."

I hefted the little thing, ten or fifteen pounds of dense gold: back before the Reagan years you could own the stuff only if it were in the form of art—Dabney had been investing, no doubt. Mr. Bournonville was beautifully done, whatever the intent, a wise-looking fellow with a blunt nose, those spherical scoops classical sculptors employed to indicate the irises of a subject's eyes, the whole thing polished and gleaming in the candlelight. Was she giving him to me? I *tunk*ed the great man on the table, turned him so he wouldn't stare. She pulled a chair close beside mine and sat such that our knees interlocked, whiff of jasmine. I put a hand on her leg—why not?—wanted very badly to kiss her. But that was not being offered: in fact the nostalgia had faded from her face.

She patted the bust. "This little man is gone missing at some point after Dabney is dead. All those crowds in my hallways all the time. I know it is after his death because for several weeks I am holding that heavy lump, trying to keep my Dabney close. And it did not work, no, and after a time I am putting it back in its place on the half-table in the High Side foyer. Under the big mirror, *ja?* And I only notice it is gone a year later, just disappeared. Desmond was donderstruck, that's what he was saying, the foyer being his domain, and each thing in it."

"Thunderstruck, you mean. Poor Desmond."

"He's very sick. *Ja,* donderstruck. You—always correcting me."

We sat a moment in silence. My hand was on her thigh. I didn't know how to move it. At length I said, "You're saying Mr. Bournonville was stolen and then he came back?"

"It comes back, *ja*. In the form of a gift from Thierry Perdhomme."

"What?" I said, emotion escalating. "Perdhomme? Thierry Perdhomme? What are you saying?"

She was a hundred elegant leaps ahead of me. Then I remembered: Dad. Kate had once told me that he'd pocketed some trinket at the High Side when they'd collected her paintings, yes—whoa—her image of his coat weighted by whatever it was, the clonking into things: Kate had not led me to picture anything like this, however, so heavy, so clearly valuable. I felt a chill, all the blood draining out of me, turned to look for the moon in the big window. Just the East River out there, the moon having risen out of sight but lighting bright waves and roiling eddies of foam. I'd heard that bodies could get stuck at the bottom, held by weeds and debris in strong currents, only emerge after years. Fire engines in the near distance. Lights on the bridges, several spans in view. I felt a fury building. Bournonville proved her connection to Perdhomme, that's all, though she didn't understand how much I knew. The gold was bait. As was all this talk of her estate, when here she was healthy and hale. She wanted me thinking of her riches, wanted me greedy. I had to harden myself, forge ahead. I pushed my seat back, erased our contact.

Suddenly, absurd timing, the whole staff came hustling in, efficient clatter, a clunky-looking apple compote nestled in a kind of whole-grain shortcake, perfect ball of vanilla ice cream adjacent. The plates were square and cobalt blue. I thought of Kate, all Kate's theories, saw Mom and Dad all tangled in one another dead, saw that hopeless pot of mums spiraling toward the fleeing car. The bust was a threat, standing there amid the food. Sylphide knew more than I thought, too.

The servers trotted out as they had trotted in.

Overheated but playing it cool, I said, "Tenke, quit messing with me. Let's talk straight. You know Perdhomme. You're friendly with Perdhomme. What was he doing at the High Side last month?"

"I invited him," she said unruffled.

"You just say it like that?"

"Of course. Keeping close our common enemy."

I studied the steaming compote, stabbed it with my fork, forced myself to look at her, couldn't keep her eye. She knew what I was thinking. She knew what she was about. The whole evening was a sham. The light right there, the exact spot she'd chosen to sit—it made her shirt transparent, showed her breasts plainly. The wine on top of the bourbon had made me dizzy. Jasmine seemed suddenly to have filled the air. I pushed back in my chair, ready to stand and flee.

She could be urgent herself: "Lizard, listen. The bust, it is important. I got a telegram from Thierry, congratulations on this or that, *ja?* David, sit—please listen. He is been a major donor at the NYCB. Very condescending, as if the money is making the art. He is having a business proposition for me. I am ignoring him for several months."

The fairy and the griffin slipped in looking frightened (the mood in the room was palpable, no doubt), dropped off coffees and small snifters. I let myself fall back into my chair, smelled the cognac, like poison. Sylphide watched her people closely as they did their work, watched after them as wordlessly they scuttled out. "Oh, Lizano, don't be mad," she begged. She'd said the same once before in exactly the same voice, but riding me all around the secret corners of her late husband's poolhouse lair.

"But I *am* mad," I said. "I'm very mad." I slammed a fist on the enormous table, couldn't help it, shouted: "You sent Perdhomme and Kaiser to my restaurant!"

Sylphide was not intimidated. She only looked unhappy, hurt that I'd doubt her. And older; she looked older. She watched me, increasingly pained. Her shirt was a theater scrim, her little sweet breasts young as ever and plainly visible, familiar still, a trick. I gulped cognac, tried to gather my wits, picked up my fork, took a bite of the compote— burning hot.

My dancer patted at my knee. "Perdhomme and . . . who?" she said.

I puffed a breath. "Kaiser," I said, marginally calmer.

"Kaiser."

"Yes, Kaiser. The man who shot my parents. You sent him to my restaurant."

The look on her face! A kind of delight!

I heard once again everything Kate had been saying for years.

The dancer didn't want to lose me: "Oh, Firfisle. Thierry Perdhomme is our common enemy. This bust? He's thinking it makes me trust him—

this priceless bust. And his note is saying, oh, Your husband give me this many years ago, and I thought I should return it to you in his honor, poof-poof. But, dear Lizard, I had that bust in my hands *after* Dabney died—I took it into my bed. It was my only comfort."

"Some comfort," I said, all I could think to say.

The dancer's chin quivered. She leaned at me. "Thierry is stepping on his own ankle. I am trusting him, always liking his gifts, always accepting his help, lots of help, financial advice, financial services, forgive me, I was stupid, taxes and hedges and this and so, but now he is handing me my own stolen property. And he is not realizing I see right through him. And then everything, Lizano-mine, it all is coming clear. And tonight even more."

"You're lying."

"Firfisle, no!" She rose and flurried out of the room, left me to darkest thoughts. Next she'd lead Perdhomme in, and Kaiser. I steeled myself. I'd kill them all. I slugged at the cognac. The gold bust would make a nice weapon. I didn't want to inherit anything. I had not come to New York to gain the High Side, nor to serve as anyone's trustee, nor to be married off. I'd come at the great choreographer's bidding, but I'd come for my own reasons, as she would soon see. I'd shake her till she told the truth, told me where the killers were.

Then again, I was a fine one to talk. I knew who had taken that bust. Kate had chastised him, so she'd told me, but Dad had taken it anyway, taken it that night they liberated Kate's paintings (really hers!), a little proprietary gesture, a fillip of entitlement, just his style: the rules were for someone else. Poor Desmond, he'd had no reason to be donderstruck: the bust had been taken during those few weeks when he was off the job after the courts had stepped in and frozen the dancer's accounts, left her to her own devices. A small thing in the midst of big disasters, no wonder it wasn't noticed missing for a year. Probably my father had told Perdhomme the dense lump of gold had been a gift to him from Dabney, a straight-out lie that Perdhomme adopted for himself. Nicholas Hoch-meyer had always made much of connections like that, no matter how tenuous. A gift from Dabney—please take it Mr. Perdhomme, take it for my debts, or whatever it was that had been going on. And the evil man took it, hoarded it, saw a use for it beyond troy ounces, made his own little lie, which depended from Dad's. Or was all this just more of the dancer's stagecraft? No bust that size was solid gold. My chest constricted. I clenched my hands. I thought to go find William, make him lead me out, no confidence I could do it on my own.

I WAS ABOUT to cycle back through my maelstrom of thoughts when Sylphide reappeared. She'd put on one of her husband's sports jackets over the silk shirt—against the offense of my gaze I realized, chagrined. She dumped a pair of large envelopes down in front of me, also a magnifying glass. I picked it up surly while she pulled all the legal papers for my executor status out of the thicker envelope, fanned them for me, proof that all Daniel's talk was no ruse. The gift and responsibility of the High Side, oversight of her foundations, the provision to wed, all of it was real—there it was in neat type, her initials on every paragraph, Tancredi's too, several witnesses as well, a notary's seal.

Clearly she was hurt that I'd called her a liar, hurt and unhappy, never angry.

"I'm sorry," I said. "I'm very confused."

"Not for any longer," said Sylphide. She slipped a giant color enlargement out of the second envelope, handled it by its edges, lay it gingerly on the table in front of me. "I was having it blown up, but still you will need the glass. Is the only image I can find."

I leaned over it, just one of a million-and-one shots of Dabney and his protean entourage, thirty or forty people, the rock star foreground with his equally famous organist just behind him, our Georges. And there was Nixie Kumar, their long-time drummer, and Ted Pounce, the wildman guitarist (and second in the band to die after Dabney, years later in a drunken brawl), all their arms around one another, lots of hilarity, famous faces, the bunch of them out in front of the High Side, some kind of publicity shot, the photographer's viewpoint lofty, perhaps from one of the High Side's enormous stepladders. Where was Pete Pounce, Ted's brother, the band's bassist, who would go on to such fame as a comic actor? Ah, over here, his back to the camera, butt sticking out—big joke—no doubt the source of all the frozen laughter. Around the core of the band, half-a-dozen dazzling young women, bangs and pigtails, microminiskirts, legs, legs, legs. I studied each face with the glass. What was it I was supposed to find?

Desmond, looking stressed. Just in front of him, Linsey, grinning broadly. And beside Linsey, *Kate,* the actual girl next door! I lingered over her image—she was just a kid, no more than sixteen, gangly, thin, her hair bright blond and falling off her shoulders in thick waves, head thrown back in laughter but responsible eyes on Linsey, all her attention on Linsey, a particular shirt I recalled, heavy blue stripes, athletic shoulders, tiniest possible blue-jean skirt (contraband at our house, so she must have put it on High Side), legs up to here, bare feet.

Impatient, Sylphide put her finger on the other corner of the print, a couple more laughing faces, but wait: the one with a fist in the air was my dad—whoa—a big screaming grin on his face, his arm around another man, who was slimmer, grimmer: Kaiser.

I must have gasped, because Sylphide nodded emphatically, *Ja, ja, ja,* tapped the photo. I looked closer, closer yet, lifted the glass higher, dropped it lower. It was Kaiser all right, nice-looking young man, unmistakable strong chin.

Sylphide said, "You recognize him, even cleaned up."

I felt a surge of violence. "Of course I know him," I said.

"Brady Rattner," she said. "The only photo of him like that I ever seen."

"No, no," I said. "It's not Brady, Tenke, it's Kaiser. Kaiser the killer."

"It's Brady," she said again. "Dabney's little stinking brother."

"You sent him to my restaurant!"

"But he is Brady, too. Don't you understand?"

"Kaiser is *Brady*?"

"We has just proven it, Lizano. *Ja, ja.* We got him."

"And you understand, right? You get that this is Kaiser, the guy who shot my folks? That you're saying he's Brady Rattner? He's Dabney's brother?" I looked closely again at the photo, used the glass. It was Kaiser all right, and wearing the sweater, the awful yellow cable sweater Kate had secured from Turkle's evidence vault. Slowly I said, "Tenke. I'm sorry I doubted you."

"*Ja!* Well, until now I wasn't being sure. Too scary when they turn up here! Brady Rattner?" I'd never seen her so exercised. She said, "Oh, he is being all *so sorry* and saying he is *changed* and how the years go by and he was an addict and, oh! Almost like a *confession*. But he doesn't confess anything. Not what we know now! Just, Oh, dear Sylphide, my manners was so bad!"

"But why would he kill?"

"For money, Lizano. For Dabney's money, don't you see? And now they are back for mine."

"But why my folks?"

"He is doing what Thierry says."

"But why is he called Kaiser?"

"Dabney and Pete Pounce, they are always calling him Brother Kaiser after a pervert priest of their childhood. They found this a scream. Brother Kaiser!"

"He killed my folks!"

"He killed his own brother, too."

Suddenly, I heard what she'd been saying. "He killed *Dabney*?"

"Now you are getting it. For the money. For the jealous. Your poppa, he didn't know how bad Brady really is. But there is a plan and in the end Dabney is dying from the plan. But Brady did not have the brains. Only the brutal nature. Your father, I am sorry, he was spineless, a stumble-bum. They use your father to get close."

"*Who* used him?"

"You're not getting it? Your Mr. Perdhomme and Brady Rattner, that's who. Dabney put up with your father because of Kate, let him get close for no other reason! So there is a plan. Who is being the boss? Who is giving the orders? Not your poppa, too weak, I'm sorry. It is Thierry Perdhomme, that's who."

"So my father brought Perdhomme to the High Side?"

"He did. And Thierry, he stay after your father was *bant*. After Dabney's murder, I mean. I trusted Thierry. Because he made it all right when your father made it wrong with Dabney's money, first time. Then after Dabney is dead, he helps me again. Thierry, he is well-mannered, very sharp, very sweet, very generous, very shy. He rescues my finances. He is becoming my financial manager, my accountant, oversight of every-thing. He is being unjustly accused in your father's case, I am thinking, and then he is cleared by the courts. And so I am trusting him. *Fahn! Fie Fahn!*"

I looked at the photo another minute—that very small representation of my father, the very small image of the man who killed him and killed my mother, too, and then ran out of bullets for me. "Tenke," I said, more tears, "I was with my father the afternoon Dabney died. We were working on the roof of the garage. He kept going up and down the ladder to take phone calls. He was wearing his own boots."

"Boots?"

"Oh. It's complicated. I think Kaiser. I mean I think Brady. I mean the killer, that's what I mean, that he tried to frame my father." But I didn't want to talk about my father anymore, couldn't defend him if he was in with all these people.

We stared a while, each trying to absorb and sort the information we were getting.

Sylphide said, "That man who ruined my shoulder? He is hired. Brady, I think, is behind it. I am sure it is Brady. Because Brady is hating me more than he hates even Dabney. Freddy tracked that man. The shoulder man. He try to tell me. Loyal, loyal Frederick. He went out to Arizona to find him and instead he was kilt."

"Freddy was killed?"

"In the desert, his head cut off."

"Oh, Jesus."

"*Ja*, hikers find him. And now they got to finish up. Brady and Thierry. Get my money, finally. Be rid of you. That's what my husband think. He thinks Thierry cannot fund his schemes anymore—all the shells are empty, all the pyramids is fallen down. Daniel's accounting group, they study all my papers—Desmond recorded everything, everything down to a penny. And fussy William, too. And then they study every Dolus transaction, and every thing Thierry is ever doing, ever. And Daniel's people discover a 'siphon,' they call it, a paperwork thing that is drain my accounts for ten years and even more through medical billing for Linsey, later for Daniel, undetectable without these forensic methods. We could take down Thierry Perdhomme and his bloody Dolus on that business all alone. But now I see it is more. Dabney, kilt, your lovely mother, kilt, your Daddy, kilt, Freddy, too. Now that we know, *ja?* Now that we know without a doubt."

"You still haven't explained. I mean, Tenke, you sent them to my restaurant."

"I did. They asked whatever became of you. I want to show no suspicion. I want you to see them. So we would be sure. Our common enemy. I am thinking, Firfisle and Tenke can take them down together."

I felt my spirit sag—I'd been through all this futile stuff so often with Kate. "And what is it you propose?"

"Thierry is coming to me with Mr. Bournonville first, and then with Brady and a business proposition. Blood Banks for India, it's called. Vast returns, untapped markets, they say. Brady is saying, Oh, Sylphide, you are like my sister and I want to make it up to you, all my foolishness! But large sums of money are required. Something they are cooking up to appeal to an old bleeding heart, mine. Thierry has checked every word of the contracts, he is saying. He is saying, 'As your financial manager, I am giving this my highest rating.' The Dolus legal team, he calls it—they've checked every document. If not for my little Bournonville I might have been fooled again. I would have been. India? Public health? Medicine? Those are things they know I already support through the foundations. Why not invest further? And if not for Daniel, who is knowing not to trust anyone, ever." She tapped the table, got my eyes back on hers. "But trust *me*, Lizard, darling Lizard, and listen. You was wanting to know. This is why they are staying at the High Side last month: I invite them. I am very good actress. I am letting let them talk about our big trip to India to inspect blood banks, how we should all travel there together. About all the papers I must sign immediately, about how my funds must be released soon as possible. People losing their life over there. Hurry! Poof-poof. We would all go to India and I would be dying there, Brady break my neck in an alley. Those papers? Three hunnert pages? Daniel's people look them over. And it all is good and straightforward except one thing: if I were to die. And then—very tricky documents—if I die, then I am giving over my entire estate to Blood Banks of India, which is the same as give it over to Dolus Investments, which is same as giving it to Thierry, which is same as giving it to Brady. They are boyfriends, Lizard. That's the other thing I realize, the other secret of their success. Brady making use of Thierry, of course, nosing out his secret life. More important thing is they are *killers*. I invite them to High Side those weeks ago because you and I must keep them very, very close. We must make a plan. And our plan must go off before theirs. Because their plan is the end of us."

I took that in, said, "But, Sylphide. Honestly. Why would they even begin to think that that estate clause wouldn't be noticed, that your lawyers wouldn't strike it?"

"Because, Lizard, like I am saying already—I am always trusting Thierry. I am never question Thierry. It's Thierry who reads my contracts, always. Thierry who okays them. Vast accounting department behind him. Head of Dolus! Always the most special attention for me! My money person, my financial manager. Why would I not be trusting him?"

"Yes, why," I said.

The new houseman entered silently, carrying a tray. He placed a small glass of water and a single sky-blue capsule at the dancer's hand. He rolled up the sleeve of her little jacket, took her pulse. He put a hand to her forehead. Had she gone hypochondriac? I put the magnifying glass back in its case, pushed the photograph aside. Out the tall windows I tracked the lights of a helicopter, watched it come closer, closer yet, watched it veer off at the last second, as if my gaze were a gale that blew it off course.

William withdrew, his shoes tapping off down the hallways back there, the maze of stairways. Tenke and I sat in silence, looking out at the view of the river, the coursing city beyond. I plucked one of the cognac snifters off the table, drank it down, aware again I was in my cook's clothes, that I smelled of the restaurant. My dancer began to slip in her chair. Her eyes drooped closed. I'd have to ring for William, soon, shout for him, however it was done in that beautiful house.

"I have a plan," she murmured suddenly. "But I don't know how to carry it out." She put a long hand awkwardly high on my thigh, intimately high, yawned extravagantly. "For that, I come to you."

I thought a moment, said, "Kate hopes we might be able to use some kind of DNA testing. Put together some evidence, link Kaiser and Perdhomme. Brady and Perdhomme, I mean. Whoa."

"DNA? *Link?* Evidence? Firfisle-mine, we are not needing any of that. We know what happen, we know exactly what happen."

"Then what do you propose?"

"We think it through, Lizano. We think it through together. Sometime very, very soon? Talk it through? Because right now, I am falling asleep." She really was, her frame twitching with it. Still she whispered: "To kill for passion, okay, *ja,* maybe I unnerstand. But to kill for *money?*" She yawned again, a vast, exhausted thing, said, "High Side? I am home there Monday. After this thing of mine they're doing, this retrospective. You'll attend—I leave the tickets. Then come see me, Lizano. Come row across your honest pond. Is time for us . . . is time . . . is for us to turn the game."

I stood, looked for some sort of bell, something to call for William, couldn't see how it was done. I said, "I don't think it's a game, Tenke. I don't think it's a game at all."

"You lovely, lovely man," she said. Her breath deepened, but still she talked, began to mutter, several sing-song sentences, something about Emily, something about Dabney, something more in Norwegian. And then something clear: "Is all written out, you know. Everything is fate. All written out in Heaven, or written out in Hell."

William's footsteps were coming up a stair back there. I picked up Sylphide's hand, brought it to my lips—a deep bow from my height down to her chair—kissed her elegant long fingers as so many fans and admirers had done before me.

23

A Tuesday night in late October, like any other Tuesday at Restaurant Firfisle, the start of our fifth year, a full book of reservations. The staff was buzzing: Sylphide's retrospective earlier in the month had been a smash, and now she was coming to Restaurant Firfisle for a private evening, party of three, her name right in the reservation book, greatest choreographer in the world. She'd been in the news as well because of Daniel Tancredi's admission to New York Hospital after the event, a coma from which he was not expected to wake. His care and prognosis was undisclosed and closely guarded, but some fink managed to get a few photos that turned up in all the newspapers of the world: Sylphide in the ambulance doors, clearly distraught, still in her gown.

Within a week William had called to say that Sylphide wanted me to know Daniel had been stabilized, a thoroughgoing stroke brought on by his cancer treatment, brain death likely; soon there'd be a decision for his children and Sylphide to make. And she wanted my advice in that. For the time being, however, Sylphide wanted me to know she was free to travel, and that her plans for India remained unchanged. She'd be in Westport one evening very soon.

My dancer let me know which evening by simply letting herself in through the glass patio sliders in my kitchen. She made her way silently to my living room, where I was deep in my new easy chair reading.

"I come to you when I'm alone," she announced.

I jumped, struggled to sit up in the face of the vision—just this girl in blue jeans and blouse, the girl of Dabney's album cover, her toes turned in shyly. I hadn't seen her hair out of its bun since our poolhouse days.

In addition to William's call, I'd been receiving messages via Dr.

Chun, destroying them in his sight after reading them, spy stuff. I'd sent my replies, which she in turn destroyed: Perdhomme and Kaiser would be coming again to Restaurant Firfisle in one week and one day—and in one week and one day and a few hours more she would accompany them to India, supposedly to investigate their blood banks proposal, whatever it was, saying she was doing it for Daniel. So Perdhomme and Kaiser couldn't kill me right away, I thought: I was needed as a prop.

The dancer climbed on my lap. She kissed my face. "I feel very close," she said.

"You are very close, Tenke. Close to me. Is that what you mean?"

"I'm not wanting to live without Daniel," she said.

"I'm sorry," I said.

"You, I am used to living without."

Since we'd last seen Perdhomme and Kaiser, we seemed to have had interlocking fantasies about them. It was like we'd torn a playing card and matched our two halves: my revenge fantasy would never have worked without hers, hers would never have worked without mine. Serious business, this transporting of fantasy into the actual world. But our plan was in place. This visit seemed to have its own purpose. Emily had left that morning, as Tenke no doubt knew, off around the world after the honestly quite moving and impressive and appropriate tribute to Sylphide, an event that had rocked Lincoln Center, rocked the city, shock waves still spreading round the world, what with Daniel's collapse as they'd arrived home.

Emily and I had had a week of harmony. Sylphide would outlive us both, we agreed, Sylphide would find the next very rich husband. All those legal documents, Tancredi's imminent death, that had had nothing to do with us. Nothing, that is, except for the idea embedded in there, Sylphide's idea, the idea that Emily and Lizard were fated to marry. We'd batted the idea back and forth. Not impossible. Not likely. But sex-drunk one evening I'd given her my mother's old engagement ring, nothing too impressive. Still, the gesture had moved Emily. We fell into a mutual warmth like we'd never had, a sense of caring, none of the usual badinage and bittersweet kisses, but something a lot like love. She wore the ring three days before giving it back, pretty considerate: she knew my mother's memory meant more to me than she ever would.

Sylphide in my lap rehearsed our plan for me one more time. It was very simple, really, and would be easy to abandon if at any stage things went wrong. Hard to see how we might get caught, though I suppose it's always hard to see anything at all with your face in the icy mists of the dish served cold. Also—she'd written this in one of her notes—if we did get caught, we'd get caught only after the fact, deed done. Well worth it, we agreed.

And that was it for soul-searching.

"I always wanted," she said reaching into my shirt, "to make love with you here in the house across the way."

"Across the wa-ayy," I sang softly, my froggy voice cracking, the refrain of Dabney's greatest ballad, one of several love songs he'd written for my sister, a number-one hit, as everyone knows, one of those chartbusters, months and months of constant play on the radio.

"I suppose it is impossible," Sylphide said.

"It would hardly be right," I agreed.

"My *Kjempe*," she said, and slipping her hands in my pants pockets, tugged her Giant upstairs and to his lair.

ETIENNE WAS UNHAPPY with me, as he is periodically, because periodically I get these urges and go off on a food mission that doesn't involve him, make executive decisions, change a supplier. And that morning I'd put Pasta Pazzo on the night's menu before he got in, sent the proof by email to the printer (a local craft-letterpress subsidized by the Tenke Thorvald Foundation, almost free to us, but always a little like writing the evening's menu in stone). We had a good supply of green tomatoes for beautiful fries, I'd checked on that. And then I'd gotten busy making wild-mushroom sausages from the exquisite load of king oysters and black trumpets and chanterelles and odd picks that Ferkie had dropped the afternoon before.

RuAngela rushed into the restaurant clacking in her heels on the old floorboards, a flood of cheer and confidence, gigantic hug to overmatch my obvious dolor. Etienne moonwalked in behind her, earphones from his Walkman loud enough for all the world to hear—Salt-N-Pepa—and the two of them danced a little, fell into an embrace, the most affectionate long-term couple I have ever known. While E.T. got dressed for the kitchen, I pulled Ru-Ru aside and told her about the menu change. She would conduct the information to Etienne, a bad-news system we'd developed over years, and I'd give him twenty minutes to calm down. I trotted out of the shop with seconds to spare, crossed the street and over into the deep-autumn garden, started pulling green hog-heart tomatoes—there were hundreds of the fat, dense things. Seconds later E.T. was behind me: I hadn't got my twenty minutes. I hadn't got two. I held a huge hog-heart up to him, scent of the plant, fantastic.

"Ha!" he shouted. "Green tomato fries? That's a no-go, mo-fo! We don't have those herbs, you kidding?" The man was genuinely scary when angry—something about that extra set of eyes, all the jewelry dangling off everything, but more than that, just the rare window on a deep fund of rage.

"We've got VIPs coming," I said gently.

"Oh, Mr. Enormous, this better be good."

"It's Sylphide," I said. "With those gentlemen from before."

"Sylphide," he said, theatrical gasp. He flung himself down beside me, started picking hog-hearts, placing them lovingly in our old olive-oil buckets one by one.

"You shouldn't call me mo-fo," I said.

"I'm sorry for that," he said.

"And the Mr. Enormous. I don't like that."

YOU WANT EVERYTHING to be normal on a big night. You want things to be normal all day. I waited till nearly two to call the staff meeting, and that was when I announced that my dancer would be coming. Back to work we went, the kitchen and dining room suddenly in performance mode, beautiful. I left, just as always, around two-thirty. Drove peacefully north, too vigilant in any case for the usual nap. I parked at a certain barn. And walked past nickering horses to a certain pasture, to a certain shaded corner Ferkie had shown me once offhand and that I'd been checking daily for a week: sure enough, the mushrooms had been there, every day more young ones pushing up through the duff, a kind of confirmation of Sylphide's and my plan, a growing galaxy of hundreds of pretty little specimens: either *Amanita phalloides* or *Amanita ocre-ata*. Death cap or destroying angel, didn't matter which, but very likely *ocreata,* given the time of year (said the budding mycologist). I picked upwards of five pounds of the youngest ones, glowing white caps still attached to veils, placed specimen after juicy specimen lovingly into one of Ferkie's large collection bags, delicious-looking knobs and stems, phallic certainly, the dick in the word *phalloides,* little flecks of leaf and dirt, faint bruises.

Back in the kitchen, I only had a couple of hours to work. Etienne and RuAngela had left, just two of our cleaning people in the dining room, the daily hiatus, vacuum running, only Colodo Doncorlo, our pasta chef, at work in the kitchen. She was irritable, having had the Pazzo sprung on her. I shrugged—wasn't I back early, too? And got to work, lovingly washing the death caps or destroying angels myself, lovingly drying them, one by one. Such robust, handsome mushrooms, compact and shapely. I chopped, one of the great pleasures of the kitchen, wielding my Masamoto, a big blade sharp as broken glass. For the sausage we kept and used the mushroom stems if not too woody; this added texture. I took the tiniest taste of the stem in my hand—it had a good bite, kind of thready, easily torn with the teeth, perfect. I swallowed it, not thinking, but not much worrying either: it had only been the most minuscule amount. Mushrooms cook down, of course, shrink terrifically, and *Amanitas p.* and *o.* are no exception, shrinking in the wine and butter and olive oil, darkening nicely, forming a beautiful stock to reduce. Each sausage might contain as much as a quarter pound of the original weight of the mushrooms, with just two ounces uncooked weight guaranteed deadly. Two ounces!

I lingered over the cooking, rubbed out some sage leaves, rolled a little fresh thyme, taking too much of the other kind of time, two trips to the garden, inefficient pleasure, dry-panning the herbs with just a little more Thai fire-pepper than I thought I should (because that's always the amount that's right in the end), attending to every detail. So much of the art of the professional kitchen comes in consistency. I chopped another round of mushrooms, adding raw to the mix for tooth, as always, but in this case for potency, potency. I wasn't nervous. I wasn't full of doubt.

And I wasn't afraid. I licked my knives constantly, kissed my fingers, added herbs, ground chilis, plenty salt, subtle spices, ate tiny morsels of the finished mixture, exquisite. But there was more to those sausages than that: they had the most subtle, lovely, rooty, earthy mushroom flavor I'd ever experienced, hints of fresh rain. I resisted eating spoonfuls of the mixture, but nibbled a little more, and then a little more again. Yes, yes, it was the single best food I'd ever tasted. The flavor would hold up a few hours, from what I'd read in the mushroom books, and I had read plenty.

Sylphide's reservation was early, six-thirty. She and her guests had one of the Tenke Thorvald Foundation's private jets reserved and waiting: overnight flight to Bombay, as the city was still called.

KATE AND JACK arrived just at five, per planning. The Firfisle staff already knew my sister from frequent visits. They knew the drill, too—she was here to serve Sylphide and her guests; the others were to leave them alone. E.T. patted my sister's still golden hair, kissed her bright cheeks: oddballs attract. Of course Brady would know her, and of course he would know she knew him: how naïve we'd seem, what pawns.

Only Sylphide and I knew the full plan. Kate and Jack and E.T. and Ru thought we were all engaged in an undercover DNA collection, something we'd all agreed we had to do although no one at the current D.A.'s office (Jack's discreet inquiry) was even slightly interested in the cold old case. The Firfisle staff was not to touch or see or know anything: no one but the core of us should be implicated in any legal issues that might arise. And we'd all expressed a lot of confidence in things going right: DNA collected, positive analysis proving connection of both men to their crimes, D.A. interested once again, case reopened, a couple of old murderers convicted. The dancer's role was simply to bring in our quarry. Even Kate had seen the wisdom of that, though none of my explanations had convinced her of Sylphide's innocence.

Neurotic celebrity, we told the staff. Special requirements. My sister was to be treated by everyone on duty just as any other waitperson, someone you were used to, no special hugs or hellos. In the wait-station she put her hair up, immediately found one of our signature green jackets to fit tight. RuAngela put her on napkin-folding duty, no special treatment and a good idea to keep Kate's hands busy, keep her nerves down: surely if there were a weak link, Kate was it. She was very, very excited that her plan had prevailed. She was very, very unhappy that Sylphide would take part, and had said so repeatedly, heatedly. It took Etienne to settle her down—look at the role the dancer was playing, bringing the marks to table!—and later Jack to keep her calm and focused. "DNA," he kept repeating, "DNA."

Jack stuck around long enough to make sure things were going to be okay, then to his car and to the Remarkable Bookshop downtown, kill an hour or so—his own reservation was for 6:15—get himself something to read over a solo dinner. Kate would be his waitress, too, so she wouldn't just be serving the one table or compromising service for actual customers by serving anyone other than Jack. And, of course, Sylphide and the killers.

RuAngela was to help Kate collect utensils, drinking glasses, napkins, anything and everything that might yield usable DNA samples, just the hostess's usual job of tidying. Kate had looked into "best practices," as the FBI manual called them, and the private lab we would use had provided ridiculous little vials and glassine envelopes and swabs and even an evidence log. RuAngela would also coat-check our PPX table, take jackets, capes, sweaters, whatever the killers were wearing, comb them betimes for hairs, flakes of skin. I had quit protesting the technicalities—all that, I hoped, would be moot.

At five-thirty Firfisle's first diners appeared, elderly regulars, Tuesday clockwork. Prep was still in progress when their orders came in, and the kitchen underwent its seamless transition to service, the daily infusion of energy. The Firfisle gang all lived for that pressure, the exhilaration of running ahead of an avalanche for a few hours every night. For me, just the usual nerves, nothing extraordinary. It was the big game, and game day had finally come. I closed my eyes and pictured a successful outcome over and over: the plates going out, the plates coming back empty. That's all I had to achieve.

There was a small fridge under each station in the kitchen, and I padlocked mine after a long look at the perfection of my sausages. They were keeping their color nicely. I tried a microscopic pinch of the filling—still in perfect taste, that exquisite, harrowing flavor. Sylphide, playing dupe to the Blood Banks of India scam and fussy diva all at once, would enforce the ordering. So there should be no surprises.

By six the dining room was full, one of those nights that won't unfold gradually but explodes.

"*Rumble,*" E.T. called out.

"*Rock 'n' roll,*" we all answered.

It was a great kitchen on a particularly good night, everyone's timing flawless, the call-and-response game spontaneous, and we all laughed easily, staying connected to one another and to the food.

Kate popped in the kitchen, marched straight to the salad table. "God damn," she said. There just wasn't enough for her to do. I could see she was crawling out of her skin, the inner Kate beginning to emerge. In our trim jacket she seemed a very beautiful matador dropped down from some unknown dimension, flushed and vibrant, much older than she looked, much younger than anyone there, a nine-year-old playing restaurant. She was close to ignition. She'd have to settle down. If anything could set her off it would be the sight for the first time in nearly twenty years of Tenke Thorvald. But what other tactic did I have?

"Just calm," I said, touching her back.

The kitchen was sizzling and popping. Zone-hot, as we used to say on the Miami Dolphins.

"Blue jeans," E.T. sang out. Kate was his 'Venus in Blue Jeans,' he meant. She'd heard it before, visibly relaxed, thumped out to the dining room, thumped back, nowhere to go, nothing to do but wait. "DNA," I said.

"DNA," she repeated. She gathered up the napkins she'd folded, pushed out into the dining room. She was my Crazy May, and might do anything. She didn't come back, five minutes, ten. I'd got salads pretty well caught up, so chanced a peek out there. Judicious Jack was in his place, probably early—I wore no watch—seated over by the coatroom. Kate was looming over him. She looked nothing like a waitperson, not even a matador. She looked how the president of the United States would look in a movie for ambitious girls. She pointed at the menu emphatically, tense as a mousetrap. Jack flirted as if they'd just met. They'd better pull it in, I thought. Jack saw me watching, got the message, said something to Kate,

something I could read on his lips: *DNA*. She made a circuit of the dining
room with the water pitcher, nice. The men's eyes followed her fanny. Jack
would order the Pasta Pazzo, of course, and that would set things ticking.

I went to my station, waited, waited interminably, polished the stain-
less steel of my counter. Finally Kate appeared with Jack's order, and
after an appropriate wait I plated the tamer wild-mushroom sausages
I'd moved from E.T.'s fridge to mine, top shelf, darker in color than the
deadly group on the bottom shelf, quick minuscule pinch—still flavorful.
Heated bowl exact timing from Colodo at the pasta station, double ladle
of her morning's beautiful pasta dressed with leek cream. Dash of salt in
the sauté pan, splash of Umbrian E.V.O.O., strips of pepper red and green,
three or four leaves peeled off a fat new brussels sprout, short heat, peak
of flavor, make a little crown atop the piping fettuccine, sausages laid like
thick petals, pretty.

Kate was back too soon, snapping and dancing like a power line down
in a storm, you could feel it. Yet very smoothly she folded a napkin over
her hand, took the bowl, turned to E.T. for the green tomato fries on
their separate plate, Pasta Pazzo complete. Jack was going to be thrilled:
free meal.

I helped the dessert table get a gooey mango cake plated cleanly, made
some adjustments at the grill, wiped my station again, triply sterilizing
everything that had come in contact with the other sausages during prep,
bursting with the tension till Kate tumbled in again. "They've arrived,"
she announced to the kitchen.

The pace picked up a beat.

E.T. looked her up and down, just as he would any waitperson under
stress. "Calm," he said, deep voice.

Kate breathed for him, came to me at my station.

Quietly, I said, "Remember, you're a plain-old waitress. You've seen it
all. So what, she's famous."

"No, no. It's him," she said. "It's fucking Brady."

"Doesn't matter, Katydid. Okay? Just like we said, exactly. He'll pretend
he doesn't recognize you. He knows whose restaurant this is. Of course
you work at my restaurant, just like we said. You'll pretend you don't
know him, too. It's a game. We'll get what we're after. They think we're

scared. Just as we planned—you don't care about a couple of middle-aged gays. Let Brady guess whether you recognize him, why you're dissing him. We play their hubris. They think we're stupid, still kids. They think the only plan is theirs. And okay to greet Sylphide. A little rueful, like we said."

"Like we said."

"Stay focused," I said. "Think DNA."

Kate took a breath, tugged down at the tight matador jacket. She said, "RuAngela's taking their coats!"

"Just as planned," I said. "Maybe help Picky Ricky." And she did, helped our headwaiter carry out a large order, table twelve over in the corner. I couldn't help it, looked out after her. In the front window, sunset in progress, every possible layer of light, Perdhomme and Kaiser just getting settled in their seats, RuAngela helping them, Sylphide already alight on hers, pleasant smiles all around.

The owner of Restaurant Firfisle should greet the famous dancer, Sylphide and I had agreed. That would be just normal behavior. Greet the dancer, acknowledge her guests, play the recognition game, we had called it—everyone pretending—act scared, in fact, someone taken by surprise and trying to keep his cool (nerves would take the place of any acting: I was scared, all right), lull them, stroke them, take my revenge face to face. I was always greeting guests. It came naturally enough. So out of the kitchen, straight to their table.

"Sylphide," I said. "Delightful."

"Ah, the famous owner," she said extending her hand.

I kissed it.

Perdhomme didn't look at me, made a point of staring out the window. I gazed at him a beat too long.

Kaiser put his hand out. "Brady," he said. "Brady Rattner."

I shook the limpish hand, braved a long look in his eye—he was one of those people who doesn't back down from a gaze.

"Thierry," Mr. Perdhomme said quickly. He didn't offer his hand, gave me the briefest look. Exquisitely awkward. He knew exactly who I was, and he knew I knew him. There was definitely something planned for me, planned for later, for after they'd taken Sylphide down.

I kept my face blank, said what I always say: "We're pleased to have you."

Little blunt sentences, tough Newcastle accent, Brady said, "We do love the restaurant. We're not meat people. How's your capitalization? We'd love to invest. We'll stop in when we're back. Yes, we'll stop in. And we'll bring some associates of ours. If you're still here. The restaurant, I mean. It's a volatile business. We have skilled associates. It may be you're gone by the time we're back, but if you're still here."

"We'll be here, all right."

"We're off to Bombay tonight," Sylphide sang, preternatural ease.

"India," I said impressed.

"She insists on the trains," Perdhomme said as if miserably, everyone acting.

"It's authentic," Brady said as if placating a reluctant partner. He had hundreds of millions of dollars in his eyes, or maybe a billion, now that Tancredi was on his way out.

"There's an endless outdoor market by the station," Sylphide said. "They fill you an enormous basket, beautiful things."

"Not an inch given to jetlag," said Brady. Brady Rattner, Dabney's rotten brother, I couldn't get over it: Kaiser.

"But first, Restaurant Firfisle," said the dancer, and we all laughed as if it were the wittiest thing we'd ever heard.

RuAngela returned with the wine list. You're lingering, her look said. Don't be stupid, it said. Perdhomme snatched the thick book, buried his face in it.

"I'd better get back in the kitchen," I said, tipping an imaginary hat. I backed away from their table, Brady's gaze upon me frigid. I looked to Sylphide, but she was touching Perdhomme's sleeve, saying something bright.

Quick hello to an older couple, regulars I was fond of, then a detour to the coat room, where I found the dancer's pea coat. I sniffed it to be sure—jasmine—then slipped our smooth little stone heart into the right side pocket, the pocket you always put your hand in first, imagined her fingers finding it, my only chance to say farewell before her trip. Fleeting thought: maybe Emily wasn't the bride that fate had in store for me.

Back in the kitchen, I cleaned my station yet again, with only a thump in my chest when Kate hurried in with the actual order. She'd calmed herself, spoke like a seasoned old waitress, all business. Autumn-vegetable stew for Sylphide, as the dancer and I had planned, no surprises. Pazzo for the boys, Sylphide imperiously ordering for them, as planned. I nodded, matter of fact. The beet and arugula salad went out first, to be split three ways, three pretty little plates. Then the warm olives and almonds Kaiser had ordered, a tiny dish.

Signal from RuAngela—time to plate the entrées. Bowls of tangled fettuccine from Colodo, smoothest timing, not a word between us, impress the celebrity. Flash-sauté the garnish, drop it in, then four fat death-cap sausages, each like petals on flowers. And Kate's rhythm a little better, a relaxed waitress now that she and RuAngela had their first genetic samples from salad forks and water glasses. Ru appeared with more exact timing, a loud joke for the kitchen. E.T. began to sing—always singing, our E.T. We'd gotten the food out beautifully, the whole kitchen knew. We were going to get the DNA we needed, our little team knew. We were just serving them dinner. Almost all of us could relax.

RuAngela nodded, collected the dressed vegetable stew from a line cook, the green-tomato fries from E.T. Kate draped her arm with a napkin, loaded up the pasta, followed RuAngela's high heels. But Kate's hands were burning—those heated bowls gripped wrong. She stopped at the door station—a tall, stainless-steel table placed for just such emergencies—got her napkin lined up properly, inspected the food, looked back at me as RuAngela rushed in.

"I touched him," Ru said as Kate pushed out into the dining room. "I put my hand on his dirty shoulder. I gave him the Ru-Ru eye."

THE EVENING RUSH heated up another notch. The kitchen clicked and whistled, splendid machine. I took up my position on the fireline as a new welter of small-plate orders came in, wrenched my mind off the meal going on out there: nearly a pound of mushrooms concentrated for each killer, if they ate all their sausage, enough for a ghastly death in every bite, a chef who took no chances.

It seemed all but eternal, but ineluctably here came RuAngela with the empty plates from our special guests. I followed her into the dish room. Our lovely dish man was a person like Linsey: very focused, competent, capable, no social graces, bottom teeth up over his lip. We'd been given a method for packaging the silverware, best practices for the DNA lab. Not, I kept thinking, that we'd need the lab or the DNA or the best practices in the end. The china went into padded plastic pouches separately—crime-lab protocol, thanks to all of Kate's research and supplies, hopelessly naïve.

Ru-Ru pushed the stew bowl toward the dish man—that was the dancer's. I helped it along the steel counter, saw the dish man take it, everything seeming particular and bright.

"I'll finish," I said to Ru.

Quickly I unpacked the Pazzo bowls—they shouldn't be going to any lab!—replaced them with others similar, rinsed them myself with the sprayer hose, rinsed them thoroughly, pushed them along the steel counter to the dish man, who took them in his impassive way. I put the evidence sack in the unused refrigerator back there, so what? No lab would ever see it. And left the dish man to his steaming tasks.

I noted only in subsequent minutes, vivid near-term memory, that there had been the knot ends of two mushroom sausages in the stew bowl, Sylphide's bowl, the kind of thing a kid or picky eater leaves. But, of course, we didn't use sausages in our autumn-vegetable stew.

Kate swaggered into the kitchen, gave me a long look. *"La* fucking *cuenta por favor,"* she said privately, the embarrassing joke Dad had always made at restaurants if the staff was foreign. A lightness had overtaken her.

"You didn't change anything about the presentation? Nothing at all?" I blurted.

"Change the presentation?" she said.

My shoulders eased, eased again.

I HAD A bellyache next day by noontime, sweated profusely, grew worried. I'd eaten no more than a quarter-teaspoon of the death angels, yet spent the night hearing their voices, a chorus of sibilant contraltos, my mother's among them: *"Something you want to tell me?"* I couldn't feel good about what I'd done, all alone in the dark.

Next morning I was fine, actually rather elated, next evening mildly nauseous again, then violently nauseous, then hearing voices and wind noises in my ears, a kind of boinging sound, sense of insects walking under my hair, and with eyes closed sharp lights under the lids. Another night's sleep and it was all over. I tried to imagine having eaten five hundred times more of the amantin poison: horrible, sudden.

Recurrences all day, all the next. Sharp lights under the eyelids. Insects in the hair. Wind in the ears. Mom's voice, repeated, repeated, not so unpleasant: *"That's how you win at tennis, David."*

And Emily's, over and over: *"We've really got no one else."*

And Sylphide's: *"Firfisle-mine."*

I COMBED *The New York Times* for a couple of days, but as it turned out, there was no need for vigilance. Because when the news came, it was everywhere, *The New York Times* first, RuAngela racing into the walk-in to find me, snapping the paper folded to the story so I might immediately see:

On that Friday, the great dancer and choreographer Sylphide had horribly died in Miraj, India, a small town on the border of Maharastra and Karnataka provinces, about two hundred miles south of Bombay. Yes, Sylphide. I gasped when I read it, fell to my knees on the walk-in floor, read the short article over and over again. Two companions had also succumbed to obvious food-borne illness, one of them her brother-in-law, the other the CEO of embattled Dolus Financial, frequent companions. An investigation was underway, but there was no real mystery—the little band of friends had carried off a huge basket of native foods from an unsanctioned Mumbai market, any number of pathogens possible, had boarded a train, almost immediately fallen ill. The trio was briefly hospitalized in the city of Pune, incompetently discharged, and died a day later on a night train heading deeply south into India. The train staff had dropped them outside a clinic in a town called Bhadravadi, southern Karnataka, but too late: death had come quickly, violently. Villagers burned the bodies respectfully per custom, the day being over one hundred degrees Fahrenheit.

Etienne, at first, was aghast at the coincidence, then for a day or two gave me long looks. Then it got worse: I wept so much I couldn't go into work, fell ill again, isolated myself, a week of severe emotion, remorse, horror, a reversion to grief and guilt I hadn't felt since the days after October 30, 1970, and could not contain, no one to confess to without turning them into accomplices.

Mr. Perdhomme no longer walked the earth. Brady Rattner, same. Let us remember that, I kept telling myself, kept repeating it through my tears: Perdhomme and Kaiser are dead.

24

I waited, and have continued to wait, but no suspicion ever fell on me in the matter of the deaths of the dancer and her travel companions. No one at all ever came to me in the matter for any reason at all. I waited for Ferkie the Mushroom Man to say something, to turn up on the likes of *60 Minutes* (four segments on Sylphide to date) but Ferkie had no interest in the lives and deaths of celebrities, continued to shuffle obliviously in the leaves of the forest floor.

I suspected Kate in the unnecessary death of Sylphide, suspected her for months, let the suspicion eat at me, keep me from her. But why? My sister hadn't been in on the destroying-angel plan. That plan had been between Sylphide and me, closely guarded. And Kate, she'd never taken the faintest interest in mushrooms, poison or otherwise, either in the field or in my kitchen, would have had no reason to draw any kind of connection between the meal she'd served and the deaths. Still, my own suspicion lingered, darkened my thoughts, already dark enough, a kind of projection of my culpability, as if it were she and not I who'd picked the poison toadstools, lovingly cooked them, packed them into sausage casings. No reason she couldn't have detected my tension around those sausages, was the logic of my whispering demon: she had always been uncannily prescient with me.

Of course our DNA project was moot. I never did my job, never delivered our samples to the lab in Bridgeport. When news of the deaths emerged, I added another layer to my deceit, pretended to call the lab and cancel the project—we knew what the results would be after all, as I kept saying. Kate didn't like that. But Jack was very much in favor of shutting the DNA door forever, and Etienne and Ru were behind me, too: What had anyone to gain?

In the months after the dancer's death my mood improved, really in inverse proportion to the growth of another suspicion: what if it weren't Kate at all? What if the dancer had asked each of her solicitous dinner companions if she might have just one from them each of those delectable-looking mushroom sausages? What if smiling with the conversation she'd eaten first one then the other right down to the nub ends, knowing full well?

Full well.

ANOTHER TWENTY YEARS are gone. Lots of football players have long hair now—even the quarterbacks, even the best, Tom Brady, for example, who's come into the restaurant five or more times with his wife, the supermodel Gisele: take that, Coach Powers. Etienne and RuAngela own Firfisle now, outright. I gifted them my share gradually, a plan concocted by our layered, double-blind team of accountants. The place is more successful than ever, a model in the industry, booms through recessions, booms through market lulls, plenty of health- and farm- and planet-conscious eaters now, at least in Fairfield County, Connecticut. Many of our sous-chefs and line cooks—the Firfisalinos, some food writer dubbed them—have started their own places over the years and across the country, nearly always with our blessing, and if so with our money behind them, and so a kind of movement has expanded across the land: great fresh food beautifully grown and prepared, reasonable prices, not much meat.

The singing from the kitchen's the same, and RuAngela's there to greet me, greet one and all. I cook occasionally, Saturday prep nearly always, but that's more to spend time with E.T. and Ru than anything else.

Because life is very busy. I'm in charge of two great charities—the Tenke Thorvald Foundation and the Children of War Foundation, trying to put money in places around the world it can do the most good, small business startups and rescues, primarily, a lot of local agriculture, thousands of small grants rather than many huge, and of course the arts, defined broadly, very broadly, even a fine restaurant here and there, and many a promising dance company. Through the much smaller and newer Lizano Foundation we are able to fund inner-city and rural children's sports leagues all over the world, building a sense of teamwork and fair play, offering an alternative to more nefarious activity.

Bhadravadi, that little town in India, has a first-tier hospital now, and yes, a blood bank. I was there for the dedications, on the eve of the millennium. The hospital director, a nervous little man quite awed by my height, had a small paper packet for me, made me to understand that these were the great ballerina's effects, those that had been on her person when she succumbed on the train in blue jeans and T-shirt. The clothing, of course, had been immolated with her. Her suitcase, anything else she might have carried on the train, all that had been lost, a very public train, he wanted me to know. There'd been no rings, no necklaces, no bracelets, he said, solemnly apologetic. I assured him our dancer never wore jewelry, and at that the kindly fellow was much relieved, clasped both my wrists. He hadn't wanted to be accused, clearly, nor have his townspeople accused. He was handing over a last responsibility, had waited too long, was heartsick over the delay. I didn't open the packet till I was on the plane home, the trip well underway.

Inside was only the great ballerina's tattered red Norwegian passport, with its wretched two-by-two Polaroid photograph, black-and-white in that era, bemused look on her face, a plain person, no hint of her greatness (though the sweetness comes through). Inside the passport was another bit of heavily textured Indian scrap paper, and inside that I found the speckled heart, polished and pale green as ever, one last secret between Sylphide and me.

IN THE END, I did get married, but that's a story for a different time, a Sri Lankan woman I met through the foundation, Aamani. Suffice it to say that I did at last receive Sylphide's bequest, High Side and all. My new bride and I didn't want to move in, however. It's a showplace, not a home, a museum of broken hearts and not only of Dabney's huge collection of contemporary art. The modest house my folks could manage across the way is plenty of house for us, steeped in memory, and now some measure of redemption.

The High Side is foundation headquarters now—Sylphide's suite of rooms and the long corridor of guest rooms adjacent to it house the front office. The Emily Bright Experience is headquartered at the High Side, too, along with the Tenke Thorvald Memorial Conservatory of Dance and Music, a newer enterprise, hundreds of kids always coming and going, always dancers, dancers, dancers across the genres, instrumentalists of every possible stripe and persuasion, the ballroom in constant use. We house the largest dance library in the country, which includes at least a hundred books on Dabney Stryker-Stewart and his music, more books than that on the great ballerina, including seventeen biographies, only one of them with any mention of me, by a writer who had access to Georges Whiteside: Georges confirms his affair with Sylphide, confirms that he was in love with her from the day they met, confirms that they became lovers after Dabney's death, that she broke his heart for Marcello Mastroianni, a short-lived dalliance. And then this quotation: "The actor hardly mattered, as the whole bloody time I was after her she's in love with this young giant, a kid she couldn't take her eyes off and couldn't stop yammering on about, lovely him."

Whoa.

Dr. Chun lives upstairs, almost a hundred years old, still mobile, still the great sports fan, no longer driving. William is the houseman, too formal and stiff for me but indispensable. Also a lot of other staff to run the place, some of whom remember Sylphide and like to offer stories.

In the grand foyer there's a secure display case with the gold bust of August Bournonville inside (it is in fact solid), also now a photograph of Desmond dusting it, found only recently by the High Side archivist in a batch of Conrad Pant's papers. I can hardly bear to look, seldom look, convinced the bust is covered in my father's filthy fingerprints.

There are other displays, too, all sorts of memorabilia, hundreds of photographs—parents waiting for kids in the dance classes often linger to look. It seems Dabney holds all his old power, as of course does Sylphide. Her diaries remained sealed and were buried in a time capsule on the grounds along with some other materials, to be opened after one hundred years and a day, as stipulated in her will.

KATE TOWARD THE end was steady as a seawall, surprisingly so, since for several years she'd been off all meds in favor of what I would like to say are kooky remedies, but they seemed to be working. Or perhaps, I thought, she'd finally outgrown her demons. Anyway, you didn't have to be careful what you said anymore, and that look of panic in her eye had been replaced with something like wisdom, also a shocking great warmth. She coached the girls' tennis team at Madison High, a volunteer position, and those young women loved her abjectly. She could still hit, too, still with the wicked backhand, that nasty spin, killer serve. Jack was almost eighty, still sailing *Deep Song,* the two of them forever off into the sunset. And the two of them, I swear, were still the great lovers, always fresh out of the shower looking kissed and bruised no matter what time you got there.

RuAngela threw a party for Etienne's supposedly sixtieth birthday, and Kate, actually and verifiably sixty, came down to be my date at Restaurant Firfisle. Aamani was on the road as always, breaking new ground for the Children of War Foundation in the borderlands of Mali. So it was just we old-timers. Etienne sang, his heartfelt, reedy tenor a cappella, heartbreaking. RuAngela came out in pants, no wig, no makeup, no false eyelashes, first time in public since I'd known her. The invitation had said come as you are, and we were as we came, a full house of friends and regulars, chefs from all over. The kitchen staff turned out sixty-one different tapas (one to grow on), all sorts of magnificent tastes. Kate drank champagne like the rest of us. I didn't intercede, wasn't thinking—still the loving, blind brother.

Back to Hochmeyer Haven late, Kate and I, the two of us full of festive fellow feeling. We watched television far too long, curled up the way we used to do on opposite ends of the couch, old shows we'd forgotten (*My Favorite Martian!*) and that brought us to well past midnight, Kate showing no signs of slowing. I went to bed, drifted off to canned laughter from the television.

I woke in the deep night to her shaking me.

"I had a dream," she said urgently.

"Katy?"

"I know where it is!"

No concession to my sleepy confusion, she pulled at the delicate chain around her neck, showed me the tiny, familiar key she'd been wearing all those years. "We've got to look," she said.

"Kate," I said. "Kate, forget it."

"'Kate, forget it!' *Please*, David. I can't go over there alone. I won't go over there alone."

Soon I found myself dressing again, found myself following her down the stairs and through the kitchen and across the lawn in balmy winds, found myself climbing into Dad's old rowboat, found myself rowing Crazy May across to the High Side, dead of night, all the years falling away. There were people still awake in the citadel, lights on anyway, a whole dance company boarding there, all the up-and-coming kids Emily worked with. But no matter, Kate and I were headed to the poolhouse. Under a particular rock she found a heavy old key to go with the tiny one, badly oxidized brass, green as grass, knew right where it was. She scraped it on the cement, rubbed it in some sand, her hair tossed violently by the wind, brushed that key in the leaves till it shone, and then she tried it on the hatch door cut into the big carriage bay, a difficult fit in the lock, a difficult turning, but turn it did, and the door was open.

We crept past the miniature carriage bays and then upstairs in faint light. Sylphide's vastly complicated and thoroughly up-to-date will and endowment had expressly required that the poolhouse remain unused but maintained. At any rate, no one had been in there but the High Side cleaning staff, and they with strictest instructions from William to keep it as it was, and it was neat, very clean, maybe a little stuffy, a pail and mop carelessly left out in the first kitchen. Right at that undersized stove the dancer and I had warmed the exquisite food that had been brought us. Right at that counter, had opened the wine. Right on that bearskin in front of that fireplace, well, a lot of stuff, those indolent days of our sojourn. The taste of jasmine came to my tongue, the taste of her sweat, her salty creases.

"You were here with Dabney," I said.

"And you were here with her," Kate said, a couple notches north of neutral.

"Yes," I said: no more lies. Or, at any rate, fewer.

She led me down the hallway past the many little bedrooms to the familiar linen closet, marched straight inside, pushed the corner of the correct shelf, swung the secret door into the beautiful bedroom, which was preserved as if it were a stage set. My grief hooked me once more, bottomless mourning, a musty wave of emotion, something emerging from behind glass, something former shaking off the dust.

"He said to look under the moss," Kate said evenly.

Dabney, she meant. In her dream. Or Daddy—she wasn't sure, rather blended the two words. Reluctantly, I helped her move a little wooden chest (we both knew what was in it—checkers, card games, ivory dice cups, antique jigsaw puzzles), lifted a corner of the dense green woolen carpet (mossy, okay, sure). Beautiful, patterned parquet floor under there, nothing else. We slid the chest back into place, moved the loveseat in the next corner (I supposed we both knew that piece of furniture very well; anyway there was a mutual hesitation), lifted the moss—nothing. I didn't want to have to move the bed, but we did, pulled it out from the wall much more easily than you'd think, expensive old casters sliding smooth as skin on skin. Kate lifted the corner of the carpet, folded it back. Underneath was a hatch as on a ship, old brass hinges, old brass handle, all of it beautifully recessed in the wood. Kate turned the latch, lifted the hatch easily, but only revealed another hatch, much lighter wood, tiny golden lock.

Which, of course, Kate's key fit, effortless clockwork mechanism. "Look," she hissed.

I could not. I only saw Dad, saw him catching one of the dozens of footballs he let me throw at him every afternoon when I was ten, eleven, twelve, felt the pop of the footballs in my chest as they came back, one by one into the hundreds, the thousands, probably tens of thousands over the years. And then Mom, of course, Mom spinning off to the club in her whites, hair mounted in a perfect pouf, legs up to here, off to slaughter the tennis ladies, merciless.

Down in the snug compartment was his briefcase, all right, unmistakable icon of my youth. Kate knelt, tried valiantly, but couldn't get it out of the hidey-hole. So I bent down there, found the handle, jimmied the thing, a very difficult fit, as if the compartment had been made just for the briefcase. Old Samsonite hard-shell, Dad's initials stamped in vainglorious gold under the handle. One of those combination locks, a row of numbers.

"Let's get out of here," Kate said.

WE SAT THE briefcase on the kitchen table, where in the old days it had often lingered. Kate, very calm now, tried Mom's birthday on the four-number lock. Nope. I tried Dad's. Nope. Kate tried mine. Nope. I tried Kate's. And the latches flipped open, familiar snaps.

Maybe I expected blue Yangtze River pearls, rare gold coins, diamonds, too, but Dad really had put all that in Perdhomme's hands, desperate to pay off whatever mistake it was he'd made, whatever deadly mistake, not even Mr. Bournonville enough. Certainly I expected that manila envelope, stuffed with everything he wanted us to know. But the briefcase was empty, each of its accordion folds empty, nothing in there but the air of another time and a packet of travel tissues, a couple of old receipts. Kate and I shared a long look, incredulous, both of us.

The famous briefcase, empty.

"Oh, Daddy," Kate said.

"Daddy," I repeated.

And it was like his spirit flew up in our faces, freed. Or anyway a sudden wind blew back our hair, fluttered the tissues, tossed the receipts, rattled the cabinets: we'd left the patio doors open in our haste, and outside it was getting ready to storm.

Kate shook her head, I shook mine. She chuckled a little. Me, too, ha. Then on cue we burst into hilarious laughter, shouts of laughter, gales of it, laughed till we cried, hooting and snorting with it, laughter funny in itself, laughter redoubled as we locked eyes, locked eyes and laughed till our innards hurt, laughed till we choked, laughed and sputtered and then laughed more. We held one another and laughed together like we hadn't in forty years.

"Since they died," I said later.

"Since Dabney died," my sister corrected.

KATE'S OWN DEATH last fall took us all by surprise. She'd been cheerful, full of life, hyper cheerful, to be sure, several phone calls a day, transcendent plans, soaring dreams, future projects in the thousands. And cheerfully one unseasonably hot morning, after a late breakfast of tortilla chips and avocado dipped directly out of the shell, she told Jack she was going for a run, just that, a run. Maybe a half hour later, he was surprised to see *Deep Song* floating off its mooring, the sails unfurling in a very fresh wind, Kate at the helm, oblivious of his shouts. Then the note on the kitchen table: *It's time.*

The Coast Guard found the boat empty with the spinnaker furled and filled, the tiller tied, old beautiful *Deep Song* preceding the wind on her own and far out to sea. Kate turned up half buried in sand on the very tip of Long Island, naked except for her necklace, Dad's golden key.

Her beach is beside an old-school stone breakwater, at the very end of which, and sufficiently under the high tide line that it's exposed only half the time, Jack has had a deeply molded bronze plaque bolted for the ages. Just one word: KATE. The rest, he felt, was nobody's business.

THE ARCHIVIST ASSIGNED to the High Side collections turned to Linsey's cache only recently, all sorts of papers and photos and works of childish art organized and labeled meticulously by Desmond—one didn't forget Desmond's handwriting. There were a great many medical records, of course, and the usual birth and baptism certificates and announcements, school notices, but also newspaper files, magazine spreads, stuff his father had kept and later Sylphide, very likely Kate as well, and of course our favorite butler. There were also several dozen large boxes of the boy's personal effects, organized by dwelling, wherever in the world they'd been. In the High Side stuff the archivist had found a folder of drawings. Linsey hadn't been a bad draftsman, perhaps a bit of a savant in that regard, endless pretty sketches of smokestacks and willow trees and vintage cars, all with vaginas—fairly innocent vaginas, but vaginas nevertheless. Tucked amongst the drawings (finest watercolor paper) was Dad's big manila envelope, neatly addressed to Kate, and carefully labeled IN THE EVENT OF MY DEATH.

The archivist brought it to me at my desk at the foundation office upstairs at the High Side. I held it a long time, Dad's familiar, long-lost handwriting. He'd meant to install it in his waiting briefcase, no doubt, safely warehoused down in that hidey hole (it could never be seen in our house again), meant to tell Kate where to look. Even desperate, his arrest imminent, he must have thought he had more time. That night I'd seen him sneaking down to the rowboat and over to the High Side, something must have gone wrong. He couldn't get in the poolhouse, probably, couldn't find the key (Kate had moved it many times, she admitted, thinking Sylphide spied on her). He didn't trust Desmond, I knew. Certainly didn't trust the dancer. And he wasn't welcome there. Had he come across Linsey? Asked for Linsey? Given the boy the envelope along with strict instructions? Strict instructions the kid would never understand? Had he been that frantic? He must have known that whomever Perdhomme sent would ransack his desk at our house if the worst came down.

I wish Kate could have held out, could have been at my side when I got home that evening. I didn't even mention the packet to Aamani—too much to explain. While she cooked (magnificent ethnic Tamil dishes, too fiery for most American tastes, sometimes too much for mine), I sat at the very desk, opened the packet in a fever of curiosity, three envelopes inside. The first held the carbon copy of a receipt from Goldberg's Shoes, the place we always went in Fairfield for my back-to-school loafers, Hyman Goldberg's clear, triumphant handwriting: *One pair hi-cut Chippewa Work Mate work boots size nine.* Under that, Daddy's more cowed script, neat as a schoolmarm's: *IOU (Goldberg) $24.99,* dated March 28, 1970, and signed with a flourish. Evocative, maybe, certainly something to puzzle over, those muddy new boots ending up in Kaiser's rental car, the one whose rear window I'd smashed, but in the end not much help: who was framing whom? Had Brady asked to borrow Dad's boots on some pretext, planning to leave incriminating prints everywhere he went? And had Dad, wise to him, bought new ones and used them but once—Kate's painting caper—and then handed them over? And had Brady put them on the day of Dabney's murder? Kate had come to think so, reimagined it endlessly right to the week of her death, and perhaps here was proof again that she'd been right.

Both brothers, she'd often told me, had their fancy cars, and in the old days often drag-raced one another out on the Merritt Parkway, more than once outrunning cops, bragging rights back at the High Side for whoever had won. Brady's car was a British model, I'm forgetting which, and that was part of the battle, too: Britain against America. Kate's theory was that Perdhomme and Brady had cooked up an emergency for Dabney to attend to, something about his money—there'd been urgent phone calls at the High Side all day—possibly, once again, something about Dad, something Dad had supposedly done or was supposedly about to do, something that required a fast, angry drive into New York City, middle of the night, Dad to be stopped, some supposed scheme, Dad as the fall guy.

The younger brother was forever bragging about his skills as a stunt driver, Dabney and the others always making fun. *Brother Kaiser, thinks he can drive!* Brady would have picked the Den Road Bridge in advance. Its old-school cement bulwark, sharp-edged and brutal, often scarred, was only a yard from the highway pavement. Intercept Dabney, engage him in one last race. *Where the bloody hell did you come from!* Realization dawning in the famous rocker's head: *Whatever the fuck is going on, Brady is involved.* Rage versus rage, the two of them side by side in their hot cars screaming toward Town, as the city was always called, middle of the night, a weekday of no importance, no one else on the highway, Brady nosing ahead of Dabney at the Greenwich line, jerking the wheel at the right moment, terrible clash of fenders, terrible screech of tires, all too late and too fast for Dabney to regain control. *Boom!*

Brady would have exited right there after the bridge per plan, calmly parked in the commuter lot up there, not a house in sight, would have trotted down to the crashed Mustang to see. He would have found Dabney still alive, and not only alive but conscious, terribly injured, to be sure, these cars with no seatbelts in them. A hero would have rescued the man, and Brady must have seemed the hero, pulling his brother through the passenger window, getting his yellow sweater so bloody in the process that he took it off and tossed it back into the wreck. Since it was crucial to the grand plan that no one find Dabney till he was dead, Brady would have improvised, walked his own brother back into the woods, this skinny man barely ambulatory and bleeding heavily, Brady leaving boot prints to implicate someone else if it ever came to that, to implicate Dad.

And then Brady would have left Dabney by the famous muddy stream, maybe with one last triumphant kick in the ribs, one last jealous curse, and back out alone to the empty parkway, back up to his car, and then on into New York and to Perdhomme to watch the media storm that would follow, attempt to reap the benefits, cold.

❑ ❑ ❑

IN THE NEXT envelope, there was only a slim box containing a spool of
Scotch recording tape from the old Wollensak reel-to-reel Dad had stolen
or borrowed from Dolus. The box was taped shut obsessively, and taped
to all those layers was a note written in a blind hurry, Dad's cramped
hand:

> To whom it may concern: If you are reading this, I am dead. All
> the evidence you need right here. I am sorry to withhold. Terri-
> fied. The voices are 1) me, 2) Mr. Thierry Perdhomme. Recorded
> from my home phone. As you hear I am not 100% innocent. Still,
> I did everything I could. To save Dabney, to save everybody. It's
> right on the tape. Let it be known that I did all I could to stop
> them. Let it be known that I wish I'd been able to do one thing
> more.

He listed ten or so index numbers for the counter on the Wollensak,
instances, apparently, where Perdhomme incriminated himself, a couple
with exclamation points. And then he'd signed the note with his full
name, none of the usual flourish.

I used a paring knife to cut open the tape, mixed feelings. I held the
reel in my hands, held it a long time, something you could throw away.

But no.

In the attic, I knew right where to look. The Wollensak was in a cardboard carton along with my old record player, both of them put away
when I'd moved to Miami, what I'd thought would be forever, a stack of
LPs, too, also a pink radio that had been Kate's. Finally, bottom of the
carton, an empty tape reel. I dug the Wollensak out, propped it on the
old costume trunk, snapped the empty reel in place, plugged it into one
of the sockets attached to the light fixture in the rafters. The old machine
hummed, its little VU meters kicking to life like no time had passed at
all. I threaded the tape, fitted the tip of the clear leader into the slot in
the takeup reel, gestures I hadn't forgotten. I pressed the big white PLAY
button.

A long, hissing silence.

Then, Mom talking: "What am I supposed to say?"

Dad: "You just talk."

Me, sounding awfully mature for my years. "I'll interview you, Mom."

"About what, life in Westport, Connecticut?"

I put on a reporter voice: "Mrs. Hochmeyer, what does it feel like to have won the club tournament seven years in a row?"

And she put on the voice of the ingénue: "Why, it feels just grand."

And rubbish like that, tears to my eyes: these lost voices. But more, of course, that Kate's was not among them.

Then there was our rendition of the Beatles song, Mom and Dad and me, heartfelt—terrible harmonies—memories of the laughter our singing evoked when we played it back, a time when there hadn't been much laughter. I listened to both sides of the tape, found a little more talk, and then a lot of music recorded off the radio—I'd stayed up half the night goofing with that machine.

Wrong reel, Dad.

AFTER DINNER, LATE, Aamani already in bed, I opened the last envelope from Dad's packet. Inside was a book he'd given me for my twelfth or thirteenth birthday, a compact little volume for budding outdoorsmen called *How to Survive in the Woods*. Inside, he'd tucked a couple of photos, images to take with him, no doubt, as he disappeared into the wilds. The first was of himself with Mom on their honeymoon, both of them tanned and ungodly attractive, twenty and twenty-one years old, a picture I'd never seen, the two of them kissing through smiles, his arm foreshortened and enormous as he holds the old Brownie reflex camera out to get the shot.

The second photo made me smile, too: Katy Hochmeyer, about five years old, holding her little brother up by the armpits to see.

ACKNOWLEDGMENTS

I'm grateful to all my many friends and to my family, none of whom are anything like the people in this book. I got lots of advice and direction and tough love from the writer friends who read the work in various stages along the way: Debora Black, Dana Chevalier, Laura Cowie, Melissa Falcon, David Gessner, Lea Graham, Stephanie Grant, Katherine Heiny, Sonya Huber, Debra Spark, and above all Kristen Keckler, who is a treasure. Warmest gratitude to my editor, Kathy Pories, for her brains and gentle forbearance, and to everyone at Algonquin, still my dream publisher. And finally, thanks and a medal of honor to Betsy Lerner, my agent, so beautiful to me. And of course to my girls, Juliet and Elysia.